IMPERIAL 109

Richard Doyle

Imperial 109

CORGI BOOKS
A DIVISION OF TRANSWORLD PUBLISHERS LTD

IMPERIAL 109

A CORGI BOOK 0 552 10845 6

Originally published in Great Britain by
Arlington Books Ltd.

PRINTING HISTORY
Arlington edition published 1977
Corgi edition published 1978 (twice)

This book is set in Intertype Period

Corgi Books are published by
Transworld Publishers Ltd.,
Century House, 61–63 Uxbridge Road,
Ealing, London W5 5SA

Made and printed in Great Britain by
Cox & Wyman Ltd., London, Reading and Fakenham

For my mother

Acknowledgements

I would like to acknowledge gratefully the help of British Airways and, in particular, of Mr. T. E. Scott-Chard for all the assistance given to me while researching for this book.

To my sister who valiantly typed the manuscript, many thanks.

Last, but by no means least, I would like to thank Desmond Elliott for suggesting the theme for this book and for much help and encouragement.

Part One

AFRICA

I

By Radio: 1310 hrs. LOCAL TIME. FRIDAY 10th MARCH 1939. PORT BELL UGANDA TO ALL AIRPORTS: SOUTH AFRICA – ENGLAND – NEW YORK MAIL PLANE, IMPERIAL AIRWAYS FLIGHT 109, REGISTRATION G-ADHO, CATERINA, LEFT HERE FOR MALAKAL – SUDAN, KHARTOUM AND CAIRO. E.T.A. MALAKAL 1700 hrs. END.

FIVE thousand feet below the flying-boat, the marshes of the Sud stretched out in every direction to the distant horizon. From the borders of Uganda the swamplands run for more than four hundred miles through Equatorial Sudan, covering an area greater than England, where the broad Nile all but loses itself in a maze of winding, sluggish channels, and creeks half choked with vegetation and mud banks. It is a region of neither dry land nor open water but of limitless green papyrus reeds, ambatch and water hyacinth, stagnant pools, quick sands and river mud. The fierce heat of the equator, the humidity and the ever present risk of disease carried by the millions of swarming insects have combined with the other natural hazards to make the Sud one of the last unexplored areas of Africa, and creating a haven for wild life of many kinds from the thousands of herons, water dikkops and plovers and other aquatic birds, to the hippos feeding on the lush weed growth and the crocodiles sunning themselves on the banks.

Earlier in the afternoon a heavy storm had lain over much of the region but now the dense clouds had rolled away eastwards in the direction of Ethiopia and the flying-boat cruised on in brilliant sunshine. The year was 1939, and with their gleaming white paint, raked prows and high wings sprouting gull-like from the crests of their hulls, the S30C Empire class 'boats' of

Britain's Imperial Airways were some of the most beautiful aircraft ever to fly, carrying their passengers in a style and luxury unmatched since the passing of the great air ships of Germany a decade earlier, and never to be seen again. Spanning the immense distances separating the British Dominions round the earth, they set standards taken from the leisured and spacious days of the previous century, as if in defiance of the new order that was already overtaking the world and would soon sweep away the last trace of the Imperial past.

From the Captain's seat on *Caterina*'s flight deck Desmond O'Neill glanced out at the scene below. A leanly built, wiry man, an inch under six feet in height, he had the dark hair, blue eyes, easy charm and quick temper of his Irish ancestry. The Sud never failed to impress him with its vast emptiness. The river at this point was more than twenty miles wide, yet it was impossible from the air to pick out the main channels in the tangle of waterways, lagoons and green patches of reeds. Considering, he reflected wryly, he must have flown over the area at least fifty times since taking command of *Caterina* two years ago, he should have grown used to the sight by now. The section between Mombasa and Cairo, two and a half thousand miles of swamp, scrub and plain desert, was the worst part of the five day Durban to England trip. Endless monotonous landscapes, the long hours in flight broken only by refuelling stops at dirty fly-blown river stations in sweltering heat. For passengers and crew alike it was a relief when they finally reached the delta.

The flying-boat lurched slightly in an air pocket and there was a momentary surge of power from the engine as the Sperry auto-pilot corrected the loss of altitude. Automatically Desmond's eyes flicked over the instruments on the control panels, registering the readings.

One caught his attention: on the main fuel gauge the fat white needle pointed to two hundred and five gallons and instinctively he knew at once it was fractionally too low. He leaned forward and tapped the dial with his finger nail. The action was a habit left over from the early days of his flying career in the frail biplanes of the Twenties whose primitive instruments had responded to such treatment, but *Caterina*'s sophisticated equipment was a far cry from its forbears and the needle remained obstinately on the mark.

'You know what that means?' he said with a sigh of resignation: beside him in the first officer's seat Kenneth Frazer shifted uneasily. 'What's that Skipper?' he asked in apparent surprise.

'You know damn well,' Desmond snapped angrily, 'We've got a fuel leak, and there's only one place it could be coming from, that portside wing tank. Did you check it out as I told you?' Frazer's face flushed, he was a tall, well built young man with pale features and carefully smoothed fair hair, more concerned with his personal appearance and prestige, it seemed to Desmond, than with attending to the less glamorous but still essential details of flying passenger aircraft. 'I followed your orders exactly,' Frazer answered stiffly. 'The engineers stripped off the wing panels and we examined the tank carefully. As I told you, we found only one small leak which was sealed. The tank had hardly been touched.'

Desmond was silent. There was no point in arguing with Frazer, and in any case the ultimate responsibility was his own. Even so there was still a strong possibility that the immediate cause was the first officer's negligence. At Mombasa on the Indian Ocean the previous evening Desmond had let Frazer bring *Caterina* in to land, providing him with useful practice. He had handled the flying-boat well, that much had to be admitted, and made a perfect touch-down, but at the end of her run in, the aircraft had struck a piece of driftwood floating on the surface of the harbour, damaging her port wing float. This in itself had not been serious, and though annoying, had been due to bad luck on Frazer's part rather than to any lack of skill. Accidents of this nature were a common occurrence among flying-boats.

On shore Desmond's presence had been required at the Imperial Airways office to sort out a number of queries about cargo schedules and passenger numbers. So after inspecting the damage he had ordered Frazer to supervise the engineers' repairs. The first officer had subsequently reported that the damage to the fuel tank in the wing above the float was not serious and would not warrant any significant delay. At the time Desmond had accepted this and, after assuring himself that the float had been properly repaired, had taken off again. Now it looked as though his confidence had been misplaced. A glance at Frazer's tight lipped expression showed that he was evidently of the same opinion.

Desmond's eyes narrowed as he made quick calculations in his head. The trouble was that their present hop was a long one – seven hundred and twenty miles from Kisumu on the shores of Lake Victoria, to Malakal at the northern end of the Sud marshes – and to save weight the flying-boat was carrying fuel for only eight hundred miles.

'Ralph,' he called out to the wireless operator at the rear of the flight deck, 'Can you give me a fix on our exact position? I want to check our fuel reserves.'

'Aye, aye, Skipper,' the reply came back above the background noise in the cockpit. Younger than the two pilots, still in his late twenties, Ralph Kendricks was a laconic, lanky New Zealander, with a lazy good humour which no amount of frustration or crisis could upset. He too, had been with the *Caterina* since her commissioning in 1937, for unlike other aircraft, the Imperial crews remained attached to one boat, forming a bond between themselves and with the aircraft they flew.

Reaching up above him Ralph unclipped the small hatch in the cabin roof. Wind whistled shrilly through the opening. Beside him, as a metal slide fixed to the bulkhead, was a loop aerial for the Marconi direction finder, on a swivel mounting. Swinging it outwards he slid it up through the hatch. The wind noise ceased, cut off by the base plate. Ralph locked it in position and tested the hand-wheel. By rotating the aerial on different frequencies it was possible to take accurate bearings on the series of radio beacons located at stations along the route. These could then be plotted together on the chart to give an accurate fix on the aircraft's position.

'218 miles due south of Malakal,' he reported, 'and 110 miles south-south-east of the emergency landing station at Shambe.' Desmond figured the answer briefly. There was still just enough fuel for them to reach Malakal provided the rate of leakage remained steady. He looked out of the window at the wing on his left. There was no sign of spirit spilling out, but that in itself was no guide; and *Caterina*'s four supercharged Bristol Pegasus XII radial engines, each of them developing 1000 horse power, were gulping down fuel at the rate of two gallons a minute, even without any extra loss.

'We'll monitor the gauges over the next thirty minutes,' he decided with a glance at the control panel chronometer. If the position gets any worse during that time we shall have to divert to Shambe.' Behind him Ralph Kendricks chuckled.

'The passengers will love that,' he said, 'an unscheduled stop in the middle of the Sud with plenty of time for sight-seeing in the swamps.'

'Damn the passengers!' Ken Frazer snorted angrily. 'London will go crazy if they hear their precious cargo is stuck out here.' There was silence at this remark; Frazer had touched on a sensitive subject. *Caterina*'s cargo was no ordinary freight load. On this flight – Number 109 on the airline schedule – she carried in the capacious holds behind them on the upper deck and astern inside the tail, more than a ton and a half of gold from the South African mines; two million dollars worth at the internationally agreed price of $35 an ounce – Imperial 109 was a bullion flight.

All the crews hated these flights; apart from the strain of being responsible for so much wealth on a journey lasting nearly a week and covering ten thousand miles over some of the loneliest and most hostile country in the world; high value cargo meant considerable extra work and inconvenience for them. A security watch had to be set whenever the aircraft touched down, the holds had to be inspected at frequent intervals, reports made and permission sought for the slightest variation from the normal flying pattern. If they were forced to make an emergency stop at Shambe, as Frazer said, the Head Office in London would be sending furious signals almost before they touched the water.

They had seen the gold being loaded at Durban. 10 lb. ingots packed eight to a crate, forty-four crates in all and brought down to the quay at dawn in a convoy of plain trucks, two armed police in each truck, and, following behind at a discreet distance, another with a squad of rifle-carrying soldiers yawning in the early light. The security had been deliberately low-key so as not to attract attention; the soldiers hadn't even got out of their truck and the whole operation had been over in half an hour, the wooden crates stowed safely away out of sight and the receipt signed by Desmond. Then Ian Haggart, Imperial's Chief Officer in Durban, a stiff, reserved man with a military bearing, handed him a canvas pouch that weighed surprisingly heavy. 'You had better take these with you,' he said gruffly and with a touch of embarrassment Desmond took the pouch without comment. Inside, oiled and wrapped, were a pair of Webley & Scott .38 calibre revolvers and a cardboard box containing fifty rounds of ammunition. On these flights firearms were issued to Captains and First Officers, a practice which made the crews feel no easier in their minds and only drove home the risks they were incurring.

For much of the afternoon the big crocodile had lain sunning itself on the edge of a small island of mud, thickly overgrown with papyrus and grasses, which rose among the creeks and sand bars on the edge of the White Nile. About it, basking themselves similarly, were half a dozen others of its species, all in identical attitudes: bellies down; crooked stumpy legs bent up against their armoured sides; long mouths slightly agape exposing their orange gums and the rows of wicked gleaming teeth. At intervals one of the great reptiles would snort and grunt and shift its huge carcass into a more comfortable position, sending the numerous plovers and water dikkops hunting for parasites and leeches, scattering for safety as the spiney ridged tail flailed round.

Among the others on the mud beside it the big croc stood out, not only on account of its immense age and size; it was starting its second century of life, was fully eighteen feet long and weighed over a ton; but also because of an extraordinary white scar, which ran from just behind the right foreleg, across almost to the middle of the back, flattening two of the protruding ridge plates. This scar was the legacy of the croc's nearest brush with death, when four decades earlier and already measuring thirteen feet from snout to tail, it had unwisely attempted to seize a small hippo calf when its mother was feeding in the vicinity.

Attracted by her offspring's panic-stricken cries, the enraged animal had surfaced to find the croc in the act of dragging the calf off by the hind leg and had instantly attacked. The shock of seeing the great beast rear up out of the water immediately beside it had momentarily paralysed the croc and it had been fractionally slow in relaxing the grip of its jaws and fleeing away. With a bellow the hippo had closed in for the kill, her colossal jaws snapping shut, grabbing the crocodile about the abdomen.

Fortunately for the croc it had managed to lash out with its tail as the hippo's jaws closed and the blow, striking home across the mother's head, had caused it to stagger momentarily, allowing the croc to wriggle free, blood streaming from its back where one of the foot long tusks had pierced the armoured skin and then ripped through in the struggle. Scuttling away into deep water, it had made for a safe place on the banks in which to rest and heal its wound. The skin had at length grown over again but the scar remained etched across its back, a permanent testimony to the narrowness of its escape.

The croc had been driven to attack the calf by hunger, and the same urge now awoke it. Too large and clumsy to hunt the fish eaten by their smaller fellows, the older reptiles are increasingly forced to attack the wildlife coming down to the water to drink, and it had been two days since the croc had eaten. Heaving itself up into the typical bow legged, high walking stance of its kind, the big crocodile lurched over the few feet of mud to the edge and slid quietly into the water.

There is no more formidable swamp in the world than the Sud, a savage hostile wilderness of fierce heat, flies, mosquitoes, snakes, mud and disease that spreads for thousands of miles, the endless tracts of reeds split by foetid pools and streams, banks of mud barely breaking the surface and islands of packed vegetation twenty feet thick drifting in the river channels. To the big croc all this meant nothing, it was merely the natural environment perfectly suited to its needs. With a few quick flicks of its tail it moved out into midstream of one of the main channels, heading northwards. Its goal was the river port and landing station at Shambe, a mile or two down-river.

The town was not large, indeed it scarcely justified the name, consisting as it did of a handful of whitewashed, stone-built bungalows for the small number of officials who administered the district and managed the station; a rest house for passengers stopping there, and the huts of a Shelluk native village which had collected round them. To the croc it simply represented a potential source of food; either from offal or garbage thrown into the river or else some unwary creature coming down to the water's edge. Unhurriedly it swam steadily on.

There could no longer be any doubt about the leak from the portside tank. Even before the half hour was up it was clear that they were losing fuel at a rate of more than two hundred gallons per hour. To reach Malakal, still one hundred and forty miles away, was out of the question.

'If the loss gets any worse we shall have enough problems reaching the emergency landing area let alone Malakal,' Desmond said as the needles slipped relentlessly back. 'Ralph, give me a course for the station at Shambe and tell them we're coming in low on fuel and request emergency services to stand by. Assuming they have any that is,' he added sourly.

'O.K. Skipper, I have the course for you,' the radio operator replied at once. 'Steer 310 degrees north, the station is approximately forty five miles distant. We should reach it in twenty minutes at our current speed.'

Desmond peered out of the cockpit windows at the featureless swamp beneath them. 'It's going to be hell's own task finding the place in all this muck,' he said irritably. 'We could circle round for hours looking for it. Every stretch of water looks the same from up here and we won't be able to see the station till we're right on top of it.' Beside him Ken Frazer said nothing but stared ahead of him, his face set and angry.

From above, the Nile appeared more like a succession of lakes than a river. An interminable series of lagoons, fringed and bordered by reeds, that stretched away into the distance on all sides making it difficult to say even in which direction the river was heading and impossible to pick out with certainty which was the main channel. The gauges showed eighty gallons of fuel remaining in the tanks, giving them another forty minutes in the air before they would be forced to ditch, assuming the rate of loss did not increase. Despite Desmond's gloomy prediction that should give them sufficient time, given that they would be able to use the direction finder to help locate the station. At close range it would be of limited value but it would at least bring them into the correct area and provide a useful check on the compass bearings.

In theory, of course, even if they did run short of fuel before locating the landing area they could simply put *Caterina* down on the nearest stretch of open water and wait until boats from Shambe came to get them. In practice, however, this could turn out to be an extremely hazardous manoeuvre. The river was so sluggish and discoloured with mud that it was impossible to tell if it was clear of obstructions. Just below the surface there could be waterlogged timbers, sand banks, even hippos. During the rainy season all manner of debris was carried along by the flood, brought down from the forests to the south and collected in the sieve-like marshes. Their present problems stemmed from a collision with a comparatively small baulk of wood in the protected harbour of Mombasa. Even that had occurred right at the end of the touch down run when the flying boat had been rapidly losing way. A big obstacle encountered here as they hit the water would be disastrous; a mud bank or a sizeable tree could tear *Caterina*'s bottom clean out of her, taking the passengers with it.

Satisfied that he was on the correct bearing, Desmond reached out with his right hand and eased back the throttle levers slightly, allowing the airliner's speed to fall back to 110 knots so as to conserve the remaining fuel in the tanks. *Caterina* was capable of cruising at a maximum of 200 knots with a minimum stalling speed of 73 knots.

'Shambe reports landing area clear and all services on standby,' Kendricks reported.

'Fine,' Desmond replied. 'I'm taking us down to 2,000 feet so we'll have a better chance of spotting the station without overshooting.' He pushed the control yoke forward as he spoke putting the aircraft into a shallow descent. 'O.K. Ken,' he said when they had levelled off at the new altitude. 'Take over and keep her on this bearing will you, I'm going to have a word with Sandy and let the passengers know about the change in schedule.'

Sandy Everett was the flying-boat's purser and the youngest member of *Caterina*'s crew. He had an office in the mail room immediately behind the flight deck and was responsible for the needs of the passengers as well as dealing with all the mail that was carried. Seeing the first officer nod his acceptance of the order, Desmond hoisted himself out of his seat and made his way off past Ralph and the radio desk.

The purser's true title was that of mail clerk although in practice he was always referred to on board as the purser, the term being borrowed from the ocean liners whose luxury and elegance the flying-boat sought to equal. Mail had been the real reason behind Imperial Airway's bold decision back in 1935 to order twenty-eight of the S23C flying-boats from Short Brothers, straight off the drawing board at a cost of £50,000 each without waiting to test a prototype despite the innovations in design, as well as fourteen Armstrong Whitworth AW27 land planes. Under the Empire Air Mail Scheme set up that year, it had been agreed that all first class mail would be carried throughout the British Empire by air on Imperial's fleet of new planes, at current surface postal rates, in return for a substantial subsidy paid by the Government. The aim was to foster the spirit of unity among the Empire's members and from the start it proved enormously successful with more than fifteen tons of mail being carried each week; a figure which had peaked to one hundred tons the previous Christmas and nearly buried the airline in the process.

The mailroom was a large compartment, some twenty feet long immediately behind the flight deck, piled high with canvas sacks coloured blue or green or white according to destination. At the far end, secure behind a locked wire grill were some of the innocuous looking wooden crates which contained the gold ingots. Sandy's desk was in the middle of the compartment directly in front of the freight hatch by the starboard wing and next to the gangway linking the flight deck to the passengers' level beneath. The spring mounted desk lamp was on but there was no sign of Sandy, evidently he was down on the lower level. Stepping round the desk Desmond began to descend the gangway.

Kenneth Frazer's hands gripped tightly on the bars of the control yoke in front of him, guiding the flight of the eighteen ton aircraft with angry concentration. The natural turbulence of the atmosphere, often met at low altitude, was being increased by warm thermals rising off the ground, and convection currents set up by the sun evaporating the moisture from the swamps, making necessary constant small adjustments to the controls. It was an exercise which he found particularly demanding, anticipating the yaw and pitch and roll of the flying-boat and catching her at exactly the right moment with just the right degree of correction.

One day in the future, probably the not too far distant future at that, aeroplanes would be built with pressurized cabins for passengers and crew, enabling them to fly at heights of 30,000 feet or more above normal air turbulence. To Frazer the prospect was a welcome one, which would relieve him of one of the most tiresome duties of long distance flight. The new developments in aircraft design: the radio beacons, the electrically operated flaps, automatic pilot and blind flying equipment, were continuing the trend towards making pilots more dependent on their aids, instead of relying on their instinctive qualities as fliers. The Captains of the future would be chosen for their technical skills, and understanding of their aircraft's equipment rather than on judgement of their flying ability alone.

By rights Frazer considered he should have been made up to full Captain already and given command of his own craft. That he was still only a first officer was due, he was sure, to the contempt felt by the older Captains in the Imperial Fleet, the barnstorming pilots of the old pioneering days when the air routes were being laid out, for the up and coming generation of carefully trained, highly qualified officers. Most of all Frazer blamed Desmond O'Neill, whose reports on his first officer's fitness to command had, he guessed, been less than complimentary. Desmond was a naturally brilliant airman with an instinctive feel for the way in which his aircraft handled, besides being a forceful Captain who firmly believed that pilots should only be given commands of their own after long experience in all conditions.

The memory of Desmond's anger at discovering the fuel leak sent another surge of bitter rage through his mind. It was all the worse because he knew himself to be in the wrong. The tank had been damaged quite badly at Mombasa, but a proper repair would have meant a day's delay and a long entry in the log, an entry which might well have found its way on to his own report and further damaged his chances of promotion at a critical time. Frazer had persuaded the engineers to do a quick patching job to last till they reached Cairo where a two day stop-over would give plenty of time for more comprehensive repairs. Now it seemed that his attempt had misfired. An emergency landing would certainly be held against him. He would have to write to his mother again and see if she could help.

The death of his father while he was still at school had meant that Kenneth Frazer had been brought up as the indulged only son of his mother, whose subsequent marriage to a wealthy London business man had in no way diminished her adoration for her boy. Recently she had become friendly with Jack Priestly, Imperial's flying-boats operations manager and a long-standing enemy of Desmond's, and Frazer hoped that with her help he might at last achieve the promotion he sought.

Originally he had been attracted into the world of flying by the glamour and mystery that surrounded the tough, daring pilots and their flimsy machines. The miracle of manned flight was still less than forty years old and very much in the public eye. Fliers were famous, their names household words. In Cairo Desmond O'Neill was a friend of King Farouk's and Ken Frazer was determined to be like him.

The reality he had found was far harder, far more demanding, more uncomfortable and at times more dangerous than he had expected. A degree of professionalism and dedication was required which rapidly palled on him. Lacking the natural abilities of many of the young men in the same intake, he began to fall behind in the struggle for promotion and bitterness had set in. He was passed from one plane to another as the crew grew sick of his grousing and laziness. He no longer had any intention of remaining with the airline any longer than was necessary to obtain his Captain's stripes. Already his stepfather had offered him a job in his own firm, the opening was ideal and he was determined to accept. First, however, he had to prove to himself that he had not wasted his ten years in the air, he had to come out as a Captain, someone to be respected and admired, somehow he had to gain promotion. It was a desire which was rapidly becoming an obsession. Bringing his attention abruptly back to the present he checked the fuel gauges once more and noted the time. The rate of loss had increased slightly; the tanks now held fifty-eight gallons with seventeen minutes to go before they would be over Shambe. The safety margin was down to twelve minutes.

With the exception of the cargo hold right in the tail and a small space forward in the nose used for storing ropes and other mooring gear the whole of the flying boat's lower deck was given over to the use of the passengers. There were four separate cabins designed to accommodate varying numbers of people according to the demands of the route, and all capable of being converted into comfortable sleeping compartments in the event of a night flight. From the passengers' point of view the immense profitability of the mail loads meant that they themselves travelled in far greater luxury than would otherwise be possible. *Caterina* was eighty-eight feet long and four double decker buses could have been fitted into her hull, yet on this trip she carried only thirteen passengers.

Stepping off the gangway Desmond was once again struck

by the lengths to which the builders had gone to ensure the comfort of the passengers.

The thick double sound proofing held the noise level well below that of the upper deck, reducing the sound of the engines to no more than a background hum. The floor was thickly carpeted in deep green and the same restful colour was continued in the covering of the walls. Chrome strip, brightly polished, trimmed the doors and panel sills. The effect was more like the first class interior of an ocean liner than an aeroplane.

He was standing in a passageway directly underneath the mailroom in the forward part of the boat. On his left looking towards the bow were the doors of the washrooms and lavatories, on his right lay the galley. In front of him the passage led into the foremost cabin, the smoking saloon, which as the name implied was the only place on board where smoking was permitted. The other three cabins, the midship, the promenade and the after cabins, all lay towards the rear.

The galley door beside him opened with a click and Sandy Everett emerged into the passage. The *Caterina*'s purser was an enthusiastic, likeable boy of nineteen who had joined the crew six months ago on leaving school. Openfaced and fairhaired, he was dressed like Desmond in the standard Imperial Airways' navy blue uniform with double-breasted jacket and white trimmed peaked cap, though without the latter's pilot wings and officer's stripes.

'Andy and I are just getting the passengers' tea ready,' he said with a smile. Andy Draper was the flying-boat's steward. 'Shall I bring some upstairs for you?' he offered. Desmond shook his head.

'You'd better leave that for now Sandy,' he said. 'We're losing a lot of fuel from that tank we holed at Mombasa and at this rate I doubt if we should be able to reach Malakal so I'm going to take us down for an emergency stop at Shambe. We shall be landing in about a quarter of an hour.'

'Will we be staying there for the night, Sir?' the young purser looked at him questioningly.

'No,' Desmond told him. 'At least I hope not. I've never

been there but according to all the stories it's the kind of place best forgotten and God knows Malakal is bad enough. If we can have the repairs done in time I'll push straight on to Khartoum.'

'You'll cut out Malakal then?' Sandy asked. 'We've no passengers to pick up there, but there's some mail to deliver.'

'We can leave that with the rest at Khartoum and they can send it up the river on the next steamer. It'll only be a day or so late which isn't going to matter to a place like that,' Desmond answered, 'and I want to reach Khartoum tonight if it's at all possible.'

'Right, sir,' Sandy said. 'I'll just tell Andy and then I'll go and inform the passengers that we'll be landing in fifteen minutes.'

'I'll do the after cabins myself,' Desmond told him. 'Most of the passengers will be there. You can tell the ones in the smoking saloon and then make sure that everyone does actually get back to their seats before we start to descend.'

'O.K. Skipper I'll see to it,' Sandy nodded earnestly and Desmond had to restrain an impulse to smile at the boy's eagerness.

'One last thing,' he said before turning back to the gangway. 'Don't mention to the passengers that we are low on fuel. Just let them think it's a routine stop so we can inspect the repairs we had done earlier, I don't want them getting worried.'

'Bloody typical!' was Andy's comment when Sandy returned to the galley to tell him the news. 'That's your engineers for you. Patch things up just enough to get us right into the middle of the swamps and then come apart. I told you we should have stayed longer at Mombasa and made them do a proper job.' He was a short, thick set, black haired man in his forties from East London, with a quick, natural shrewdness, who so frequently expressed his utter lack of respect for the airline and its passengers, as well as his superiors, that Sandy was often amazed that he managed to keep his job. He had a particular contempt for the passengers, whom he considered to be both brainless and a nuisance, although Sandy noticed, he spared no effort to make their flights comfortable and ran the lower deck with considerable efficiency.

He had taken Sandy in hand from the moment of his arrival, looking after him, showing him what to do and how to go about it, and giving him a great deal of useful advice; all in the same tone of tolerant contempt with which he treated everyone, Desmond included. Andy was expert at anticipating problems and sidestepping them, at smoothing over difficulties and blocking complaints. Sandy found him invaluable in dealing with the ground staff at the various stops along the route; there was no trick of the quarter-masters or supply clerks he did not know.

'The captain says Shambe is worse than Malakal,' Sandy remarked and the steward snorted derisively.

'Let me tell you my lad,' he said, 'I know all about Shambe and it's worse than anywhere. For a start we don't normally let passengers ashore there if we can help it, in case they catch yellow fever. It's got mosquitoes that bite deep enough to draw blood as well as giving you a bad dose of malaria; it's hot as a turkish bath and it stinks of mud.' He began tidying away the trays of cups and saucers he had been preparing.

'So we keep the passengers on board while the engineer looks at the tank?' said Sandy. 'They won't like that.'

'Can't, not while they're working on a fuel tank,' Andy replied, bending down to stow away a teapot. 'The rules say all personnel must be taken off the ship before any work is started on a fuel tank, it's the fire risk,' he explained. Andy was an expert on all airline regulations, 'which means,' he continued 'that you and I will have to go ashore with them and make sure they don't do anything stupid like eating the local fruit and make themselves sick, which some of them are bound to do anyway,' he concluded with grim satisfaction.

'O.K.' Sandy turned to the doors again. 'I'll go and tell them the good news.'

'One more thing,' Andy called him back, 'we shall have trouble with the female passengers when we land. The natives round here don't wear any clothes. Not unless you count a string of beads round their waists and they only wear them if they're married. The time I was here before, a general's wife fainted getting into the launch and fell in the river. Stupid cow said afterwards it was the heat, but I know what she saw.' With a chuckle Andy went back to his work leaving Sandy to go off and inform the passengers.

The promenade cabin, located immediately aft of the wings, was the flying-boat's greatest attraction and an understandably popular feature among the passengers. The largest of the four cabins, it contained not only seating for eight people but also a wide area running the full length of the port side which was left free for passengers to stroll about and admire the view through the row of panoramic windows let into the hull at standing height. On long journeys this freedom to move around and stretch the legs was a great relief and people tended to congregate there.

Laura Hartman had been gazing out of one of these windows on the promenade deck at the flat green scenery sliding past below, for the past quarter of an hour. She was a pretty girl in her late twenties, small and slightly built, with short fair hair curling neatly into the nape of the neck. Her face was narrow and high cheek-boned and tanned by her recent stay in South Africa. It was an attractive, even beautiful face, but with an air of sadness about it. She wore a short sleeved yellow cotton dress and white shoes. Despite the aircraft's lower altitude which enabled her to get a better view of the country over which they were flying, she was bored.

Laura had been bored ever since she had entered the cabin and was now bitterly regretting that she had been so foolish as to leave the smoking saloon where she had been sitting a short while ago. The cause of her annoyance was standing beside her in the shape of a young man in the uniform of a British Royal Navy Lieutenant. Fresh faced, pop eyed, and, for all his youth, unbearably pompous, Ian Thorne had striven manfully to impress her from the moment they had both joined the aircraft at Durban, when his opening remark 'I say you're American aren't you? I can tell, you know, by the accent,' had earned him a look which would have dropped a more sensitive man where he stood. Since then he had plagued her with his constant attention and a never ending flow of increasingly inane conversation. He was either incredibly thick skinned she thought to herself wearily, or simply too stupid to notice how off-hand to him she was being. Unfortunately, there was seldom any way of avoiding him during a flight.

'It's such a pity Mrs. Hartman,' he was saying, 'my having to leave the aeroplane at Alexandria while you go on to New York. It's so nice talking to you. I say,' he had a sudden thought, 'we stop for a day in Cairo first. Perhaps I could show you around the sights. I've been there before you know,' he added proudly.

'Thank you but so have I,' Laura replied dryly, 'and in any case I shall have a lot of work to do when we get there.'

Thorne looked crestfallen, but before he could reply, to Laura's relief they were joined by another passenger. Dr. Van Smit was a small wiry man of about fifty, dressed in a neatly cut brown suit. Very sunburned about the face and hands, and with clever, sharp features, he described himself as a consultant geologist although he appeared to earn his living primarily from card playing and gambling. Both his name and his pronounced accent proclaimed him to be a South African, a descendant of the original Dutch settlers. 'I understand you have been visiting my country Mrs. Hartman,' he asked politely, 'did you enjoy yourself there?'

'Yes very much, but I'm afraid I only saw a little of it,' Laura confessed. 'I was only there a week and I had to spend most of that time in Durban. I'm secretary to Mr. Stewart Curtis,' she explained.

'That would be the Mr. Curtis who is chairman of the Klerksdrop Mining Company? I have heard a great deal about him. I gather he is travelling with us, is that not so?' the Doctor inquired.

'He's taken a private saloon in the after cabin,' Laura told him. 'He likes to be able to work in the aeroplane so as not to waste time.'

'And you have both flown down to Durban from London for a week and now you fly back again, that is a long tiring journey for so short a time,' the Doctor pursued, his small dark eyes watching her intently.

'Oh no,' Laura shook her head firmly, 'Mr. Curtis had been spending the winter in Cairo with his wife, but he had some urgent business in South Africa, so we flew down. Mrs. Curtis didn't want to make the trip and she stayed behind.'

'Do you travel a lot with him?' Ian Thorne broke into the conversation. He had been standing stiffly by the window resenting Van Smit's intrusion. 'I mean, it must be quite interesting I should think.'

'He doesn't make that many trips, most of his business is in the United States now or else in South Africa, we just travel between the two mostly. It depends more where his wife wants to be than anything else I think.'

'It is unusual if I may say so Mrs. Hartman,' Van Smit was looking out of the window as he spoke, 'for an English business tycoon to employ an American secretary. Normally it is the other way around is it not?'

The tone of his remark irritated Laura somewhat. It was hard to say whether there was some innuendo behind it or just plain inquisitiveness.

'My husband used to work for Mr. Curtis in South Africa. He was a mining engineer and when he was killed in an accident last year Mr. Curtis offered me a job as his personal secretary. He said he needed someone who understood a bit about the business. It was very generous of him.'

The flat tone of her voice was enough to tell the two men that the subject of the recently dead husband was still too painful to be touched on lightly. For a short while they gazed out of the windows in silence. It was Ian Thorne who spoke first.

'Are you yourself interested in mining Dr. Van Smit?' he asked as a frown of reserve passed over the South African's features.

Before he could reply however, Desmond O'Neill stepped through the cabin doorway and came over to them. 'I'm sorry to spoil your viewing,' he said, 'but I'm afraid you will all have to return to your seats very soon. We are going to make an extra stop on this flight and the aircraft will be landing on the river at Shambe in a quarter of an hour.'

'Shambe,' the Doctor echoed his words, 'Shambe, that is a

most unusual place to stop. Is there something wrong with the aircraft?' Desmond hastily reassured him.

'We just want to take the opportunity to check on the repairs that were made yesterday,' he said, 'we shan't be delayed very long.'

'Well I'm glad,' Laura peered forward out of the window. 'It looks nice down there, green and cool, and Khartoum will be so hot. It will be nice to rest here for a while.'

'It may appear pleasant enough from this height Mrs. Hartman,' Dr. Van Smit replied grimly, 'but you are looking at one of the most terrible regions in all Africa: the marshes of the Sud. Fifty thousand square miles of fever and mosquito ridden swamp. Captain O'Neil must indeed be concerned to be bringing us down in such a place. Less than sixty years ago a well equipped expedition of four hundred men was almost wiped out here by starvation and disease.'

Desmond looked at him sharply. Van Smit had a knack of making disconcerting remarks, and there was no need to make the other passengers aware of the discomfort of the Sud.

'I think you exaggerate a little Doctor,' he said, keeping his tone deliberately casual. 'Certainly Shambe presents no problems as far as flying-boats are concerned, and the company has maintained a rest house and servicing facilities there for many years.' Van Smit gave an enigmatic smile and did not reply. Desmond transferred his attention to the other occupants of the cabin.

To the right of the far doorway leading through into the after cabin sat an elderly English couple, the Finlays, returning home after a lifetime spent abroad in the colonial service. White haired and thin, both seemed dried up by the climate in which they had lived for so many years. They sat upright in their seats, books open in front of them, dressed in stiff, old fashioned clothes, unsuitable for travelling. During the only conversation he had had with them so far, Desmond had felt that their often expressed pleasure at being at last on their way home rang a little false. He suspected that secretly the old couple were dreading the prospect of ending their lives in a country they no longer knew and where their friends were all dead or had long since forgotten them.

The two seats immediately in front of the Finlays were occupied by a pleasant faced, dark haired rather plump woman in a floral print dress and her ten year old daughter. Their name Desmond recalled with an effort was Johnson, the woman's husband, at present up at the front of the aircraft in the smoking saloon, was a civil engineer from Kenya, taking his family home on leave. The mother he was glad to see, had not been in the least disturbed by Van Smit's ominous remarks. The child appeared to be asleep.

With a quick word to each of them Desmond broke the news of their imminent descent to those who had not realized it already from his conversation by the windows. None showed more than a casual interest with the single exception of Mr. Finlay, who asked several erudite questions about Shambe and, when he saw that Desmond could not give him the answers, began to consult a guide book. Satisfied that all was well, Desmond went through into the after cabin.

Running back into the tail of the aircraft, the after cabin was the most luxurious on board. It measured nearly twelve feet in length, with a nine foot ceiling, and since it was the furthest from the engines, it was also the quietest and most vibration free of the four lower deck cabins. On this flight, it had been booked as a private stateroom and its sole occupant was the financier Stewart Curtis.

Entering the cabin from the promenade deck Desmond found the tycoon seated at a table working over some papers. To Desmond's surprise, the news of the unscheduled landing appeared to irritate Curtis immensely.

'We shouldn't be delayed very long,' he attempted to explain. 'And we hope to make up any time we do lose before we reach Cairo, but I think it advisable to inspect the repairs.'

'This is a confounded nuisance,' Curtis snapped in reply, laying down his papers, 'any delay will be extremely inconvenient to me. I have some most important business to attend to. Surely this inspection could be carried out at Malakal?' He was a big, heavily built man with a square thick jowled face, somewhere in his fifties, dressed in a Savile Row suit cut from tropical weight cloth. Desmond tried to remember what he knew about him: a multi-millionaire with big holdings in mining, steel and armaments, who had worked his way up from the office boy and made his first big killing by selling off war surplus material in the twenties, survived the depression to become a leading industrialist and a key figure in the new move by British and American finance houses into the South African mining market. A sportsman, art collector, and member of high society on both sides of the Atlantic; so far Stewart Curtis had impressed him only as an arrogant, demanding bully of a man, who seemed to derive a perverse pleasure from terrorizing his inferiors.

'It's damned inefficiency,' Curtis snorted, 'none of you people would last ten minutes working for me. We were delayed at Mombasa so that damage caused by your crew's carelessness could be put right. I see we shall have this excuse brought out the whole way to New York.'

'I couldn't say about New York, sir,' Desmond responded tight lipped, 'you will be changing planes once you reach England, but in any case I am sure this will be the last delay.'

'It had better be Captain,' the financier retorted. 'Because if it isn't I shall be making complaints to London that will have you back on the ground loading luggage.' Indicating by a dismissive nod of the head that the interview was terminated, he returned to the study of his papers. Desmond however stood his ground.

'Mr. Curtis,' he said quietly, with difficulty restraining the anger that boiled up inside him, 'I don't know what your understanding of modern aircraft is, but I can only assume it to be extremely limited. Any extra stops or delays will be caused by consideration for the safety of this flight and its passengers. If I decide that such delays are required then I will make them, regardless of what you or anyone else may say or do about it.' Curtis gazed at him open-mouthed with astonishment. 'And furthermore,' Desmond continued, 'if you are ever again as rude as you just have been, either to me personally or to anyone else on board, I'll put you off at the next stop and leave you there.'

It had been a long time since anybody had dared to speak to Stewart Curtis in such a manner, and the shock left him speechless. Seeing the mingled rage and utter surprise evident on his face, Desmond judged it prudent to withdraw before the financier found his tongue. Closing the door quietly behind him he made his way back to the flight deck gangway.

Never before had he spoken to one of the company's passengers like that, and it was quite likely that Curtis might cause trouble over it. Nevertheless he was justified in his outburst he considered, however much Curtis might want to reach America, and he was obviously in a great hurry about something, there was no cause for such rudeness. There had been a certain satisfaction in telling him so.

Returning to the galley passage, Desmond paused at the foot of the gangway, glancing back down through the doorways of the midship cabin into the promenade deck. He recognized the slight figure of Laura Hartman standing by the window, half hidden by the bulkhead between them. She was talking to the young naval lieutenant and he felt a momentary regret that he so seldom got to know many of his passengers. Collecting himself he commenced climbing back up the stairs. Even after a year of divorce the freedom of bachelorhood still came uneasily to him at times.

Perhaps it was just as well, he reflected. Relationships were hard to hold together in this profession. In his pocket at the moment he was still carrying Pamela's last letter, addressed to him through the Imperial Airways office. Even after all this time his wife's bitterness remained undiminished. Now, it appeared, she had taken a job in London as fashion editor of a woman's magazine and wanted to sell the house. She had had a valuation done and, of course, he thought, had taken legal advice. As usual Pamela had it all worked out. She had decided on a price, hired an estate agent, found a buyer; all he had to do was sign a form of consent which she enclosed. 'I'm sorry to push you,' the letter ran, 'but I am anxious to move

33

back to London and you certainly don't require a house that size to yourself.'

The words were typical of Pamela. Reading them he had pictured her standing there, head tilted back imperiously, eyes aglitter with intensity, the blue black hair he so admired tossed in disorder and her small determined mouth compressed in a tight line. Pamela made up for her lack of inches with a ferocious energy that carried her against any opposition. He could hear her snapping out the points of her argument, 'In the first place I hate Southampton, secondly I can get a better job in London, thirdly it is ridiculous for a divorced couple to own a house together, fourthly . . .'

In the beginning Desmond had worked hard at his marriage, blaming his frequent absences on duty for the difficulties that had arisen. Looking back, however, he could see that in reality a much more fundamental weakness lay at the heart of their problems. The periods between flights for rest were generous, other pilots were away from home no less often, yet their wives coped. The trouble was, he realized, that for all her attractiveness, her intelligence and the stylishness so many people envied, Pamela's confidence in herself was very superficial. Unless the constant centre of attention, a basic insecurity within her would well up, frightening her into savage attacks on any competing attraction.

In this respect Desmond's job had proved to be an opponent she could not match. Unable to enter into the masculine world of flying and aeroplanes and pilots, Pamela had first tried to separate him from it, and then when she saw that this was impossible, had set about tearing their marriage apart about them. The result had been inevitable. Their increasingly violent quarrels had driven Desmond to escape more and more into his own world from which his wife was barred. A reaction which only served to magnify Pamela's sense of frustration and grievance. When the divorce came they had been married for exactly three years. He wondered whether Pamela ever felt the regrets that he still experienced. Probably she did, although it was hard to tell, and always had been, what feelings ran underneath the efficient carapace she presented to the world. Certainly there were times when he missed the quick abrasive companionship and the eager passion she had brought to their love-making.

As if the problems with his wife were not enough trouble, another letter had reached him at the same time. This had been a communication from the Admiralty and although the envelope had read Captain D. M. O'Neill, the letter inside was addressed to Flight Lieutenant O'Neill, Royal Navy Flying Corps Reserve. Arrangements had been made, the message ran, with Imperial Airways for him to spend his summer leave undergoing further training on carrier aircraft with the Fleet Air Arm. Under an Act of Parliament and Orders in Council passed during the previous year the Ministry possessed the authority to order him to report at Portsmouth for duty on July 15th for four weeks. As a sop the letter added that during this time he would receive payment at the rate of eleven shillings per day, in addition to his keep.

Reading the dry official phrases the threat of war had suddenly seemed very near at hand.

Back on the flight deck Desmond saw at once from Ken Frazer's face that there had been no change for the better during the short time he had been below. Resuming his seat hurriedly he ran his eyes over the instruments. Their safety margin was dropping all the time.

'I've cut our speed to 105 knots,' Frazer told him, 'but it doesn't seem to have made any difference.' Desmond thought rapidly. The tanks were draining at an increasing rate and on the main fuel dial the needle had swung past the red danger mark. The gauges were notoriously inaccurate at very low readings and it was quite possible that the position was not as serious as the gauge indicated, equally though the engines could run dry at any second.

An added complication was that in heading straight for Shambe their course had taken them away from the main river which had bent sharply off to the east for several miles; the aircraft was now flying over an area where the water was thickly clogged with reeds and mud and other obstructions. Here there were none of the open stretches which before had offered the possibility of an emergency touch-down should it become suddenly necessary. A ditching here would almost certainly result in the total wrecking of the aircraft, with severe loss of life among those on board.

'How long before we reach the open river again?' he asked, taking over the controls from Frazer. *Caterina* was still flying sweetly, her four engines in synchronization with each other and as yet without a trace of the falterings which would signal the presence of air in the fuel leads. Once that began they would have only a minute or two in which to select some place to ditch.

'We shall be over the river in approximately twelve minutes,' Ken shouted to him, 'just before we hit Shambe.' That was little help. There would be no prospect of making a safe landing before they reached the station on this course, and it was too late now to turn away and head directly for one of the main channels; to do so would only increase the risks. Twelve minutes. If the fuel gauge was reading correctly they had barely sufficient reserves to reach the river.

'I'm going down to 500 feet,' he said to the others, 'send a message to Shambe that our fuel situation is now critical.'

Down below, ignorant of the danger they were facing, the passengers peered excitedly from their windows at the startled flocks of birds that rose on every side, scattering swiftly away from them as the great plane winged low over the marshes.

Siegret lived with her widowed father David Wienzman who was head of the Department of Medicine at the University of Vienna and one of the most respected men in the city. Together they had lived in a pleasant house in the grounds of the university, and as she grew older Siegret had begun to assume more and more of the responsibilities for running their home, looking after her father's needs, and acting as hostess when he entertained other members of the faculty, or the groups of students.

They had been happy years. Vienna had been free from many of the ugly events taking place in neighbouring states.

Both Siegret and her father had many friends among all shades of opinion. There had been parties, visits to one another's houses, travel abroad. Then abruptly all that had ceased one terrible day in March 1938.

Anschluss. In a single instant the borders of the hated third Reich had leapt forward one hundred and fifty miles to encompass the people of Austria.

Files of troops, and lorries, motor cycles and armoured cars. And they had come not parading openly down the great main avenues of the city, confident of a popular welcome. No, that had come later, when they were sure. First they had slunk in silence through the side streets, lorryload after lorryload, of grey uniformed men, grim faced and alert. And all in utter silence. Neither the soldiers nor the watching people had said a word, made a noise or gesture, while all the time the endless columns rolled by.

Later of course, had come the great parade, the buildings hung with the huge red banners with the crooked swastikas on them, the crowds issued with flags and carefully policed, instructed to wave them. Siegret herself had had a flag thrust into her hand as she waited in Parliament Square to see what would happen. She had even seen the great man himself drive past, standing very upright in the huge black and silver car at the head of a phalanx of military vehicles. He had been waving and beaming with pleasure, and to Siegret's amazement some of his fierce joy had been communicated to the crowds.

The speed of the changes which followed had been bewildering. Uniforms and arm bands were all at once to be seen everywhere all the time.

Vienna took on the air of a besieged town. A host of regulations was issued prohibiting and governing the people's lives down to the smallest details. New passes and identity cards had to be obtained from government offices where bullying officials demanded to know every insignificant fact about people's lives. Travel was restricted, newspapers censored, young men and woman conscripted for state work camps.

The Jewish decrees had started a little later, when the authorities had the country firmly in their grip. Already there was a feeling of unease among some sections of the population; rumours of what was already happening in Germany were current, it was noticeable that numbers of men and women from all races, who might have been opposed to the new order had dropped from sight, but even so it was a great shock for Siegret to learn of decrees aimed at her and her father, to discover that they were no longer part of the ordinary mass of people but a separate and suspect minority.

Certain streets were banned to them for they contained monuments or memorials before which all Germans saluted, Jews were not allowed to give the Nazi salute and were therefore prevented from passing. Their passes were now stamped with the word Juden and the letter J imprinted on every page. Vile cartoons appeared in the press, backed up by ranting articles.

The attitude of the people around them had begun to change too. It was now a common occurrence for Siegret to find uniformed thugs daubing obscenities on the walls and windows of Jewish owned shops, and to see their owners, decent respectable men she had known all her life, being openly abused and roughly handled. It was common too, to hear groups of youths calling out at her jeeringly as she passed: 'Little Jewess, Jewish whore, dirty Jew.'

Even before the take-over her father had been worried about their future should the Nazis seize power in Vienna. He had memories of the troubled times immediately after the war, when chaos had reigned in the defeated empire. Also, though he scarcely ever referred to the matter, Siegret knew that he had had some dealings with the Nazis, or their leaders, from those days. For the past six years, ever since the rise of Hitlerism, he had refused to enter Germany on any pretext whatever, or to allow his daughter to do so.

When the Anschluss came he was prepared. Taking advantage of a day soon after, when gangs of youths had stormed the university to censor and burn all books and other works which the Nazi party had declared to be of a degenerate, non-Aryan nature, he dispatched a letter of resignation to the University Governors.

While the chanting crowds piled thousands of irreplaceable volumes on the bonfires, in an orgy of vandalism, and members of the faculty stood by helplessly, the Wienzmans had packed up their belongings and set off for their old family home in St. Veit. Seigret could never recall the memory of that journey without a shiver of fear. The two of them slipping away through the mob, dressed as inconspicuously as possible so as to escape attention, carrying with them only a few of their most valued possessions. Her father's small, upright figure, still dignified even in an old and shabby coat, guiding her safely out towards the station, all the time clutching the parcel containing his precious research records tightly to his chest, as though afraid someone would try to snatch it from him.

The journey had been long and wearying. Forbidden to own or drive a car, the old man and his daughter were banned from all but the cheapest of the third class trains and for much of the trip were forced to stand, packed tightly among scores of others. At every stop it seemed police had boarded the coaches to check papers and each time some unfortunate individuals had been dragged off for further questioning. In order to obtain permission to travel to an area so close to the frontier, special passes were necessary and Siegret had been in terror lest theirs should be in some way defective. Each time one of the strutting guards had examined the precious documents she had been gripped with numbing fear, her limbs trembling, her mouth dry, scarcely able even to whisper the answers to the curt questions.

Not till late at night did they finally reach the town. Siegret nearly cried with relief when they stepped out on to the familiar old station and saw the streets and houses she knew so well, clustered together at the head of the valley beneath the slopes of the mountains. The station master himself had greeted them and driven them to the house in his car and that night Siegret had slept soundly and unafraid for the first time in many weeks.

For a little while the spell remained. It did appear that the poisonous atmosphere of the cities had failed to reach the hearts and minds of the independent mountain villagers. The

Jewish decrees went ignored and forgotten and in any case the majority of the regulations were irrelevant to the countryside. Local officials were helpful and kindly, the ranks of the police free from the vicious thugs who had terrorized them in Vienna. With Munich and the threat of war over Czechoslovakia it seemed that the Nazis had turned their attentions eastwards and would perhaps be less concerned in future with the spectre of internal enemies.

The respite, however, was brief. As always it was among the children and youths that the first signs of trouble appeared. Subjected daily to intensive propaganda through the schools, educated in the politics of hatred and violence and encouraged by those in authority to indulge in every kind of outrage against the helpless section of the populace, already cowed by police action, bands of youths carried the campaign against the Jews even into the most remote areas of the country which, as yet, had been free from their activities.

The first Siegret had known of it had been when a gang of boys from the local school had shouted names after her in the street as she was walking home one afternoon. They were boys she knew, in their early teens for the most part, though with several older youths among them, and all had run off at the approach of an adult. But the pattern she remembered so well had begun again. The older boys in particular took to persecuting her, deriving particular pleasure in making her blush with shame by following her about making lewd and filthy suggestions to her, or leering at her in public when she went shopping for her father.

Soon life for the young girl had become worse than it had been even in Vienna. Her natural prettiness, which had increased with the clean air and good food of the mountains, served only as an added incentive to the louts who grew in number and appeared everywhere she went. One youth in particular she was especially afraid of. Heinz Gerdler was a big fair-haired boy, heavily built, and the leader of one of the gangs whose tactics was to pursue and trap her, forcing her to listen to his stories of what he had done to other Jewish girls and would soon do to her. Standing round they would jeer and laugh at her humiliation, till desperate and in tears she broke through their circle and fled home.

Though the youths had so far not dared to extend their attentions to himself, Professor Wienzman had observed their behaviour towards his daughter with anger, and a bitter frustration at the realization that he was powerless to do anything to prevent it. The chief of police for the St. Veit district was an old friend, Hans Meyer, and Wienzman went to ask his advice; that morning someone had daubed a crude slogan in whitewash on the fence in front of the house. Could not something be done to prevent such behaviour?

The policeman was a big, square faced man, with a slow phlegmatic temperament suited to his twenty stone weight. He listened in silence to the Professor's complaints. 'My friend,' he said shaking his head sadly when Wienzman had finished, 'I will do what I can but I must tell you that that is very little. These young louts,' he rolled the word contemptuously in his mouth, 'have official backing for their acts. It is incredible but true. If I try to arrest them, or even hinder them I shall lose my job. I know,' he held up a hand as the old man started to protest, 'that should not matter, I should be prepared to do my duty, and I am. But here in St. Veit I am responsible for many people. If I go someone much harder will be put in my place and then things will be much worse. There is nothing I can do for you here. My advice is that you leave this country and go away until these terrible times are over and the streets are safe for decent people again.'

'I am too old to leave my home,' the Professor answered, 'nor will I be driven from my own country by these hooligans. This persecution cannot last forever, it will pass.'

'Professor,' Meyer leant forward across the desk and spoke urgently. 'It is going to get very much worse and very quickly. Already in the cities there are killings and murders every day which go unpunished. This evil is spreading through the whole land. If war comes then who knows what the Nazis may do to people such as you? Take my advice and leave while you still have time; for your daughter's sake if not your own. In that at least I can be of some help with travel documents and passes.'

'We shall lose everything we own,' the Professor replied tonelessly, 'they let you take nothing out with you. Even taxes must be paid in advance for a full year after leaving. What would happen to us both? We shall be penniless.'

'Professor, a man of your reputation and qualifications will soon find a post in any country. England or America would welcome a distinguished doctor like yourself,' Meyer tried to reassure him. 'If you stay the Nazis will take everything anyway sooner or later, and you may lose your freedom as well, perhaps even your life.'

Reluctantly the Professor admitted that there was much sound advice in his friend's words and, after some delay, began to make preparations for departure. Even with the police chief's help the difficulties placed in the way of anyone wishing to emigrate were immense. No fewer than thirty-four separate permits and certificates had to be assembled, in addition to the usual passports and visas, all of them involving lengthy visits to the provincial government offices in Klagenfurt. Sometimes the Professor went alone, but frequently it was necessary for Siegret to accompany him and take her place in the long queues, or in the ever crowded waiting-rooms. The interviews, with churlish, overbearing officials were exhausting and dispiriting, and there seemed to be no end to them.

Nothing which might conceivably be of any value might be taken out of the country unless such huge sums were forfeited as to make the exercise worthless. Their home in St. Veit was sold for a nominal sum to a relative of Siegret's mother, who, since her family was not Jewish, would be safe, with the understanding that the Wienzmans were to continue to live there until their departure and that it was to be resold to them if they ever returned.

Again with the help of Hans Meyer a letter was smuggled to an old friend of the Professor's now working at the University of Rome, Dr. Augusto Farenzi. Through his aid Italian visas were obtained and he also promised to use his influence to persuade the United States Embassy in Rome to grant the pair visas for America.

Their preparations occupied the whole of the winter months,

but by March all was virtually complete and they awaited only confirmation of the American visas from Farenzi. Now that the time to leave had drawn near the Professor realized that he found the prospect infinitely more alarming than at first. For all its dark side, Austria was his home, and had been so for sixty years. He had little experience of travel abroad, and to throw up his life for the uncertainty of a new world, seemed to him a tremendous risk, and one he was reluctant to take unless convinced it was truly essential.

Yet at the same time he sensed that round him the time was running out.

In both ordinary daily affairs and the official press the tone of anti-Jewish feeling was becoming more strident. The persecution to which Siegret was subject had grown so bad that she scarcely dared leave the house. Even in St. Veit some shops would no longer serve non-Aryans and many private homes were barred to them. The decrees issued by the government were increasingly severe, their demands more humiliating.

Then, without warning, during the second week in March, while the Professor was recovering in bed from a chill, there came a devastating and unexpected blow which appeared to shatter all their plans. It came in the shape of a peremptory letter from the new Chancellor of the University in Vienna. It was brief and to the point. A recent review had shown that the Professor's research programme on disease immunization was of national importance, he was directed therefore to return immediately to continue his work.

The shock of this sudden message, when he had begun to believe that the authorities had forgotten his very existence, struck fear and dismay into the old man. Not so much for himself, he would be safe so long as his work was important, but for his daughter. Now the authorities would never let him send her to safety, she would be a hostage to his co-operation. They had waited too long.

'We shall have to go back,' he told her helplessly, letting the letter drop from his hand down on to the floor. Siegret picked it up and regarded him anxiously. The strain of the past eighteen months had told on them both, but in her father it was particularly marked. His hair had become totally white, where once there had been only silver streaks among the grey, and was thinning rapidly exposing the scalp beneath. His face, naturally aquiline, had always been lined about the nose and mouth and across the brow, but these had deepened into long creases in the skin while at the same time his cheeks had shrunk and hollowed. Propped up in bed on the pillows she had arranged for him, his hands lying listlessly on the coverlet, he had become, she realized, an old man.

Silently he drafted a telegram message of acceptance and gave it to Siegret to send.

'I will get up and come with you,' he said to her bitterly, 'since it is not safe for you to be out on the streets by yourself.' But Siegret refused to let him.

'It will be alright at this time in the afternoon,' she assured him, 'and there won't be any boys about outside in this weather. Besides that it's much too cold for you to go out Papa.' She tucked the bedclothes firmly around him as she spoke. 'I shall be perfectly safe,' she promised him, 'it's so dark outside I doubt if anybody will even be able to see me.'

Despite her protestations, Siegret was secretly more than a little worried at the prospect of a trip into the centre of the town. For a fortnight she had not ventured further than the end of the road in which they lived, and twice in recent days she had caught sight of Gerdler there. Putting on her boots and the thick furlined coat and hat her father had bought for her in Vienna the previous winter, she prayed that the gloom outside would indeed shield her from hostile eyes as she had said. The back way would be safest, there was less likelihood of being seen there and there would be plenty of side streets to duck down if she heard people coming. Tucking her father's message into her pocket she slipped out through the back door and set off down the road.

Ungainly and vulnerable on land, once in its natural habitat, the crocodile is a devastatingly formidable predator, so well adapted to its environment that it remains one of nature's most successful creations. A design that has been virtually un-

44

changed for more than one hundred and fifty million years, stretching back into the Triassic era with a direct link to the gigantic crocodilians of the age of dinosaurs, whose fossilized remains have been found to exceed forty five feet in length. With his savage jaws, heavily armoured back, his claws and enormously powerful tail, his tremendous strength and speed through the water, coupled with an ability to stay submerged for an hour or more at a time, or to float on the surface in perfect mimicry of a piece of driftwood, the crocodile is one of the most dangerous and lethal creatures in the world, and each year claims a greater number of human victims than any other species except the snake.

Its four foot jaws slightly agape, throat membranes closed to prevent the entry of water and its ton weight of armour-plated muscle floating virtually invisible, with only the nostrils, eye humps and the crest of the back protruding above the surface to betray its presence, the big croc drifted steadily downstream on the current making scarcely any movement save for an occasional swing with its tail to correct its course.

Its eyes scanned the banks on either side of the channel for any sign of prey near the river's edge, while its scent organs were alert for traces of food within the water itself. Shambe was now less than a mile downstream.

At 500 feet every detail of the swamplands was visible from the windows of the flying boat. At intervals flocks of ibis, plovers and scarlet waders still rose from their feeding grounds as the plane's shadow passed overhead. In one place Desmond caught sight of a group of hippos splashing hurriedly into deep water. He was holding down the speed to 90 knots with the rev counter showing a bare two thousand in a desperate effort to conserve every drop of their remaining fuel. The gauge was flickering about the zero mark and it was no longer possible to make an accurate guess of how much longer they could remain in the air.

'We should sight the station in the next three or four minutes,' Kendricks told him, 'we're about nine miles due south of it by my reckoning.' Nine miles, six or seven minutes

45

flying time, Desmond thought to himself. The moment was fast approaching when they would discover if their navigation had been accurate. If it had not, if they failed to sight the station when they expected, then they would have no choice but to ditch and pray that they and the passengers survived and that somehow, a rescue party would find them. All three of them were silent, concentrating on the ground ahead, their searching among the waving reeds for the first sign of their goal.

'Shall we ask London for permission to start jettisoning the cargo skipper?' suggested Kendricks behind and they laughed, the tension on the flight deck easing momentarily as they did so.

They had flown on for another two or three minutes when the inboard port engine coughed suddenly several times and commenced to run with a stacatto, irregular stutter. With the loss of power *Caterina*'s nose dipped sharply towards the ground. Instinctively everyone braced themselves. Desmond's hands moved swiftly over the controls, pulling back on the stick to lift her head again and opening up the throttle on the three good engines to boost the power and restore stable flight.

At the same time he began feathering the port engine, cutting it out completely for a second and allowing the airscrew to spin freely in the slipstream. Then turning up the fuel mixture and punching the ignition button he restarted it. The hope was that this would clear out any airlocks in the leads and set the motor running freely again. The engine gave another series of explosive coughs and the racketing stutter shook the wing again. Sweating Desmond switched off and repeated the manoeuvre; again the engine refused to fire properly. The strain in the cockpit was intense. Desperately he punched the ignition button a third time, expecting all the while to hear the same ominous sounds from the other engines. The altimeter showed they had sunk to less than 350 feet. Involuntarily Ken Frazer began looking for a place ahead in which to bring the aircraft down.

Again they heard the familiar stutter as the engine struggled to catch on the weak mixture. Ralph Kendricks' hand strayed to the radio emergency switch ready to get off a PAN signal, the airman's S O S, before they had to crash land. All three of them were about to give up hope when the engine suddenly burst out into a deep satisfying roar. With sighs of relief they relaxed. Synchronizing the engine into tune with the other three Desmond knew the danger was not yet over. The fault might have been only an air lock caused by insufficient pressure as the pumps sucked out the very dregs of the tanks, but at this height and speed any prolonged engine failure could be fatal. Unless they sighted the station within the next two or three minutes he would be forced to ditch in the best available stretch of water, praying as he did so that there were no hazards beneath the surface.

He checked the rev. counter and air speed indicators again. *Caterina* was flying at only just over stalling speed now. His hand was poised ready to open up the throttle the instant he felt the nose begin to drop, while his ears strained to catch the faintest hint of a check in the rhythm of one of the engines.

A sharp exclamation from Frazer jerked his attention back to the ground immediately ahead. The sound of the flying boat sweeping in low over the reed beds had surprised an enormous herd of elephants which had been browsing knee deep in the mud. The whole windscreen seemed full of heaving grey backs, streaked with mud, and massive heads tossed up in fear as the great beasts wildly plunged through the swamps, flinging up gouts of spray and muck, scattering in all directions.

'Christ! there must be hundreds, I've never seen so many together,' Frazer blurted out. 'Look at those tusks!' One huge bull, maddened with fear and enraged by the clinging mud which held him back had broken into a frenzied gallop and as the fliers watched in amazement, charged down a young calf, sending it crashing over amid the muck. The unfortunate beast struggled to rise but even as it did so others careered into it from behind, soon several of the herd were brought down struggling in the mire, their great limbs flailing desperately in their panic.

Then the flying boat was past and the vast herd lost to sight, leaving the men on the flight deck awestruck. All three had heard stories before of these herds to be found in the Sud, sometimes they roamed the swamps a thousand or more strong, secure from attack by hunters in their impenetrable sanctuary. The sight they had just seen must have been common all over Africa a century ago before the advent of white hunters with heavy game rifles.

'If we had come down in the middle of that lot . . .' standing behind them Ralph left the sentence unfinished. If the engines had given out back there a minute ago and had failed to respond to the feathering, Desmond thought grimly, they might well have found themselves gliding in to do just that. Low down, without power, they would have been unable to prevent an appalling crash right among the herd. It was quite possible that in their terror many of the beasts might actually have turned on the wrecked plane and attacked it. He could picture only too graphically the enraged elephants storming through the wreckage of the crashed flying boat, crushing to death anyone who remained alive.

'We must see the station soon,' Ken Frazer muttered under his breath. 'It can't be more than a mile or two away at the most by now. Where the hell is it?'

He glanced at the instrument panel again. Speed 81 knots, height 200 feet, fuel zero, below the gauges a line of five lights glowed red indicating that all four main tanks and the reserve were at danger point. Outside the wilderness still flashed past with no sign of the landing station. A flock of scarlet ibis rose before them and wheeled away to starboard, climbing rapidly, revealing the delicate pink underfeathers on thousands of wings.

'We shall have to ditch,' he told the others, 'unless we can spot the station within the next sixty seconds. I can't risk being forced down anywhere when the engines give out. So keep your eyes open for any stretch of water that looks at all usable.'

'Aye, aye Skipper,' Frazer replied mechanically, it was evident that he had been expecting such an order for the past five minutes. Immediately below the flying-boat the river channels were split by hundreds of small islets and banks to which vegetation clung thickly, nowhere that Desmond could see, was there sufficient length to hazard a touchdown. He reached out to flick on the switch of the lower deck intercom system and warn the passengers that a crash landing was imminent, as he did so a crackle of static from the radio sounded behind him.

'Skipper,' Kendricks called out, 'Shambe report they can hear the sound of our engines. They estimate we are approximately two miles south east of them. The landing area is clear, wind speed seven to eight knots from the north east.' The relief in his voice was plain to hear. For the second time in the space of a few minutes they felt themselves relax a little.

'O.K. We should be able to spot them soon enough now.' There was no need to tell the others to keep a sharp look-out. Beside him Ken Frazer was straining his eyes forward through the windscreen.

'There it is,' he cried thankfully, 'ahead at two o'clock,' as he and Desmond sighted the cluster of low, white houses almost simultaneously. No more than a couple of miles away the water opened out and at the tip of a bend in the river, the station lay half hidden among the surrounding reeds and a few bushes and stunted trees. The site allowed them a clear run in at a point where the Nile opened out into a broad unobstructed channel. A narrow jetty of wooden pilings had been built out into the water with a pair of white motor launches tied up alongside and a knot of people had gathered on the shore.

Pushing forward the levers controlling the electrically operated wing flaps, and slipping the airscrew into course pitch, Desmond brought *Caterina* down in a long slow sweep towards the river. Throttling back on all four engines he let her sink gently through the last few feet of air, checking carefully as he did so, that he had judged the height correctly.

At landing altitude the instruments were simply not precise enough to tell the pilot exactly how many feet he was above the water and the most careful judgement was called for in putting the heavy craft down on to the surface at the right moment. In certain conditions this could be extremely difficult, especially at times like this when the river surface was very calm and the afternoon light deceptive. An error of only a few feet could easily result in catastrophe.

If the pilot came in too high at the moment he throttled back and reduced speed the flying-boat would literally drop into the water, certainly causing herself serious damage, perhaps even breaking up. After one such accident another of Imperial's fleet had recently had to be crated up and sent back to the makers to have every one of the two hundred and fifty thousand rivets in her hull replaced.

Equally serious was the risk involved in coming in too fast and striking the surface at too high a speed, or at the wrong altitude. Then there was a strong chance of a wing dipping and catching in the water causing the aircraft to capsize.

A fresh bout of coughing vibrated throughout the flight deck as another engine, this time one on the starboard wing, faltered. Praying that the power would hold out long enough to get him down Desmond ignored the sound and closed the throttles still further. Water flashed past outside the windows, there was a slight jar, a burst of spray, a trembling and hissing as the keel split the surface and trailing a long stream of foam, the aircraft breasted down on the river and settled gently on her planing bottom while one after another the remaining engines spluttered into silence.

II

By Radio: AIR TRAFFIC CONTROL CAIRO TO IM-
PERIAL AIRWAYS LONDON. 1640 hrs. LOCAL
TIME. RELAYED FROM KHARTOUM. IMPERIAL
AIRWAYS FLIGHT 109 G-ADHO FORCED TO
MAKE EMERGENCY LANDING AT SHAMBE-
SUDAN FOR FUEL TANK REPAIRS. PASSEN-
GERS AND CARGO SAFE. ESTIMATED DELAY
TWO TO THREE HOURS. WILL ADVISE
FURTHER WHEN REPAIRS COMPLETED. END.

EVEN before *Caterina* had stopped moving, the two launches
from the station had started towards her across the river; the
channel at this point was about three hundred yards wide and
the aircraft came to rest a little over half that distance from the
shore. Directly beneath the flight deck and right in the prow of
the flying boat was a small box-like space where ropes and
fenders, and other tackle used for mooring, were stored.
Reached by a ladder from the flight deck, it also had a hatch
opening out from the prow and a retractable mooring bollard
let into the hull. Ralph Kendricks lifted up the trapdoor in the
cockpit floor directly behind the pilots' seats and dropped
through. There was a bang and a loud click as he undid the
hatch and a draught of warm air filtered up into the cockpit
bringing with it a smell of mud, and the sound of water slop-
ping against the hull outside.

Sandy Everett came hurrying through from the mailroom
clutching his cap and handful of letters. 'Will you be sending
the passengers ashore, Sir?' he queried and Desmond nodded,
'Yes, they'll have to land while we take another look at the
tank. You and Andy had better go along with them and see
they don't get into any trouble. Make them all go straight up to

the rest-house and don't let them start sightseeing and wandering about more than necessary.'

Since Shambe did not possess the special Braby mooring pontoons which enabled passengers to disembark directly on to dry land, *Caterina* was towed to a fixed mooring buoy thirty yards out from the shore and made fast. The two white launches, surprisingly smart and well cared for, for such a remote spot, at once began ferrying people off under the supervision of Sandy and Draper the Steward, while in the cockpit Desmond and Frazer completed the landing check.

'Do you want to write up the log now?' Frazer asked with apparent unconcern.

'No,' Desmond told him, 'I'll wait till I hear what the engineer has to say first.' A scowl passed briefly over the First Officer's face. He was anxious to try and discover exactly what Desmond intended to say about the reasons for the break of the itinerary.

A third boat, loaded down with tools and equipment approached, bringing out an engineer to look at the ruptured fuel tank and Desmond went out on to the wing to talk to him, glad of an excuse to escape from the atmosphere inside the cabin. Frazer's attitude annoyed him, the more so since it was based on bad judgement. However much Desmond might berate him privately for his inefficiency, when it came to writing up the log he would never have considered for a moment trying to shift the blame on to a junior officer. The responsibility was his as the Captain. The inability to realize this was just another reason why Frazer had a long way to go before the time came to give him his stripes.

The engineer was a small, dark skinned man, in an oil stained shirt and trousers, who spoke a mixture of English, French and Portuguese. His usual tasks, Desmond guessed, were confined to repairing the engines of the boats or overhauling the few motor vehicles in the station. He examined the tank with care for some minutes and shook his head pessimistically.

'Well?' Desmond demanded of him, 'how long will it take to plug the leak?' The engineer came back along the wing, ducking under the wire of the dipole radio aerial and the two of them stood on top of *Caterina*'s hull.

'It will not be easy Captain,' the engineer pronounced the rank in the continental manner, 'in order to make the repairs correctly I must weld a new patch into position along the seam. The patch there now is too small. Even that will not be a permanent repair, but it will last you until you reach Cairo. There the facilities are better.' He glanced apologetically down at the boat with his own equipment which had tied up to the wing float. 'How long will it take to do this?' Desmond asked him impatiently. The flight to Khartoum 550 miles away took two and a half hours. The time was four-thirty already, unless they could get away within the next three hours they would have to stay at Shambe for the night. Even as it was he would have to make a night landing at Khartoum and the passengers would be lucky to reach their hotel before midnight.

'Maybe three, four hours,' the engineer shrugged. 'It is difficult to say. The leak is very bad.' That much was certainly true. Even from where they were standing the smell of spirit was clearly detectable, and when they had opened up the wing to look at the tank the fumes had nearly choked them. The whole of the inside of the wing must have been swimming with fuel. It was a miracle that there hadn't been a fire. That too would have to be cleaned out and made safe before they could take to the air again.

Leaving the engineer to start getting up his tools, Desmond climbed back inside the aircraft through the mailroom hatch and returned to the control room. Frazer was still in his seat inspecting the river banks through the flight deck binoculars.

'See anything interesting?' Desmond asked him.

'A couple of native canoes are putting out towards us,' Frazer told him, passing over the glasses. 'An official from the station was talking to them but he's just left. You can see him walking back along the bank.'

'He was probably making sure the canoes kept out of the way while the launches were busy,' Desmond twisted the focus adjuster and the image became suddenly sharp and clear. Two canoes, more like rafts really, made from bundles of reeds

lashed together were coming towards them. The natives pad-
dling them were tall, magnificently built, proud looking men,
apparently completely unclothed. On the leading craft one of
them stood up and waved his paddle in greeting.

From down below in the mooring compartment came the
noise of someone moving about and Ralph Kendricks' head
emerged through the trap door.

'All secure down below,' he reported scrambling out. 'I've
wedged a fender right up under the nose ring so the cable
shouldn't run out at all.' Tying up in open water in this fashion
tended to result in badly flaked paintwork on the flying-boat's
prow caused by the mooring cables chaffing with the swell,
giving the aircraft a slovenly appearance which Desmond
hated.

'I'll have to go ashore and get off a report to London,' he
told them, 'before they start calling us. I want you both to stay
on board and keep an eye on things.' There was no need to say
why. 'You had better each keep one of these with you,' opening
the metal locker behind his seat, he took out the canvas pouch
which Ian Haggard had given him at Durban. Frazer and Kendricks received the pistols without enthusiasm.

'Must be one hell of a big demand for gold round here,'
Ralph remarked sardonically, looking out at the tiny group of
houses and the vast wilderness that surrounded them. 'I reckon
there's a bigger risk of being eaten.' He indicated the natives
who were circling the flying boat uttering shrill cries. Desmond
smiled. 'I'll be back as soon as I've sent the message,' he said. 'I
want to supervise the work on that fuel tank myself.' This
last remark brought an angry flush to Frazer's face. If the rest
of the trip continued in the same manner Desmond thought to
himself, as he descended the gangway, he was going to be
heartily thankful when they reached New York.

The smaller of the two launches was waiting for him at the
main entry port. About twelve feet long it had space for six or
eight passengers beneath the canvas awning and was crewed by
a pair of cheerful natives who, in deference to European sen-
sibilities, wore smart white shorts.

Taking off his jacket, he undid his collar and loosened his tie.

The heat must be about ninety five degrees he guessed, but it was the humidity which was making him uncomfortable. It was the beginning of the rainy season in Equatoria, the very worst time to be there, but even so he felt glad of the chance to see it. Very probably this part of Africa would never see regular tourists or visitors. In fact with the improvement in range of aircraft fewer rather than more planes would call.

The shore line was littered with canoes and rafts and piled baulks of timber, evidently flotsam picked up from the river. The small jetty gave access to the rest house; beyond it, tied up to the remains of a rotting wharf, the derelict hulk of an old paddle steamer, bore silent witness to the station's vanished traffic of the past.

Rain had fallen recently, presumably it did so each day at this time of year, and a line of duckboards led across the muddy ground to the rest house and airline office. Desmond stepped out of the launch and dismissed the crew, as a tall, gangling man in khaki shorts and shirt came down to meet him.

'Keeling,' he greeted him holding out his hand, 'Barry Keeling, I'm the station chief. Welcome to Shambe.' He was a tough, wiry looking man, aged about forty-five, though his thinning hair made him seem older, deeply tanned and with the fit, agile movements of someone used to strenuous existence. He was one of those men, Desmond guessed, who deliberately sought out posts in remote places like Shambe, where they could indulge their passion for hunting and exploration, away from the cares and pressures of the rest of the world.

Briefly he explained the trouble with the fuel tank and repeated what the engineer had said. Keeling listened gravely. 'I'm sorry to add to your problems,' he said when Desmond had finished; 'But I'm afraid we've come across an added complication. The fuel in one of our storage tanks has become contaminated by rainwater. We've had heavy downpours for the past week but it was only discovered today. Anyway the result is we haven't enough here to get you up to Malakal. I've radioed Malakal however and they are sending us down five hundred gallons on board a Calcutta they've got up there, but I'm afraid it won't reach us till seven o'clock at the earliest.'

'Everything's going wrong today,' Desmond said with exasperation, 'how many gallons have you got still useable?'

'Two hundred, one of the tanks was more than half empty, but the Calcutta will be carrying enough to get her home again without refuelling here, so you should be able to carry right on through to Khartoum if you want to. You can tranship the mail for Malakal here.'

'Yes, that's what I was thinking,' Desmond agreed. 'If I can have the repairs completed and the fuel on board by seven thirty I'll make the trip tonight.' Keeling grinned.

'Sure we can't persuade you to stay?' he asked, 'I mean, just look at what we can offer in the way of sightseeing and entertainment.' He indicated the buildings of the little town with a wave of his hand.

'Personally, I wouldn't mind at all, neither would the rest of the crew,' Desmond grinned back, 'but I can imagine some of our passengers not being too happy at the idea.'

'No,' Keeling admitted as they began to walk back up to the rest house. 'That's very true. One of your female passengers has already complained at our allowing the natives to go about naked. Still, it's a pity you can't stay, we might have been able to offer you some shooting, if you enjoy that. Elephant, lion, buck, hippos, crocodile, buffalo. It's a hunter's paradise.' His eyes glowed as he spoke. 'Crocs too?' Desmond asked with a backward glance at the river. 'I should think this must be just the place for them.'

'They grow to greater size here than anywhere in the world,' Keeling answered. 'I've seen more than one twenty footer and fifteen or sixteen feet is quite common. We lost a woman from the village to one last week,' he added. 'It took her while she was bathing in the shallows. Sometimes they even attack boats and overturn them to get at the people on board.'

Laura Hartman had come ashore in the launch with the middle aged couple she had met on the plane, Mr. and Mrs. Harold King of Phoenix, Arizona. Mr. King was a short, stout man clad in grey trousers, a white gaberdine jacket and a white shirt open at the neck, wearing a straw hat with a black ribbon. His wife was about the same height as her husband, though much lighter in build. She was more formally dressed in a neat but old fashioned brown suit and cotton blouse. Her face, creased and wrinkled by the dry summers of her home, was shrewd but kindly.

Their landing had been nowhere near as quiet and uneventful as Desmond's was to be a few minutes later. A small crowd of white officials and residents and curious native on-lookers had gathered to meet them at the jetty so that the moment they stepped ashore they were surrounded by a jostling excited mass. Laura and the Kings travelled in the same boat as Mr. and Mrs. Johnson and their daughter. The little girl was fascinated by the strange, new country and danced about the launch impatient to reach the land after the long period in the air. Hastening along the jetty after her Mrs. Johnson suddenly found herself in the centre of a chattering throng of stark naked natives of both sexes. For a moment she stood speechless with embarrassment and indignation, then, letting out a sharp cry she rounded on poor Sandy Everett who had also been in the launch.

'How dare you allow such a disgusting display?' she demanded furiously. 'It's obscene and horrible! You knew I had a child with me. Clear these people away at once.' Her face was bright red with anger and shame and Sandy felt himself turning crimson as the woman's husband, a serious faced man in a brown trilby, joined in the outcry and threatened to take his family straight back to the aircraft.

'I'm terribly sorry,' he apologized, 'I honestly had no idea about it. I think they always dress like this. It must be the heat,' he said helplessly. Everywhere he looked he seemed to see quivering breasts and genitals displayed by their owners without the least trace of concern. To make matters worse many of the women in the crowd were young and extremely attractive.

'Well, you should have known,' Mr. Johnson told him angrily. 'And don't just stand there, do something.' Mrs Johnson broke into loud sobbing.

Fortunately the situation was saved by Mrs. King, who

pushed forward and took the weeping woman and her now equally tearful daughter by the arm and began leading them up the path to the rest house.

'I know just how you feel,' she said firmly as they went, 'but you must remember that these people are quite innocent, they haven't learned our standards of decent behaviour yet and I think the only thing we can do is ignore them.' The remaining passengers followed her along the path and Sandy shot Harold King and Laura a look of heartfelt gratitude. Andy Draper brought up the rear.

'See,' he hissed to the young purser, 'didn't I tell you there'd be trouble. Stupid woman! The way she carried on you'd think it was us that wasn't wearing any clothes.'

Facing on to the strip of bare, muddy ground that bordered the river were a number of white-washed, single storied, square stone buildings with flat roofs. The largest of them an L shaped bungalow with a screened verandah beside which grew a tamarisk tree, was the airline and river service rest house. The others were houses belonging to the handful of local officials stationed in the town, the river pilots, a mission school and a general store. Behind these, lay a sizeable village of mud huts and shanty dwellings which had grown up around the station. Around the edge of these huts a few acres of land had been cleared and drained in an attempt to scratch a living from the poor soil, and supplement the efforts of the fishermen and hunters. Beyond, the great marshes stretched away to the horizon in a forest of apple green reeds. The air was hot and sticky, heavy with the smell of rotting vegetation and stagnant water, and from everywhere there came the ceaseless whine of insects, and the cries of birds.

To Siegret Wienzman's intense relief the streets on her route to the centre of St. Veit were all but deserted. Although snow was not actually falling, the sky was dark with its threat and a bitterly cold wind was driving up the valley from the north keeping the inhabitants firmly indoors by their fires. She had chosen this particular time for her sortie because she knew she could count on a clear space of half an hour between the emptying of the schools after the afternoon lessons, and the appearance on the streets of the first of the homeward going workers.

The pavements and roadway were covered with frozen snow and slush, interspersed with treacherous patches of black ice. Siegret picked her way carefully, hurrying as best she could, watching all the time for any sign of danger, and ready to duck down a turning or into a doorway the moment she caught sight of anybody she did not trust. With luck, even if she were seen she thought, in her long dark coat and fur hat she might well escape recognition in the poor light.

Besides the danger of being seen and pursued, the other thought which occupied her mind was what she and her father would do in the future. The telegram the old man had given her simply informed the University governors that he had received their letter and would be returning to Vienna at once to take up his work again. That much he had to do even if only to buy time for them to escape. A refusal to undertake the work designated 'of national importance' would certainly lead to imprisonment in labour camps for both of them.

Even doing such work would not necessarily ensure their safety. The authorities might perhaps change their minds about the value of the Professor's research. Equally the Nazis might decide to send Siegret herself to a camp as hostage for her father's good behaviour. Whatever happened, at the very best she and her father would have to face all the dangers of Vienna from which they had been trying to escape, and from which hundreds were still fleeing every day. Professor Wienzman had never been a particularly devoted Jew, indeed he had married a Christian, Siegret's mother, and until the Nazi rise to power had regarded himself simply as an Austrian, but the persecution had driven him and many others of similar beliefs, into closer ties with the Jewish community. Through this they were kept aware of what was happening in the cities and in other parts of the country.

News of increasing severity in the persecution, of the notorious 'Crystal Night' when the synagogues were destroyed and the Jewish shops smashed, of the ever-growing numbers of arrests, of the beatings and murders and rapes was passed on to them even in Villach. More than half of the Jews of Vienna, Siegret knew, had already left the city or been driven away.

The Professor had considered returning alone and leaving his daughter in the care of some family in the mountain town. One or two were still friendly towards them and would help as Hans Meyer was doing, but Siegret had refused even to discuss such an alternative. The very thought of remaining behind alone in St. Veit while her father went off to the capital appalled her. She would have virtually no means of knowing if he were safe, or when she would ever see him again and she would have to face the harassment of Gerdler and his gang by herself.

As she approached the town square the streets grew wider and less deserted. Cars passed by several times and she met people hurrying about, muffled up against the cold. Fortunately everyone appeared to be too anxious to finish their errands and get home to the warmth to worry about the slight figure that slipped by, head bowed to hide her face.

The Post Office itself was the part of the journey she had dreaded most of all. There were three or four people inside but fortunately they were engrossed in their own business and none of them took any notice of her. Nervously she filled out the telegraph form, mis-writing it in her haste and having to begin again, before handing it in across the counter and starting back.

All the while she was near the busy part of the town her heart started violently each time a figure came towards her. The youths often spotted her in this area and then followed her back to the house. Usually they waited until the street was clear before beginning the taunts and jeers but lately they had become bolder and less afraid of a rebuke from an adult hearing them. If she could only gain the safety of the narrower, less frequented back streets she stood a good chance of getting back unobserved. If Gerdler or any of the others were near the house she could then simply rush past them.

She was halfway there when the boys saw her. Six of them came out of a road on her right so suddenly that they practically walked into her. They were wearing the brown shirts and shorts of the Hitler Jugend movement and among them Siegret recognized at least three members of Hans Gerdler's gang. Obviously they had been delayed after school attending some meeting.

Instantly, without thought she turned and ran frantically back in the direction of the nearest main street. At least there in the open, however much they might tease and leer at her they would not dare to molest her physically. Though the youths had been momentarily as taken aback as their quarry and were slower to react, they took up the chase with eagerness. Siegret heard their feet pounding swiftly after her and the quick cries of pursuit. The lane she was fleeing down was long and narrow, along one side ran the backs of a row of houses, the other was fronted for two thirds of its length by a high wall surrounding the local primary school, empty now that the day was over. Panic-stricken and without knowing what she was doing, Siegret ran in through the gate at the far end and up the steps to the main doorway with the mob at her heels. They caught her as she grasped the handle.

The youths were all in their middle teens, two of them no more than schoolboys, and now that they had caught her they seemed to have no clear plan of what to do next. They held the trembling girl against the wooden panels of the door while they regained their breath and very probably had she had the strength then to tear herself free and run on she might have escaped with no more than a fright. The long months of fear and persecution however had successfully sapped her will to a point where such an experience left her incapable of resistance. So terrified was she that the youths literally had to hold her up on her feet.

The cries and noise of the chase had attracted others from the gang and it was not long before Hans Gerdler arrived with others of the older boys. He pushed his way through to stand in front of her and grinned evilly at her.

'So what have we here?' he demanded, seizing the girl by the chin and forcing her head round to look at him. 'A little Jewess out on the streets, what were you doing Jewess? Why did you run away from our patrol?'

Too frightened to answer, Siegret remained silent. Gerdler released her and began slapping her lightly across the face. Her fur hat fell off on to the ground. He turned to his followers.

'See how rich these Jews are,' he declaimed, 'with money they extort from honest Germans. This Jewess is wearing furs while the rest of us have hardly got a coat to our backs.'

'Get it off her and let her see what cold's really like,' called someone. There was a chorus of agreement and several of the gang began pulling off her coat.

'Let me alone!' Siegret screamed, 'I wasn't doing anything. I was just going home. You haven't the right to do this to me.'

'Haven't the right, we'll soon show you what your rights are,' Gerdler retorted. 'Take her coat off,' he ordered. There was a brief struggle but against so many hands the girl was powerless. In a few moments she was shivering before them in a thin cotton blouse. The youths tossed the coat away with a laugh.

'That's better,' Gerdler said with a sneer. 'Now we can have a better look at you. Oh no you don't!' With a sudden desperate effort Siegret had twisted free from the hold upon her and had made a dart for freedom. Grabbing her by the arms he pushed her back up against the doors, pressing his great body against her as she squirmed beneath him. The others stood round laughing.

Powerless against his strength, Siegret felt his hands start roaming over her body, pinching and squeezing. Her struggles served only to arouse him further.

'Let's get her inside,' he called to the others, 'and see what little Jewesses are made of.' Siegret let out a scream at his words, but a hand was clamped over her mouth. There was a fumbling at the lock of the door behind her and she was dragged through into the passage. 'In here, take her in here,' Gerdler said as the boys paused. 'Put her down on the table,' he panted still holding her tightly. Several more of them grasped her and she felt herself lifted up and flung down on her back on the hard surface of a classroom table. She could see the wooden beams of the ceiling above her and the faces of her attackers leering down at her. Someone tugged off her boots.

'High and mighty Miss Wienzman, who walks about with her nose in the air and thinks she's too good for the rest of us because she comes from Vienna.' Gerdler hissed viciously. 'Now we're going to show you how to be nice to us.' Taking her blouse by the neck with a single jerk he ripped it open to the waist.

'Hold her down,' he snapped as Siegret fought violently. Reaching out again he tore down her slip and brassiere. The other boys crowded round breathing fast with excitement, their faces flushed. Hands pawed at her breasts. 'Quick,' said another voice she did not recognize. 'Pull off her skirt.' Clumsy fingers fumbled at the fastening at her waist, she tried to kick out but her legs were pinned tightly to the unyielding table. Her skirt and slip came down, stripped eagerly off over her ankles. Desperately she bit hard at the hand over her mouth, her teeth meeting in the flesh. There was a shrill cry of pain and the hand was snatched away. Instantly she let out a scream.

'Bitch!' Gerdler snarled, and struck her violently in the face with his fist. 'Keep her quiet. We don't want people coming in.'

Someone else gripped her mouth shut tightly, the nails clawing savagely at her cheek, stifling her cries. Her head was spinning with pain and shock. Fingers scrabbled urgently at her panties, there was a sound of tearing fabric and she felt cold air strike her skin. Hands were touching and feeling all over her body, she heard Gerdler call out harshly, 'spread her legs open!' and her thighs were forced apart.

The other boys were still pawing at her. Gerdler pushed them aside. 'I'll go first,' he panted, 'the rest of you can follow.' His weight descended heavily on top of her, crushing her against the table. Siegret was aware of his face pressed up against her own, his breath in her nostrils. The hand over her face was released and his grinning mouth clamped fiercely down on her lips, their teeth grinding together, his fingers were probing between her thighs.

There was a sudden confusion of noise, voices raised, shouts and swearing, cries of alarm. The hands that had been holding her down let go. She heard the sound of running feet. The boy on top of her was pulled away. Sick and faint, and scarcely realizing that she had been released she tried to sit up. A face bent over her, a man's. Siegret screamed chokingly and shrank away.

'It's all right,' she heard him say. 'It's the caretaker, Stortman. They've gone away, I've got rid of them all. You're safe now.'

Dimly, through a haze of shock and nausea Siegret found she remembered him. They were alone together in the classroom. The youths must have fled when they heard him coming, ashamed to be caught actually trying to rape someone, even a Jewish girl. The caretaker was a middle-aged, shabby looking man, he fussed about trying to help, unable to take his eyes off her body. Looking down at herself Siegret saw that her blouse was in ribbons, the whole of the front entirely torn away together with all her underclothing and one of the sleeves, and from the waist downwards she was completely naked, her stockings hanging in shreds about her ankles.

Feebly she tried to cover herself. Her grey skirt lay in a bundle by the door where one of her attackers had dropped it. The caretaker fetched it for her and turned away while she pulled it on and drew the torn fragments of her blouse together to hide her breasts.

'You'd best put my coat round your shoulders,' the man offered kindly, 'and come round the back to my room. You can tidy up there and then I'll take you home to your father. They ought to be punished those boys,' he added as Siegret began sobbing quietly, her tears streaming down her scratched and bruised face. He managed to retrieve both her boots and with an effort she put them on and gathered up the scattered remains of her underclothes which lay about the room. Her skirt was badly ripped and she had to hold it up with one hand.

'This way,' the caretaker took her gently by the shoulder and he led her away, still trembling from her ordeal.

Despite Dr. Van Smit's remarks about the unpleasantness of

the swamps and the dangers to be met there, neither Laura nor the Kings were at all put out by the extra stop. Indeed Laura herself felt intrigued by the idea of visiting so notorious an area. Although the air was close and sticky and the ground covered with patches of mud, the opportunity of looking round the little town attracted her far more than the proposal of iced drinks and easy chairs in the rest house.

Mr. King had brought his camera ashore with him and Laura decided to ask if she could borrow it before they returned to the aircraft. She had just reached the entrance to the rest-house when she met Mrs. King coming out in the company of Lieutenant Thorne.

'Laura, my dear, I shall have to go down to the launch,' Mrs. King told her, 'Lieutenant Thorne has kindly offered to run me out to the aeroplane to get my travelling case. I've gone and left it under my seat.'

'There's really no need for you to trouble yourself Mrs. King,' Thorne assured, 'If you just describe the case to me I'll fetch it for you easily.'

'No, no, I shall most certainly come,' she replied firmly, 'I'm afraid I'm not entirely sure where I put it. You might have difficulty finding it.'

'Mrs. King, why don't you let me go across and look for it?' suggested Laura, 'I know what your case is like and it's silly for you to tire yourself in this heat.'

'I say, that's a splendid idea,' Thorne said eagerly, delighted at the prospect of a few minutes alone in Laura's company, 'Mrs. Hartman and I will have your case for you in a jiffy.'

The landing stage and jetty were deserted when they reached the shore and there was no sign of the launch crews or of any of the station staff on the banks.

'Don't you think we ought to find someone to take us out?' Laura said, but the young man dismissed the idea at once. 'I do know how to handle a boat Mrs. Hartman,' he replied a trifle petulantly, and without waiting to see if anyone would come to stop them he handed her down into the launch, and followed her aboard.

With the departure of the passengers for the rest-house the

crowd on the foreshore had dispersed and peace had returned to the river. At this time of the day few people were normally stirring from their rest, and the water-dikkops and plovers, no longer disturbed by the noise of the launch engines, had returned to the reed beds near the banks and resumed their feeding. A pair of grey herons flew silently in, their long legs trailing behind them in the air, and alighted near the beached canoes and rafts of the village to search for scraps of fish. Only the faint sounds of the engineer and his assistants working on the flying-boat in mid-stream disturbed the quiet of the afternoon.

Emboldened once more by the calm, the big croc pushed out from the shallows where it had been waiting and let itself be carried down along the bank with the current, moving very slowly and at a slight angle to the line of the river. Its resemblance to a drifting log was perfect. Its eyes scanned the banks for prey. Nowhere was there anything in sight near the water. One or two figures moved about among the huts of the village, a pig squealed from somewhere. Unhurriedly the croc steered closer in towards the bank, aiming for the end of the wooden jetty.

It was about ten yards away when it first spotted Laura and Ian Thorne approaching. Instantly the muscles of its body tensed, its pulse quickening as it prepared to strike. Watching the two intently it moved in nearer.

The launch had been made fast at both ends. Thorne went forward to cast off the bow rope before going back to release the stern and start the engine. The rope was tied to one of the pilings on a level with the low gunwale of the deck. He stooped down to loosen it.

Seeing him stoop the croc quickened its pace, diving below the surface and thrusting forward.

The rope was wet and greasy from long use, and tightly tied. Its end slipped out through the young man's fingers and fell back into the water between the stern of the boat and the jetty.

As he bent down lower to retrieve it, the crocodile came gliding unseen past the head of the jetty and saw the figure dabbling in the water above it only a few feet away, the white

66

uniform making a clear mark. With a powerful double thrust of its tail, it shot forward swiftly to the attack surging through the murky liquid round the pilings, jaws opening wide.

By a fraction of a second it was too late. Thorne had recovered the rope and was already straightening up when the attack came. His hands and arms were out of reach at the moment the huge jaws came level with him.

This time there could be no mistaking the danger. The croc's head broke the surface of the water, and the passage of the great reptile driving forward and upwards was clearly marked by a long eddy and a trail of bubbles. Thorne had a sudden vision of the huge creature lunging for him out of the depths.

With a cry of alarm he leapt back and his sudden action upset the equilibrium of the boat, it swayed violently, throwing him off balance and making him clutch wildly at the gunwale for support. It was this action which gave the crocodile an unlooked for second chance. Its jaws were now too far past to be of use in the attack but, seeing out of the corner of its wide-angled eyes, the white figure once more bending low over the water, it lashed upwards and outwards with its tail.

Like an enormous club, this terrible weapon, six feet of bone and hard muscle, encased in a carapace of armoured plate, sharp ridged along the crest, and making up almost one third of the animal's weight, whipped out at the helpless man, smashing him clean off the launch and into the water beyond the jetty.

Instantly the croc arched round, its body banking steeply in a tight turn against the boat. Massive jaws agape, it thrust furiously forward for its prey. No longer concerned with stealth and silence, its tail thrashed the water again, and its limbs paddled furiously as it swept round. The river's surface erupted in an explosion of foam and spray.

Ian Thorne never had a chance. The blow from the huge tail had broken his left arm and two of his ribs and knocked him half unconscious. Choking on the water entering his throat, he struggled weakly to regain the boat, even as he did so the croc was upon him.

The savage jaws clamped shut on his left thigh in a bone

crunching grip that ripped through the flesh, severing the blood vessels and bursting the femoral artery. A dark trail of blood began to stain the surface as the croc started to drag its victim off into mid-river.

Appalling screams broke from the doomed man, his arms flailed in the water with all his remaining strength in a desperate fight to free himself from the relentless grip on his leg and resist the creature's attempt to carry him away from the shore.

Badly injured and half drowned as he was, Thorne might perhaps have stood some hope against a beast of more normal size. Laura's cries, his own screams, the loud smack of the croc's tail on the river's surface, the splashing and struggles in the water, had all attracted the attention of people on shore. With a croc of perhaps only eight or twelve feet long he might have been able to fight long enough for help to reach him.

He was hopelessly outmatched in strength by the ton weight of the white-scarred monster however. Shaking him as a dog might shake a rat, it drew him out into the main channel. In a matter of seconds it was in deep water once more. Then clamping its jaws even more tightly about the man's thigh, it dived steeply downwards towards the river-bed thirty feet below. Its prey was weakening fast and it sensed that the battle would soon be over.

The water closing over his head spurred Thorne to make one final despairing effort to free himself, wrenching with panic-maddened strength against the teeth which had bitten agonizingly through to the bones.

Infuriated by this final show of resistance, the croc went into its most fearsome and terrible manoeuvre. Ceasing its attempts to pull its victim into the mud at the bottom, it allowed itself to float upwards for a few feet. Then, even as Thorne, fast losing all consciousness, gained a moment's hope, it tightened its grip again and suddenly flung itself into a violent spiral twisting motion, its whole body rotating over and over rapidly along its length.

The terrific force of this action splintered the man's thigh bone from hip to knee, mangling the leg till it was virtually torn from his body. A cloud of blood and fragments of flesh and bone spurted out. The croc twisted again with all the leverage of its enormous weight, and then backed away, tugging the now completely severed leg clear of the torso. The man's remains had become invisible behind a screen of blood and particles of debris, mixed with mud from the bottom, stirred up by the fight. More blood was pumping from the ragged stump and it took the croc a moment to locate its victim again.

It mattered little, Thorne was finished. Shock, loss of blood and drowning had completed their work. Before the crocodile laid hold of him a second time he was dead.

From the shore and from on board the *Caterina*, the attack had been witnessed in horror and amazement. The suddenness and its speed had caught everyone unawares, even those from the town who had experienced them before. Barry Keeling kept a heavy hunting rifle in his office and the instant he had realized what had happened, he had seized it and raced down to the water's edge. Desmond had reached the jetty already and was supporting Laura Hartman in his arms. When the first cries had brought him running from the rest house, he had found her collapsing in a state of shock in the launch, and his immediate thought had been for her safety. Now he stood holding her, and watching in impotent fury while the crocodile overcame Thorne's resistance.

By this time the trail of swirling blood-streaked water already ran a long way out into the river. When he had got there the struggle had still been taking place near the surface in a furious welter of foam and splashing. Through this, for one brief instant he had caught a glimpse of the young man, the uniform showing very white and slashed across with bright lines of red where the great brute had clawed him. Coiled round him had been the enormous green-black body of the reptile, its tail lashing at the water and the man it had seized with impartial frenzy.

Then both had sunk from view as the crocodile gained the depths of the main channel. The frothing and splashing on the surface had ceased abruptly and only a strong churning of the water marked where the final phase of the struggle was being fought out below and Thorne's death throes overcome.

Keeling flung the rifle to his shoulder and the crash of the heavy weapon echoed across the marshes and reed beds. Clouds of birds rose shrieking into the air and flapped hastily away as he fired twice more, but the crocodile was too deep now to be frightened off and the echoes died uselessly away. The surface of the river became calm again, the churning from below ceased, and the bloody tracks in the water diffused and disappeared. Before a boat could set off from the shore, all traces of the tragedy had vanished and the river had returned to its former tranquillity.

David Wienzman was hardly able to recognize the battered girl brought home by the caretaker as his daughter. Siegret had made a brave attempt to clean herself up, but the bruises on her face had already begun to swell and darken, her eyes were puffy and red from crying, her lips bleeding. She was covered in deep scratches all over her body and still nearly hysterical from what she had been through.

Helping her upstairs to her room he sent the caretaker back to summon first the town Doctor and then Hans Meyer from the police offices. The Doctor was a woman and would be better able to see to his daughter than himself.

'But Father,' Siegret cried at him when he told her what he had done. 'Don't you understand? It's no use going to the police, it's no use asking anyone to help. Those boys are from the Hitler Jugend, they can do what they like to us, we're Jews, we have no rights. Nobody can protect us,' and she burst into renewed sobbing.

The Doctor arrived and examined her carefully and dressed her wounds. Where the youths had gripped her, ugly marks had developed in which the imprints of fingers and nails showed clearly in the skin. The blow she had received on the face had split both lips and bruised the whole of one side of her face. Livid marks and blotches covered her chest, stomach and thighs, interscored with deep scratches, where the youths had pinched and scrabbled at her.

'Your daughter has suffered no serious physical injury,' she told him when she descended to the sitting-room. 'Fortunately

70

she was rescued in time before those young louts could have their way with her. As for her mental condition,' she shook her head, 'it is too early to be sure. Sometimes a person recovers quickly from such an ordeal, with others it may leave permanent damage. I have given her a sedative and she is asleep now but if she is to have a chance of a complete recovery she needs rest and peace and freedom from fear. I strongly advise that you take her somewhere where these may be found.'

'What can I do?' he asked the Police Chief helplessly when the Doctor had left and the caretaker, suitably thanked, had returned to the school. 'You see what that letter says. I have to return to Vienna, perhaps even go into Germany. What peace of mind will Siegret find there?' With a low moan of distress he collapsed into a chair.

'Herr Professor,' Meyer addressed him with energy, 'there is only one course for you to take. You must go, leave Austria at once. Tomorrow morning you must take your daughter and cross the frontier into Italy. From there you must somehow make your way to some country where you will be safe.'

'But they will stop us, the Nazis will never give me a visa now. They want me to stay,' Wienzman protested.

'You still have time, as yet no word has been sent through to my office ordering that you be refused an exit permit. You are not on the prescribed list, and it is very probable that the same is true of the frontier police. You already have the necessary documents certifying that you have paid your taxes and have no debts. I can issue you with a permit and provided you have no valuables with you, you will almost certainly be allowed through. In any case the Italian frontier is the easiest to cross.'

'No,' the Professor replied firmly after a moment's pause. 'You are very kind but I could not accept your offer. It would only put you in grave danger and neither my daughter nor I will buy our freedom at such a price.' The policeman made a gesture of exasperation.

'Don't you see? If you go at once I shall be in no danger. I have received no order to detain you and we are allowed to permit people, refugees and Jews, like yourselves to leave the country, provided they take nothing of value with them.' He leaned forward and spoke earnestly 'Tonight I shall order the arrest of this boy Gerdler and the others. I can do this because under the Nazi laws sexual relations between Aryans and other races are forbidden, even in the case of rape. I doubt very much if the charge will succeed, but at least it will enable me to keep them out of the way while you make your escape. The authorities in Vienna will receive your telegram and will not become suspicious about you for at least two days I hope, by which time you will be in Italy. Of course I shall be questioned, but there will be no proof that I shall have acted improperly. Everything will have been done exactly according to the rules. There may be a reprimand but no more than that.'

Siegret's father was silent for a moment, when he spoke again his face was grave. 'There is something else, I have not told you about,' he said, 'there is another reason why I am afraid to return to Vienna, or worse still to go to Germany.' His voice sank lower and Meyer had to lean forward to catch his words. 'Many years ago, not long after the War, I was working in a clinic in one of the poorer areas of the city. I was one of three doctors who spent some time there each week in order to assist those who could not afford to come to the hospital for treatment in the ordinary way. We got all kinds of people, suffering from many different illnesses and complaints. Pneumonia, typhus, diphtheria, tuberculous cases of course, we had a great many of those,' he hesitated again, then went on, 'I was already specializing in virus infections and I worked mainly on the venereal cases. One day a man came to me to be treated for syphilis. I remember him quite well, it was in the winter of 1924, he was a strange man, full of wild, irrational talk. At that time I thought he was mentally unbalanced, possibly as a result of his illness.'

'And this man?' Meyer was conscious of a dryness in the mouth as he spoke. 'Where is he now?'

'Can you not guess? He is so powerful now that to possess such knowledge as I have is certain death, and he must know I kept records of all my patients. If I am forced to stay on in Germany, if I am taken by the police while trying to escape,' he shrugged, 'the secret police, the Gestapo have their files. Probably they are searching for me already, maybe that is why I have been ordered back to the University.'

Meyer sat up in his chair. 'What you say makes it more than ever imperative that you both leave at once. I agree that if you return to Vienna you will probably never get out alive. If you leave tomorrow, you stand a good chance, a very good chance, of escaping altogether,' he said earnestly.

'Yes, it is possible I suppose,' the Professor's tone was more hopeful. 'You are sure we would not have trouble at the frontier, and shall we be safe in Italy do you think?' His friend gave him an encouraging smile. 'It is unlikely that you will have much trouble. Make sure you are wearing your oldest clothes and appear very poor. The guards only bother with rich people. Above all take no valuables with you of any kind. If you do they will certainly be confiscated and very possibly you yourselves will be arrested. As for Italy,' he shrugged, 'I do not know. It is not as bad as Germany and Austria are today, but it is probable that the Italian police might arrest you and send you back if they were asked. For that reason alone I advise you to travel on as soon as you can. You have friends who can help you there, do you not?'

'Yes. In Rome. A man I was once a student with who is now a doctor. He will help us I know, it was through him that I obtained the visa for Italy.'

'Good, then there is nothing to prevent your leaving tomorrow. I will make out your exit permits myself and you can collect them tomorrow morning.' Meyer stood up and reached for his hat.

'Yes certainly, and yet,' the Professor hesitated, 'what if Siegret is not ready to travel, perhaps we should wait at least another day?'

'Listen, you heard what Frau Muller said, there is nothing wrong with Siegret that rest won't cure. The sooner you get her away from here the better for both of you.' He spoke sternly and was glad to see that his words had an effect. The old man rose to his feet and together they went towards the door. In the hall Meyer stopped for a moment and placed a hand on the other's arm.

73

'My friend,' he said quietly, 'it is wrong that this should happen. That an innocent girl can be molested by these young thugs and decent people be powerless even to punish them. It saddens me that you should be driven from your home when it is my duty to protect you, but it would grieve me far more if you were to remain and suffer worse things. At least I can be of some use in this way.'

There was little in the way of packing to be done. As Meyer had suggested he left behind everything of value, placing the few pieces of jewellery that his wife had left to Siegret, in a box to be desposited with the police chief for safe keeping. They would take only what they could be sure of carrying themselves in suitcases. There was a small supply of Swiss currency which he had managed to keep through the Anschluss, not a large sum, but enough to take them as far as America. How they would live when they got there unless he could obtain an academic post he had no idea. He was the leading authority in his field, how much interest there was in that field in other countries he was not sure.

The most vital items were his notebooks. There were a dozen or more of these, thick volumes crammed with the results and records of the past twenty years' case histories. He was strongly tempted to destroy their dangerous contents, but to do so would not save his life and they would be essential to him if he were ever to start work again. Yet they were too bulky and heavy to conceal and the guards would be sure to question their value. He was still wondering what to do about them when there was a soft sound at the study door and Siegret entered in her dressing-gown.

She was still a shocking sight even after her sleep; the bruises on her face had risen in huge purplish and blue patches, her mouth was badly swollen and her eyes had sunk back into dark rings. Her father rose and took her by the hand as she moved stiffly towards him, she was very weak and shivering, whether from fear or cold he could not tell.

'I woke and heard you moving about,' she told him, steadying her voice with an effort. 'What are you doing?' She gazed round apprehensively at the books and papers that littered the floor.

Gently the doctor explained the plan Meyer had proposed. 'We shall leave as soon as possible in the morning,' he said, 'by the afternoon you will be safely across the frontier in Italy.' To his consternation Siegret buried her face in his chest and wept, her thin shoulders shaking with uncontrollable sobs. The old man stroked her head and talked to her softly, trying to re-assure her, but the tears continued unabated. For the past year and a half Siegret had bottled up her feelings, refusing to accept the full impact of the life she was forced to lead. Now it was as though a block had been lifted away, and she could realize how much she had been suffering and that at long last it had come to an end. The pent-up emotions burst from her, releasing the pressure of fear and pain that she had suppressed for so long, but they were tears of relief that wiped away much of her anguish and when eventually she ceased to cry, she found she had begun to recover some of her former spirits and was able to smile at her father again.

When she had dried her face, and tidied herself, they dis-cussed the details of their proposed escape together. 'Pack a few of your best and most useful clothes,' her father said, 'what we take with us may have to last a long time, and no more than two small cases, light enough for you to carry. And nothing of value, no rings, or necklaces or any such things.' Siegret laughed, 'father you talk to me as if I were one of your stu-dents,' she said kissing him. 'How many rings and necklaces do you think I possess? Mother had a few pieces which you have taken and no-one, not even a Nazi would care about the things I have bought myself. Now give me your notebooks. I will label them as school work books. No-one will know that I am not still using them and I shouldn't think a frontier guard will be able to tell the difference between research notes and 5th grade biology class studies.'

The idea was a good one, so much so that the professor was prepared to accept it. Siegret scooped up the pile of books in her arms and made to return to her room. At the door of the study she halted and looked back at him. 'Father,' she said in a hesitant voice, swallowing hard, 'those boys, Gerdler and the others. They didn't succeed, I wasn't . . .' she coloured, searching for a less emotive word than the one which sprang to her mind.

'I know,' her father answered tenderly, 'I know, the Doctor told me while you were asleep. We shall be all right, do not fear.' Coming back into the room she kissed him once more and the old man hugged her to him.

The aftermath of the crocodile's attack left *Caterina*'s passengers and crew with only one firm desire; to get away from Shambe and the river station, to get out of the whole of Equatoria as quickly as possible. Where originally Stewart Curtis had been the only traveller to be irritated by the extra stop, now he was joined unanimously by the others.

The chances of their being able to take off again before dusk had never been good, and with the delay imposed by a prolonged search for Thorne's body, a search which, perhaps fortunately, he thought, had yielded nothing to upset the passengers further; and the complications of the official report on the incident composed by himself, Keeling and the local magistrate, a night on the river became inevitable.

Finally, after a lengthy argument with Johnson, the civil engineer whose wife had taken the opportunity to resurrect her complaints about the practice of allowing travellers to be greeted at the jetty by naked villagers. Desmond called all the passengers together in the lounge.

'I know all of you have been upset by the tragic accident which took place this afternoon,' he told them, 'and that like me there's nothing you want more than to get away from here and up to Khartoum and Cairo. If I thought there was any chance of our being able to have the aircraft repaired and tested in reasonable time I would take it, but the engineers tell me that there is no possibility of being ready before nine o'clock this evening at the earliest, and frankly, I think a night flight over the swamps would be foolhardy. So I suggest we all settle down and make the best of our night here.'

'This is all very well Captain,' Stewart Curtis stood up to speak and looked round at the other passengers to gather support, 'but we shall have wasted a whole day here in that case. Naturally we are all appalled at the tragedy, but I fail to see how our remaining here will help. You were apparently prepared to land at Khartoum in the dark before, why can't you do so now?' He spoke with an arrogant rasp to his voice that irritated Desmond exceedingly.

'I was prepared to land at Khartoum at night only if we could take off from here and get beyond Malakal and clear of the swamps before dark,' he answered, 'you've all seen what the terrain is like round here, it would be too easy to get lost and impossible to make a safe touchdown if something did go wrong.'

There were a few murmurs of dissent from the Johnsons and Mr. and Mrs. Finlay, as well as Curtis at this, but to Desmond's surprise this was crushed by help from Dr. Van Smit.

'Since we have only recently witnessed the dangers to those who are careless in these swamps,' he remarked in his dry manner, 'I for one am only too happy to take Captain O'Neill's advice and remain here. I personally have no wish to find myself struggling in the dark with another crocodile.'

An awkward silence greeted this last statement and the passengers began to drift away, Stewart Curtis still scowling angrily. Van Smit walked over to the bar and Desmond followed him.

'Thanks for your help,' he said, feeling a little self-conscious as he did so. For some unidentifiable reason he found it difficult to be at his ease in the presence of the enigmatic Doctor. There was nothing he could put his finger on as being wrong, or out of place, except perhaps the man's faculty for stating unpleasant truths, yet all the same it was hard to find things to say to him which did not seem trite.

'It was nothing,' Van Smit answered him, 'they were being most foolish, but at times like this, such people often are. Also, even after this afternoon's display they have still not fully appreciated the dangers of the Sud. It is better to arrive at one's destination a few hours late than dead.'

The barman came forward to serve them both and they took their drinks out on to the verandah. It was past seven o'clock and dusk was falling swiftly as it always did in these latitudes Desmond remembered. The cries of birds which he had listened to earlier had been replaced by a steady unceasing sound of frogs croaking in the mud, and the shrill buzz of cicadas and other insects.

The verandah door opened and Stewart Curtis came through. He too carried a glass in his hand and as the two watched he drank deeply, draining it in a single gulp and commenced pacing up and down on the far side of the verandah, his hands thrust deep in his pockets and his head hunched between his shoulders in thought.

'There is a man with a great deal on his mind,' Van Smit remarked softly, 'I wonder what it is that makes our Mr. Curtis so eager to continue his journey.'

This time there was no chance to ask what he meant by his words for Keeling stuck his head round the door at that moment. 'A radio message has come in for you Captain,' he said, 'it's London again.'

The message was the third since Desmond had sent off his first report of Ian Thorne's death. It was signed by Priestly, one of Imperial Airways senior managers, and consisted of a bald demand for fuller details of the accident. Since these had already been sent off a short time previously, it seemed likely that a further reply was unnecessary, so after dispatching a brief acknowledgement, he returned to the verandah to finish his drink.

Night had now fallen completely, but the sky was clear and a full moon shone brightly on the river, turning the water to silver and gleaming on the reeds. On an impulse Desmond unfastened the doors with wire mosquito screening and let himself out. The air was very still and warm, with only a faint murmuring and rustling among the rushes. The sound of the frogs seemed extraordinarily loud and close.

Young Thorne's death still weighed on his mind, despite repeated efforts to assure himself that it was in no way his responsibility. As Captain of the aircraft it had been his duty to safeguard the passengers and anticipate behaviour which could bring them into trouble. Perhaps, he should have warned them all of the risk of crocodiles before they disembarked, or seen that Keeling posted a guard on the launches.

Quite aside from the personal tragedy of the accident, there was the knowledge that the remaining passengers would be on edge, nervous and irritable for the rest of the flight, and the same would probably be said of the crew. Then, even when they reached England, there would be further inquests to be faced and questions answered. Head office in London was already burning up the wires with its messages, an incident like this could be counted on for an immediate reaction on their part.

Moreover his relations with Imperial management, never easy at the best of times, had of late been hitting a fresh nadir. In the eyes of Desmond and of most other senior captains and pilots, the company treated its crews shockingly badly. Low pay, long hours, and scarcely any say in the design of aircraft or the routes to be flown, had been the rules throughout the airline's history. Three years ago, he and a number of others had founded a pilots' union to try and put right some of these faults. A prolonged struggle with the senior management had followed, a struggle which had become increasingly bitter. Demands for the installation of de-icing equipment and other safety features had led to several pilots being sacked, ostensibly for disciplinary reasons or inefficiency, and Desmond was well aware that there were men high up in the company's hierarchy who would welcome an excuse to treat him in a similar manner.

In fact, matters within the company had already reached a position where the government had been forced to step in. A commission of inquiry had recommended nationalization and the recognition of the pilots' union. By the end of the year these would have to have been put into effect, but in the meantime there was every indication that the airways board was digging its heels in for a last ditch battle, and was making a determined effort to rid itself of the most persistent critics among its employees.

The loss of a passenger, however accidental, would be a

heaven-sent opportunity for the board either to dismiss him altogether, or else to down-grade him to one of the junior routes, his next trip could easily be on the cross-channel service, or on one of the internal routes to Scotland or Ireland. At least if that were the case, he thought ruefully, he would be justified in rejecting Pamela's demand that he sell the house.

A small movement in the shadows caught his eye, a figure detached itself from one of the tamarisk trees and came towards him. It was Laura Hartman, the moonlight softening her face.

'It's all so peaceful,' she said when they were close to one another, 'I can't believe that only a few hours ago,' she shivered, unable to complete the sentence, 'I keep feeling that it was somehow my fault, that if only I had asked one of the boatmen to come with me, or you, or anyone who realized what could happen, then Lieutenant Thorne would be alive still.'

'If anyone is to blame it's me,' Desmond told her gently, 'I should have warned you all before you went ashore.'

'Oh, no,' Laura looked up at his face, 'not you. How could you be to blame. You didn't know what we were going to do. You couldn't possibly be responsible.'

'No more than you could, I agree,' he said, 'but my superiors certainly don't seem to think so, judging by the cables they have been sending.'

'Are you flying straight back to the United States?' he asked her as they drew abreast of the landing-stage, 'or will you be stopping off in England.' He asked the question in an effort to turn her mind away from its morbid trend, but to his surprise he experienced a momentary feeling of disappointment at her answer.

'We're going right through to New York.' She sighed. 'In a way it's a pity, I'd have liked to stay over in Europe for a while, but Mr. Curtis thinks the political situation too dangerous and I guess he's right. Do you think there will be a war soon?' she asked suddenly.

This time it was Laura's turn to be surprised. Desmond stiffened.

'Perhaps you are right Mrs. Hartman,' he said, 'though it

seems a pity if, so soon after the last war, we still have not learned enough to avoid another.'

'You might try telling that to the refugees and Jews they imprison and torture in Germany,' she countered sharply, angered by the rebuke.

'And you might try asking how much misery, how many more deaths would result from another great war,' Desmond replied, 'and maybe too there would be a better chance of settling the problems of Europe, if people didn't go around saying that war is inevitable.'

Laura glared at him angrily for a moment in the dark, and then turning on her heel with an angry sniff, started back to the rest-house.

Stewart Curtis had a great deal on his mind. The enforced delay at Shambe, was to him a cause of acute anxiety. Throughout the evening he was seen to pace up and down on the verandah or in the lounge, chain smoking Egyptian cigarettes, and at dinner, served by Andy Draper and the rest-house staff, he drank heavily and was almost offensively morose.

Returning immediately after the meal to the bedroom that had been prepared for him, he flung himself full length on the bed and lay, staring up at the slow turning fan hanging from the ceiling. He was tired from the journey and half drunk as well but he knew that sleep would be a long time coming. Instead he began turning over in his head once more the problems that faced him.

The first of these, and certainly the most pressingly urgent, was the mine at Klerksdorp. Klerksdorp! He cursed the day he had ever heard that name. His experts had sworn to him that there was gold there. They had been unanimous in their forecasts. The richest mine in the country, they had said. Unlimited reserves of gold waiting to be extracted. And he had believed them. Millions he had sunk into Klerksdorp, he had hired the best men and bought the latest, most sophisticated machinery. The crushing and extracting plant was the most efficient installed anywhere in the world. It was the envy of every other mine operator. All it lacked was gold.

At first, four years ago, the project had started well. A massive surface stripping operation in which huge excavators had sliced away the top soil, had revealed several veins of ore, and digging had begun in earnest, to an impressive fanfare of publicity. True there had been a few doubters, mainly from among the more conservative of South Africa's mining community, but for the most part Curtis had been hailed as one of the new Czars of the Rand and spoken of in the same breath as Rhodes and Oppenheimer.

So Klerksdorp went ahead with the utmost speed. Of course not all the money was his, the undertaking was too vast for that, but he had invested a substantial part of his fortune in the company, was its chairman and the person whose name was identified with it. Far more of his money had been put into buying up land around the concession. From studying the history of other great mines he had come to realize that there was certainly as much and possibly more money to be made from speculating in land values as the area filled up with thousands of people attracted by the gold.

On paper Stewart Curtis was one of the wealthiest men in Africa. Companies under his control were valued at tens of millions of dollars. His prestige had never been higher, and yet there was one fatal flaw which in a few days would bring the entire structure of his empire crashing down in ruins.

There was no gold in Klerksdorp! The one critical factor on which all else depended was missing. Without the gold his shares in the mine were valueless, no longer security for the loans he had raised against them. Without the gold his enormous land holdings were worth only a fraction of their current price. The moment the news was leaked out, his vast assets would shrink to nothing overnight as overdrafts and loans were called in, deals suspended, credit refused.

The mineral lodes which at first had seemed so promising had petered out uselessly after a few hundred feet. New shafts had been sunk and further seams uncovered but the ore was too low grade to be profitable even with the equipment that had been installed. Trusting the advice of his experts Curtis had ordered fresh shafts sunk to even greater depths, and a further range of galleries opened. He drafted in more men and cutting gear, pushing the work ahead at a furious pace, hoping for some indication of success before news of the fiasco broke. As the position worsened he had resorted to more and more desperate means.

Before long he was issuing deliberately misleading statements to the press, going out of his way to show off the mine itself and its new machinery, and by dint of an energetic public relations company, had managed to keep up the fiction that gold was being produced in large quantities.

More difficult were his dealings with official bodies, the banks, insurance companies, the representatives of the world's stockmarkets. Here he had been driven to juggling assay reports and monthly production figures, actions which might well make him liable to criminal charges if he continued.

The crisis had come a fortnight ago, while he had been on holiday in Cairo with his wife. Summoned south by an urgent cable from the Klerksdorp board he had arrived to find that the company's principal bankers in the Cape, no longer content with the deliberately vague reports they had been receiving, had demanded to be allowed to send in their own team of inspectors.

Curtis closed his eyes, he could picture the scene now. The panelled boardroom in the mine's Durban offices, and old Stuttenheim, the fat, bald President of the bank, leaning back in his chair and puffing at his cigar and assuring Curtis in his heavy, guttural accent that the request was 'only a formality in the interest of my shareholders you understand'.

Curtis had understood all right. The smile on Stuttenheim's face had not reached as far as his eyes. The old Boer had guessed what was happening and now he was sending in his men to make sure. There was no urgency about his request, he had readily accepted Curtis' suggestion of a date ten days away for the start of the inspection. That afternoon, when the banker had left Curtis had telephoned his stockbrokers to confirm what he already suspected. There had been steady but persistent selling of Klerksdorp all day, nothing heavy, nothing the market couldn't absorb, but it was there all the same. The shares had closed a few points down as a result. Stuttenheim was unloading his holdings before the news broke.

Once that happened the panic would be instantaneous, the share price would collapse overnight and Curtis himself would be ruined. There was no way to prevent that or even to delay it for much longer, but there still remained one faint chance of clearing something from the wreck, an American consortium in New York was paying a high price for mineral options on his property interests around Klerksdorp. If he could complete the deal before they heard about the failure of the mine he would still have something left. Stewart Curtis had come a long hard road to wealth. The memory of those early, bitter days of poverty was still vivid, and now they loomed terrifyingly near once more. At all costs he had to reach New York and complete the land sales before Stuttenheim pulled the world from under him.

There was a low table beside the bed. Reaching out for his cigarette lighter his eyes rested for a moment on the silver framed portrait of his wife, and inwardly he cursed again. As if he had not enough on his plate, Charlotte had chosen this moment to start being difficult. That was an added incentive to get back to Cairo as quickly as he could. He looked again at the calm patrician face and the cloud of dark hair that surrounded it and felt a squirm of jealousy. Charlotte was not the kind of woman to be left alone with safety. In Cairo there were any number of men ready to pay court to a woman like her.

Fifteen hundred miles to the north, amid the formal splendour of a dinner party at the Residency of the British Ambassador to Egypt, Jacquetta d'Este was watching her husband flirting with Charlotte Curtis.

It had been a tiresomely hot day in Cairo, unusual for this time of year when the mild climate drew the wealthy and famous in society from every country to the city which had become the world's most fashionable winter capital. Even now, towards the end of the season the hotels and palaces were still full. Film stars and millionaires mixed with Egyptian Pashas and the aristocracy of Europe on the terrace of Shepherd's

Hotel and congratulated themselves on staying beneath the same roof as kings and princes.

Inside the Residency, however, the high ceilinged rooms with their silent slow turning fans had contrived to maintain a pleasant coolness despite the considerable number of guests. Normally, the party, consisting as it did of the smartest and most important Cairenes and visitors, would have been enjoyable for Jacquetta. The Ambassador and his wife were old friends, she knew just enough of the guests to feel at home and not so many as to be bored, she was wearing a new dress brought over from Paris and was conscious that she was appearing at her best, added to which there was at present a carnival atmosphere of excitement and anticipation in the city, as the preparations for the marriage of King Farouk's sister to the Crown Prince of Persia drew to a climax. The pleasure of all this, however, was spoilt by the behaviour of her husband.

A tall, strikingly attractive woman whose dark colouring was set off against the whiteness of her skin, her face was rounded and gentle, at times so much so as to appear sad, as it did at the moment, though in face she was merely pensive. Her husband's antics were annoying rather than hurtful. In the ten years since Luca d'Este had taken her from her father's home in Tuscany she had learnt to live with the knowledge of his constant infidelities, what was less easy to put up with was his indifference to the embarrassment he caused her in public.

Across the table he caught her eye upon him and raised a quizzical eyebrow in rejoinder. At forty-seven Baron Luca d'Este still believed himself to retain the attractiveness of his younger days, and remained sublimely indifferent to his thickening waist line and thinning hair. The dashing Italian cavalry colonel had been replaced by an ageing provincial governor, whose affections were rapidly becoming ludicrous.

That Charlotte Curtis was finding them acceptable rendered her all the more obnoxious in Jacquetta's eyes, although presumably the fact that Stewart Curtis, her husband, for all his great wealth was both older and less attractive than Luca, made some difference. There could be no denying however that the English woman was beautiful in her hard, superficial

85

way, Jacquetta thought vindictively. A lot of men ran after Charlotte and to judge by the stories she let a good many of them catch her. Tonight she was looking very glamorous in a close fitting green silk evening suit from Schiaparelli, hand embroidered in gold with a Jean Cocteau design; taken together with her dark eyes and carefully fluffed up jet black hair, the effect was stunning.

There was a stir and bustle behind the chairs and footmen began removing the dishes. Here in the Embassy, the regal pomp of British Imperial splendour ran unchecked. Egypt, nominally an independant state united to Britain only by treaty of friendship, was in actual fact virtually a British fief, just as much as India, or Kenya or Hong Kong. Until a short time ago the Ambassador had actually been known as the High Commissioner, and it was still common for references to be made in the world's and Cairo's press to 'the real ruler of Egypt'.

Footmen behind the chairs, splendid silver and gold heaped upon the table, candelabras, salvers and vases, the finest crystal gleaming against the dazzling white of the cloth. At her right shoulder a hand descended removing her wine glass and replacing it with another; another course, another wine. Jacquetta had experienced a hundred such dinners before in her life, when Luca had been assistant Governor in Tripoli they had been an almost nightly occurrence, only tonight the glinting luxury and wealth jarred within her.

The guests were faithful mirrors of the finery of the table. White collars and waistcoats for the men, crossed with ribbons and sashes, the breasts of their tail-coats shining with stars and decorations. Some, like the Egyptian Pasha on the opposite side, sported diamond studs and cuff-links as well. The wealth of this city was staggering, many of the women here were literally weighed down with the most astonishing jewellery. One princess, sitting on the Ambassador's right was wearing a pink diamond like a piece of candy suspended from a necklace of more huge brilliants. Rubies, emeralds, ropes of pearls, there must be several fortunes in gems round this one table.

Her husband and Charlotte were talking again, Luca with

the ridiculous, gross leer on his face, his eyes fastened greedily on Charlotte's bosom as he spoke. Perhaps it was the title that attracted her, certainly it could not be his conversation or his looks. She saw the English woman rest a gloved hand lightly on his wrist for a moment in a coquettish gesture, and glancing up and catching sight of Jacquetta watching her, give an over-friendly, condescending smile.

Turning away, trying to hide her anger, Jacquetta realized that the man on her left had been speaking to her.

'I'm sorry,' she apologized, inclining her head towards him. Courteously the man, an elderly and important member of a visiting French delegation, repeated his remark.

'I understand,' he said carefully, 'that the government here is concerned at the numbers of Arab tribesmen who have been crossing the border into Egypt. It is said that several sheikhs from the great Senusi family have arrived recently.'

Even though her mind was preoccupied with Charlotte Curtis, Jacquetta caught the allusion behind the diplomat's words. The Italian colonies of Tripolitania and Cyrenaica to the west of Egypt were maintained over a hostile population by the presence of a sizeable army. Periodically the land erupted into warfare as one tribe or another rebelled against their European masters.

The Arab raiders were hard, ruthless men, accustomed even in days of peace, to an existence on the very edge of survivial. In their perpetual inter-tribal forays no quarter was given or expected. Enemies were slaughtered pitilessly, wounded abandoned to die. The fight against an invading, conquering enemy was even more vicious and the troops had responded in kind. Torture and brutality were commonplace, occasional bloody reprisals permitted to demonstrate the futility of revolt. On both sides a degree of hatred had brewed which nothing could extinguish.

Luca d'Este had been assistant military governor in Tripoli when they had first been married. To Jacquetta the post had meant no more than the comfort and ceremony of colonial life and the satisfaction of knowing that her husband was one of the territory's senior officials. Italian rule had made Tripoli into an attractive town, its surroundings planted with groves of olives and citrus trees and great vineyards. The fighting in the desert had been hundreds of miles away, utterly remote from the tranquil life of the capital, and its rounds of parties and horse races and receptions.

Only later had she learnt of the part Luca had played in the suppression of one rebellion. Of the ferocious atrocities committed against the families of the ruling sheiks, atrocities carried out on his orders to cow the populace, but which had only succeeded in creating a legacy of hatred and desire for vengeance that had almost threatened to engulf the province, till Luca himself had been precipitately recalled a year ago, and successive administrations had succeeded in restoring peace to the area.

Jacquetta's neighbour was evidently pressing for further news on the latest outbreak of violence. It was common knowledge that the Arabs sought refuge in Egypt when hard pressed, and the Senusi were the Italian army's most persistent foes. Luca indeed was under the sentence of death by them for the execution of a former chief sheikh of the tribe carried out by the airforce and police on his orders. The Egyptians at present were torn between a natural desire to help their brother Arabs throw off the yoke of colonization, and a wish to preserve friendly relations with Italy as an insurance against British failures in any coming European War.

'It is more than a year since my husband resigned from colonial government service,' she replied to her neighbour's question, 'I'm afraid I am quite out of touch with the news from the colonies, but I thought things were generally supposed to be quiet there now.'

'Will you be watching the race on Sunday?' she asked, changing the subject from politics, a topic she had found uninspiring even when she and her husband had been involved in them.

'The motor race to Fayum?' the Frenchman took a careful sip of wine, 'I shall watch the start, of course, but I fear I am no longer young enough to follow behind through the desert to the finish. Since your husband, the Baron, is taking part in the race, I presume you will be expected to see it through to the end. I hope for your sake the weather remains cool.'

'So do I,' Jacquetta echoed fervently. 'Fortunately we shan't be following the exact course of the race, we shall cut out a large loop in the official track and be at the finish in time to see the winner past the flag.'

'I wish the Baron good fortune, I am told he is highly favoured to win.'

'You are most kind,' Jacquetta finished eating and placed her knife and fork neatly together on her plate. At these banquets she invariably found it impossible to finish more than half the courses put in front of her. 'It would make Luca very happy to win. On Monday we leave for New York and it would be nice to end his stay in Cairo with a victory.'

On the opposite side of the table Luca and Charlotte Curtis were laughing at some private joke. The irony was that Luca had asked her to invite Charlotte to watch the race with her. The two of them would have to spend the whole day together. There was irony in that somewhere.

In their suite at the Italian legation that night the events of the dinner came to a head in a bitter row.

'I fail to see what you are complaining about my dear?' Luca answered blandly when she had protested over his behaviour during the evening. 'I was simply being polite. It is true Charlotte Curtis is a beautiful and charming woman and it is natural that I should be attracted to her. What of it?'

'You were pitiful,' Jacquetta was brushing out her hair and was watching him in the mirror as she spoke. 'Contemptible, she was playing with you, anyone but a fool could have seen that.' The expression on Luca's face hardened. 'I will not have you speak to me in that fashion,' he snapped. 'What do you know about how people think? Till you married me you were nothing but a little country bitch living in a shack.'

'And not content with making a fool of yourself,' Jacquetta continued, ignoring his retort, 'you make me look stupid by inviting that woman to drive out after the cars for the race. The whole of Cairo will be laughing at us.'

'Bitch, when I met you your father was so poor he'd have

sold his daughter to anyone who'd have offered to repair his roof.'

'Your money, my breeding,' Jacquetta answered easily, putting down her brush and going over to the bed, 'you had to have someone to show you how to behave after the Duce had given you your title and was sending you off to play dictator with the Arabs.' The moment the words were out of her mouth she knew she had gone too far. Like many of the new upstart breed of politicians and party bosses, Luca d'Este was exceptionally sensitive to any criticism of his birth and background. Swearing savagely between his teeth Luca stepped in towards her and hit her hard twice, aiming for her face. Ducking away she caught the first blow across the side of the head while the the second slammed into her neck.

Choking for air, her head singing, she fell to the floor on her knees, while her husband stood over her venting his fury. 'You will never again dare to criticize myself or my family! Do you understand? Or speak disrespectfully of the Duce and the work he is doing for Italy, or allow your infantile jealousies to make you impolite to my friends and my guests.' His voice was high pitched with rage, his face flushed. He must have drunk heavily during the meal.

'Do you think I don't know what you were doing in Tripoli all that time?' she spoke with difficulty, her breath still coming in gasps. 'Do you think I didn't hear what they said about you when we were there. "That butcher d'Este", that was what they called you when your back was turned: Oh, you were so brave fighting a few bands of unarmed tribesmen, and showing off your uniform in parades. Well, it may impress women like Charlotte Curtis, but to me you're nothing but a posturing bully.' She half turned herself for another blow, but Luca's anger seemed strangely to have burnt itself out.

'I shall sleep in my own room tonight,' he announced curtly, drawing his dressing-gown about him, 'and trust that in the morning you will have recovered your manners,' and with a click of the door he was gone.

On the other side of the world, where the ice and frozen

snows of the long winter months had only just begun to give way before the onset of Spring, Pat Jarrett stood at the head of a small lake, lying in a bowl among the pine covered hills of New Hampshire and let out a deep breath of satisfaction.

It had taken a month of laborious searching before he had found what he was looking for. Warren Lake, a five mile stretch of clean deep water on which the ice had already broken up and was now fast melting.

Every feature about it was perfect, a good North South lie, among hills which were not high enough to pose difficulties for an aircraft, yet at the same time provided an effective screen against the outside world; a dirt road sufficiently clear to enable him to bring the truck up yet which would still discourage other drivers from making use of it. By renting one of the houses he could ensure himself a legitimate cover among the inhabitants of the nearest village and at the same time obtain shelter for himself and the plane. Finally, and most important of all, Warren Lake was only a few miles off the direct route between Montreal and New York's La Guardia Marine Terminal.

There was still some snow lying on the shore line and Jarrett had to pick his way between the deeper patches as he made his way back to the truck. Physically he was not a particularly large man but he moved with an energy and determination that made him appear bigger than he was. Striding through the slush he revelled in the clean, cold air, already he felt invigorated and fresh again after the long drive in the pickup. With the discovery of the lake his plans had at last really taken shape, now he could go ahead at once to make ready for the first flight.

The dirt track wound back along the eastern shore of the lake past the big house on the point which he had already picked out as his base. Standing out a short way into the water it possessed a small natural anchorage out of sight of the head of the lake, as well as a sizeable wooden boathouse, large enough to conceal a small float plane and a good long jetty. Here he would live and work for the next eight days.

He had parked the pick-up under the trees so as to be out of sight of any unexpected observer, though in point of fact he doubted whether anyone at all had visited the lake during the past five months. Perhaps an occasional hunter in late fall or a workman repairing one of the houses after the summer visitors had left, but certainly none since then.

On an impulse he opened the door of the cab and stepped out again. Where the snow had been, much of the ground had turned to mud which clung to his boots as he walked the few yards back to the shore line. The sensation brought back a host of memories. France 1917 and his first visit to the trenches to see the kind of war they were fighting on the ground. The mud and the stench of those dirty, shivering grey-faced men were as fresh in his mind as if it had been only a few hours ago instead of more than twenty years.

It had been good in those early days, the best he had ever known. A nineteen year old pilot with the newly formed Army Air Corps, an ace with six kills to his credit, a boy hero, the favourite of his squadron. Jarrett's family had been proud of him, especially his mother, struggling to keep up appearances among the neighbours on a tiny pension after her husband's death. Even when they had had to sell the old house in Chicago and move into rented accommodation she had still had her son's fame to hold up to the world.

But two years later Pat Jarrett had returned to the United States from the battlefields of France to find that the world had changed in his absence. With the coming of peace people wanted only to forget about the war, they had no use for heroes any more and anyway every bar held half a dozen willing to tell their stories for the price of drink. Jobs were scarce and money tight and Pat Jarrett, former flying ace was just another unemployed veteran.

He had tried, of course, to stay on in the air force. Flying was the only thing he knew and the discipline and demands of the life had suited him, while the hours in the air had given him the chance to excel at individual combat. He had enjoyed too the comradeship and toughness of body and spirit which the service instilled. Back at home he found himself despising the soft civilians with their slack habits and easy existence. He resented having to defer to them, to plead for jobs from men whom a year ago he would not have deigned to notice.

He had been good-looking before he had sailed off to Europe, and more than one girl from the neighbourhood had cried the night he left. On his return, the glamour of his decorations and wound stripes had worn off as soon as the money in his pocket had gone. Now the girls wanted men with cars and fat wallets who could take them to places where they could have fun.

Abandoned and rejected, Pat Jarrett had turned inwards on himself. Leaving Chicago he drifted from town to town, hanging round airfields, picking up odd jobs, begging a flight from a friendly pilot when he could no longer afford to buy one. He became morose and bitter, scarcely talking to others, living in a private world of his own imagination preparing for the day when the air force would need him again.

Discipline, both mental and physical, became an obsession with him. Each day he exercised himself thoroughly, gradually building up to a point where he was spending more than two hours a day in weight-lifting sessions and calisthenics. In his personal appearance, he was scrupulously neat, his clothes always cleaned and pressed, his coats brushed, shoes polished even when he himself could hardly afford to eat. Remembering the ignorance of most pilots about the mechanics of the aircraft they flew, he went to night school to study and took jobs in airline repair sheds, while all the time he read avidly following every development of aircraft and flying, learning the characteristics of every plane.

Paradoxically, Jarrett's intensity was the very factor which prevented him from obtaining a job with the airlines, when passenger aviation and mail flights sprang up in the twenties and thirties. By this time there were any number of hungry young pilots available, and the directors were suspicious of the taciturn, stern faced veteran, who was so desperate to get into the air that his hands shook uncontrollably in the interview.

Then last year Britain had started to re-arm in preparation for another European war. The crisis had died away in September after Munich but the expansion of the armed forces

93

continued and in pilots' mess-rooms around the States the word went out that the Royal Air Force was signing up American flyers for combat training. When he heard the news Jarrett had applied at once, travelling to Washington to the British Embassy at his own expense.

The result was a foregone conclusion and a less obsessive man would have realized it. The British wanted pilots, but they wanted young men, not forty-two year old relics from a previous war with limited experience of modern aircraft. The interview panel had been quite kind and had taken time to explain their reasons for turning him down. They had even held out a faint chance of a posting on the supply staff, 'but I'm afraid what we're really looking for are qualified airline pilots,' a young wing commander told him, 'we don't even recruit our own people beyond thirty-five.'

Jarrett surveyed the lake again. He had better be moving, there was much to be done and not over long to do it in. The date was Saturday the 11th of March, in eight days time the first of the bullion flights, Imperial 109 flying-boat *Caterina*, Commander Captain Desmond O'Neill, would be passing overhead en route for New York.

III

By Radio: AIR TRAFFIC CONTROL CAIRO TO IM-
PERIAL AIRWAYS LONDON – RELAYED FROM
KHARTOUM 0720 hrs. SATURDAY 12th MARCH.
IMPERIAL AIRWAYS FLIGHT 109 – G-ADHO
CATERINA LEFT SHAMBE. E.T.A. KHARTOUM
1015 hrs. LOCAL TIME. ENDS.

THE passengers were still gathering themselves sleepily
together and cursing the night's delay which was responsible
for the early start when Desmond came down to the jetty to
take a launch out to *Caterina*. Dawn was only just breaking
over the river, revealing a scene of great beauty. The whispering banks of reeds, tipped with silver and gold in the light,
and reflected in the mirror-like surface of the water, where
dense masses of purple hyacinth drifted among the channels.
Patches of mist still hung over much of the swamps heighten-
ing the sense of remoteness.

The villagers were going about the first of their daily tasks.
Desmond saw a boat-load of three muscular black fishermen
pulling towards the entrance to one of the smaller channels.
Naked as they had been the previous day, for even this early
the temperature was in the seventies, they waved their spears in
greeting as he watched.

'A fine looking people Captain,' the sound of the voice made
him turn with a start to find the American Mr. King standing
behind him, smiling politely. 'I beg your pardon if I startled
you,' he said apologetically.

'Not at all,' Desmond told him, 'and you're right they are a
fine-looking people. I think I rather envy them their way of life
here.'

Harold King stopped and faced Desmond squarely. 'I
should like you to know Captain, how deeply upset my wife

95

and myself are over Lieutenant Thorne's death, it was a terrible tragedy, a shocking thing to have happened. Mrs. King feels very much responsible for what took place. If only she had not forgotten to bring her case off the aeroplane, or had not asked Lieutenant Thorne to fetch it for her, he would still be alive.'

The American was evidently quite genuine in his distress. 'Of course, it was in no way any fault of your wife's,' Desmond assured him, 'as I told Mrs. Hartman, that crocodile was waiting in the vicinity for the first person to come near the water. It was just Thorne's bad luck to be the one it caught, but it could just as easily have taken someone else. In any event Thorne was quite wrong to have tried to take a boat without a crew on board, and if there had been two more people with him I doubt if the croc would have attacked. I'm afraid he was very largely to blame for his own death, that is if anyone is,' he added. He felt awkward speaking ill of Thorne so soon after the accident. Even if the words were true they sounded more than a little callous.

'That's very kind of you Captain,' King's voice was plainly relieved and he began to walk on once more. 'I know Mrs. King will feel greatly eased in her mind when I repeat your words to her, Mrs. Hartman will be happier too I am sure.'

He stood on the jetty watching as the launch pulled out from the shore and moved in the direction of *Caterina*.

The repairs to the fuel tank had finally been completed after dark the previous night and Desmond had gone over every inch of the work with the engineer, and grudgingly pronounced himself satisfied. Even so, he took care to make the launch take him round underneath the wing to allow him to check for signs of any fresh leakage since the tank had been refilled. Satisfied that all was as it should be he boarded the aircraft and went straight up to the flight deck. On his way he met Andy Draper directing a pair of boys sent out to scour the cabins before the passengers arrived.

'Everything's fine Skipper,' the steward reported. 'Passengers are being assembled now. Purser's sending them on board at half past seven.' Desmond glanced at his watch. Six fifty, that gave him forty minutes to go through the pre-flight checks and send a radio report off for transmission to London. 'Were there any complaints about the accommodation or food?' Andy shook his head, 'No sir, barring Mrs. Johnson's that is. She was still shook up about seeing all them natives undressed sir, if you'll pardon the expression. Nothing was right for her, wouldn't eat and said the bed had bugs in it.' Andy spoke with feeling, evidently he had had a trying time, 'but in the end we got her off with a nice bowl of soup and then she quietened down.'

'Glad to hear it, let's hope she stays that way. You'll be serving breakfast as soon as we're airborne I take it?' Desmond suddenly realized that he was very hungry.

'Aye aye sir. Shall I bring one of my specials upstairs?' Andy's special cooked breakfasts, bacon, eggs, kidneys and all the trimmings were legendary. Desmond shook his head. 'You can certainly bring me one, but I'll have it in the smoking saloon.' The previous night he had dined with Keeling after the two of them had drawn up a detailed report on Ian Thorne's death. It was time he showed himself among the passengers again. Breakfasting among them was as good a way as any.

'No problems of any kind Skipper,' Ralph answered his captain's look of inquiry. 'Andy's got a pair of boys cleaning ship below and he's keeping an eye on them, Ken Frazer went out and had another good look at the portside wing but it's still there and no sign of any leakage. We've just started the pre-flight check. Oh, and I've had a Met. forecast from Khartoum, it should be fine all the way up the delta.'

'And how's our cargo,' Desmond asked, 'is it still there?'

'Any mice you mean?' Ralph laughed as he led the way through to the mail room. 'Not a sound all night. Andy rigged a bed in here last night. Ken and I tossed to see who should sleep in it and he lost. He said he never slept better in his life. We counted the boxes as soon as we woke up just to be sure and I'm glad to report all present and correct.'

'Forgot to mention one thing,' Ralph said as they returned to the flight deck, 'there was a signal passed through from Khartoum late last night after you had turned in. It seems the Canadian people have been getting worried about our falling behind on the schedule. Anyway London has had some query or other from Botwood, Newfoundland, over whether we were cancelling or not. London say they've answered that we will be making up the time on the route and sticking to the original schedule. They passed the message on to us for information.'

'As a polite way of telling us to get moving I suppose,' Desmond replied moodily. There was no reason for Botwood, a tiny airfield on the remote Newfoundland coast to start worrying. The place was no more than a refuelling stop for the handful of transatlantic flights, used as Foynes in Southern Ireland was, as a stepping-stone to the main airports on the continent.

So far he had received no less than fourteen separate signals from London, first on the fuel tank delay, then, and more copiously, over Thorne's death. Even though he had told both Laura and the Kings that the accident had been nobody's fault, it certainly appeared that Imperial's London office had no doubts on the subject. Aircraft captains were not supposed to lose passengers in their care, no matter how foolishly or irresponsibly they behaved. The Navy was evidently of the same opinion, having chimed in at 11 p.m. with a curtly worded demand for 'fullest details to be forwarded to the Admiralty forthwith'. It was becoming very obvious that he was in for a hard time as soon as the plane reached England. Mentally damning Thorne for his cursed stupidity he went through into the cockpit.

Ken Frazer meanwhile had come to the same conclusion. In other circumstances he would have welcomed any event which might possibly damage his captain's career and thereby open the path for his own promotion. This case however was different. That there would be an inquiry into Thorne's death he was sure. Unfortunately he was equally sure that the reason for *Caterina*'s unscheduled touch-down at Shambe would come out, and the board might well delight in having a second scapegoat on which to load the blame. As soon as they reached Cairo he would have to send off a telegram to his mother in London, telling her to use all her influence to have his part in the business hushed up.

During the latter part of the evening he and Ralph Kendricks had not unnaturally discussed the tragedy and its consequences. Like Desmond, the radio engineer held Ian Thorne largely responsible for his own misfortune and was angry at the thought that the blame might be cast elsewhere. The New Zealander had been nervous and preoccupied during the evening, and subject to fits of irritability. Unusually too, he had drunk quite heavily before turning in for the night; all of which Frazer had put down to reaction to the killing.

The galley was only eight feet long, and less than half the width of *Caterina*'s main cabins, yet from it the steward was capable of producing at only an hour or so's notice, a full four course meal for up to twenty people.

In his mind he planned out the breakfast he would offer the passengers as soon as they were in the air. Fruit juices to start with, they would have to be tinned, the supply he had taken on at Mombasa was no longer fresh enough, and he did not trust the local fruit. Nothing was more annoying than a passenger with an upset stomach and the airline was acutely sensitive to complaints of this nature. The fish was still good though, a fine Kingfish caught while they had been in the harbour, Andy had seen it cleaned and gutted and placed on ice in the refrigerator within a quarter of an hour of its being landed. Originally he had intended to serve it for dinner, it would have made an excellent centre piece on the serving trolley, surrounded by a nice salad garnish. Now, however, he would make a kedgeree. His eye flicked automatically to a shelf, yes there was plenty of rice.

Then there would have to be bacon and eggs, as well as kidneys, both cooked with all the usual trimmings, fried bread, tomatoes and sausages. The passengers had a right to expect a choice of several dishes, and besides which Andy was firmly convinced that any traveller with a good meal inside him was likely to be far more contented and less trouble for the remainder of the flight.

Of course, some passengers, particularly the women, would prefer cereals, he had seven different varieties of these, and all would finish with toast and marmalade or honey. Mrs. Hartman, he remembered, had told him she enjoyed a continental style breakfast and he had bought some small bread rolls for her during the wait in Kenya.

It was fortunate that Sandy was a friendly, easy-going young man, quite willing to do a share of the kitchen work. Andy had been working the airline for twelve years and before that he had spent very nearly as long serving as a cabin steward with Cunard on the trans-atlantic run. A lifetime spent ministering to the comforts of wealthy travellers had taught him to sum up a passenger's character after only the briefest acquaintance. He could spot at a glance the troublemakers, 'the professional moaners' as he referred to them privately, who liked to occupy their hours in the air in making him run to and fro at their whims, having him fetch first one thing then another. Their cushions would never be comfortable, their drinks would never be mixed correctly, and this always annoyed Andy who prided himself on his cocktails, they themselves were constantly either too hot or too cold.

There was one such person on board every flight and this time Andy had even less trouble than usual in picking him out. From the first moment he had stepped on board Stewart Curtis had had him running about like a tame dog. Arrogant and highly irritable, Curtis made no attempt to allow for the time the steward had to spend attending to the other passengers. Whatever he wanted had to appear at once and preferably before he even asked for it. Convinced of his own supreme importance he treated those he thought inferior with contemptuous disdain and his attitude towards anyone who had to serve him was that of a man who appeared to enjoy humiliating people.

So far Curtis had complained of the service on board twice to Sandy Everett and once to the captain. In fact Andy worried not at all about the effects of such behaviour. He knew his captain well enough to be sure that Curtis would be listened to politely and no more. Desmond O'Neill made it a cardinal rule never to interfere in the handling of the passengers, leaving them firmly in the hands of his steward. Nevertheless, Andy resented the financier going behind his back. Had Curtis but known it he had managed to ensure for himself the maximum of discomfort and inconvenience during the remainder of the voyage. The steward of a flying-boat was in a position to make life very difficult indeed for his enemies.

Desmond sat at the flying-boat's controls, watching the distant shore through the wide panoramic windows of the cockpit. Despite the fact that every window that could be opened was fastened back the air inside the plane was still hot and oppressively heavy. Judging by the heavy clouds spreading across the sky from the east, another torrential downpour would reach them soon. With luck they would be away before it struck.

Fine view or not the atmosphere in the cabin was tense and not solely due to the weather. The entire crew was sensitive to the fact that they had lost a passenger and the nerves of all of them were on edge. Ken Frazer had greeted him monosyllabically on his return to the boat and had gone about his tasks with an angry defiance, as if determined to show that he did not consider himself in any way responsible for what had happened. Ralph Kendricks on the other hand had been all too obviously upset and was clearly worrying as to what the reaction of the London Office might be when they reached England.

Although the repairs had been properly completed, and the port side wing tank refilled, there had still been the incredible delays in starting. The passengers had been slow in getting ready, and even slower in coming down to the pier to embark. Then one of the launches was discovered to have a defective engine and had to be withdrawn so that one boat had to fulfil the dual role of ferrying out passengers and their baggage and also transporting supplies of fresh water, mail and clean linen out to the aircraft. Then, too, there had been some final and grisly arrangements to be agreed with Keeling on what to do if Thorne's body should be recovered.

Now they waited only for the final clearance to be received over the radio from the station before starting up the engines and taxiing out into mid-stream. Together Desmond and Frazer had gone through the pre-flight procedure, running over the course they would follow up to Khartoum and on up to Cairo, and estimating the fuel loads required. This last was important, for an excess of fuel meant increased weight to be carried aloft and hence increased consumption and greater costs. On really long flights such as over the newly opened trans-atlantic route, the aircraft burnt up so much fuel getting into the air that they had insufficient reserves left to reach the far shore. Consequently they had to be sent up with half-empty tanks and be refuelled in mid air from another aircraft, an experiment which seemed to work surprisingly well, though Desmond could well recall his own trepidation during his first attempt at this manoeuvre.

A slightly bigger wave than usual rocked *Caterina* and Desmond saw the starboard float dip and touch the surface of the water for an instant. She was listing a trifle to port, resting part of her weight on the port side float, it was seldom possible to trim an aircraft so exactly that she would lie evenly, and the slightest motion of the water would send her rolling to the swell. He could feel the tension building up within him, a growing impatience to be off, to be back at the job he should be doing.

'She's all yours Skipper, they're ready to go,' the words were hardly out of Kendricks' mouth before the two pilots had their hands on the controls.

'Switch on master,' Ken Frazer leaned forward and pulled the master ignition switch. At once the dials and gauges in front of them came alive, as needles flickered behind the glass. 'Master on,' Frazer confirmed.

'Check fuel levels in all tanks.' Together they both scanned the separate gauges for the main and reserve tanks. 'Five hundred and fifty gallons total,' Frazer answered, *Caterina* had taken on a much less than full load, but they had enough on board to see them safely to Khartoum.

'Oil pressure normal?'

'Affirmative,' Frazer echoed.

'Radios functioning?' there was a series of clicks behind

them as Kendricks tested the three separate sets. 'All radios functioning Skipper,' he sang out.

'Fuel pressures normal?'

'Affirmative.'

'Ready with the pyrene gun Sandy?' Desmond called out over his shoulder, and again it was Ralph who answered, 'he's all set skipper, I can see him standing by the hatch.'

'Starting No. 2 engine.' Punching the ignition button, Desmond heard the nearside starboard engine spring into life with a clatter, propeller blades twirling slowly at first, then vanishing into a single spinning disc. The aircraft gave a surge forward and began to slew round towards the far bank as the screw bit into the air.

Back in the mailroom, Sandy Everett crouched by the open hatchway peering out at the spluttering engine. This was always an anxious moment for him. If an engine should overheat and catch fire as they sometimes did from the rich fuel mixture fed in for ignition, then it was the purser's job to crawl out on to the wing and pump foam from the pyrene fire extinguisher into the cowling. This was no easy task at the best of times, with the aircraft pitching through the water and the slipstream tearing at his fingers clutching the slippery wing, while trying to keep hold of the heavy pyrene gun and praying he wouldn't be left standing by a burning engine having dropped the extinguisher into the water.

For the rest of the crew the purser's antics on these occasions were always something of a joke, especially when the weather was bad, although the airline had actually lost one purser this way at Rome when Bill Claridge slithered off a wing and disappeared forever into Lake Bracciano. Drowned, it was popularly believed, because he had not dared to let go of the pyrene gun. Had he done so, the company would have made him pay for it.

This time, however, there was no trouble and the engine settled down to run smoothly.

When all four engines were firing, Desmond worked the throttles, making sure that each one ran smoothly, feeling the power surge and die away beneath his control.

'Check for carburetter heat.'

'Aye aye sir,' there was a momentary drop in revolutions on each engine as Ken Frazer pulled the switches which pumped warm air from the engines into the carburetters via a small hatch. In freezing conditions, or at high altitudes such a facility was vital to prevent ice from forming round the inlets.

'Carburetter heat functioning correctly, switching back to normal.' Frazer closed the switches as he spoke and the aircraft's speed increased with the restoration of power.

'Check alternator load.'

'Check oil pressure,' this could never be done too often, a fall in the oil pressure gauge was often the first and only warning of imminent engine failure.

'Check fuel pressure.'

'Check oil temperature.'

'Check manifold pressure.'

'Check suction gauge.'

'Check exhaust temperature.'

'Close throttle.' The power died away, the noise ebbing from the cockpit as the engines returned to idle and the needles on the rev. counter sank back to the 500 mark.

'Test power flaps.' With his right hand Desmond worked the levers controlling the electrically operated wing flaps.

'Flaps operating normally,' Frazer confirmed.

'Set gyros.' This was the second officer's task and Desmond waited as Frazer fiddled with the setting of the gyro compass and flicked up the cover of the magnetic compass beside it.

'Open artificial horizon and direction indicator,' both these instruments, like the compass based on gyroscopes, were shielded by metal flaps. Frazer now snapped these open.

'Check turn and bank indicator.'

'Set altimeter.' This last was a crucial item and one which Desmond always checked very carefully himself. Contrary to popular belief the altimeter did not tell a pilot how high he was off the ground. A careless pilot could easily fly into a 1000 foot hill with his altimeter reading 1500 feet. What an altimeter did was to give a height reading based on the air pressure outside the aircraft, but it was essential the instrument be set at the correct ground pressure for the particular area. A wrong setting, or a sudden change in the general pressure below an aircraft, such as could be caused by moving from flight over land to over the sea, could bring about a totally false reading.

Under his captain's watchful eye however, Frazer took the readings and made the setting correctly, and went on to check the proper functioning of the airspeed indicator, and the rate of climb and descent indicator while Desmond brought *Caterina*'s head round in to the wind and prepared for the final take-off run.

'Request take off clearance from shore,' he asked Kendricks, and the radio operator bent over his microphone, 'Hotel Oscar to Shambe station, Hotel Oscar to Shambe station,' he repeated, 'Imperial 109 requesting clearance to take off.' There was a crackle of static, 'O.K. Skipper,' he called out, 'we're cleared to go.'

Trailing a long streak of white foam *Caterina* raced along the water, spray flying from her sides. As her speed increased she rose on to the planing step of her keel, and she seemed to skim along the surface. The vibration, severe at first, became easier as she went faster, the water flashed by outside the windows, the banks sped past, then, as though severed suddenly by a knife, the foaming trail was cut off, the vibration ceased, and the great plane rose slowly from the river and climbed away into the sky.

'Withdraw boost,' the engines quietened as Frazer obeyed and the superchargers were shut off. Watching the revolutions steady out at two and a half thousand per minute Desmond set about the task of synchronization, setting all four engines running smoothly in time together.

'Autopilot on sir?' Frazer's hand was on the switch but Desmond shook his head, 'No,' he said, 'I'll fly her myself for a while.' In truth it was a relief to have his hands on the controls again, to feel the aircraft responding to his touch, sensitive to the slightest movement of the rudders or steering yoke. They were still climbing slowly towards cruising height. With no high ground between the marshes and the scrub and desert plains through which the Nile ran for the next 2000 miles, 5000 feet would be easily sufficient altitude. Already the sun was warming the air, creating powerful thermals which now and then caught the plane lifting her and then, with equal suddenness dropping her back through a hundred feet or more. Anticipating such forces and compensating so that the passengers were scarcely aware of any break in level flight, was a source of pleasure and satisfaction to him.

'Winds east-south-east, at 12 knots skipper,' Kendricks told him as the forecast from Khartoum came over the radio, 'I've given them an e.t.a. at Khartoum of 10.15.'

A little over three hours to Khartoum at the junction of the two Niles, then another seven up to Cairo, with a stop at Wadi Halfa for more fuel. With luck they should reach Cairo at dusk, but it was going to be a long day.

A sudden lurch as the flying-boat struck an air pocket recalled his attention to the present. At least for the next few hours he could concentrate on his job and leave worrying about the future. Settling himself more comfortably in his seat he eased the aircraft back towards her cruising height.

By common, though unspoken, consent among the passengers it had been agreed that no mention would be made of yesterday's tragedy and that the day's journey would proceed as though nothing had happened. Accordingly, once they were in steady flight and Andy was handing round the menus for breakfast, and passing from cabin to cabin taking orders, the passengers began to move about and talk much as they had on the previous day.

Their attitude was noted by Sandy Everett with relief as he helped the steward to organize the meal and made his round of the cabins to see that everybody had what they wanted. Most of all he was worried about Laura Hartman and the Kings. For these three the picture of normality was less easy to maintain. Unlike the rest of those on board they felt a degree of personal responsibility which could not simply be ignored.

Today they had resumed their seats in the midship cabin and were sitting in silence, eating mechanically, without noticing the food, and staring out of the windows. Several times during the flight Sandy went in to talk to them and to try and bring them out of the fit of gloom which possessed them. The tragedy seemed to have driven the three Americans closer together, reinforcing the natural ties of race and nation. Their talk was almost exclusively of their homes, and of events taking place there, and he suspected, all of them were counting the days till they were back in their own country and away from the nightmare into which they had fallen.

Early on in the journey to Khartoum Laura was summoned to the after cabin by Stewart Curtis for a session of dictation and letter writing, and during conversation with the Kings Sandy realized that the couple had adopted the protective attitude of parents towards the younger girl.

'I don't like Laura working for that man,' Mrs. King said openly, with a defiant glance in Sandy's direction. 'I don't care how rich he is he makes her work too hard and take on too much responsibility.'

'Now Louise,' her husband reproved her, 'we have no reason to speak against Mr. Curtis. He is Laura's employer and that is a matter between them privately.'

Louise King sniffed, 'A good employer doesn't keep a girl up till all hours, or make her travel about with him alone. I think he behaves much too selfishly, and if I see him I shall tell him. He doesn't even let her use his cabin, he just keeps the whole place to himself. I'm surprised the airline allows one man to take up an entire cabin like that,' and she looked hard at Sandy.

'Mr. Curtis's wife is joining him in Cairo,' he explained to her apologetically, 'and she's travelling with her maid. I suppose it is easier for them to have a separate cabin. We only allow it when there are plenty of other seats, but if someone is willing to buy up all the seats in one particular cabin there's not a lot we can do.'

Harold King gave a low whistle. 'What's that, four seats? And one for Laura Hartman, that's five, and then you say his wife is bringing her maid, six seats in all and they're flying right through to New York. That makes one expensive trip.' He shook his head in slow disbelief.

'It's even more than you imagine sir,' Sandy told him. Like Mrs. King he disliked Laura's employer and was glad of a chance to criticize him. 'I know for a fact that Mr. Curtis has booked luxury suites at every hotel we stop at on the route. He must be spending a fortune.'

To his surprise Harold King did not seem pleased at this revelation. 'I am not sure you should be telling us this young man,' he answered gruffly, 'Mr. Curtis's travel arrangements should be his own private business.' Sandy flushed at the rebuke and shortly after found an excuse to leave them and return to the upper deck.

At his seat at the flying-boat's radio desk, Ralph Kendricks was gripped by nerve breaking panic. Every muscle trembling in an uncontrollable spasm, his two hands gripped the metal edge of the table fiercely, his face contorted with effort as he fought back the attack, sweat pouring from his body.

Soundlessly he sat, locked and rigid for nearly half a minute, before the fit passed, leaving him weak and spent. Mopping his face he looked across to his right at the other two, noting their motionless, unseeing backs with relief. That was the third attack since the trip began, how much longer could he conceal them from the rest of the crew? Desmond had already begun to notice that he was behaving differently.

He ran his tongue over his gums, his mouth felt parched, another three and a half hours to go before Khartoum. He needed a drink badly. Automatically his eyes strayed to the locker by the radio spares box. There were the remains of a bottle of whisky in there, hidden among the repair tools, left over from last night, when the strain of the forced landing and Thorne's killing had driven him to seek relief in alcohol. Almost half of the bottle had been needed to steady his nerves. Now he dared not run the risk of Desmond smelling the spirit on his breath this early in the morning. He would have to wait.

That damned trans-atlantic crossing. Just when he had thought he had finally laid the ghosts of the past. The ghosts of a flight seven years ago. He shivered at the memory as his mind relived those hours again.

It was almost six o'clock, they had been in the air ten hours and were more than eleven hundred miles out over the North

Atlantic. Now they were flying at about 5000 feet between banks of violet cloud, which gradually deepened in shade as night drew nearer.

'Carl, be a good fellow and switch on the panel lights,' Bell had asked, and Carl had leant forward to comply. There were three of them on board the Junkers monoplane. Bell the captain, Carl Huisson, the German co-pilot, and Ralph as radio operator. Their task was to make a survey flight over the route between Ireland and Newfoundland preparing the way for the airliners of the future.

It was a good aircraft the Junkers, solid, reliable, all metal, a similar plane had already flown from Dublin to Labrador in April 1928, but no plane can be too good for the Atlantic and they had spent days testing every piece of equipment.

Yet when Carl switched on, the instrument panel remained unlighted.

'I'll check the connections, it's probably only a fuse,' he said, but when he tried the switches again, it brought only the same result. Bell swore irritably.

'It's a nuisance that's all, either you or Kendricks will have to shine a torch on the compass so I can see where we are headed.' The others said nothing, this far out over the open sea, even so small a failure as this seemed ominous. Ralph looked down at the rapidly darkening expanse of the Atlantic below them. There was a heavy swell running, the crests of the waves foaming white, far off to the left a lone iceberg drifted with the current. Huessen checked their speed. 'Ninety miles per hour. We must be hitting head winds. Fuel consumption is steady though.'

Then the Canadian weather bureau had come on the air. 'Severe storm moving eastwards over Nova Scotia, high winds and some snow.'

'That means we may have to fight these headwinds all the way to the coast. Let's hope they don't get any worse.' There was no need for Bell to elaborate on his statement. If the wind strength against them increased and their speed dropped further they might run out of fuel before they reached land.

Ralph did some calculations, 'Seven hundred miles to go to

the coast of Newfoundland, about eight more hours at this speed,' he told them.

'Provided we're on the right course,' Bell grunted, 'I don't trust this compass much.' He stabbed at the dial with a stubby forefinger. By the light of the torch beam Ralph saw that the needle was flickering and jumping beneath the glass. He felt a knot of fear tighten his stomach at the sight. If the compass were faulty out here then they were indeed in trouble.

The train had been halted at the approaches to the pass for the past three quarters of an hour, at the small siding in the Carnic Alps which held the frontier control post for Germany's border with Italy. The platform outside, covered in frozen snow, like the roof of the low grey cement building, was crossed through with muddy tracks. A few passengers had descended, and were walking about in the cold clear air, gazing up at the mountains around them, whose peaks glistened in the sunlight. Among them moved the watchful figures of the frontier police in their dark green uniforms.

The majority however, preferred to stay inside the heated carriages. It was still only eleven o'clock and the sun had not yet succeeded in warming the day which in any case had started cloudy. More than that a significant number were refugees reluctant to abandon the train on which all their hopes of survival were pinned. Instead they waited nervously while the inspecting police worked their way slowly through the carriages checking the complex documents and permits needed to allow a citizen of the Third Reich to travel beyond its borders.

Siegret and her father sat in silence, occupied with their own thoughts and too tense and nervous to speak. The professor held his daughter's hand in a gesture that brought her some comfort. Already they knew, some people had been ordered off the train. These could be seen from the window, standing in a miserable, pathetic group on the platform under the eyes of two guards, surrounded by piles of baggage. Among the huddled figures Siegret could see a child of eight or nine years old, its eyes round with anxiety.

There was a noise of doors opening nearby and the murmur

of voices. The police had reached the next door carriage, very soon she should have to face them. She felt herself begin to tremble with the strain of waiting and the fear of what might happen, and her father squeezed her hand reassuringly. The others in the carriage seemed equally apprehensive, these days any encounter with the authorities was a matter to be feared by all but the most powerful. One was a businessman most probably, she thought, he was too well dressed to be a refugee. He was travelling with his wife, a stout, brassy blonde in her forties who smoked incessantly. Further down by the door an old couple sat facing each other. Man and wife, both were frail and worn out and, like the Wienzmans, shabbily dressed. The old man caught Siegret's eye watching him, and gave her a fleeting smile.

The voices next door rose and fell interminably. Once or twice Siegret heard snatches of some kind of regular dialogue as one or other of the occupants was interrogated, but both questions and answers were too faint to be understood. Then there was more slamming of doors and there were uniforms in the corridor. The door was pulled back and two guards and a plain clothes police officer entered the carriage.

'Ausweisse bitte.' With the peremptory demand for their papers Siegret was at once acutely conscious that their whole escape depended on this one moment. All the elaborate plans, the sacrifices they had made, the risks taken, would have been in vain if these men were not satisfied. All the work she and her father had put into collecting those passes and permits, in obtaining their passports and visas had been directed to this one instant. This was the final and crucial barrier.

On the journey up to the pass her mind had been occupied in speculating what their fate would be if they were caught at the frontier, either through some error or deficiency in their papers, or because the guards had already been warned to watch out for them and not to let them through. In the eyes of the Nazi authorities their actions would certainly be treasonable. Even if they needed her father's work too badly to harm him, they would have an excellent excuse for sending her to a labour camp for 'political re-education' as they termed it, where she would be held as a hostage to guarantee his co-operation. The thought had made her sick with fear. In Vienna she had heard about the camps and knew how savage the conditions there were, and the brutalities of the guards. Her chances of ever being released again, once inside, would be non-existent.

The old couple by the door were the first to be checked. The plain clothes man took their papers and ran his eye over them with a frown, 'Jews,' he remarked wearily, 'more Jews, I see nobody but Jews on the trains these days. Do ordinary Germans never travel?' The old man and his wife looked frightened and made no reply, but sat watching him. 'Baggage?' he asked curtly. 'One trunk,' the man answered in a quavering voice, 'in the passage, and my wife has a basket.'

'Go and take a look,' the policeman gave a nod of the head to one of the men with him. Apparently satisfied that their papers were in order he moved on.

From their answers to questions put to them, Siegret learned that the blonde woman and her husband were German nationals employed in Italy and returning there after a holiday in their homeland. Their visas had evidently been counter-signed by some important official for they were subjected to only the most cursory examination and their baggage left untouched. The policeman handed back their papers with a small bow of respect. Finally it was the turn of the Wienzmans.

Siegret's father handed over the two bundles of documents to the plain clothes policeman who started to examine them page by page, reading each one carefully right through from beginning to end, checking every detail for mistakes. Siegret watched out of the corner of her eye, not daring to look at him too closely. He was a man of about forty, solidly built, with a barrel-like chest and a small head on which the hair had been cropped very short, who wore a raincoat undone to reveal a dark suit beneath. His face was sallow and impassive, concentrated on his task. He turned the pages of the passports slowly, creasing each one down with his thumb as he went, to read more easily.

At first he was silent, studying the elaborately printed papers without comment. Then abruptly without raising his eyes from the page he spoke in a quick flat tone, 'Purpose of journey?' he demanded. Taken by surprise, Siegret's father stumbled over his words. 'Emigration, we wish to emigrate,' he managed at last, his face pale and sweating. The policeman ignored him and turned another page. 'More stinking Jews,' he said contemptuously. 'Search their baggage carefully,' he told the guard, 'they probably have property stolen from the Reich concealed there.' The Professor lifted two of their suitcases down from the rack above on to the seat and undid them. The guard began pulling out the contents, shaking the folded clothes loose to see if anything had been hidden among them. Siegret and her father watched apprehensively. Their sole contraband, the notebooks, were at the bottom of Siegret's suitcase which was still to be searched, but the police might easily take exception to something else.

'It says here,' the policeman spoke again, this time his voice was slower, as if puzzled by something he had found. Both instantly recognized it as a sign of danger. 'It says here,' he repeated, tapping the page he was reading with a finger and glaring at the Professor, 'that your profession is that of doctor and lecturer at the University of Vienna, but in your passport,' he turned back to the reference he was seeking, 'you call yourself a Professor. Which of these is the correct description?'

The man's tone was casual but the inference behind the question was only too apparent. It was clear that he suspected that he had here a highly qualified intellectual who was trying to slip out of the country by pretending to hold a much lower grade post. Siegret's father however was prepared for the trap. He had, indeed, realized that as a mere lecturer he would arouse considerably less interest when applying for permits than if he did so as a Professor. Only his passport revealed his true status. 'Lecturer is my correct title,' he answered, forcing himself to speak calmly, 'I was provisionally made professor of my department in 1938, and at that time I applied for the passport, but after the Anschluss my appointment was not confirmed and I remained a lecturer until I was dismissed later in the year.'

'So you had to go back to your old job,' the policeman sneered, 'you must feel bitter towards Germany,' he suggested, but the Professor was not to be caught out so easily.

'No,' he said, 'I am not bitter, but since I am unable to find work in Germany I am forced to go abroad.' At the quiet way in which he answered, disguising the deep loathing she knew he held for the régime, Siegret felt a surge of respect for her father. The policeman snapped the passport shut and tossed the whole bundle back into the Professor's lap.

The guard meanwhile had finished with the two cases the Professor had got down. 'Put that stuff back,' he told Siegret, pointing to the belongings that lay strewn over the seat. 'Which are your cases?' Siegret stood up and lifted her two small suitcases down. The injuries she had received the previous afternoon had stiffened, making her movements painful and awkward. To her alarm, this caught the attention of the plain clothes man.

'What's wrong with you?' he asked sharply, giving her a hard look. Siegret made no reply and turned her head away, pretending to be busy repacking her father's belongings. She was terrified that the guards would become suspicious of the bruise on her face where Gerdler had hit her. Before setting out she had done her best to disguise the marks with powder and make-up, and had wound a scarf round her head, but there was no hiding them from close inspection.

The man was not to be put off however. Grasping her by the shoulders he pulled her round towards him. 'Answer when I speak to you Jew,' he snapped angrily, 'what happened to your face?' Before she could reply her father intervened. 'My daughter was attacked in the street by some youths,' he said, 'she was beaten about the face and body. I must ask you to speak gently to her, she is still very upset.'

'Shut up,' the policeman retorted viciously. 'What are you, some kind of whore that you fight in the streets?' he demanded of Siegret. 'Did one of your clients give you a beating? You filthy Jewish bitch.' His harsh voice and bullying tone brought back all the horror of the assault upon her by the gang in St. Veit, she was seized by a fit of uncontrollable trembling, tears began to stream down her face, she tried to speak but the words would not come. The two police laughed jeeringly at her, and the plain clothes man tugged the scarf loose from her head.

'Leave her alone!' Siegret heard her father's voice above the jeers and laughter and saw that he had risen to his feet. 'How dare you say such things to an innocent girl. Have you no children of your own that you behave like this? Is this the greatness of the new Germany we are told about?' Anger and disgust at the treatment of his daughter leant a power to the old Professor's voice that stopped the two men short. For a moment they stared at him, amazed at his outburst, that anyone should dare to rebuke them.

'Listen old man, your daughter is nothing but a dirty little Jewish whore and you're her pimp,' the senior of the two retorted, 'you keep quiet unless you want to be arrested and sent off to a camp.' Placing his hand on the Professor's chest he pushed him down so that he fell on the seat. The uniformed guard laughed again. 'What do you want to do with the girl—' he asked, 'shall I send her back to the post for questioning, maybe we could find some more bruises on her,' he said leeringly.

Siegret waited, transfixed with fear, for the policeman's decision. His eyes flicked over her as though she were no more than an article of baggage. Plainly he was undecided on what to do with her. Then just as he opened his mouth to give his answer, there came a noise and commotion from outside in the corridor. 'What the hell's going on there?' he barked angrily. Another guard put his head round the door, behind him Siegret recognized the anguished face of the old man who had been sitting in the corner.

'We've found a whole load of silver, this old nut was trying to get away with,' he informed the plain clothes man.

'It's not true,' the old man shrieked in protest, 'I have certificate of ownership!'

'Take them away and put them under arrest, we'll sort it out when the train's gone.' The second guard took the man's wife by the arm and dragged her to her feet still clutching her basket. 'Put them with the others,' the policeman ordered following them out. At the door he paused and looked back at Siegret and her father. 'Stinking Jews, how anyone can sit in the same carriage with you I can't think,' he spat, then he was gone, and the cries and protests of the old couple, interspersed with shouts from the guards, receded down the corridor.

Siegret's father hugged her to him, patting her shoulders gently. The train gave a short warning blast on its whistle, and began to pull slowly out of the station. The last thing Siegret saw was the old man and his wife standing with the other prisoners. With hopeless expressions they were watching the train leaving them behind as it steamed off towards the frontier and into Italy.

The train's smoke was still hanging in the air above the pass when the telephone in Hans Meyer's office in St. Veit rang shrilly. 'There is a call for you from Berlin,' the operator informed him 'a Herr Rintlen from Gestapo Headquarters, Prinz Albertstrasse.' With sudden foreboding Meyer waited for the connection, it was impossible that the Gestapo should already have heard of the Wienzman's attempt to escape. They could scarcely have reached the border and in any case had they been arrested his own office would have been the first to receive the news. All the same the call was ominous.

A voice on the line cut across his thoughts, 'Superintendant Meyer of the Kriminalpolitzie, St. Veit?' it demanded curtly. 'This is Standertenfuhrer Rintlen of the Sicherheitsdienst. I wish to speak to you on a confidential matter concerning a person known as Professor David Wienzman at present registered as a resident in your district, formerly lecturer in medicine at the University of Vienna.'

Hans Meyer's mind was racing as he listened to the words. The Sicherheitsdienst, the SD, was the secret intelligence division of the SS itself, controlled by Reinhard Heydrich, the most feared man in the whole of the Third Reich, the evil genius behind the rise of the black shirted SS and, many said, in reality more powerful that Heinrich Himmler, his nominal master. It had been Heydrich who had masterminded the slaughter on the terrible Night of the Long Knives in 1936.

when Rohem's brown shirts had been purged of all opposition to Hitler. The SD, the innermost, most secret and most powerfull organization within the Nazi state apparatus, was the means whereby Heydrich maintained his hold upon the SS and the Gestapo.

'I am instructed to inform you Superintendant,' Rintlen continued, 'that the work of this man Weinzman is considered to be of the highest importance. It is essential that he and his family be sent here under guard at once.'

Meyer could picture the man on the other end of the line. The harsh, arrogant tones he had heard so often before from the blond Aryan supermen of the blackshirts. Although the previous evening he had spoken to the Professor so confidently of the ease with which he would be able to deal with the inquiries of such men, he felt a cold fear in his stomach as he answered.

'I very much regret, Herr Standartenfuhrer, that the man you refer to was permitted to emigrate recently. He obtained the necessary permits from the Ministries in Vienna and I issued him with a frontier pass myself several days ago. By now he will certainly have left.'

'You idiotic fool,' a torrent of abuse came over the line, 'you allowed a man of vital importance to Germany to leave the county. My God but you'll pay if this is true.'

The best way to answer this attack was to brazen it out. 'Whatever has happened,' Meyer responded, 'the fault is not mine. Wienzman was in possession of permits from your office in Vienna, as well as from the Foreign Ministry, the Economics Ministry and the Office of Emigration, I merely issued the frontier pass for which he already had authority. You must look to those higher than me if you wish to find someone to blame.'

'Tell me this much,' Rintlen snapped, 'since you have so signally failed in everything else. When and where did the Professor cross the frontier and who was with him?'

At all cost Meyer realized, he had to delay the pursuit which the SD and Gestapo were bound to launch after the Professor and his daughter. He glanced at the clock on the wall opposite, a quarter to eleven, they were probably crossing the border at this very moment. A single telephone call might stop them.

'The Professor was to travel with his daughter,' he answered carefully, 'the pass allowed them to cross into Italy at any point within this police district. As to the time of their departure,' he hesitated, 'of that I am not sure. Would not the best course be for me to check at once with the border guards. It may even be that they are still on Austrian, that is German soil. In which case I can deliver them to you.'

'Do that, and telephone me back here the moment you learn anything.' The line went dead as Rintlen slammed the receiver down. Meyer turned his gaze thoughtfully towards the window. Above the roofs of the town the tops of the mountains stood out clearly against the bright sky. With luck he thought he could delay any pursuit for a couple of days at least, and that would probably give the Professor and Siegret a chance to get out of Italy and beyond the reach of the Gestapo.

In Berlin Paul Rintlen sat for a moment in thought, then picking up the file of papers in front of him, he went out into the corridor and along to a door at the far end. Unlike Hans Meyer's idea of him, he was dark and slimly made, with the light build of an Austrian rather than the traditionally Nordic appearance of the North Germans. His face was intelligent and would have been good looking were it not for too narrow and pointed a chin, an awareness of which had given him the habit of constantly stroking and kneading at his jaw with his fingers, as though trying to hide the defect.

The door at the end of the corridor opened into a large room containing a leather sofa and several chairs for visitors and, at one end a small desk behind which sat an officer dressed like Rintlen in a grey uniform, trimmed with silver.

'Is the Chief free, Lindeman?' he asked, 'there is a problem with the Wienzman case.' With a nod Lindeman rose and knocked softly on a door behind him, 'Standartenfuhrer Rintlen,' he announced and standing back motioned him forward.

Hated and feared more than any other single man in the Third Reich, Reinhardt Heydrich epitomized in the eyes of many everything the nation's government stood for. Tall, blond-haired, strikingly handsome, he had an air of irresistible power and vitality and a ruthless, driving ambition which had brought him to the topmost circle within the state. In some quarters it was whispered that Heydrich, by far the cleverest mind among the Nazi hierarchy, was the only man in Germany feared by Hitler. Certainly the chief of the SD had over the past years amassed detailed and incriminating files on every other person of significance including both his current boss Himmler and Prime Minister Herman Goering. Perhaps, too, among these carefully guarded papers there were records of secrets that the Fuhrer himself would wish to hide.

Rintlen had been a little surprised to have been given so routine a task as the tracing of the man Wienzman, and even more so when he had been ordered to report the results directly to Heydrich. There must, he realized, be some special aspect of the case which had yet to be disclosed to him and it was with some trepidation that he related the failure of his efforts.

For a moment Heydrich remained impassive, then his face twisted in a scowl and he swore once, with such venom that Rintlen started.

'There is a good reason, Obergruppenfuhrer, to believe that this man and his daughter are now in Italy. If that is so a special request to the Italian ministry of police should produce results.' Heydrich waved him to silence. 'This is not a case of some little Professor fleeing the country,' he said thinly, 'Professors are two a penny, the Gestapo can take care of them.' He paused, staring out of the window in thought, Rintlen was aware of the noise of traffic in the Prinz Albertstrasse beneath the window. Abruptly Heydrich switched his attention back.

'Wienzman is important not because of what he is or does, but because of who he was,' he lit a cigarette and tossed one to Rintler who smiled inwardly. As far as the general public were concerned his master was a man without indulgences such as tobacco and spirits. 'Wienzman is being sought by Goering's people, ostensibly because the Luftwaffe want him to continue his work on medical research. That, however, is only a cover.

For myself I am certain that Goering has discovered a relationship between this man and a high state official. Naturally it is
my duty to investigate.'

Rintlen felt a shadow of fear fall on him at this. The risks of
entering a struggle between such antagonists were terrifying.
Whatever the result he would be bound to offend one of the
country's most powerful men, both renowned for their ruthlessness and implacable hatred. Heydrich's next words
confirmed his suspicions.

'You will go out to this place St. Veit,' he said, 'and find this
man Wienzman and arrest him and any member of his immediate family. You will go alone, and if you are forced to use local
police support you will tell them nothing. No record will be
kept of the arrest, or of any associated action. You will also
bring away unread all personal documents you find.'

'And if he has already crossed into Italy?' Heydrich gave him
a cold hard glance. 'You will follow him wherever he goes and
carry out your task, our missions abroad will be instructed to
give you any assistance you require.'

'I understand Obergruppenfuhrer. You may rely on me.'
Rintlen rose and saluted 'Heil Hitler.'

'Heil Hitler,' Heydrich smiled grimly. 'Our salutes demonstrate our reverence to our leader. Nevertheless I trust that in
this particular mission you will at all times remember to whom
you owe your immediate loyalty, even should this appear to
conflict at times with your loyalty to the Party and its officers,'
again he paused momentarily, 'perhaps even conflict with the
supreme authority.'

Back in his own room Rintlen poured himself a stiff measure
of schnapps, gulping it down he refilled the glass. His fingers,
he noticed, were actually trembling slightly. There had been
enough difficult, brutal jobs in the past years which he had
carried out without qualms. The road to power in Germany
had been tough and merciless, but this one, he shivered again
and took another swig from the glass, savouring the fiery liquid
coursing down his throat; of the implication of Heydrich's
final words there could be no doubt. Wienzman was to be elim-

inated and the incriminating documents of his background placed in his hands, and not even the supreme authority in the state was to be allowed to prevent it.

Desmond had already guessed at Ralph Kendricks' fears. The radio operator's growing nervousness had been apparent to him ever since the news of the Atlantic flight had been broken to them, two days ago at Durban. As yet he was not sure what to make of it. All flyers were afraid at times, they would be inhuman if they were not. Bad weather, night flights, faulty equipment, engine failure, at any time one might be only seconds away from death. Desmond remembered some of his own experiences, flights which had gone wrong or nearly so. A crash landing in the Pyrenees en route to Lisbon, when forced down by a storm, he had found himself hemmed in on all sides by the steep walls of the mountains rising above him through the clouds. He had known fear then, and only luck had enabled him to find a way through the tortuous valleys, skirting the rock faces in the failing light. There had been engine failure over the sea off the coast of France, a fire in the air at Croydon in England during one of his first trips for Imperial.

Every flyer had similar memories. If modern techniques and equipment were rendering their tasks less dangerous, this was being more than compensated by the constant striving after ever more difficult achievements. Night flying, trans-saharan flying, flights across the Andes and over the Pacific. Always longer and more arduous journeys, and the most difficult and dangerous of all was the North Atlantic; the route with the worst weather in the world.

Ralph had had a bad crash. The fear would probably always remain with him, just as for himself, the fear of those terrible shoulders of rock in the Pyrenees surrounding the aircraft would remain. Far more to the point was whether he possessed the toughness, the determination of the spirit, to push back the fear and carry on. One way or the other, Desmond thought, this flight would provide the answer.

Privately he was sure that his Radio Officer possessed those qualities, the dedication to duty that made a good flyer. A trip might be good or bad, easy as sleeping or so hard and exhausting that when you finally stepped down from the cockpit it was all you could do to stand upright. None of these things mattered, one seldom ever mentioned them. What counted was getting through, delivering those coloured canvas sacks of mail, those precious crates, the infinitely more precious and more complicated human cargo, and keeping to the schedule. Private fears and hopes, private lives, everything came second to this. If a man could not accept it then there was no point in his flying any longer.

The rain was sleeting down on the road, blowing in off the Chesapeake Bay.

Jarrett paid off the cab and squelched across the yard to the office. Outside stood a couple of cars and a battered pick-up painted red. The windows of the hut were steamed up and inside he found three men sitting round an oil stove on wooden chairs, drinking coffee in a thick, stale atmosphere. They looked up at him with hostility as he entered.

'I've come to pick up my plane,' he told them. 'The Supermarine S4.' None of the men made a move but sat staring angrily at the visitor who had disturbed their retreat. Eventually one of them, a fat balding man in a much dirtied white overall, heaved himself to his feet and approached the paper-strewn desk.

'A Supermarine S4, the Supermarine,' he repeated to himself, sifting through the mess until he came to some kind of registration book. 'Yeah, I remember,' he ran an oily finger down a list. 'Ain't seen yer for a week or two Mister Jarrett, yer used to be down most evenings working on her. What you aim to do with her? Only got one seat 'n no space for baggage. Heavy on the gas and been smashed up once.'

'Ach, she's a fine bird for all that,' one of the other two men threw in unexpectedly, 'sister to the one that won the Schneider Trophy in '27.'

'She was smashed up on trials though,' the older man answered without raising his head, 'that's why they sold her.'

'What you planning on doing with her then?' the second man asked.

'I collect historic aircraft. I buy them up and try to restore them to their original condition. Got a Curtis Navy Racer CR3 and a Fairey F17 Compania.' As he had expected this explanation established him as a wealthy fool with more money than sense and the men's interst in him disappeared at once. 'Is the plane ready?' he asked, 'I'm short on time and I've got a long way to go.'

'She's ready,' the fat man admitted reluctantly, squinting through the window at the rain dancing on the tarmac outside. 'You want to take her out in this?' Seeing Jarrett nod his head he reached for a black oilskin with a sigh, 'O.K. then fellers, let's get the man his plane.'

It took the combined efforts of all four of them to roll back the hangar doors. The metal was freezing cold to touch, with water cascading down the gulleys of the corrugating. Inside, in the gloom Pat saw two light amphibians, and towards the rear the silver-white outline of the Supermarine sitting in its launching cradle.

'We'll hook her up to the tractor and back her down the ramp till she floats off,' the foreman wiped the rain off his face, his voice echoing hollowly in the vast empty space of the roof.

Some twenty-seven feet in length with a slightly greater wingspan, and standing just over twelve feet high at the tail, the racer's sleek, powerful fuselage, long floats, and wings placed below and forward of the pilot's seat, gave her an impressively streamlined, businesslike appearance. The nose, float struts and upper wing surfaces were all plated with polished duralumin; the remainder of her body glistened a freshly painted white. Just to look at her, he thought, made one realize the speed and power she was built for. A fact all the more extraordinary when one considered she was more than fourteen years old.

Three quarters of an hour later, with the aeroplane fully fuelled, and the last pre-flight checks complete, he was sitting in the tiny cramped open cockpit, tightly wrapped in a heavy leather flying coat, furlined helmet, goggles and gauntlets.

The little aircraft increased speed and she began to skim across the surface of the water. Jarrett was conscious of the wind and spray flying up at him over the tiny cockpit rim. The engine noise now rose swiftly to a high keen pitch as they howled across the bay.

For the next few minutes, oblivious of the rain flung back at him over the cowling, Jarrett put the aircraft through her paces, climbing, diving, banking, loops and rolls, lost in the exhilaration of flying a single seat high performance plane. Not since the end of the war had he known such single-minded pleasure.

Khartoum was hot and humid. The air, once the doors were opened, struck the flying boat's occupants like an influx of steam. Set on the point of the triangle where the swift moving waters of the Blue Nile, flowing down from the mountains of Ethiopia, meet the slow turgid, discoloured White Nile, the Bahr el Abyad, heavy with silt from its long straggling journey through the Sud; the city of 'Chinese' Gordon, of Speke, of Livingstone and the Mad Mahdi, impressed them as no more than a stifling harbour, whose peeling waterfront sheltered only a handful of dhows and a solitary river steamer. The town had been rebuilt since its destruction by the Mahdi's fanatics and its subsequent recapture by Kitchener forty years earlier, but it still remained a remote colonial outpost, the capital of one of the world's emptiest lands, and everyone was relieved when Desmond announced that they would resume the flight as soon as refuelling was complete. Lunch would be served aloft.

On they flew in the harsh sunlight, the desert unfolding slowly, in a vast carpet of brown and yellow, streaked and mottled with the marks of hills and dried watercourses. Beneath them the endless bright ribbon of the Nile flowed steadily northwards, its banks fringed with a green that ran for a short distance inland, turned yellow and vanished in the sands.

The weariness of the long flight coupled with the strain of the previous day's events was telling on them. With the auto pilot on, and no hills to avoid or course changes to observe, they sat in tired silence, each occupied with his own thoughts, their minds numbed by the noise and shake of the engines, and their eyes aching from the endless glare.

One-fifteen in the afternoon saw them taking off once more, this time from the Egyptian waters of Wadi Halfa after the final refuelling stop of the day. Here again there was little to see and do except sit in the aircraft and wait while the tanks were pumped full for the six hundred mile flight up to the delta, and the sacks of mail transferred and sorted. The thousand or more miles they had already covered since dawn, seemed to have made only a slight difference to the heat and humidity. There was a hot wind blowing out of the Nubian Desert and the air was heavy with dust.

'The hot weather's returning early this year,' the airline's representative told Desmond resignedly. He was a thin dispirited man, with a grey, unhealthy face despite his years in the sun. 'We shall have a long summer of it.' He gazed out over the river towards the low brown hills in the distance to the south east. 'I hear you're taking the flight across the Atlantic this time,' he remarked suddenly, giving Desmond a quick look from under his heavy brows, 'Good luck to you in that, you'll need it.'

'I've flown the route before,' Desmond answered him shortly. The old man looked away again. 'It'll be winter out there, and here the summer's starting. Wonder if I'll ever see a real winter again, back home I mean. Do you reckon there'll be war this year?'

'Who can say,' Desmond shrugged. He felt a sudden dislike of the man and a longing to be away.

'Heard about your spot of trouble down in the marshes, bad thing to happen. These crocs, never see 'em coming.' Years of loneliness and too much of his own company had left the man with an oddly clipped manner of speech, it was hard to decide if he was talking to himself or not. 'Company won't like it, never do, especially a passenger. The rest of us, you and me, we're not so important.'

That much was probably true, Desmond thought as he climbed back through the hatch to the flight deck. Crews and pilots were far less indispensable than passengers or freight. It was still very likely that command of the Atlantic flight would be taken away from him. And he would be left to work his way back and forth along the Cape to Cairo route, passing and repassing the scene of Thorne's death. The thought angered him and his mouth tightened grimly as he settled himself in behind the controls. At all costs he was determined to make that flight. If the board tried to pin the blame for the accident on him he'd fight them every inch of the way.

The other three on the flight deck noted the signs of their captain's anger and kept silent, going carefully about their duties so as not to bring down rebukes on themselves. Only when they had been flying for several minutes did Ralph Kendricks tap him on the shoulder. 'Think you'd better see this Skipper,' he said passing him a slip of paper, 'it's a weather report just in from Cairo. It looks bad I'm afraid.'

IV

'That's a hamsin,' Ken Frazer commented when Desmond passed the flimsy across, 'it must be moving right into our path judging by this.' His eyes strayed to the map open on his knees where a moment earlier he had been marking off their progress, 'I suppose there's a chance we might outrun it,' he said doubtfully.

'That's what we'll try for,' Desmond agreed. It had, in fact been his own immediate reaction on reading the message. With a little under three hours to go till they reached the delta, there was a chance, if they flew at maximum speed, that they might be able to cross the path of the storm and get ahead of it. The winds would be operating in their favour; the only questions were how far the storm centre was from the city and the speed at which it was moving.

'Give me our exact fuel requirement for maintaining maximum cruising speed to Cairo,' he told Frazer, 'and check that we have sufficient reserves.' Frazer moistened his lips with his tongue, 'you won't worry about the wing tank then?' he asked, the nervousness just evident in his voice.

'I'd rather take a small risk on the repair holding up than try to land through the middle of a hamsin,' Desmond's tone was curt, he felt in no mood to pander to his Second Officer's anxieties, 'the tank has given us no trouble so far today.'

For the flyer the storms were even more terrifying. Caught

in one, a plane's engine was swiftly choked and stopped by the fine particles blowing in through filters and inlet ports. Tossed and buffeted by the air pockets the pilot would strain his eyes in vain to see through the impenetrable dirt which swirled around him. In such conditions it was impossible to tell even which way up the aircraft was flying let alone the direction to take for safety. Planes had disappeared in these clouds never to reappear, even their wreckage having been swallowed up by the sands.

The alternative was to land on the river and wait till the hamsin had passed over before taking to the air once more, but this course, simple as it seemed, was to Desmond the less attractive of the two. At ground level the effects of the wind and sand were felt at their worst. Besides the difficulty of mooring *Caterina* securely in such conditions, there was a very real possibility that the engines would be so clogged with dust that re-starting them would be impossible, and at all costs he was determined to avoid another day's delay.

'Of course if we meet it in the open desert we should be able to fly above it,' Frazer continued hopefully. Desmond made no reply. Although in theory Frazer was right that if they were to meet the storm within the next hour or so, then they would have a fair chance of being able to escape by increasing their altitude, it was far more likely that the storm would strike them as they were nearing Cairo and having to lose, not gain height.

'We'll continue at maximum speed,' he announced when they had checked the fuel figures. To Ralph Kendricks he said, 'Tell Cairo I want everything they hear about the storm as soon as they get it.' The drone of the engines altered to a slightly higher pitch with the increased power.

For the present the surface of the desert continued calm and undisturbed, the horizon a flat clear line, unbroken by any hint of cloud, but an hour, perhaps a little more, would see the full weight of the hamsin bearing down towards them upon a converging track. With all possible speed they raced on into the north.

'Have we not seen enough? Why do we wait?' The howl of

the sandstorm snatched the words from the Egyptian's mouth, rendering them barely audible, muffled as they were already by the cloth he had wrapped around his face as a protection against the flying dust.

Crouched near the top of the dune Rashid al Senussi peered down on to the road two hundred feet below. There was no denying that conditions were rapidly becoming impossible. Great gusts of wind were tearing sand off the crests of the dunes around them in long ragged streams, and driving the dust furiously across the open plain. The two of them were shielded to some extent from the worst of it by the small hollow in which they sheltered, but even so their position was exposed and uncomfortable, a fact which the Egyptian evidently felt keenly.

'We have seen everything, why waste time,' he repeated. 'Let us go back. We will return tomorrow,' he gave a tug at Rashid's robe, 'let us go back.'

Rashid struck the man's hand away angrily. 'Be still,' he said curtly, 'And watch the road. It is only a little wind.' Damn these Egyptians, he thought to himself, peasants and farm dwellers they were useless in the desert. A few hours without water, the threat of a storm and they were finished. Generations of easy living near the delta and the banks of the great river had softened them to a point where they would be of less account than a woman among the nomadic tribes of the true desert.

Thank God he had a few of his own people with him. Tough raiders out of the Sahara, men who could travel all day on a handful of dates and half a cup of brackish water and still fight hard at the end of it. Men who were not afraid to risk death in battle rather than submit to the rule of an alien master.

For himself the fight had lasted so long he could no longer conceive of any other life. Almost his earliest memories were of trekking off into the passes of the hills with his father's tribesmen, out of the reach of the shells of the Italian artillery, clinging flat against the rock faces as the planes swept the narrow valleys with machine gun fire and shrapnel bombs. He could recall as vividly as though it were yesterday the terrifying roar of the aircraft engines diving down at them, the crash of the explosions as the bombs blasted the column, the sound re-echoing off the sides of the gorge, the sharp smell of cordite, the screams of the women and other children around him, wounded men and horses struggling together on the ground, their blood mingling in the sand.

The enemy had overwhelming strength and it had been a long time before the Arabs had come to terms with this new method of fighting. Rashid had ridden in more than one mad horseback charge against Italian forts, charges that had turned into bloody routs when the machine guns and mortars had opened up. In the last of these he had seen his three closest friends blown into rags a scant ten yards ahead of him when a salvo of the bombs landed at their horses' feet.

After that they had fallen back on the old ways, of raiding in small groups, attacking by stealth at night, laying ambushes, and melting away in the vast empty regions beyond the coastal strip. Harrying the convoys and farms and the small outposts of the occupatation army. A boy warrior at thirteen, by the time he was fifteen Rashid was a battle-hardened guerilla veteran with a price on his head.

That price had been collected one day in 1933 when a military detachment had surprised him at his father's home near Tobruk in Cyrenaica. Seized and captured before he had been aware of what was happening, by decree of the military governor the young Sheikh had been dispatched back across the sea to Italy as a hostage for the good behaviour of his father and his people.

Somewhat to his amazement he had been well treated. There was a new policy in force at that period under which the sons of Arab chiefs and sheikhs from troublesome areas were to be educated and instilled with an understanding of the Italian way of life in the belief that this would make them sympathetic to colonial rule on their return. In Rashid's case it faced him with the dilemma of being determined to continue his fight for freedom, and yet at the same time being filled with a passionate desire to acquire the knowledge which brought his enemies so much power.

In the end it was his father who had decided for him. 'My son,' he had written in a letter, 'for us the war is lost and to fight on would be useless, bringing death, hardship and misery to our people. For the present we must wait and trust that with our children the times may change, that our enemies may grow weaker and that you will one day return and show our people how to throw off the yoke which has for so long lain upon our necks. Take what your captors offer, accept what they have to teach, but never forget that you are of the desert, that you are a Prince of the Senussi, and that your home is with us.'

From that day there was no more dedicated student of European culture than Rashid. So pleased were his superiors that they even allowed him to be sent to the Victor Emmanuel Military College in Rome.

'd'Este will come by this road tomorrow, of that I am sure,' the Egyptian pleaded, plucking once again at Rashid's sleeve, 'it is always the same course.' There could no longer be any doubt that they were about to experience a full hamsin, the strength of the wind had increased markedly in the past few minutes and furious gusts were cutting across the dunes, driving the sand off them in solid sheets. Already the road below was entirely obscured, and visibility was all but impossible. 'He will come as you say,' Rashid turned angrily on his companion who cringed back against the wall of the hollow, 'unless your information is a pack of lies.' There was a note of real menace in his voice and the unfortunate man whined with fear.

'No, it is true, I swear it, my Sheikh, upon my mother and my sister. d'Este will drive in the big race, his car is a red one. It is said he may win.'

d'Este, d'Este, the memories evoked by the name grew more bitter each time he heard it mentioned, renewing the force of the oath he had sworn. A year, no more, since an urgent message smuggled secretly past the guard of his supervisors had transformed him into a hunted rebel once more as he fled back to his homeland, a message which carried that name, and whose contents were to remain forever burned into his brain.

'd'Este must come,' the Egyptian pleaded, his face a mask of anxiety, fear of these hawk-like desert rebels had long since swallowed up his natural greed which had first persuaded him to act as guide. 'He leaves the country for America in two days, and his wife goes with him. Tonight he will attend the King's ball at the Palace, tomorrow he drives in the race to El Faiyum. There, I have told your Highness all that I know. Believe me!'

'Is there any reason why I should not?' Rashid demanded. 'Since you know that your life depends upon it.' He rose to his feet, pulling the hood of his robe over his head. 'I have seen enough, we will collect the horses and return to the city to fetch my men. When d'Este comes past tomorrow we will be ready for him.'

Jacquetta d'Este had been wrong in supposing that her husband was already having an affair with Charlotte Curtis. So far they had not progressed beyond the stage of mild flirtation. Which, while most enjoyable, could hardly be considered a great romance, Luca thought to himself as he sat alone with his brandy after lunch on the terrace of Shepherd's Hotel, and it was a state of affairs he was determined to alter.

Jacquetta had left to go riding, a frequent pastime of hers of late. Indeed so frequent, that at one point Luca had begun to wonder if she were meeting a lover during these long periods of the day when she was absent. For a time he had even felt jealous; his wife was certainly beautiful enough to have attracted any number of admirers, and he doubted whether in the light of his own past behaviour, she would suffer any guilt in deceiving him. Discreet surveillance had, however, revealed that her time was genuinely spent riding among the sand dunes and watercourses on the edge of the desert; country which she evidently preferred to the more popular areas around the river or among the citrus groves in the watered parts near the city.

The wide, marble floored terrace of Shepherd's Hotel was the most celebrated rendezvous in all Cairo, and equally famous throughout the whole of the Middle East. A carpeted stairway led up from the street where among huge potted palms and exotic plants the guests lounged at their ease, idly watching the pavement below where there milled a crowd of snake-charm-

ers, donkey men, souvenir hawkers, touts, dragomen and itinerant pedlars, preying on passers by, and prevented from
entering the hotel itself by the gorgeously uniformed suffragi
standing at the doors.

'Good afternoon Baron, you honour us with your presence, I
trust everything is to your satisfaction?' The speaker was a
man of medium height in his late thirties, dressed with impec-
cable elegance in a formal dark suit.

'Your cooking, my dear Freddy, is far superior to that of the
Embassy,' Luca greeted the newcomer affably, 'will you join
me in a brandy?' He indicated the chair beside him as he spoke,
and the hotel manager took it with a small bow. 'Some brandy
for Mr. Muller,' Luca turned to the suffragi who approached
soundlessly.

'And so Freddy,' he went on as they sipped their drinks,
'another season in Cairo draws to an end. It has been a good
one I think.' Freddy Muller reflected for a moment.

'Yes,' he answered at length, 'it has been a good season, one
of the best, indeed I should think the best for ten years at least
if not more, but perhaps . . .' he hesitated.

'Go on,' Luca was watching him carefully. Freddy collected
his thoughts.

'I was going to say,' he continued, 'that this last season has
been the brightest and gayest for many years. Cairo has never
seen so many distinguished visitors; kings, noblemen, states-
men, film stars, millionaires, men of letters, a true gathering of
fashionable people. The women have never been so beautiful,
nor their clothes more elegant. This season has seen the most
lavish and glittering parties that I can ever recall, hardly a
night has gone by here at Shepherd's without a ball or a dance,
or grand dinner party being thrown, and now with the marriage of the King's sister to the future Emperor of Iran, the
celebrations have become more spectacular still. And yet
behind all the gaiety and wit, all this carefree enjoyment, I
seem to sense an undercurrent of urgency, almost of desperation, as though people thought in some way it could not last
forever.'

'Come, come Freddy,' Luca gave a laugh, 'like all Swiss

133

you're a national pessimist. People are happy now because last summer they all thought there would be war in Europe, and now that has been avoided. I agree it's been a marvellous season, but this air of desperation as you call it, no, I don't find it anywhere.'

'Well, Baron, perhaps you say I am a pessimist and an oversensitive one at that. You do not believe there will be war then?' He took another sip at his brandy.

'War, there is always war somewhere,' Luca responded carelessly.

'No, I meant . . .' Freddy began.

'You mean a big war, between Germany and France say, or Britain.' Luca dismissed the idea with a wave of his hand. 'I think there is small chance of that. Hitler's eyes are to the east. It is Germany and Russia who may fight one day, but there will be no war in the west for a while I think.'

'But the British and the French are re-arming.' Freddy murmured as he watched a pedlar selling flowers on the pavement, holding a pot in each hand and balancing a third on his head.

'So are Germany, and Japan, and Italy, it does not mean they are about to go to war with one another. Enough of this depressing talk,' Luca answered with some asperity, 'tell me how do you vote my chances in tomorrow's motor race?'

'It is said that you have the fastest car,' Freddy responded suavely, 'with perhaps Captain O'Neill as the next challenger. As to driving skills,' he spread his hands, 'I am no judge, but the betting is lying in your favour.'

'Well if I win Freddy,' Luca told him jovially, 'I shall give a great party at Shepherd's to celebrate. Everything in the colours of my car. With a dinner and dance in the gardens afterwards.'

'I confess we are already making preparations to accommodate the winner,' Freddy told him with a grin, 'and I shall pass on your intentions to the chefs. I only hope that the wind will have dropped in time for the race.'

'It will have passed by this evening and tomorrow the day will be clear and cooler.' Luca said optimistically, 'so tell your chefs to have everything ready. And now I must go.' He rose to

his feet and the hotel manager at once stood up. 'I have promised to escort Mrs. Curtis to the palace of Prince Suleiman.'

Prince Suleiman was an Egyptian of unequalled wealth who
lived in a fairy-tale like roccoco palace on the western side of
the river, beyond Bulak bridge, in a poor, predominantly Arab
quarter, whose mean and crooked streets and squalid homes
served to emphasize the extravagant lines of what was said to
be the most beautiful of Cairo's many palaces. Though a wid-
ower, and in his seventies, the Prince had formerly been one of
the leading figures in Cairo's society and invitations to his
palace were still much sought after. Luca, who knew the old
man well, was hoping that the grandeur and luxury of the buildings and its splendid gardens would assist him in his seduction
of Charlotte.

The Prince had sent a boat to fetch them, a marvellously
oriental affair powered by a dozen oarsmen with gilded timbers,
and a silk canopy over the high carved stern to shade the
guests. The wind was now stiffer, but not yet unpleasantly so,
though Luca could see that the return would have to be made
by road, and on the river itself the air was cooler and less
dusty. ·

Charlotte leant back against the stern and looked back over
the river. Beneath the white façades of the buildings on the
front, the banks were fringed with tamarisks and palm trees
and bright with the colour of bouganvillea and oleander;
nearby, on the shore the opulent house-boats of rich Cairenes
rode at anchor. A string of feluccas moved slowly upstream
ahead of them, their huge single sails bellying out in the wind.

Luca eyed her keenly, barely suppressing the desire he felt.
His gaze lingered on the firm outline of her body beneath the
thin silk of her dress.

Was it simply the desire for physical satisfaction or aesthetic
attraction that made him crave for her so? Was it because his
instincts told him that she would be an exciting lover, or was he
merely aroused by the difficulty of the conquest and by the
thought of her stripped of her beautiful clothes and robbed of
the coolness and poise with which she kept him at bay?

'It's such a pity there should be a hamsin,' Charlotte remarked with a frown, 'I should have loved to come here on a really perfect afternoon.'

Luca did not reply. In his experience a woman's complaints on such matters were best ignored; treated with respect they tended to assume an exaggerated importance. He put his faith in the splendour of the Prince's palace to make her lower her guard. This afternoon was his last chance before her husband returned and he intended to make the most of it.

The boat drew in at a point where luxuriant gardens ran down to a marble faced embankment, in the middle of which lay a white marble pier set with silver lamps and handrails like an enormous piece of jewellery. The sound of music reached them faintly over the water; concealed musicians, Luca realized, must be stationed nearby to greet the arriving guests. Liveried servants waited on the pier head to receive them.

The scene could not have been more perfect, he heard Charlotte give a small gasp of amazement at the beauty of it. Taking her arm he conducted her up through the water-gate and into the grounds of the palace.

Jacquetta d'Este had not found the wind too troublesome at first. She had driven out beyond the suburbs some twenty miles to where her horse was kept at stables on the edge of the desert. The horse was a fine bay gelding named Balbo whom she had brought over with her from Italy for the season, a present from Luca on her birthday three years ago, during one of his rare spells of affection.

The majority of riders from the stable invariably made for the Pyramids and the Sphinx whose colossal bulks rose from the sand not far away. Today, however, only a few tourists were defying the blowing dust. Even so Jacquetta turned Balbo's head away towards the open ground to the south west. This afternoon she felt a need to be as far away from others as possible, she had even made the groom who normally accompanied her, remain behind with the chauffeur.

As soon as they had left the vicinity of the stables, Jacquetta gave the horse his head and at full gallop they sped towards the hills. Exhilaration swept through her as she felt the wind flying through her hair and heard the swift drum of Balbo's feet on the sand. Sensing her excitement the horse responded, quickening his pace still further.

When at length they pulled up and she slowed him first to a trot and then to a walk, she realized that she was already halfway to the hills and that the dust blowing into her face was considerably more unpleasant than she had at first thought. The fact annoyed her, just as anything which threatened to interfere with the pleasure of her daily ride annoyed her, and urging Balbo back into a trot she pressed on towards the shelter of the broken ground. In a few minutes she came upon the course of a dried stream which wound tortuously back towards the hills, its wide bed offered an easy path for a horse to follow, and though the banks on either side were not high they nevertheless gave a fair amount of shelter.

Finding a way down into the channel presented no difficulty and very soon Jacquetta was following the stream back up towards its former source. She rode slowly, partly to give the horse a chance to pick its way among the stones which littered the ground, and partly to allow herself time to think.

Her thoughts ran, as they so often did these days, on Luca, and their future together. Increasingly over the past years, and especially during the last two or three months, her position seemed to have become intolerable. Her husband's affairs had become more and more blatant till now he appeared to care nothing about the impression he gave in society. He humiliated her constantly in public and in private he abused and ill-treated her. At heart a bully, he seemed to derive an actual physical pleasure from watching her suffer, a pastime which his constant heavy drinking was causing him to indulge even more frequently. Sexually he ignored her for months at a time, and judging by the stories being bandied about, Luca was rapidly degenerating to a point where only the stimulus of a new conquest was sufficient to arouse him to potency.

Physically a highly sensuous woman, to whom lovemaking had been one of the chief delights of marriage, Jacquetta hated him all the more for making her spend the nights alone and unsatisfied while he debauched himself with his latest mistress.

Of course the obvious answer was to do as several of her friends did and take a lover herself, but Luca was watchful and somehow she felt she wanted a more final solution, some form of separation which would allow her to live apart from her husband, though she knew Luca would never permit that.

Preoccupied with her thoughts she rode steadily on. The shallow channel turned into a small ravine with sides that were steeper and rockier than before but she scarcely noticed the fact. In her mind she was running back over the first happy days of her marriage, contrasting these with the present. Overhead the sky had darkened as the dust clouds rose to cover the sun. The wind was howling outside the ravine driving the sand before it in a stinging spray, but so far, sheltered by the rock walls, Jacquetta had scarcely noticed the approach of the storm.

'Why must it be d'Este who must die, Highness?' the Egyptian asked when they had covered nearly half the distance back to the city outskirts and were taking a temporary shelter with their horses from the hamsin in the ruins of an abandoned village. Outside the mud walls, the sand was blowing thickly enough to choke anyone unprotected by a head cloth and they had been forced to rest the horses. The Egyptian was reluctant to move on and kept up a flow of questions in the hope of putting off the moment when Rashid drove him out once more.

'Why do you hate this Italian so much, Highness?' he asked again. He crouched, huddled in a corner, watching Rashid anxiously.

'He murdered my father and my sister,' Rashid told him in a flat, dead tone which carried nothing, and was meant to discourage further conversation. The Egyptian, however, broke into voluble comment on the iniquity of such a deed and the understandable need of revenge. Rashid paid him no attention. It was impossible to convey to this little man his feelings when the news had reached him in Italy. 'Your father is dead, murdered by the soldiers, they took him up in an aeroplane and threw him out over the village. Your sister, Rathine, they have carried off to the palace of the Governor in Tripoli.'

Once when he had been a boy he had seen a killing done that way. The Italians had surrounded the village with soldiers during the night and moved in at dawn. They were looking for rebels and arms and to begin with the pattern had been familiar.

He had stood and watched while the tents and houses were searched and their possessions strewn over the ground outside. The soldiers had picked them over taking any articles or small trinket that might be of value and smashing some of the others with their boots or the butts of their rifles. The men meanwhile had been separated from the others and made to stand in lines. Rashid remembered them shivering with cold and whispering nervously to each other, striving to appear unafraid. Then an informer in a black hood had been brought out and he walked along the lines with two of the officers, stopping at intervals to reach out and touch the chests of the men he betrayed.

The beatings and interrogations had gone on for most of the morning. The cries of the tortured men had been audible all over the village, and the rest of the people had waited and listened and the smell of pain and fear everywhere. For the most part the soldiers had lolled about in the shade, smoking and drinking wine from flasks but near one edge of the village Rashid had seen two of them rape one of the girls, stripping her at knife point and taking turns to hold her down. Later that evening that same girl had hanged herself from the branch of a thorn tree.

Not that the soldiers would have cared; the purpose of the expedition had been punitive, to teach these tiresome rebels a lesson, rather than to capture large numbers of men and guns. After the interrogations were over one or two of the men were released and the remainder loaded into a truck. The villagers noted this with a certain degree of relief. According to previous experience the prisoners would be taken off to one of the forced labour projects near the coast. At least they would be allowed to live.

The sound of the aircraft's engine came as a surprise. The Arabs had learnt to fear the machines which scattered death from the air in the form of shrapnel bombs and tracer bullets and watched the movements of the tribes as they crossed the sands.

The plane landed in a patch of firm ground beside the camp and switched off its motors. It was an obsolescent twin-engined bi-plane, but to the villagers it was symbolic of the conqueror's power and the soldiers knew it. Now with much shouting and blows with their rifles they drove everyone into the centre of the village, where the officers stood and beside them, between two guards, the Sheikh of the tribe.

One of the officers then spoke for a while. Rashid hadn't been able to follow his words for the man's Arabic was poor. Instead his eyes had been fixed on the Sheikh. The old man, until that day the undisputed master of his people, their Judge, Leader and Prophet, still retained his dignity. He held his head high and his eyes still held their accustomed pride, but now Rashid saw confusion and bewilderment in them too. Something was about to happen that even the Sheikh did not comprehend and this frightened the boy greatly.

The officer stopped speaking and for a brief moment there was silence. Then he motioned to the guards and they fell upon the Sheikh with ropes, binding him, not in the normal fashion to prevent escape, but trussing him up bent double like a turkey being taken off to the market.

Amid the laughter of the rest of the troops and the horrified cries of the women and children they dragged the old man across the sand to the aeroplane, lifted him up to the door and bundled him in. The door was slammed shut, the engines started up with a clatter, the plane raced across the ground and lifted off into the air, climbing swiftly to disappear towards the north.

Their task apparently complete the soldiers climbed into their lorries and began to move off in the direction they had come from, with their prisoners. Soon only a slowly disappearing cloud of dust marked their progress.

The villagers remained together in a group, many of the women bewailing the loss of their menfolk, the others attempting to comfort them. With their Sheikh and half of the men taken away, their homes looted and ruined nobody had a clear idea of what to do.

When they heard the plane again the first reaction of many had been the thought that their Sheikh was being returned to them and they had waited eagerly for the buzzing speck in the sky to descend.

But the plane had not descended; approaching from the north it circled high above the village, while the eyes of those on the ground strained to follow it. Rashid had not seen the tiny black missile drop suddenly towards them, but others must have done, for he heard cries of horror and there was a scattering away for cover. There had been a sound in the air above like that made by a bomb and he had been expecting a loud bang but instead there had been only a heavy thud on the ground behind him and he had turned his head just quickly enough to catch sight of the tattered bundle leaping high into the air again as it bounced on the blood-spattered sand.

And the Egyptian asked why he hated the men who had condemned his own father to this shameful death. Baron d'Este had cared nothing for justice or treaties, nothing for the feelings of the people he governed, his only concern was that his province remained quiet, and so he had given orders that Rashid's father be thrown out from a plane above one of his own villages.

At least his father had died quickly. Rashid still felt an impotent fury when he thought of his sister's fate. The Governor had a great palace in Tripoli, with golden domes and marble fountains set in the gardens, and the officers had liked to force pretty Arab girls to dance naked in the fountains for them, and Rashine had been very beautiful. She had died on her second evening in the palace, hurling herself from a balcony in a grim parody of her father's death.

She and Rashid had been very close. Their mother had died when they were still young and their father had been occupied with the affairs of his tribes, so they had looked to one another for company and comfort throughout their childhood. Later when Rashid had been fighting with the rebels he would return to see her as often as he could. Now her death struck him even more deeply than his father's.

Desmond O'Neill made his way forward to the smoking saloon for lunch, his mind still preoccupied with his crew. As far as Frazer was concerned there could be no doubt that he would have to go. Desmond was fairly confident that for all the young man's boasted influence with the board he would be hard put to block an official request for his transfer. Perhaps some other captain in the fleet would find him easier to stomach, though personally Desmond doubted whether anyone would willingly take on the arrogant first officer. One thing was certain though, he was not going to remain on board *Caterina*.

Of Ralph Kendricks he was much less sure. Ralph was a steady, reliable radio officer whose solid qualities he respected. Yet he was obviously suffering acutely from nerves at the prospect of another flight across the Atlantic, across the ocean which had once nearly claimed his life. Of course the simplest way out would be to suspend him from duty when they reached England. Any pretext would do, he could be sent off for a medical check or on a familiarization course with some new equipment. The trouble was Ralph needed to beat his fear; if he took, or was given, an easy way out, then for the rest of his life he would be a failure in his own eyes. The question was how far Desmond was justified in risking the safety of the aircraft in order to give the radio operator the chance to prove himself.

In the passageway he met Sandy returning from the smoking saloon. The purser was looking flushed and angry.

'Mr. Curtis is in there having lunch sir,' he said with a backwards nod of the head. 'He's been wanting to know if you'll be cutting short our lay-over in Cairo in order to make up for the time we've lost. I told him that I thought if anything we would be saying longer while the engineers did a thorough inspection job on the fuel system and when he heard that he really hit the ceiling. You'd have thought we were doing it just to spite him.'

'All right Sandy, I'll see to it,' Desmond assured him, 'are the rest of the passengers behaving themselves?'

'All except Mrs. Johnson, she's complaining Draper's been rude to her. He probably has but that's only because she's been giving him hell all morning. I told her she must have misheard him and made Andy apologize but she's still pretty cross.'

'Do we lose her at Cairo?' Desmond asked. Several of the passengers, he knew, were due to leave them at the delta while a number of others would be boarding.

'No such luck,' Sandy answered gloomily. 'The Finlays are leaving us there, and an Italian couple are joining, as well as Mrs. Curtis. I just hope she's not as bad as her husband.' Desmond smiled. 'Cheer up Sandy, at least then he'll have someone else to complain to beside you. Who are the Italian couple?'

'A Baron and Baroness d'Este,' Sandy had done his home-work and had the facts at his fingertips. 'He's some kind of big-shot in government circles apparently, he and his wife are going all the way to New York with us and I've been told to see they get red carpet treatment. They're friends of the Curtises, I think.'

Leaving Sandy, Desmond passed on into the smoking saloon. Here, as he had been told, he found Curtis together with Laura Hartman, the South African Dr. Van Smit and Mr. Johnson. As he entered Curtis was holding forth to the others on the short-comings of the Airline and especially the flight they were now on. He greeted Desmond's arrival however without any trace of embarrassment.

'Captain, your Purser tells us we can expect further delays when we reach Cairo. I should like to know if this is, in fact, true?' he demanded, 'I should have thought you would want to push on as quickly as possible so as to make up for lost time.' There was a murmur of assent from Johnson. Laura and Van Smit said nothing.

'You're correct Mr. Curtis in thinking that I intend to make all possible speed,' Desmond answered him equally, 'just as soon as I am satisfied that the aircraft is safe to fly.' His eyes glanced towards Laura as he spoke.

'You were apparently sufficiently satisfied to fly nearly two thousand miles up the Nile,' Curtis said rudely, 'why should you change your mind.'

'I have had temporary repairs made to allow us to reach the nearest port with proper servicing facilities,' Desmond answered quickly, 'since, when we leave Cairo we shall have to cross open sea as well as fly over the Cevennes Mountains. I would have thought you would be glad of my taking extra care.'

'How long will these further repairs in Cairo take?' Curtis asked. Desmond shrugged. 'That depends on what they find, but I don't expect that we shall be delayed for more than about half a day. We shall probably leave in the afternoon on Monday instead of first thing in the morning. After that it depends very much on whether or not we have a clear run right through to Rome or have to stop for a night in Athens.'

Dr. Van Smit gave a low chuckle. 'But at least Captain there will be plenty of time for you to drive in the motor race in Cairo on Sunday. Your purser was telling me earlier that you have a Hispano-Suiza. A magnificent car, you are most fortunate. How did you find such a car in Egypt?'

'Magnificent but old I'm afraid,' Desmond said, 'she doesn't have a great chance against some of the new machines that will be competing. I managed to buy her off King Farouk, his father left him more than a hundred cars when he died three years ago.'

'Ah, then you know the king?' Van Smit remarked.

'Hardly at all,' Desmond told him, 'but like a lot of people he's interested in aeroplanes and I've flown him on a couple of occasions.' He did not add that one of his most serious quarrels with Pamela had been over his refusal to accept Farouk's offer to become his personal pilot.

Stewart Curtis's voice cut across the conversation. 'You apparently fail to realize Captain,' he said heavily, 'that I have important business commitments which make it imperative that I reach New York without delay. As it is you have already seriously inconvenienced me, I am due to attend a ball at the King's Palace in Cairo tonight with my wife and thanks to your tardiness I may well arrive late. What excuses will you have me make then I should like to know?' he demanded in a hectoring voice. Desmond's jaw tightened.

'I can assure you Mr. Curtis that you will be in Cairo in plenty of time for the King's ball,' he paused for a moment before adding: 'Quite apart from any other considerations, I have been asked to attend myself.'

There were smiles from the others in the cabin at the financier's visible discomfiture. For a moment he appeared about to retort, instead however, he rose abruptly to his feet and stalked out of the door.

'I think Captain, that you have just made an enemy,' Van Smit said in his soft voice. 'Our Mr. Curtis is not used to being made a fool of in front of others.'

At this remark the third passenger in the cabin, Johnson, who had been sitting quietly in a corner with his pipe taking in the conversation, bridled unexpectedly. 'I see every reason to sympathize with Mr. Curtis' feelings,' he said pompously, 'it is extremely annoying and inconvenient for some of us to have our travel arrangements upset in this manner.'

Laura Hartman leapt instantly to Desmond's defence. 'I call that a very selfish viewpoint Mr. Johnson,' she said with spirit, 'why! you're asking Captain O'Neill to put your personal convenience before the safety of the rest of the people on board.' Johnson looked taken aback at this sudden attack and Desmond intervened hastily to cool the situation.

'It's annoying for all of us,' he said, 'for myself and the crew every bit as much as for the passengers. Lost schedules mean a lot more work and less off duty time. We had been hoping we'd be able to push on fast enough during this part of the trip to allow us time to make an extra stop over at Bastia in Corsica. There's a special landing area there by a little fishing village where they give us fresh lobster tails for dinner washed down with local wine. It's a tiny place, so quiet and remote you can almost imagine you're on a private island.'

'But can you do that?' Laura asked with surprise. 'Stop and come down just anywhere you want like that?'

'Not quite anywhere,' Desmond smiled back, 'we're supposed to stick to the scheduled ports, but I like to vary the trip a little if I can, so I admit I tend to look for excuses.'

'Yes. We were warned of that in Durban,' Van Smit showed his teeth in an answering grin, 'the Imperial Airways officer told us that there was no alternative landing area you had not used at least once.'

Desmond made a wry face, 'Unfortunately they were wrong, I hadn't been to Shambe,' and an awkward silence descended on the cabin as they recalled the events of yesterday.

'We should be having a news bulletin after lunch,' he said to change the subject, 'since there wasn't any recent newspaper at Khartoum or Shambe we thought you would all like to have the four o'clock broadcast from Cairo put through on the intercom.'

'Ah yes,' Johnson agreed at once, 'I shall look forward to that. I regard it as most important to make an effort to keep up with the news at home when one is abroad.'

'It's all so gloomy these days I sometimes think I prefer not to hear it,' Laura said, her eyes glancing involuntarily at a Pictorial News magazine on the table in front of her.

Andy Draper entered with the dining trolley and set about serving lunch while they continued the conversation. The meal had been put on board by the best restaurant in Khartoum and was surprisingly good.

'Nile perch,' Van Smit commented with appreciation, 'your caterers certainly know their job Captain, I shouldn't have expected such excellence from Khartoum. Will you have some wine?' He proffered a bottle.

'Not when I'm flying I'm afraid,' Desmond thanked him. The fish certainly was good. 'We may not always run to time,' he said, 'but we do our best to give you a good meal.' Van Smit he remembered, had been in the Sudan before.

The Doctor filled Laura Hartman's glass and Mr. Johnson's before attending to his own. 'And tell us Captain,' he went on, 'what kind of weather can we expect to find in Cairo? It is starting to get hotter there at this time is it not?'

'At this particular moment they are experiencing a hamsin

sandstorm.' Desmond told him, 'but with luck,' he added, seeing their faces fall 'the weather will have cleared soon. These storms don't usually last long, though they can be nasty while they do. By this evening it should be fine again.'

'Just right for your ball,' Van Smit remarked, 'and Mrs. Hartman tells me that she will be there as well. Mr. and Mrs. Curtis are taking her in their party. You will be able to show her over the Abdin Palace, Captain.'

Desmond and Laura looked at one another with some embarrassment at this, and Desmond found himself once again resenting the South African's sardonic sense of humour. Laura gave a nervous smile and began to ask about the forthcoming race.

'We drive out to Fayum on the morning after the ball,' he explained, 'it's a small oasis in the desert about sixty miles from Cairo, but the course takes a big sweep out into the desert, so that the total distance back to the finish in the City is about one hundred and eighty miles. Part of the way is tarmac and the rest is dirt track across the sand. It should be a good race.'

'Will you have much competition, I mean, will there be many other cars in the race?' Laura took a sip of her wine, 'I won't know until I get to Cairo,' Desmond said.

The flying boat gave a slight lurch in the air as he spoke and instinctively he glanced at the window opposite him. Outside the horizon was clear, there was still so sign of the storm they were heading towards. They must be passing through a patch of local turbulence. As if in response to his thoughts he felt *Caterina* lift as upon the flight deck Ken Frazer increased altitude to take them up into smooth air again.

There was still plenty of time before they could expect any marked deterioration in the weather but all the same he was anxious to return to the controls. Turning back to his food he began to hurry through his meal, while the three passengers talked among themselves.

Jacquetta d'Este stumbled over the desert lost in a suffocating world of sand and dust. Around her she could see no more than a few yards through the storm. Blindly she kept

147

going, head bowed to escape the stinging blast of particles. All sense of direction had vanished long ago, now all she could concentrate on was keeping the wind at her back and holding on to the bridle of her horse, forcing the unfortunate beast to stagger along in her footsteps.

Somewhere not a great distance from her, she knew lay the fields of the irrigated land that fringed the desert, only a few miles away at most, yet in the choking clouds that surrounded her she no longer even knew in which direction to turn. It was very possible that she was actually heading away from safety and out into the empty wastes to the south.

Terrified as she was by the thought, Jacquetta found it hard to accept that in the space of only two hours conditions had changed to a point where they now threatened her life. When she had first climbed up and out of the dry wadi bed, she had found that it was hot and the sand was blowing uncomfortably hard, but not so as to alarm her. In fact she had ridden on at first, hoping to find shelter among a line of dunes and from there make her way back straight across the desert to Mina, rather than go to all the trouble of retracing her steps along the path she had taken.

Among the dunes themselves the wind had not been too bad, their huge masses affording some protection from the blowing dust. It was only when she got past these and out on to the flat plain beyond, that she first became aware of the severity of the storm which was about to hit her.

As far as her eyes could see, the whole of the horizon and sky behind her were blotted out by an immense dark wall of dust, towering thousands of feet into the air. Even as she looked she realized that this monstrous vision was travelling towards her at great speed, devouring the ground in front of it, sucking up the surface of the desert in great twisting spirals of dirt that billowed up out of sight into the sky.

Urging her horse into a gallop Jacquetta had made a futile attempt to outrun the storm, but the hamsin had rolled inexorably after her. With frightening speed the wind had built up and with it the fury of the driven sands. Almost before she knew it she was enveloped in a stifling cloud of dust that swallowed up the landscape about her, burning her face and eyes, and leaving her hardly able to breathe.

It became impossible to ride in such conditions, and slipping down from Balbo's back she began to lead him by the bridle, trying all the time to head in the direction in which she thought the city lay. The sandstorm had become so dense around her that even the sun was hidden and very soon she knew that she was hopelessly lost.

She tried to remember the features of the land she ought to be crossing. Although at first sight it had appeared to be quite flat she knew this was deceptive and that quite soon she should reach an area of hilly ground with outcrops of wind eroded rock. The land rose there also for a space before falling away again into another long level stretch beyond which lay Mina and the Pyramids.

The Pyramids; for all it mattered she might have been hundreds of miles deep in the Sahara instead of only a couple of hours ride from the tourist hotels and monuments of the Nile. Jacquetta had no illusions about her chances of survival should the hamsin continue. It was frighteningly easy to become lost in the desert even in fine weather and when no more than a mile or two from safety. Unused to the sands, people wandered off into the dunes, lost their bearings and turned in the wrong direction. The sun did the rest. Nineteen hours the experts always said, nineteen hours a man could last in the desert without water. If she was headed in the wrong direction now she would wander in circles all night, and by midday tomorrow she would be dead, her body shrivelling and buried in the sand drifts.

Already the heat was taking its toll of her. In Cairo the temperature in spring rarely climbed above seventy degrees, but out here in the heart of the hamsin, it must be at least thirty degrees above that. The effort of walking in the wind was draining her fast, Balbo too, she could tell, was tiring, several times during the past minutes he had tripped and stumbled. Very probably if she let him go now he would simply lie down and die.

Grimly she forced herself on. To stop, even for a moment

would be fatal. Like the frozen deserts of the poles, the Sahara would seize the first instant of weakness and turn it into surrender. The urge to give up, to stop and rest where one was must be resisted at all costs. There was still a chance, still some small hope of coming through alive; if she could only keep going till the storm blew over or she managed to reach the edge of the desert; and meanwhile it was possible that search parties would soon be starting out to find her.

Though the hamsin was a severe one, it was in fact travelling in a path which would cause its centre to pass some way to the south west of Cairo and only its trailing edge ever reached the city itself. Nevertheless, this alone was sufficient to bring hot stifling winds, and dry dust laden air into the streets and houses. Everywhere the inhabitants retreated inside if they could, fastening their shutters and windows. From long experience they knew that these periods of discomfort were brief, and that by the evening the city would be cool again, and the winds still.

Luca and Charlotte however had found that it was too hot to wander far in Prince Suleiman's palace gardens and had retired inside to join the other guests.

The interior was truly sumptuous. Tarboushed retainers in white robes opened magnificent doors of beaten copper to reveal rooms whose floors were inlaid with beautiful mosaics, from which slender columns of alabaster rose to painted ceilings with chandeliers of coloured crystal. They passed through a seemingly never ending succession of rooms whose walls were hung with fabulous paintings by every artist from the Italian old masters to Dali, and in each of which the furniture was more perfect than the last.

Brancusi sculpture, Giancometti figurines, ottoman costumes, jewellery, carved fountains, golden goblets, tapestries, polished weapons gleaming in the afternoon light, so many and so wonderful were the displays that it became hard to take them in. They crossed floors inlaid with ivory and stood beneath strange stalactite ceilings and saw themselves reflected in a hundred mirrors as they followed the silent feet of the palace servants.

The old Prince received them in a small salon decorated in the ottoman style, with hanging carpets, rugs scattered on an alabaster floor, and panels of muchrabia, the fine fretted wood-work of carved tracery studied with coloured glass, let into the windows. The Prince, an elderly, but still bright and alert figure, reclined amongst a heap of embroidered cushions on a divan at one end of the salon, listening to the talk of his guests who seated themselves similarly around him, watching them shrewdly, while all the time sucking at the pipe of an elaborate silver hookah.

This was the first time that Charlotte had come in contact with an Egyptian nobleman who still clung to the old oriental style of behaviour, rather than following the western fashions adopted by the Courts of King Farouk and his father, and Luca was gratified to see that she was pleased and not a little awed by her surroundings. The other guests, as was usually the case, were part of the smart clique of wealthy cosmopolitans with whom the exotic and unashamed opulence of the Prince's living, as well as his disregard for the conventions of society, were much in vogue.

Perhaps surprisingly, in view of the Prince's age, the palace was a meeting place for the radical and anti-British element in Egyptian political life, an element with which Luca was familiar. With popular pressure for the withdrawal of British troops increasing, and the rapidly rising power of the fascist regimes in Italy and Germany, there were those close to the King who were urging him to safeguard his throne by adopting closer relations with these new powers, especially with Italy whose army of one hundred thousand men on the border with Libya, constituted the most formidable force in North Africa.

Beneath the veneer of tranquillity and sophistication in the capital, a fierce struggle was taking place for the hearts and minds of the Egyptian people, between the pro- and anti-British parties, with the Court attempting to hold a middle course between the two. Already a number of leading politicians had been assassinated openly in the streets, while scores of others had been threatened. The stakes were colossal, despite the desperate poverty of the majority of the people, the country was prosperous, a small number of men and women staggeringly rich. In Cairo there were estimated to be more than five hundred millionaires alone. The King himself personally owned one seventh of the land in the country. Nowhere else in the world did such magnificent displays of wealth contrast with such misery, disease and starvation. The rewards of power in Egypt were very real.

More than this, Egypt was of the most vital strategic importance. With control of the Suez canal, the gateway to India and the east, as well as to the oil of Arabia, a nation could place a stranglehold on the British and French colonial empires, and even perhaps control Africa as well. Small wonder that the spies and agents of half a dozen governments swarmed through the city and that the King's secret police watched everyone. Corruption, treachery and savage torture raged unchecked behind the cultured façade.

Today the conversation was more guarded than usual, a swift glance about the room soon told why; in a corner opposite the Prince, in an elegantly cut grey suit lounged the plump, pampered figure of Yousouri Pasha light featured and soft haired, more like a woman in appearance than a man, the Albanian blood in his ancestry proclaimed by the pallor of his skin. Behind the indolent mask he presented to the world, Luca knew, was one of the King's most trusted advisers, and for that reason one of the most powerful, and most feared men in Egypt.

Presenting Charlotte first to the Prince, who bowed amiably and waved them to seats among the cushions. Luca found them places next to Yousouri. Half an hour or so of gentle conversation he planned would suffice before he would suggest to her a tour of the Palace. Behind the principal rooms there were secluded suites designed for just such a purpose as he had in mind.

'You are both leaving shortly I am told,' Yousouri greeted them as he proffered a bowl of sweetmeats to Charlotte. 'It will be a sad loss to our little community,' he added with elaborate courtesy.

'Your Excellency's presence is an unexpected pleasure,' Luca responded with equal politeness. 'We had not expected to see you before the ball tonight.' What twist and turn of local politics brought so sinister a figure here at this moment, he wondered.

'His Majesty sent me with greetings to His Highness,' Yousouri took a sugared pastry from the bowl and examined it idly. 'I am no more than a humble messenger who has remained out of curiosity to meet the guests.' He popped the pastry into his mouth, flicking his fingers to remove the sugar which had stuck to them. 'It is coincidental that I should meet you here though, Baron,' he continued when he had swallowed, 'for a little earlier your name was mentioned in my presence in an unusual context.'

He spoke casually, smiling at Charlotte as he spoke, but Luca was conscious of a hollow feeling in his stomach nevertheless. As a foreign diplomat he was theoretically beyond Yousouri's reach, but in these times one could never be sure, and there had been unpleasant rumours in the past of unexplained disappearances. An English officer had once told him that blinding the eyes with red hot wires was a common practice of Egyptian tortures, and his mouth went dry at the recollection.

He forced himself to speak naturally, 'I trust you heard nothing to my disadvantage.'

Yousouri transferred his smile from Charlotte to Luca. 'It was merely an expression of interest in your person. A man who was here had met another man, quite recently it seemed, who knew you and had asked after you. It is of passing interest, nothing more.' He leant back against the cushions, closing his eyes for a moment. Around them the mutter of quiet conversation continued, in the background a lute was being played with exquisite skill. Mentally Luca cursed the necessity for this elaborate indirect form of speech. Why could none of these Egyptians ever say what they mean? he thought angrily.

'I meet so many people,' he replied, 'it is not always possible to remember them.'

'It seems that the man of whom we speak was until recently in your country, which must, of course, be where he met you. He himself however is a native of Libya, although his family is related to that of the Prince here,' Yousouri indicated their host with a wave of his hand. 'His name is Sheikh Rashid al Senussi,' he said looking intently towards Luca.

'I have heard of the man you speak of, though to my certain knowledge we have never met.' Luca said shortly. 'His father was a noted rebel during my appointment in Libya and was dealt with severely.' He could not quite bring himself to admit that on his orders the old man had been put to death.

'Then it is clear that the man I spoke to must have been recently in Libya, for where else could he have met Sheikh Rashid? Certainly not, I am sure, here in Egypt.'

'Your Excellency would be better placed than I to know that,' Luca answered, and the Egyptian nodded.

'That is true, and in any case the day after tomorrow you yourself are leaving. Before that however I hear that you are to take part in a motor race,' he said, 'it is to be hoped that you will exercise great care, these events are dangerous and accidents can easily happen.'

'Thank you. I shall heed your advice, and now if you will excuse us,' Luca rose to his feet, 'I should like to show Mrs. Curtis some of the beauties of the palace.'

The Pasha made a regal gesture of dismissal. 'By all means, and if I may advise,' he said to Charlotte with a bland smile, 'the galleries on the first floor are particularly worth viewing, but I am sure the Baron knows that already.'

Luca led the way out of the salon and into the hall beyond. 'This is the most beautiful place I have ever seen,' Charlotte whispered slipping her arm through his, 'but who was that man you were talking to? He seemed very odd even for an Egyptian. Did you say he was a Pasha?'

Like a great many newly wealthy women, Charlotte Curtis believed that the possession of a title was indicative of personal merit, an attitude which Luca hoped would soon prove to be of use.

'Yousouri Pasha? He's just one of the King's advisers,' he told her with deliberate casualness. 'Quite a powerful figure in his way.'

'And what was all that about the Sheikh from Libya? I couldn't follow that.' The hall was lined with huge mirrors in ornate gilt frames and Charlotte was looking at her reflection as she spoke. At least, thought Luca, he could make some use of the Egyptian's remarks, although he still couldn't decide whether they had been intended as a warning or a threat. 'Sheikh Rashid al Senussi?' he shrugged, 'he is just someone who has sworn to kill me, that is all.'

As he had expected this produced an immediate effect. 'Darling, how terrible,' Charlotte squeezed his arm excitedly, 'why ever should he want to do such a thing?' This was playing straight into Luca's hands, giving what he hoped was a regretful sigh he said, 'Rashid's father was a criminal,' he almost said murderer, which would have made a stronger impression but changed his mind at the last second, there had, after all, been no evidence that the old man had ever murdered anyone in his life, and he had only been a criminal in that he had refused to acknowledge the authority of his conquerors. 'His father was a criminal whom I was obliged to sentence to death several years ago. I did not wish to do it,' he went on, striving to convey the impression of a misjudged ruler, 'but he was guilty and it was my duty to enforce the law.'

Charlotte gazed up into his eyes with exaggerated wonder. 'But aren't you frightened at all? I know I should be.' Looking down into her upturned face, with its dark eyes full of admiration, and red lips parted Luca felt his pulse quicken, they had reached the door leading to the first of the private suites, opening it he drew her through into the seclusion of the room beyond.

'One is more sorry for the young man than afraid for oneself,' he said, anxious to maintain a role which she evidently found attractive. 'If he goes about saying he is going to kill people like me, he will be arrested and sent to prison.' Charlotte was still looking up at him, her eyes shining. Greedily taking her in his arms Luca kissed her hard on the lips.

In the salon they had just left, Yousouri Pasha heaved his corpulent body to its feet and made his way across the room to the Prince's side. The other guests withdrew a little at his approach to allow the two men a degree of privacy, though Yousouri knew that for all their apparent disinterest they would strain to hear every word.

'And so?' the Prince said quietly when he had sat down on the divan beside him, 'you delivered your warning?'

'I delivered the warning. Whether d'Este will heed it or not is another matter. For the moment I think he is too busy to concern himself with so mundane a business as a threat to his life.'

The Prince took a long suck at his hookah and passed the coiled pipe across to his guest. 'He would he wise to take precautions, Rashid is no simple desert youth, he has been educated abroad, as well as spending time in my own household.'

'I explained the close links with your Highness,' Yousouri put the pipe to his mouth and drew deeply on the smoke, feeling the narcotic fumes pass into his lungs. 'Yet I doubt if he realizes the danger.'

'Then you will take precautions?' the old man queried. Yousouri nodded assent.

'Yes, such as I can. Rashid must certainly be thwarted, at least while he is on Egyptian soil. As to what happens afterwards ...' He left the sentence uncompleted.

'You are right,' the Prince agreed, 'I have no love for this Italian. Whatever these fools may think,' he gave a contemptuous glance at the rest of the room. 'I wish to see the British out of our country for ever, but I do not wish simply to replace them with Mussolini's governors.'

'Nevertheless we do not wish to anger them needlessly, and the British themselves would give us no peace if d'Este were killed.'

'Then you had best see he is not,' the Prince answered. 'Find Rashid if you can and lock him up till d'Este has left the country, but take care you treat him well. I will not have a kinsman of mine ill-used as though he were a common criminal, and Rashid is fighting for a cause many of us believe in.'

'His Majesty's instructions are similar to your own, High-ness. It shall be as you ask.'

Jacquetta had lost count of the number of times she had stumbled and fallen during the past half hour. For what seemed like an eternity she had been clawing her way up the slope of a hill, the wind tearing and buffeting at her. There had been no such hill anywhere within sight when the dust clouds had closed around her that she could remember; but there could be no doubt that the ground was rising steeply.

She slipped and fell heavily once more, dragging at Balbo's reins, causing him to toss his head and squeal. At least if she could keep him with her she might stand a better chance of making her way back when the storm eased. With a tremendous effort she heaved herself to her feet once more. The heat and long exertion had given her an appalling thirst, her eyes, mouth and nostrils were caked with sand, so that she was forced to drag herself along half blind, while the dirt caught chokingly in her throat. She was very nearly exhausted; according to her watch she had been lost for two hours and she doubted if she could last much longer. The realization that she must have wandered far off her intended course had all but drained her remaining willpower.

Her repeated falls had torn her hands to shreds on the sharp rocks that littered the surface of the desert and the spines and thorns of the tough scrub plants. She was thankful that she was wearing leather riding boots and breeches. Without them she would have given up long ago.

Abruptly the terrain in front of her flattened out and Jacquetta pushed forward with relief. She had no idea of how high she had climbed or of how steep the descent might be, she was only thankful to be released from the desperate uphill struggle. Moving onwards she encountered a shallow slope, and she began to follow it, fighting the wind which was now coming in sudden savage gusts rather than with the steady pressure she had encountered earlier, and which if she were caught unawares was sufficiently strong to knock her from her feet.

When she had progressed a few hundred yards she found that her descent had brought some shelter from the sand which was now blowing from directly behind the hill. Wiping the dirt from her eyes she saw that in front of her lay a wide valley. Her heart sank as she gazed down at it. The far side was very largely obscured by long fingers of sand blowing off the ground beneath but from what she could make out there was more of a gorge than a valley in that direction, with high, nearly sheer walls of rock, occasionally split by sharp vertical fissures. There would certainly be no escape there.

To her left the valley flattened out into what appeared to be an endless void of dunes and sand drifts, across which the dust was driving. There was no obstacle in that direction but the very emptiness of the vast wilderness that opened up there frightened her. Even looking at it made her feel lost and hopeless in the immense and desolate land.

The only alternative was to follow the valley back up to its head. To her right the floor narrowed and the sides grew steeper. At least there would be more shelter there and shade and there was even a faint chance that she might find some water. Her thirst was almost unbearable. Scrambling down the hillside she began to make her way up the valley and into the gorge.

Once on level ground she found that it was possible to ride again. Provided the wind dropped by morning and she was able to hold out through the night, then there was a fair chance that she might be spotted by a search party or by an aeroplane.

As she came near to the cliffs at the start of the gorge she realized that these were much higher than she had at first thought. Great crumbling cliffs, their sides split and pierced with cave-like openings loomed above her in the swirling dust, drawing gradually closer together as she ventured further and further inwards, till at length she was riding down a deep narrow canyon whose walls stretched far above her.

Although there was less wind here than in the open there was still a great deal of dust and sand being blown in from above, or being wafted up the pass in both directions. Stones and pieces of rock crashed down from the cliff faces from time to time alarming her and startling the horse. Her spirits which had risen when first she had remounted and entered the gorge fell again. She felt dead with exhaustion and lack of water and even the effort of guiding Balbo was almost more than she could manage.

Then suddenly, without any warning, the ravine opened out, the walls fell back and she came out into a wide open space. Some great geological upheaval of the past had opened up a vast natural amphitheatre in the desert floor. There was much more dust and sand in the air here but Jacquetta could distinguish several smaller defiles opening out into the one in which she was riding. The cliff faces of these were all heavily pierced with caves, and in the gloom of the storm these had a sinister and unwelcoming appearance.

She had halted instinctively at the sight, now she rode on slowly, keeping to the centre of the pass, hoping to see a way out on the far side. The ground was littered with piles of old rubbish, and the crumbled remains of what had once indeed been dwellings of some sort she guessed.

Jacquetta was still taking this in and wondering what the history of this place had been and what kind of people had lived in so lonely a spot when, out of the corner of her eye, she saw a movement near the dark mouth of one of the nearby caves. Instantly her heart leapt in fear and instinctively she spurred the horse onward. As she did so a wild, tattered figure, clad in grey rags sprang out at her through the swirling dust from behind a heap of rocks and made a grab at the reins.

She let out a scream at the sudden attack, and, alarmed, Balbo shied away from the creature and made a break for one of the nearby ravines. At once, from every cave and hole more figures appeared, leaping down from the rocks and swarming towards them from all sides like rats. More hands reached out clutching for her. The horse reared and snorted in fright at their darting movements and for one terrible second Jacquetta thought she was about to fall. Hideous faces leered at her through the dust, their features distorted repulsively it seemed to her bleared vision. Maimed, fingerless hands waved in front of her eyes, agile cripples hopped across the ground, waving their stumps from beneath the rags that bound them. Shrill cries resounded dimly in her ears above the noise of the wind.

Jerking Balbo round she made a vain attempt to get back down the gorge the way she had come, but the creatures were too many for her. Blocking the path they drove her back with flailing arms. Jacquetta struggled desperately to control the horse and force him to charge through the mob, but his strength and rising fear were too great for her and in panic he swerved aside and raced blindly round, along the valley wall among the refuse tips and broken hovels.

An opening in the cliff face looked briefly ahead amid the storm and seizing her only chance she steered Balbo for it, urging him on past the figures at the entrance. The way was only a little less wide than the path she had originally come down and she prayed frantically that it would prove to be a way out. She could hear the sounds of the chase close behind as the inhabitants of the caves hurried in pursuit.

Balbo gave a sudden start of alarm as they rounded a bend in the canyon. In the dust they had all but run into a horse and rider coming down the pass towards them. At the sight of the tall, hooded and cloaked figure Jacquetta's nerve broke. There was no room to turn and in any case the path behind her was already cut off. Screaming with terror and lashing out with her free arm she tried to force a way between the rider and the sheer wall of the canyon.

The newcomer was too quick for her, however, as she drew level with him he reached across and grasped her reins. Jacquetta cried out and beat furiously at his hand with her fists, but the effort was futile and the iron grip did not relax. Helplessly she collapsed sobbing on to her horse's neck.

Charlotte Curtis responded to Luca's embrace with a readiness that surprised and gratified him. Pressing her open mouth against him she kissed long and passionately, her body moving urgently into his own. Excitement flared within him as his hands caressed her back and fondled the soft curves of her bottom, he could feel her thighs close against him and the pressure of her breasts on his chest.

His tongue probed between her lips and over her teeth. Luca was aware of his own body stiffening with desire as her passion aroused him. His heart beating swiftly with anticipation, he drew her over to a wide, silk-spread couch, in a window alcove shielded by half closed, embroidered drapes.

Drawing the curtain behind them he lay beside her on the couch in the dim light from the stained glass. Eagerly their hands explored each other's bodies, touching and stroking, their hunger removing all barriers between them. Unfastening the zip of her dress he let his hands roam over the warm naked back, feeling the play of the muscles beneath the velvet soft skin.

At that very moment, to his fury and surprise, there came a loud tap at the door of the room. 'Baron d'Este,' a voice called, 'Baron d'Este please come quickly. A messenger from the embassy has arrived. You are needed urgently.'

'All right, all right, I am coming,' Luca swore viciously in Italian under his breath. What a moment to choose. Charlotte was already sitting up on the couch, hastily doing up her dress and tidying herself.

'Come quickly Baron!' the voice called again.

'Yes, yes I will, damn you!' Luca shouted back with exasperation. He stood up and helped Charlotte to her feet. 'I am sorry,' he apologized, 'why do these things always happen at exactly the wrong moment? There will be other times I promise you.'

Putting her face up to his she gave him a hard quick kiss on the mouth, 'Lots of times,' she grinned as she checked her make up with a vanity mirror. 'Although,' she gave a sly chuckle, 'it would have been fun in a real palace. You had better go and leave me here. It will be quicker for you and look better for me. The Prince will send me home in a car.'

Her self-possession was truly incredible Luca thought as he hurried from the room after one final embrace. Most women in similar circumstances would have been angry or upset, and very possibly both. Yet Charlotte was able to sit down and repair her make-up as though nothing out of the ordinary had happened. Such coolness and imperturbability on the surface, such fire and passion underneath. What more could a man ask for in a mistress?

An anxious major-domo in the Prince's livery was waiting outside. 'The messenger is in the main entrance hall, Baron,' he said in English with a deferential bow. 'It appears that your wife the Baroness has become lost on her ride. There are fears for her safety in the hamsin.'

Once again Luca swore under his breath as he followed the major-domo to the hall. It was ironic that his wife should succeed in thwarting his plans at the very moment of success. He found himself vengefully hoping that Jacquetta would not be found. His marriage had long since ceased to bring him pleasure and nowadays he was conscious only of its inconveniences. Far from accepting the state of affairs which had grown up, Jacquetta was daily becoming more critical of his behaviour and more openly hostile to her rivals.

After listening briefly to the courier's message, which in fact was no more than the information that Jacquetta had failed to return after her ride and that there was now a severe dust storm blowing in the vicinity, he left immediately by car for the Embassy.

On board *Caterina* the first signs of their approach to the area of the hamsin came as a long dark line on the horizon like a smudge of dirt, which appeared shortly before four o'clock when they were still one hundred and eighty miles short of Cairo. As they drew nearer the men on the flight deck saw it grow until it extended right across their line of sight. The massive clouds of the storm became more distinct and the slowly sinking sun tinged their crests with ominous fire. They had experienced similar storms before and were only too well aware of the battering the aircraft would receive if they were forced to descend through it.

'What's the latest word from the Met. people?' Desmond asked when they had been watching it for a while. 'Tell them I want the exact speed and course of the storm Ralph, as well as the strength and direction of the winds.'

'Looks to me as though it's heading almost due east,' Frazer muttered as Kendricks began tapping out morse on his key, 'in which case it may be missing Cairo altogether and we shall be O.K.'

'We shall know that when we get the weather reports,' Desmond replied with asperity, 'there's no sense in arguing about it beforehand.' Even the simplest discussion led to bickering between them nowadays it seemed. Frazer had an uncanny knack of putting his back up.

'Storm moving west-south-west at approximately thirty-five knots on a front estimated to be 100 miles wide,' Ralph Kendricks informed him. 'Wind speeds at the front averaging fifty knots plus with gusts up to seventy.' He bent over the charts on the table beside him. 'Assuming it holds this course for the next hour,' he said, 'we should be able to fly over it and land at Cairo without any particular difficulty. The Met. Office estimate the limit of air turbulence at 12,000 feet.'

Frazer's face flushed with triumph as his forecast was vindicated. 'Very well then,' Desmond said, 'you had better go and ask Sandy to warn the passengers that we shall be climbing to high altitude shortly. He'll want to make sure they all have blankets and sweets to suck.' The co-pilot's face darkened with annoyance.

'You could put it out over the intercom loudspeakers.'

'And I could send you off to tell Sandy quietly, which is how I'm going to do it,' Desmond answered. For a second the First Officer appeared about to make a retort but the look in Desmond's eye made him bite it back.

When he had left the deck Ralph Kendricks let out a whistle of amazement, 'I don't know how you take it from that man. He's got the biggest chip on his shoulder of anyone I've ever met and he unloads it all on the rest of us.'

'I know Ralph,' Desmond said, 'but he's the only co-pilot I've got and we'll have to live with him until we can find another.'

'And in the meantime he's down below kicking hell out of poor Sandy just because he's been put down up here.'

Sure enough, as Ralph had predicted, Frazer sat down on his return and began at once to complain about the purser's behaviour. 'He's useless that boy,' he said spitefully, 'the least upset in the normal routine and he goes into a flap. He had no idea of what to do down there.'

'Maybe it's just you who puts him into a flap Ken. He seems fine to the rest of us,' Ralph answered with an edge to his voice.

'That's because I'm not soft on him like you are,' Frazer snapped

'Break it up you two,' Desmond told them. 'We're all tired after this last couple of days, let's not take it out on each other because of that. Anyway shouldn't that news bulletin be on soon Ralph? It's almost four o'clock.'

'Coming up in a couple of minutes Skipper,' Kendricks replied, 'I'm tuned in already.'

'What about the storm?' Desmond had his eyes on the dark clouds ahead, 'will that cause interference?'

'Uh, uh, it's non-electrical. Here we go.' He flicked down the switches of the intercom and they heard the familiar hiss as the loudspeaker circuits warmed up. There was a crackle of static and then the voice of the announcer came over the air. *This is the Overseas Service of the BBC. Here is the British Empire and Foreign News. Drastic measures have been taken in Czechoslovakia to suppress Slovak separatism. The autonomous Slovak government has been dismissed and Czech troops are mobilizing.*

Siegret Wienzman and her father were doing what they had dreamed of night and day for the past six months and yet never really believed would be possible. Together, arm in arm they were strolling round the Piazza San Marco in Venice in the evening sun. It was chilly, the sky was overcast and puddles from rain earlier in the afternoon still remained. Most of the tourists had returned to their hotels and with them had departed the seed sellers, the pavement artists, the postcard sellers and other itinerant traders. To the two refugees however the scene could not have been more beautiful.

After the nightmare of the previous day, the tense journey through Austria and the harrowing experience at the frontier, Siegret had refused to believe at first that it might at last be over. To be able to walk about freely in the streets, without listening for the sounds of pursuing feet or hearing the jibes and insults of the Nazi bullies was an incredible joy. She felt intoxicated with her new freedom, and her release from fear. Grasping her father's hand she danced round the square at his side, bubbling over like a child with happiness and laughter.

For the Professor there could be no surer proof that he had acted rightly than the change which their escape had brought about in his daughter. In the space of the few hours in which they had been on Italian soil a fair measure of her former high spirits had returned and the colour was returning to her bruised face.

'Remember we are still not completely safe yet,' he cautioned her, 'we still have to reach America.'

'Yes I know, but Papa, you have already spoken to Dr. Farenzi and he said he was sure it was going to be all right about the visa.' This was true, immediately on their arrival the Professor had telephoned his old friend in Rome who had been delighted to hear of his escape and had assured him that he had already contacted the American embassy authorities and these had expressed their willingness to grant a visa. 'Of course there are formalities to go through, it will take a little time, perhaps two or three weeks, but you will both stay with me in my house.'

'All the same,' the Professor repeated his warning, 'we must still be on our guard. If the Nazis knew we were here they might persuade the Italians to send us back to Germany.'

'Oh they could not do that.' Siegret's face went pale again with fear. 'Oh say they could not do it Papa!' Her father felt instantly contrite at the effect of his words. 'There, there,' he squeezed her shoulders, 'we are too small fish for them to bother about, and even if they did they could never find us now.'

His daughter's tense body relaxed and the anxiety faded from her eyes. 'Don't ever talk about going back again Papa,' she said in a hushed voice, 'I couldn't bear it. It would be the end of us both.' They stared at one another for a moment and then with a laugh Siegret shed the seriousness that had fallen on her and they walked on. 'Papa,' she said when they had reached the other side and were preparing to return to their hotel. 'If we really are safe, can't we stay here a few days? There's so much to see and do, and if we go to America we may never have a chance again.'

'Stay here, in Venice you mean and not go to Rome?' her father asked.

'Only for two or three days. Just to give us time to look around before we go on. It would be like a holiday together. Oh do say we can Papa,' she begged.

The Professor smiled down at her indulgently. 'Two days will be enough? You're sure?' he said.

'Yes, yes, oh Papa thank you! I'm so happy,' and flinging her arms about him she burst into tears. Two days will make no difference, her father thought, as he held her close and patted her hair, he would telephone Farenzi in Rome and warn him of the delay. It would be good for the child to rest and tomorrow was Sunday anyway. They were safe enough here in Venice, there was no need to worry.

The horseman made no move to touch Jacquetta, but neither did he relax his hold upon her reins. Instead, he shouted in Arabic past her at the pursuing mob. Gusts of wind were whistling and shrieking over the canyon walls, but his voice sounded clearly above the noise. A chorus of cries and shouts rose in reply, but the man shook his head decisively and repeated his words, letting go of the reins of his own horse as he did so and unslinging the rifle which he carried on his shoulder.

'You are safe now, they will not come near you.' At the sound of the words spoken in English she looked up with a start. The man bending over her horse wore a loose white cloak stained with dust from the hamsin and a bedouin headdress bound with black braided tassels. To protect himself against the sand he had covered his face with a fold of black cloth but he had pulled this aside to speak. It was a young handsome face with finely drawn aquiline features, but with such a look of pride and fierceness that she felt afraid to speak.

'You are safe,' he repeated. 'Who are you and what are you doing out here in this wind?' his voice was authoritative and with surprisingly little accent. The cloth of his face mask was shot through with gold thread she noticed.

'I was riding and lost my way,' she answered in the same language when she found her voice. To allow him to believe she was a British subject might be more sensible. 'I am staying at the Embassy in Cairo,' she added in the hope of impressing on him that she possessed friends who would be searching for her.

There was another man behind the rider who now pressed forward saying something urgently, glancing at Jacquetta as he spoke. He was a smaller, less attractive person, with quick, shifty eyes. Dismissing him with a few words, the rider turned back to her.

'Come with me,' he said, 'I am going back to the City and I will show you the way. If you remain out here you will certainly die.' Releasing her reins he handed her a leather water flask and Jacquetta drank greedily. 'Ride between us,' he ordered, 'I will keep these creatures away.'

Together they retraced her steps back into the main gorge. The mob gave way before them as they emerged into the circle of cliffs. There were more than two hundred of them, she guessed, of all ages, crowded into the caves and passages. Now that she dared look at them properly she realized that every one of them was deformed or crippled in some way.

'Who are they?' she asked her rescuer. Even with his protection they still inspired her with fear and loathing. The servant evidently felt the same way for he rode close behind them. 'Who are they and why do they live out here?' she repeated.

The man looked at her with scorn. 'Can you not guess?' he said. 'They are lepers and they live here because they have been driven out from the city and from their villages. There is nowhere else for them to go except for these holes, so they live here like rats.'

Jacquetta shuddered. As a child she had always been horrified at tales of the disease. Met with in reality it was even worse. 'You will keep them away won't you?' she cried for the lepers were showing signs of coming closer. 'You won't let them touch me? Can't you frighten them off with your gun?'

Her companion did not answer; putting a hand inside his robes he produced a small leather pouch of money, and taking out a handful of coins he flung them in a wide arc behind the crowd. At once they scattered scrabbling in the sand and scuffling with one another over their finds. Pausing only to toss another handful, the rider led them on, across the centre of the clearing and into a cleft in the far wall.

'That is easier than using a gun,' he said as they went 'and they can give money to their families to buy food for them.' Jacquetta tried to thank him but he brushed her words aside. 'We must ride quickly,' he said, 'you had best put this over your face, it will keep out the sand,' and he handed her his black head-cloth. 'It is two hours or more to the city by the route I must travel. There are men hunting for me on the desert road.'

Jacquetta accepted the cloth gratefully. It was wonderfully fine and light, woven with gold thread and perfumed with some scent she did not recognize. At his words, however, some of her alarm returned.

'Who are you?' she asked, 'and why are people hunting you? Are you a bandit?'

'I am called Rashid al Senussi,' the man answered, 'I am not a bandit but men hunt me all the same.'

At the mention of his name Jacquetta gave an audible whimper of fear, which, thanks to the wind and the sound deadening clothes they were wearing, went unnoticed by Rashid and the Egyptian. For the whole of the past year, since she and Luca had left Libya they had known of the young Sheikh's threat to revenge the deaths of his father and sister. For a while, in Rome they had lived under armed guard, in case Rashid, with his European schooling and military training should be capable of seeking them out and killing them even in Italy.

Luca, she had to admit, had never shown the slightest fear in this respect. So great was his contempt for the Arabs, whom he had never fought except when the odds were overwhelmingly on his side, that he refused to take the assassination risk seriously. On the contrary, she suspected he rather enjoyed describing himself as a marked man as though this brought him additional glamour in the eyes of the world.

Even the news that Rashid's men had systematically hunted down and, in a succession of attacks ranging from stealthy murder to full scale ambush, killed a high percentage of the soldiers and airmen who had taken part in the raid on his father's village, had not worried him unduly. When the security police had suggested that he might be unwise to spend a month holidaying in Cairo before taking up his new appointment in Washington, he had dismissed their advice without a thought.

Jacquetta's feelings towards this then unknown desert prince who so desperately wanted her dead had been mixed from the start. Although Luca himself had been reticent about the reasons which had sparked off Rashid's desire for revenge, she had learned the details from other members of the Governor's staff, and what she was told had horrified her. When she had faced Luca with the truth he had brushed her accusations aside, refusing either to confirm or deny the story, and claiming that he had acted for reasons of state which a woman could not be expected to grasp.

Confronted with him in person she was at a loss to know what to do. The reality was very different from what she had ever imagined. She was utterly dependent upon Rashid's help to get back to the city alive, yet once there, if he were to learn who she was, she would be in greater danger than she was already.

Wild plans flashed through her head, of making a break for freedom when they reached the edge of the desert or of trying to seize the rifle which he carried negligently on one shoulder. There was a faint hope that they might run into the men who were looking for him, whom she presumed were the Egyptian or British authorities, but the man ahead of her appeared too competent and assured to be captured easily.

For what felt like an eternity they rode in silence, heads bowed against the wind. How Rashid could find a way in such trackless sands, where the dust blotted out all features in the landscape, and had shuffled the dunes over the face of the desert, she did not know. Occasionally he paused to confer with the Egyptian and once he made a sudden, unexpected detour back on their tracks after he had climbed alone to the crest of a low rise and scanned the ground ahead. Jacquetta guessed that this unexplained manoeuvre was connected with the need to avoid interception.

She was at first surprised and finally a little annoyed to discover how little interest her rescuers displayed in her. Apart from turning his head a few times at the beginning of their journey to check on her riding ability, Rashid scarcely looked at her again. Instead his eyes searched restlessly through the desert, the hawk-like leanness of his face emphasized by the emptiness of the land.

She felt ashamed to recall how feeble and weak she must have seemed, her fear and loathing of the lepers must have made her ridiculous in his eyes, justifying the contempt which he displayed for her presence. Jacquetta had never before met a true Arab from the deep sands, her previous acquaintance had been only with the degenerated tribes of the town and she was unprepared for the concentrated self-discipline, the sheer physical and mental toughness which marked them out from other men. She felt overpowered in Rashid's utterly self-reliant, ruthlessly masculine world.

Towards five o'clock she realized that the wind, which had been dropping steadily for the past hour, had virtually ceased. They were walking more easily now, the horses hooves thudding monotonously on the packed sand, on what appeared to be a path of some sort. The sun was sinking in the sky and the coolness was a marked contrast to the suffocating heat earlier in the afternoon. Shadows crept out from the sides of the dunes, carving the scenery into strange geometric shapes, sculptured by the wind.

The first signs of their approach to the city outskirts came when she realized she could distinguish the squat outline of the pyramids like regimental toys against the horizon. For a long time these grew no closer then, quite suddenly they rode out from behind a low ridge and saw in front of them, about a mile distant, the beginnings of the cultivated land.

Rashid reined in his horse beside her. 'Do you see that building ahead?' he pointed to where a few sparse and stunted trees marked an attempt to create an olive grove on the very edge of the desert, among the scrub and thorn bushes. Shading her eyes against the dying rays of the sun Jacquetta saw a square white blockhouse standing beside a road. 'That is a police guard post on the road between Fayum and Cairo,' he said, 'the men there will take you back into the city.'

Jacquetta's heart stood still at the thought of what was going to happen when her identity was revealed to him, but Rashid's next words removed her fears. 'It is not possible for me to go with you for the final part of the way,' he said, 'since the men at the post probably have orders to arrest me, but you cannot lose yourself now.'

Her relief was so great that she was profuse in her gratitude. Rashid cut her outpourings short. 'I have been honoured to have been able to help you,' he said dryly. 'Farewell and take care you do not ride alone in the desert again. I may not always be on hand to rescue you.'

Frazer and Kendricks were discussing the implications of the news from Czechoslovakia with Sandy Everett who had returned to the flight deck and was sitting on the radio spares box behind the co-pilot's seat. All three were drinking coffee brought by Draper at Frazer's request.

Desmond listened to their conversation with half an ear. With *Caterina* only a few miles from the edge of the storm zone, the ground beneath them had become hazed with dust, at times obscuring completely the line of the river and the green strip of cultivation that clung to it. He was flying on manual, concentrating on the feel of the controls, alert for the first signs of air turbulence that would mean the time had come to climb to 12,000 feet or more.

'What do you think Skipper, will Hitler go in?' Sandy appealed to him.

'It'll be war if he does,' Frazer put in before Desmond could reply, he was making a visual check of the instrument panel as he spoke. 'Starboard fuel tank is nearly dry. Shall I trim the other tanks?' Desmond nodded his assent.

'I don't see Chamberlain taking the country to war over Czechoslovakia,' Kendricks replied to Frazer's remark, 'he didn't at Munich and anyway there's nothing we could do to help them.'

'We're preparing for war some day soon,' Frazer continued, 'you heard what it said on the news. "Expansion of the Fleet, Air raid precautions, plans to evacuate children from London, two hundred and fifty thousand pounds a day being spent on aircraft for the R.A.F. National service". What's all that for if it's not for war with Germany? Don't you agree Skipper?'

'You're probably right, I don't know,' Desmond said non-committally, though as he spoke he knew this was untrue. He thought of what he had heard and seen during the past six months, of the letter from the Air Ministry. However unwillingly, Britain was moving towards war. Even so, he could not bring himself to admit it.

He was still thinking in this vein when the aircraft trembled violently and immediately afterwards dropped sickeningly through a hundred feet or more as they struck an air pocket. Loose items of equipment rattled across the cabin floor and Sandy cursed as hot coffee was spilled down his uniform trousers.

'You had better go back to the passengers,' Desmond called to him over his shoulder as he pulled the stick back, 'I'm going to take us up above this but it may be rough for a while.'

Opening up the throttle to counter the fall in speed as the plane's nose lifted, he set her into a steady climb of 300 feet per minute. At that rate they ought to be above the worst of the turbulence in a quarter of an hour. All sight of the desert below had vanished, covered by a thick barrier of black clouds shot with streaks of lighter brown.

'Must be one hell of a storm down there,' Ralph shouted above the engine noise, watching the cloud base receding beneath them as they climbed away. 'They say a wind like that can strip the paint clean off a car in a couple of hours.'

'Or choke an engine within a few minutes,' Desmond suggested watching the needle swing round on the altimeter, twelve thousand feet. He swallowed to clear his ears, this would do. Easing the control yoke forward gently he brought *Caterina* back to level flight once more and throttled back to normal speed.

Mentally he calculated the distance and times involved. The weather report had said the storm front was one hundred miles deep, if they were flying at 165 miles per hour, they would be clear to descend in forty minutes, by which time they would be only another fifteen minutes flying time from Cairo. For all Frazer's casual dismissal of the hamsin as weather one could fly above, that left them little room for manoeuvre. At low altitude the winds could play some nasty tricks.

Now that this leg of the journey was nearly over he realized for the first time how tired he was. There had been little sleep the previous night, the shock of Ian Thorne's death and its subsequent complications, Kendricks' nerves and Ken Frazer's foul temper, to say nothing of the behaviour of passengers like Stewart Curtis, had all taken their toll of him. He half wished that he did not have to attend the ball in the evening after their arrival, then remembering that Laura Hartman would be there, he changed his mind.

Fortunately *Caterina* encountered little more turbulence as she skimmed over the storm front. Once or twice she was buffeted by small airpockets but each time Desmond caught her smartly and lifted her back to resume her steady course. Almost to the minute of his prediction they reached the limit of the clouds and began a slow descent to bring them down to 3000 feet preparatory to making a final approach when Cairo came in sight. Beneath them the Nile, wider than at any previous point in its length as it neared the end of its four thousand mile journey, flowed between green and fertile farms, dotted with groves of trees and sliced by tiny irrigation channels, a sharp contrast to the desert that began when the irrigated land left off, and ran on as far as the eye could see.

'E.T.A. Cairo twelve minutes,' Frazer reported, 'we should be able to see it by now.' The light glinting off the city's countless minarets and domes was visible miles away. Today the dust between them was obscuring it.

'Coming down to 2000 feet,' Desmond set the aircraft on the path that would bring them down on the river thirty-five miles away. The altimeter wound slowly back as the plane descended through the heated air.

'Speed down to 140 knots' he ordered and Frazer eased the throttle levers back.

'Revolutions 2000,' he reported.

A descending aeroplane with a nose down attitude would automatically pick up speed as she came down and unless corrected, this would bring them in at too fast a speed for a safe touchdown.

'Cairo acknowledged our E.T.A.' Kendricks reported from the radio desk, 'winds 20 knots from the south west. Visibility clear.'

'Then why can't we see them?' Frazer asked, then, 'Christ! What's that?' he exclaimed with alarm. Ahead of *Caterina*, at the same altitude but a little to starboard a small dense cloud had appeared out of nowhere in the otherwise clear air. With incredible speed it mushroomed outwards, sucking up dust from the surface of the desert far below and spewing it out into the sky.

Before they could do anything they were upon it and at once the aircraft was enveloped in an opaque, yellow cloud of swirling sand. 'Hold tight!' Desmond shouted to the others, as he did so they felt the giant hand of the pressure bulge lift the flying-boat dizzily upwards as though it were no more than a chip of wood. 'Give me full revs!' he called urgently, struggling to hold *Caterina* against the fierce cross-currents. Frazer slammed the throttle levers open again, holding them hard against the stops to ensure that every ounce of power came through.

Engines screaming, Desmond banked the aircraft steeply to port, seeking the safety of calm air once more. In a dust bubble of this intensity it would be only a matter of minutes before choked valves and air intakes left them with multiple power failure. Within seconds however a monstrous air pocket opened beneath them and the plane fell four hundred feet with stomach-wrenching speed.

A red light glowed on the control instrument panel in front of him. 'No. 3 engine overheating,' Frazer called out, 'shall I reduce power?'

'No!' Desmond shouted, 'Keep it on full.' Their best hope lay in breaking free from the grip of the pressure spiral as soon as possible, before they suffered serious damage. Through the rudder bars and control yoke he could feel that the flying-boat was taking a terrific hammering. Again he made a tight banking turn to try and bring them clear. Another air pocket struck them and then a third and this time the fall was truly frightening. Before their horrified eyes the needle of the altimeter, wound back to less than 1000 feet.

Another warning light lit up showing a second engine overheating to danger point. Props clawing at the air, *Caterina* fought to shake herself clear of the tenacious squalls. Again they fell as the pressure vacuum snatched the support from around the plane.

The nose dipped violently, threatening to throw them into a spin. Hauling back on the controls Desmond's eye was on the altimeter. 700 feet, 650, 600, there were only seconds left in which to pull the flying boat out of the dive before she smashed herself and them to pieces on the ground. 550 feet, 500, the jerking needle was slowing, 480, *Caterina* was responding to his weight on the stick; 450 feet, the needle was hovering, the nose was coming up, she was levelling off. He eased the stick back thankfully.

So thick was the dust cloud that it was only by watching the instruments, the artificial horizon and the altimeter that it was possible to tell if the plane was flying on a straight course. Outside the windows the sky was the colour of pea soup. Both remaining engine temperature warning lights came on simultaneously. The next two or three minutes could decide whether *Caterina* was to be brought down by engine failure due to dust choking or fire. Unless that was, Desmond thought grimly, another air pocket like the last one dashed them to the desert floor. He was climbing steeply, but with less than 500 feet beneath them there was little chance of pulling *Caterina* out of a spin, and he dared not reduce his engine speed and lessen the fire risk until he had gained some height.

Beside him Frazer was white and set with strain, his eyes glued to the altimeter dial and the engine temperature gauges. Every few seconds he made a quick glance out of the windows to check the engines for smoke, although in the murk they were flying through, it was impossible to see beyond the inboard motors.

Then, as abruptly as it had begun, they were out of the cloud and into clear sky again. As if a curtain had been suddenly pulled away, the men on the flight desk found themselves blinking in the sunlight again.

'Jesus!' Frazer wiped a hand over his face, 'what on earth was that?'

He had relaxed his grip on the throttles and was easing them back.

'Don't shut them off more than a quarter way Ken,' Desmond said, 'all four engines are probably so chocked with muck after flying in that dust they're probably just waiting for an excuse to die on us. I'd rather risk a fire at the moment.'

'Understood,' Frazer adjusted the settings on the levers accordingly. 'There's Cairo coming up,' he said pointing ahead. Surprisingly, all their wild gyrations had thrown them only a few degrees off course. 'What caused that squall back there?' he repeated.

Desmond shook his head. 'I don't know,' he said, 'it's some kind of rare pressure phenomenon met with over desert. For no reason at all the sky just seems to bubble like that, carrying the sand up to immense heights. You find them in the Sudan, and in Jordan in the desert beyond Lake Tiberius, but I've never known one as strong as that before.'

'Ralph,' he called out, 'get down below will you, and see if Sandy needs any help, the passengers must be feeling pretty shaken up after that little experience.' There was no reply from the radio desk and he strained round to look over his shoulder. Ralph Kendricks was sitting ashen faced, staring rigidly out of the side porthole next to him. His mouth was working convulsively, his eyes distended.

'Ralph!' Desmond called sharply again, and with a huge effort the Radio Operator took hold of himself, and turned to face him. 'Did you hear what I said?' Desmond ordered, 'Go down and help Sandy.'

'Aye, aye Skipper,' Ralph whispered hoarsely; he rose wearily to his feet, 'I'm sorry, I felt a bit sick back there for a second.'

'Did you see his face?' Frazer demanded unnecessarily as soon as he was gone. 'He's cracked up, his nerve's gone.'

'Maybe,' Desmond answered coldly, 'we shall see.'

'But you can't let him go on like that,' Frazer persisted, 'he isn't fit to fly.'

'I'll decide that, not you,' Desmond replied witheringly. 'Keep your mind on your own job and leave me to deal with the crew.' Biting his lip with rage Frazer turned away, the knuckles of his hands clenched white on the bars of the control yoke.

A short while later Ralph was back to report, the traces of the spasm gone. 'Luckily Sandy and Draper had them all strapped in and the breakables stowed away on the off chance that we might hit trouble. I think they were more surprised than anything else. The Johnsons' child was crying and she was upset. There were a few glasses smashed in the galley. Mr. Curtis' papers on his table were scattered all over his cabin and he's cross about that.'

'Somehow I can live with that,' Desmond said. 'O.K. Thanks Ralph. You had better call Cairo air traffic control and tell them we are coming in.'

Part Two

CAIRO

V

IMPERIAL AIRWAYS. LONDON TO BRANCH OFFICE LA GUARDIA MARINE TERMINAL NEW YORK 20.30 hrs. G.M.T. IMPERIAL 109 DELAYED 24 HOURS AT CAIRO FOR SERVICE AND FAULT CHECK. WILL CUT OUT ATHENS STOP-OVER TO MAKE UP TIME. TRANS-ATLANTIC FLIGHT WILL DEPART AS SCHEDULED AND E.T.A. NEW YORK REMAINS UNCHANGED AT 1600 hrs. EASTERN STANDARD TIME SATURDAY MARCH 18. ENDS

IT was the custom of Imperial Airways whenever possible to book their passengers into Shepherd's Hotel. This was by no means always easy. During high season the hotel was frequently so overcrowded that numerous people had to be turned away, and yet so great was the attraction of this, the most famous hotel in the East, that guests were often prepared to pay simply to be allowed to spend the night on the couches in the lounges.

Luxury hotel, fashionable rendezvous, gentleman's club; with its bars and its restaurants, its ballrooms, its night-clubs and celebrated terrace, Shepherd's was the unquestioned centre of Cairo's social world. Indeed to many people it was Cairo, the first place they wanted to see, the only place they wanted to stay.

'You wouldn't believe the trouble we had getting you in this time,' Keith Payne, the company's local manager, told Desmond when the latter came ashore to report. 'It's this blasted wedding, the world and his wife have come to Cairo this week, they've actually got two kings staying at Shepherd's, two! Can you imagine that? There's so much bowing and scraping and "yes your Majesty" and "no your Majesty" that no ordinary person can get a look in.'

'What about the bullion?' Desmond asked, 'what happens to that while we're here?' The manager frowned. 'We were going to leave it on board under guard, but when you said the plane would need servicing we decided that was too risky so it's being transferred to the army barracks under cover of dark,' he said.

'We heard about your trouble down at Shambe,' he said, 'I'm sorry that had to happen.'

'Have you any idea what the company wants to do next about it?' Desmond asked. Though he could be a bit of a pedantic old woman at times, Keith Payne possessed a shrewd insight into the minds of Imperial's management back in Britain, he also kept his ears open and could be relied upon for advance warning of action likely to affect an individual personally.

'There's to be an inquiry held by the airline when you reach Southampton,' he told Desmond, 'I've been instructed to let you know that officially. Unofficially . . .' he paused, and looked serious.

'Go on, tell me the worst,' Desmond said.

'Unofficially then,' Payne went on, 'some of the top men see this as a chance to crucify you. They want to pin you with the blame and get rid of you. On the other hand they need you badly because they are short of pilots to fly the transatlantic run and they can't afford to let the Americans go ahead on their own without them. So the general feeling is that you may come out of it relatively intact. For the present that is, and so long as your passengers and crew are prepared to support you.'

The formalities at the pier head complete, he left *Caterina* to be unloaded and then towed off to the service wharf. The rest of the crew had already left to go their separate ways and now Ralph Kendricks took his leave shamefacedly after his performance during the storm.

'We had better have a talk together,' Desmond said to him, 'and see if we can get things sorted out. Why don't you drop by my room before I go off to this party tonight?'

'O.K.' Ralph agreed unhappily. 'I'll come by at about seven,' and left without another word.

In the taxi on his way up to the centre of Cairo Desmond thought over what he had learnt from Payne. From the sound of it the inquiry in England on Thorne's death could be the breaking point of his career. Desmond was under no illusions about the lengths to which his enemies among the Imperial management would be prepared to go to get rid of him. They would never have a chance like this again and they would make the most of it.

His job threatened, perhaps his flying career, as a result of one foolish act by an idiot of a boy trying to show off, and none of it need have happened, he thought savagely, if only Frazer had bothered to do his work properly. If he somehow managed to come out of the inquiry still in command of a plane, that young man was going to go, he resolved.

The familiar sights and sounds of this, his favourite city, drained away some of the anger and tension which had built up inside him. The night was falling fast, hectic neon signs pulsated over the squares and the bridges were glowing with lines of pale amber light. The time was after half past six and the city's night life was beginning. In an hour's time he would have to set off for the palace. At least, Desmond reflected as he leant back against the cushions of the taxi's seat, he could put aside all the worries and decisions for the next forty-eight hours and enjoy himself in Cairo.

Rintlen's interview with Superintendent Hans Meyer of the St. Veit police district had gone well. In fact, he thought to himself, as he sat over a glass of schnapps at the town's sole hotel, it had not gone at all. The big policeman had been apologetic for the unfortunate error which had resulted in the Wienzman father and daughter being granted permits to cross the frontier, but had been careful to point out at the same time that his own part in the business had been a small one, and entirely covered by the orders of his superiors in the various ministries.

No-one, Meyer had assured him, could be more anxious than

he was to secure the arrest and conviction of the enemies of the Reich. Had he known that Wienzman was needed for questioning he would have had not the smallest hesitation in detaining him. As it was . . ., Meyer had shrugged, it was not his fault that Rintlen's call had come too late to enable the train to be interrupted. Of course, it would have helped if they had known which route the fleeing couple were intent on using, thus avoiding the delay which had ensued when the more westerly passes had been contacted first. But this had been a legitimate assumption based on the knowledge that the majority of escapers crossed as near to the Swiss frontier as possible.

Rintlen had not visited the Austrian mountain provinces before; his previous experiences had been confined to the major towns of Germany, with a brief spell in Vienna immediately after the Anschluss, and he was finding the sturdy independence of the people a shock after the easily cowered Berliners. Meyer, he had no doubt, was concealing something, whether the police chief had actively assisted the Wienzmans to get away or was simply covering up his own inefficiency was impossible to say, but so long as he stuck to his facts and put the blame on the officials in the government ministries, he could not be touched.

He swallowed another mouthful of the schnapps and signalled the hovering waiter to refill the empty glass. The worst feature of the affair was that so far he had nothing worthwhile to report to Heydrich, and the Chief of the SD was not a man who took failure lightly. Besides Rintlen had an instinct that this case was not one in which any failure or half measures would be possible. If the stakes were really as high as he suspected, Wienzman had to be tracked down or he, Paul Rintlen might suffer in his place.

Lighting a cigarette he tried to decide what to do next. The long flight up in the plane and the interview with Meyer had left him tired and the cold air had sapped his strength. Probably he ought to go on into Italy and search for Wienzman there. He took out a map of the border area and northern Italian cities and spread it out on the table.

The railway line which the Professor and his daughter had

184

taken crossed over the border at Tarvisio hard by the Yugoslavian border and then wound through the Venetian countryside as far as Treviso. Here the two tracks divided; one line ran eastwards to Trieste, another west to Verona and Milan, from both of which there were connections down to Rome, and a third continued south for twenty miles or so till it came to Venice.

Venice. The more Rintlen gazed at the map the more certain he was that Venice must be his starting point. Not only was it a convenient day's journey from the border, making it an ideal place for the escapers to rest after their recent ordeals, it was a seaport with excellent connections by rail and road to other parts of the country. It was highly likely, he thought, as he continued to stare at the map, that the Wienzmans would remain in the city until they could board a ship to take them on to another country. Either that or they would make for Rome where the same would apply. Rintlen was inclined to dismiss the possibility of their taking the westerly route towards the safety of Switzerland. If that had been their intention all along, he reasoned, then they would indeed have attempted to cross over there straight from Austria.

Having decided where to begin his hunt there were still other problems to be faced. The first and most important of these was the difficulty of finding and identifying Wienzman. The only photographs available to him were either of the passport type or else scaled up extractions from group portraits and none were of good enough quality to be of any real use. There was a strong chance that the two Jews would have registered in a hotel under an assumed name, or even taken rooms in a private house as paying guests to avoid detection.

What was really needed was a full scale police hunt using all the resources of street identity checks, hotel and boarding house searches and checks at every port, railway station and highway exit. Heydrich however had specifically forbidden calling upon the Italian authorities for help. At the very least however he would need to have a better picture of the Professor or his daughter.

An idea struck him as he considered the problem. Folding up

the map he replaced it in his briefcase and drained the remainder of his schnapps. 'Here you,' he growled at the waiter. 'Take for the drinks out of this.' Tossing a single one mark coin down on the table behind him he strode out into the snow. The money he knew, was insufficient to pay his bill but no innkeeper would dare to bring a complaint against an officer of the SD over so small a matter.

At the police headquarters he found Meyer in his office. The police chief welcomed him cordially back and insisted on Rintlen seating himself so as to catch the warmth of the fire he had burning. 'How can I be of assistance Standartenfuhrer?' he asked. 'My staff and I await your orders.'

Keeping his temper with difficulty, Rintlen answered, 'the youth Gerdler who led the attack on the Wienzman girl. You say you have him under arrest.'

'Yes indeed,' Meyer responded, 'under the new laws governing racial purity, relations between Aryans and non-Aryans are strictly forbidden, but then I expect you know that Standartenfuhrer,' he said with a trace of irony. 'I have Gerdler here in the cells.'

'Good, bring him out. I want to talk to him.'

'To Gerdler?' Meyer looked surprised. 'I doubt if he will be able to help you. He was certainly no friend of the Wienzmans.'

'Nevertheless, I want to speak to him, and quickly.' Rintlen snapped, 'have him brought to me at once.'

Heinz Gerdler, on first sight, proved to be an unprepossessing young man, strongly built with heavy loutish features. There was however, Rintlen noticed, a gleam of sly cunning in his coarse features.

'Very well, you may leave us,' he dismissed Meyer when the latter returned with his prisoner. His deliberately casual tone towards the police chief made a visible impression on Gerdler who stood in the centre of the room watching the newcomer with a mixture of apprehension and admiration.

'Do you know what authority I represent?' Rintlen asked him. The youth ran his eye swiftly over the grey and silver uniform taking in the unit badges and the flashes of rank. 'Yes,

Standartenfuhrer,' he replied nervously, 'Sicherhietsdienst.' He pronounced the name dry-lipped. Rintlen nodded his approval. 'Yes, the SD. That is correct, and do you know why I am here?' Gerdler shook his head violently. 'I am here to find out what has become of a man called David Wienzman and his daughter. You know of them at least I take it.'

'Yes, Standartenfuhrer,' Gerdler's voice was hardly more than a whisper.

'Very well. Now it seems that Wienzman left the country in great haste this morning. This may have been because he discovered that he was wanted by the authorities in Berlin, or,' he paused to give weight to his words, 'or it may have been because a gang of half-wits tried to rape his daughter.' He let the last part of the sentence ring out harshly and the youth wilted in the face of his anger.

'I swear, Standartenfuhrer,' he stumbled, 'we were only playing with her a little. We didn't know, nobody knew, she was wanted. It was just a bit of fun,' he ended lamely.

'Possibly,' Rintlen said dryly, 'the question is, are you prepared to make up for the trouble you have caused us? Good,' he cut short Gerdler's expostulations. 'Would you be able to recognize Wienzman and his daughter, even if they were attempting to disguise themselves by wearing different clothes, or by cutting their hair for instance?'

'Certainly, Standartenfuhrer,' the boy agreed. 'The girl more easily than the old man,' and he flushed.

'Excellent.' Gerdler was exactly what he needed. Having experienced the humiliation of having his quarry snatched from him, he would be tireless in his efforts to find her again. 'You will return home therefore and meet me here again at nine p.m., bringing with you ordinary civilian clothes to last you a week, do you understand?'

'Yes, Standartenfuhrer, I mean no, Standartenfuhrer. What is it you want me to do?' the boy asked desperately.

'I want you to come with me to Italy to search for the couple your actions frightened away. You are being offered a chance to perform a special service to the Reich. Do you refuse?' Rintlen demanded.

'No sir, of course not. At nine o'clock I shall be here.' Drawing himself up hastily Gerdler saluted, 'Heil Hitler.'

'Heil Hitler,' Rintlen acknowledged with a half-wave of the arm. Now at least he reflected as Gerdler hurried out, he had a means of identifying the Wienzmans. It only remained to find them.

Laura Hartman and the Kings arrived at Shepherd's while the light of evening still lingered. The sun was slipping down below the hills to the east in a brief but spectacular glow of red, pink and gold, while the temperature, which had been uncomfortably hot for much of the afternoon, due to the hamsin out in the desert, had eased and a slight breeze from the north had cleared the dust and lifted the stale atmosphere which clung to the streets.

With the change, the bars and street cafés had begun to fill, and the heavy traffic of the day, the lorries and carts and jostling, noisy crowds had given way in the smart districts of Gezirah and the Garden city on the Nile's eastern bank, to an ever-increasing flow of expensive limousines, taxis, and the innumerable horse-drawn gharries, conveying wealthy Cairenes off to their evening's enjoyments. While from the minarets of the mosques, the high wailing cries of the muezzins echoed out above the streets, calling the faithful to prayer.

Imperious doormen drove off the herds of pedlars and beggars who surged round the taxi as it drew to a halt at the red carpeted steps. Efficient clerks entered their names in the register and detailed bell-boys to convey their luggage. 'What a place,' whispered Mr. King to Laura as they went up in the lift, 'did you see the flags on the roof as we came in? Royal standards! They say there are two monarchs staying here.'

'Bulgaria and Albania,' his wife snorted derisively, 'hardly among the world's great kingdoms and one of them has lost his throne anyway. The staff needn't think they can ignore the rest of us because we have not got titles to our names. I don't hold with them in any case,' and she glared severely at the nearest bell-boy.

'Now Sarah,' her husband said mildly, 'I'm sure we shall be very well taken care of.'

'Maybe,' Mrs. King responded, 'but they might as well understand right away that I shan't stand for being treated second best.' The lift came to a halt and the doors were pulled back. 'I guess we separate here,' she said to Laura, 'you be sure to come and show us your gown, mind, before you go; it's not often we see a girl going to a royal ball.'

'I thought you didn't approve of monarchs,' Harold King reproved her with a wink at Laura.

'I don't approve of them, but that doesn't mean the girl shouldn't enjoy herself,' his wife replied with conviction. Promising to do as she was asked, Laura left them to find her own room.

On the previous stay Laura had been given a bedroom and bathroom across the passage from the Curtis' suite on the third floor, but on this occasion, in order to make room for the royal contingents, the whole of that floor had been cleared and the Curtis' were now staying on the second floor and Laura's rooms opened off the private hall of their suite. Charlotte Curtis had not been at the pier to greet her husband when the plane landed, but Laura heard her voice coming from the sitting-room, raised in argument.

'Every time I turn my back you're off playing around with a new man,' Curtis was shouting angrily, 'I'm away for two weeks and you're so busy with d'Este you haven't even time to come and meet me when I return.'

'I was having tea at Prince Suleiman's if you must know,' Charlotte snapped back, 'and your flight was delayed so how did I know when it would reach here?'

'You could have found out easily enough,' Curtis said furiously, 'and I know damn well that Prince Suleiman is a crony of d'Este's. You were there with him, and the whole of Cairo knows the kind of tea parties they have at that palace. First it's a German ski instructor, now it's this slimey wop. Well I've had enough do you hear?'

Quietly Laura slipped into her own room and shut the door behind her. The cause of their quarrel was a familiar one to her. Surprisingly, to those who did not know him well, Stewart Curtis loved his wife and was passionately jealous of her frequent affairs.

Laura had never quite been able to decide what to make of Charlotte Curtis. She invariably treated Laura with kindness, and at times with generosity, whereas her husband was thoughtless and selfish to all his employees alike. It had been Charlotte who had asked her to the ball with them and even provided a dress for her to wear. Yet she was also hard, to the point of ruthlessness, and a greedy unscrupulous woman who frequently admitted that she had only married Stewart for his money, and who made a point of refusing to accompany him on business trips so as to be able to enjoy her affairs unhindered. In a way Laura supposed Stewart Curtis and his wife were well matched.

Leaving his room to go downstairs for a drink in the Long Bar before the ball, to his surprise Desmond came face to face with Laura Hartman coming out of a suite on the same corridor. So great was the transformation in her appearance that for an instant he almost failed to recognize her.

In place of the grey suit she had been wearing during the day she had on an evening dress of heavy cream coloured silk embroidered with flowers, with puffed sleeves, a low neck and a long close-fitting waist. Her arms were bare and she wore matching gloves and a small necklace of pearls.

'Why! Captain O'Neill,' her face lit up with pleasure, 'how smart you look,' Desmond gave a deprecating glance at his evening tails. 'Beside you I am very ordinary. You look magnificent,' he said with sincerity, 'that is a most beautiful dress.' Laura laughed self-consciously. 'Yes isn't it just,' she admitted, 'the Curtises gave it to me. It's by Mainbocher, do you know,' she said with a trace of awe in her voice, 'it cost more than my whole salary for a year? I feel a bit strange wearing it.'

'Well it was worth every penny,' Desmond assured her. He held out an arm to her. 'I'll take you down the stairs. You can't possibly go in the lift in such a dress.'

The Curtises were sitting in the main lounge, a large dimly

lit room, with a vaulted ceiling, thick Persian carpets and alcoves arranged with couches and low tables. Several parties of guests in evening dress were waiting there, talking in low voices among themselves. Desmond led Laura across to the Curtises' table and was introduced to Charlotte.

Beautiful, proud, wilful, cunning and sensual were the reactions that sprang to Desmond's mind. She sat, very upright in a white satin dress trimmed with black velvet, the thick folds of the skirt spread out on the seat of the couch beside her. Unlike most of the other women in the room that evening, her black hair instead of being pinned up had been brushed back off her face to hang in Pharonic style on either side. The whole effect was striking and dramatic and she knew it. She was the centre of a small circle of admirers who were hanging on her words.

'So you are the aviator who will fly me across the Atlantic,' she said, when Desmond had been introduced to the rest of the party and Laura complimented on her appearance by everyone present. She appraised him thoughtfully, 'tell me, is it safe?'

'No,' Desmond returned her gaze steadily, 'it is not safe.' There were disconcerted murmurs from the others, but Mrs. Curtis remained unmoved. 'Not safe?' her eyes widened in feigned astonishment. 'How is that Captain. Surely you would not take us on a journey that was not safe.'

'Professional pessimism,' a man sitting next to her commented in accented English. 'People always want to make us believe their jobs are dangerous.' He gave Desmond a contemptuous glance and began screwing a cigarette into an enamelled silver holder. 'The crossing is safe or the airline would not be making it.'

'Hush Luca,' she tapped him on the knee with a crimson nailed hand. 'I am sure Captain O'Neill has excellent reasons for saying what he does. Is that not so Captain?'

'No flight over two and a half thousand miles of ocean where the worst weather conditions in the world exist can be called safe.' Desmond said flatly. 'We try to keep the risks to the minimum, but they remain nevertheless.'

'You make it sound exciting, don't you agree Stewart?' Charlotte questioned her husband.

'I think Captain O'Neill's superiors,' Stewart Curtis emphasized the word, 'would be displeased to hear him talking in this manner, and I confess I personally am surprised,' he continued frowning heavily, 'to find him going to a ball so soon after a tragedy in which he was involved.'

'Then you feel that any regret on your part is unnecessary?' Desmond suggested and Curtis's frown deepened to a scowl, 'I fail to see . . .' he began but his wife cut him off.

'I see you are no mean opponent Captain,' she laughed, 'certainly not a man to be trifled with. Baron d'Este here will be worried. You and he are competing against one another in the race tomorrow.'

'I'm afraid I haven't had time to examine the lists,' Desmond said politely. D'Este, he remembered was one of those joining the flight at Cairo according to Sandy Everett. 'What car will you be entering?'

'A Delahaye,' Luca inhaled his cigarette. 'The same car as the one which won the Le Mans Twenty-Four Hour Race last year. She has the fastest acceleration of any car on the road today,' he told the party proudly. 'From rest to sixty miles per hour in eleven seconds.'

'The Captain is driving a Hispano-Suiza,' Laura Hartman entered the conversation for the first time since their arrival. 'An eight litre sports racer. He'll give you a run for your money Baron.'

'Ah yes, the Hispano, an excellent car,' Luca answered complacently, 'but no longer modern of course.'

'Its top speed is equal to a Delahaye's and it's a race proven design,' Laura responded warmly, 'I'd back a Hispano-Suiza any day.'

'Do you see the interest your presence arouses?' Charlotte said to Desmond with a smile. 'You must join us for the evening. I do so want to hear more of the dangers of flying the Atlantic with you. Shall we wait for your wife?' she turned to Luca d'Este who was still disputing the merits of the two cars. 'Baroness d'Este was caught in the hamsin while out riding and almost lost in the desert,' she confided to the others.

'No thank you. She is still resting at the Embassy and may

192

join us later. Fortunately some Arabs found her and brought her back to the city before she suffered any harm,' Luca said amid general expressions of concern. 'She was foolish to go riding alone without her groom.'

'Then let us be setting off for the Palace,' Charlotte announced, 'Captain O'Neill shall escort me in the car because I want to talk to him about flying. Stewart, give Mrs. Hartman your arm.'

Desmond obeyed reluctantly, feeling that he was being asked to desert Laura. To judge by the expression on Stewart Curtis' face he too, disapproved of his wife's behaviour. Whatever happened, it seemed he was fated to arouse the financier's hostility.

What worried him most though, as they left the hall, was the fact that Ralph Kendricks had failed to meet him in his room as they had agreed down at the pier.

In the hotel's famous long bar, the haunt of generations of travellers and explorers Ralph Kendricks was getting drunk. He had left the flying-boat with the firm intention of drinking himself into oblivion by the end of the evening in an attempt to silence the memories which wracked him the only way he knew.

Staring glassily into the bottom of his whisky on a stool at one end of the bar, he told himself for the twentieth time since coming in that he was finished. His utter collapse during the aircraft's battle with the squall had finally removed any hope he might have had of maintaining the fiction that he was going to be fit to fly the Atlantic again. The violent lurches of the air pockets, the shaking of the aeroplane caught in the fierce eddies of the wind currents, the sightless windows of the cockpit had brought back to him more acutely than ever before, the memory of his seven year old horror.

Ralph shuddered. Whisky spilled from his glass with the action, spread over the surface of the bar. Taking another long swig, he watched the trickle reach the edge and drip to the floor. The bar was filling up with people having their customary pre-dinner drink. The barmen hastening to and fro with cocktail shakers. No one cast more than a casual glance at the morose figure sitting by himself.

He felt badly about letting Desmond down, failing to turn up at his room as he had promised, but when the moment had come he had found he couldn't nerve himself to face him. Though there would be no real escape, he thought, sooner or later Desmond would come looking for him. Quite apart from his responsibilities as flight Captain he was relying on Ralph to act as engineer and navigator in the race tomorrow.

The bar was becoming too noisy for comfort as more and more people filtered in on their way to the restaurant. It was time to move on. Shepherd's was no place to get oneself drunk in alone, and beside Ken Frazer might show up at any minute and at all costs he wanted to avoid running into him.

Weaving his way through the throng he went out past the great pillared hallway and on to the terrace steps. The night was warm and unclouded and scented with the smell of bougainvillaea and the oleanders from the gardens opposite. A tout approached him offering his services but Ralph brushed him aside. Three or four streets away he remembered, there was a quiet bar where a man could drink in peace and forget for the space of a few hours, that his nerve was broken.

Ken Frazer was not, in fact, contemplating coming down to the bar, though he had ordered the room service waiter to bring him a pink gin. He was not, like Kendricks, seeking to avoid the company of his fellow crew members, but first he had important business to attend to.

Weighing on his mind was the thought that he might be held in part responsible for the emergency landing at Shambe and thus by extension for Ian Thorne's death. An unemotional man by nature, he had had no difficulty in absolving himelf of any possible moral blame, but there was still the nagging doubt that the committee of inquiry might think otherwise.

The solution, as he saw it, was to make sure that Desmond took the whole blame for the incident on his shoulders, and was thoroughly discredited. Not only would this relieve Frazer of any criticism, but it would also open the way to have Desmond transferred, perhaps demoted and possibly even dismissed. In which case, Frazer considered, he himself would stand a strong chance of being given command of *Caterina*.

The essential thing was to see that the board and senior management of the airline were made aware of Desmond's general failings, as a Captain, as well as his personal and sole responsibility for the tragedy at Shambe. If Desmond could be made to appear in their eyes as incompetent and irresponsible, then the findings of the inquiry would be a foregone conclusion.

To this end Frazer was composing a letter to his mother in London, to be sent by tomorrow's mailplane. In it he presented her with a catalogue of his Captain's faults as he saw them, and his errors of judgement during the flight up the Nile, and urged her to do her best to bring them to the attention of Jack Priestly.

'I am utterly convinced,' he wrote, 'that Captain O'Neill means to make me the scapegoat of this whole dreadful affair and duck his responsibility. More than that, his behaviour throughout the trip has been disgraceful. In particular, as well as being rude to several of the passengers and causing unnecessary delays by demanding extra servicing to the aircraft so as to give himself time to take part in motor races here in Cairo, he is also allowing a crew member, our radio officer, to continue his duties even though the man's nerve has gone completely and he is drinking heavily. You can imagine the danger into which this puts us all, both passengers and crew, and I only hope that this state of affairs is brought before the management prior to our setting out across the Atlantic.'

Altogether, he decided as he sealed the letter and took it up by hand to the purser of tomorrow's aircraft, with a request to have it delivered by special messenger on arrival in London, he had provided his mother with ample ammunition to bring Desmond O'Neill's career to a halt for ever.

Given the limited forward vision permitted from the cockpit

of the Supermarine, manoeuvring close enough inshore to enable him to reach the platform of the boathouse took Jarrett longer than he had thought, and darkness had fallen by the time he had the plane safely berthed within the enormous interior. He used ropes to tow her in for the last part of the way, being very careful not to scrape the wing tips against the side. With the doors shut and the overhead lighting on there was ample room to work whenever he wanted, undeterred by conditions outside or the risk of being observed.

He began bringing his tools and other equipment down from the house and stowing them in one of the rooms in the back of the boathouse, listing the tasks that lay before him in his mind as he did so. The engine had not been running as smoothly as he would have liked on the way up; one of the problems with such a race-bred machine was that she needed very careful tuning before each flight to extract the maximum performance. That would be a half-day's work, but it was a job which could be left till last.

Far more important was the radio. The telephone transmitter receiver had to be installed somehow in the cramped cockpit so he would be able to operate it during flight, and that was going to mean cutting away part of the instrument panel, and possibly repositioning some of the gauges as well; a couple of days work at least, even if there were no snags.

Finally, from underneath a pile of rubbish in the cellar he pulled a long narrow wooden box, grunting with the effort as he lifted it. Inside the boathouse he laid it on a bench top beneath the lights and set to work to prise open the lid. The wood had been tightly fastened down with nails hammered home every few inches and it took him much levering with the point of a chisel before it came clear with a wrench. Inside a number of cloth-wrapped bundles lay packed in shavings, held in place by battens fastened to the sides, impatiently Jarret levered these aside and lifted out the contents.

A moment later he was gazing rapturously at the oiled gleaming metal lengths of two air-cooled, electrically fired .50 inch Colt machine guns, complete with ammunition trays, mountings, remote firing control gear and optical sights suit-able for use in a single seat fighter aircraft. The Schneider racer was about to be given some teeth.

The festivities at the Abdin Palace were at their height when Dr. Van Smit, using a locksmith's key prepared on his arrival in Cairo, opened the door of the Curtis' suite without difficulty, paused momentarily to check for sound within, and entering, shot the bolt firmly home behind him.

The suite was laid out in the form of a small hallway, off which opened two bedrooms and a bathroom used by Laura Hartman and Charlotte Curtis' maid, and opposite doors lead-ing to the suite's sitting-room and master bedroom. These last two were large, specious rooms with balconies luxuriously, if ornately, furnished in the style of the Third Empire. The sit-ting-room especially would have graced one of the city's finer residences, occupying as it did a corner of the hotel over-looking the gardens at the rear.

It was to this room that Van Smit turned his attention first, setting to work to pick the lock of the massive desk situated immediately to the right of the door. He had little fear of being interrupted, for Laura, he knew, was at the ball with the others, and earlier in the evening he had seen the maid slipping out of a side entrance of Shepherd's in the company of a valet belonging to another guest.

The lock, like those on many seldom used pieces of fur-niture, proved stiff and troublesome, and to the Doctor's an-noyance yielded only a handful of unimportant papers; passports and travel documents and the like. Glancing at the bundle of airline tickets he noted that the entire group had been booked right through to New York, before replacing them carefully so as to make the contents of the drawer appear undisturbed.

Evidently Curtis kept his more valuable possessions else-where and Van Smit turned his attention to the rest of the room. An impressive walnut sideboard yielded only a selection of spirit bottles and glasses, a cupboard beneath a bookcase was empty and unlocked. Van Smit was about to move through into the bedroom, when the sound of the hall door being tried froze him where he stood.

The door rattled and shook as the person on the other side turned the key this way and that in an effort to get in, and the Doctor held his breath, thankful that he had remembered to fasten the bolt. A chambermaid would have possessed a master key, capable of overriding it, but wisely he had waited until the rooms had been prepared for the night. With luck he reckoned, whoever was outside would abandon the attempt after a while and go off to find help. Most probably it was Charlotte Curtis' maid returning unexpectedly early.

As he expected, the noise ceased and instantly the Doctor moved swiftly into the hall and put his ear to the door to catch the sound in the corridor outside. The thick carpeting, he knew, would absorb all footsteps, but voices nearby, or other doors being opened would be audible. Satisfied that all was clear as far as he could tell, he took a deep breath and striving to appear as normal as possible, unlocked the door and stepped out into the passage.

To his intense relief it was empty and at once he closed the door behind him and made off in the direction of the stairway. Rounding the corner he saw he had not been a moment too soon. Coming towards him along the corridor was the Curtis' maid in the company of the second floor waiter brandishing a pass key.

Inside the Byzantine Hall of the Abdin Palace, Laura Hartman and Desmond O'Neill stood side by side among more than a thousand other guests waiting for the entrance of King Farouk and his royal household. A while earlier they had both been reluctantly released by Charlotte Curtis when her husband had insisted on exercising his right to escort her up the marble steps of the main entrance, and now they talked quietly.

'I've never seen such a fantastic place in my life,' Laura whispered, 'it's as though Hollywood and Versailles had got together to throw a party.'

In the great hall gilded columns soared towards a many domed ceiling studded with intricate stained glass panels and hung with alabaster lamps. Along the walk were ranged chests of bronze and sandalwood, holding the jewelled costumes of the palace dancing girls. Sculptured marble fountains, surrounded by flowers, played among the richly dressed throng gathered to meet the King.

'They say the Royal apartments are even more unbelievable,' Desmond told her, 'staircases with crystal banisters, and floors inlaid with ivory and mother of pearl. And this is only one of Farouk's five palaces.'

Laura transferred her attention to the clothes of the people around her. 'It's like a fancy dress ball,' she repressed a laugh with difficulty, 'and the men are much worse than the ladies.' Desmond followed her gaze. Representing as it did a cross-section of the cream of Cairo's high society, the guest list encompassed more than twenty different nationalities, providing a glittering array of military and diplomatic uniforms, as well as Egyptian court dress.

Tarboushed pashas moved among Indian rajahs in jewelled turbans and arabian sheikhs in gold spun robes, the light sparkling on diamonds, pearls, and rubies. There must be fortunes in precious stones here tonight Desmond thought to himself. To Laura he said, 'I feel very ordinary in such a dazzling collection. You on the other hand are outshining all competition.'

Laura coloured with pleasure. It was certainly true that she had noticed a number of the women looking with envy at her dress. 'When do you think the King will enter?' she asked.

'I'm afraid that's anyone's guess,' Desmond said, 'Farouk is notoriously unpunctual and in any case he hates functions like this. Sometimes he keeps audiences waiting for hours.'

'You know him quite well don't you?' she asked, 'I mean as a friend not as a King.'

'Not really, I'm not sure anyone can know him like that. I've only taken him up flying a few times and gone shooting on the marshes at Dahshour with him when he's asked me. I think he likes to get away from all the grand people surrounding him occasionally.'

'You sound as though you feel sorry for him,' Laura said.

They were both speaking in undertones to avoid being overheard by those around them.

'A nineteen-year-old boy who has inherited one of the world's greatest fortunes along with one of its poorest lands? Everything in the country depends upon him, and yet he isn't really master of Egypt. He's surrounded by fawning, corrupt courtiers and condescending foreign diplomats who laugh at his attempts to impress them.' Desmond said, 'Yes I am sorry for Farouk.'

'A very convenient attitude for one whose nation rules Egypt virtually as a subject colony,' Luca d'Este's sneering voice behind them caught both Laura and Desmond by surprise. Looking round they saw that the Baron had approached through the crowded hall, in company with the Curtises. The others looked embarrassed by his remarks and Charlotte interrupted before Desmond could reply.

'My husband does not dance Captain,' she said smiling at him winningly, 'so I turn to you for an escort on the floor when the music starts.'

'I should be delighted Mrs. Curtis,' Desmond answered sincerely, 'though I am afraid I have already engaged the first dance of the evening with Mrs. Hartman.' Charlotte's smile remained unchanged at his reply, but a momentary glint of annoyance came into her eyes. 'That will be nice for you Laura,' she said patronizingly, 'I see I shall have to take second place,' she added sardonically.

'My dear Charlotte, I should be honoured . . .' d'Este pressed forward. Charlotte's expression hardened. 'Yes, yes of course Luca, of course,' she said shortly and turned to say something to her husband. Luca fixed Desmond with an angry stare and seemed about to speak, when from the far end of the room there came a sudden buzz of excitement and looking up they saw that the massive bronze doors were opening.

Down the steps there came first a pair of trumpeters who took up station on either side of the door. Behind these followed a double line of courtiers wearing red tarbooshes and dark blue, tight fighting jackets so stiff with gold frogging it was hard to see the cloth beneath. Walking with a grave dignified demeanour they filed out into the hall, pressing back the crowd of eager guests, creating a clear avenue into the centre of the gathering, over which an expectant silence had fallen.

At a signal from one of their number, the trumpeters raised their instruments and blew a series of ringing peals. As the echoes died away the figures of the King and Crown Prince appeared at the head of the steps. The ball was about to begin.

For all her husband's promises, Jacquetta d'Este had no intention of joining the celebrations at the Palace. Arriving back at the Italian Embassy Residence in the police car, she had given Luca and her hosts only the barest outline of her adventure, before pleading utter exhaustion and retiring to bed. In particular, she had not mentioned Rashid al Senussi in any way, except to say that she had been found and brought in by a party of wandering Arabs.

Lying back against the silk pillows in the dimly lit bedroom, she tried to analyse her motives for shielding Rashid in this manner. Gratitude certainly came into it, but gratitude alone was not enough to explain her reluctance to expose a youth, who, after all, had sworn to kill her.

Now that her ordeal in the hamsin was over she found it difficult to dismiss the lean figure and proud features of the young Sheikh from her mind. For the space of a few hours she had glimpsed a world very different from her own; a harsh, uncompromising world where the smallest weakness of body or spirit meant death, and yet where men still followed a code of honour and chivalry in the midst of a ruthless struggle for survival.

The shallowness and dishonesty of men like Luca with their endless pursuit of wealth and power, their trivial amusements, vulgar intrigues and pathetic displays of arrogance and temper, paled beside Rashid's fierce thirst for revenge, his savage pride in himself and his people, the single mindedness and self-discipline with which he pursued his aims.

Rashid she realized had attracted her more as a woman than any other man she had ever met, and by some strange twist of fate he had also rescued her from death and was intent on killing her husband.

King Farouk had spared no expense for the climax of his sister's wedding week. Four separate bands of musicians, specially imported from Europe and America, played in different rooms throughout the night. There were cabaret dancers, troupes of acrobats, jugglers, fire-eaters, magicians and singers. A sumptuous buffet at which every kind of exotic and expensive delicacy was served, was followed by an hour of brilliant fireworks, set off in the garden behind the palace. The bursting stars, silver rain and brightly coloured rockets exploded over the domes and minarets of Cairo in a display of extravagant beauty, while the guests watched awestruck from terraces lit by the flare of torches.

Desmond and Laura had spent the evening together, dancing in the ballroom and talking with the many friends which the Irishman had made during his frequent visits to the city. 'This is almost like home to you. Cairo I mean?' Laura said to him as they strolled out on to one of the balconies in the warm night air. 'I suppose you're right,' he agreed, 'Cairo's full of people like me, men who come and go all the time, without any fixed place to live.'

'Do you have a home to live anywhere?' Laura asked him and almost before he realized it, he found himself telling her about Pamela and the house in England and the bitterness of the divorce.

'She sounds as though she feels very angry and hurt,' Laura said, 'I guess I would if I hadn't been able to make my marriage work.'

'We were mad to try in the first place,' Desmond answered, 'you can't expect a marriage to succeed when the man is away flying half the year.'

'That's not true and you know it. All round the world there are thousands of people with jobs like yours, taking them away from home and they don't all get divorced,' she spoke with a firmness which surprised him. 'I'm sorry,' he apologized, 'I shouldn't be boring you with my problems.'

'You weren't boring me,' Laura answered, 'and anyway I owe you an apology. For being angry when you said you didn't believe in war,' she explained, 'Sandy Everett, the purser, told us about your brother being killed flying in the last one. It must have been terrible for you.'

'Yes a terrible tragedy and terrible waste.' For a moment his brother's laughing face flashed into his mind as he had seen him for the last time alive, waving jauntily from the car on his way back to the front. 'Mark was nine years older than me and I worshipped him. When he died it was the worst day of my life.'

He stopped abruptly, remembering too late that Laura herself had lost her husband little more than a year ago. Their eyes met and they smiled at each other in understanding. Instinctively and without noticing, they had stopped walking and moved closer together. In the flickering light of the torches Laura's upturned face was very beautiful. He felt an enormous desire to take her in his arms and kiss her.

'I should quite like to go back soon,' Laura confessed when, having stepped apart a little self-consciously they began wandering back into the ballroom. 'It's nearly one o'clock and I'm afraid I didn't sleep very well on the river last night.'

'I'll see you back to Shepherd's,' Desmond said, 'I want to make sure of a good night's rest myself before the race tomorrow.'

Reactions from the rest of the party when they announced their intention were mixed. Luca d'Este and Stewart Curtis appeared pleased, Charlotte however was less happy at the news. 'I simply must have another dance before you go,' she insisted, and brushing aside the protests of the Italian who had been promised the next turn, she swept Desmond off to the dance floor.

She was an excellent dancer, they moved around the ballroom as one, swiftly and lightly, and just as in their first dance of the evening, she held herself close against him, flirting with an intimacy which embarrassed him. In more normal circumstances Desmond might have been susceptible to her overtures, for Charlotte was an undeniably attractive woman and there was a certain honour in being singled out for her attention in this way. As it was however with Laura Hartman looking on, as well as the lady's husband and friends, Desmond felt only annoyance at her behaviour.

'You're very stiff and formal tonight,' she whispered, 'has something offended you?'

'Not at all,' Desmond said hastily, 'I'm afraid I really am just very tired. We had a long flight up and not a lot of sleep the night before.'

'I know, you poor man,' Charlotte's eyelids fluttered as she gazed at him in feigned sympathy, 'and tomorrow you are driving in the race. Poor Luca is furious,' she laughed, 'everyone is saying you will win, even the King himself told me.' Earlier in the evening Desmond had seen her dancing with Farouk in the main ballroom. Evidently the King's praise of him had raised his desirability in her eyes.

The music changed to a slower rhythm and Charlotte settled herself more firmly into his arms. 'Tell me, how are you getting on with little Laura Hartman?' she asked with too obvious casualness. 'Do you like her?'

'I like her very much. She is a very sweet girl,' Desmond answered shortly, angered at being asked to discuss Laura behind her back. Charlotte gave him a sudden intent glance, 'I see I shall have to put you in the picture there,' she remarked obscurely. He was still trying to puzzle out the meaning behind her words when the music ended and they rejoined the others.

At Charlotte's insistence, they took the Curtis' limousine back to Shepherd's. The main courtyard was packed with an endless array of expensive motors and they had a lengthy wait before the chauffeur was summoned and the Curtis' Packard was steered out from among the ranks of Cadillacs, Rolls-Royces, Hispanos and Mercedes which stood gleaming in the moonlight and the beams of the Palace lamps.

Most of the hotel's guests had gone up to their beds, or left for their homes, but the pavement beside the steps was still crowded with beggars hoping for generosity from late returners. Laura shivered as a blind cripple and his child keeper were turned away by one of the doormen.

'Egypt still horrifies me sometimes,' she said, 'I don't know how people can accept the contrasts between the very rich and the poor so easily. It's awful to think that we can leave a palace where a King is staging a fabulous dance and less than a mile away find the most desperate poverty and misery.'

'It's the same everywhere in Cairo,' Desmond said, 'there have always been a handful of immensely rich and millions of poor. The villas of the Garden City right next to the hovels and slums of the City of the Dead.' He was about to add that Shepherd's itself backed on to a huddle of shanties and vermin infested tenements when he heard his name called loudly from across the street, and looking round, saw the figure of Ralph Kendricks lurching towards him.

'Skipper,' he cried again, as he stumbled up the stairs to where Desmond and Laura waited for him beneath the canopy, 'Skipper, I'm sorry I didn't make it this evening,' he slurred, clutching at the pillars of the awning for support. 'I couldn't come, just couldn't come,' he repeated drunkenly, 'wanted to, but just couldn't.'

Shepherd's was used to high spirited revellers returning late at night, but Desmond could see that the doorman was looking doubtfully at Kendricks, who had taken off his jacket and tie and was carrying them in his hand together with a half empty bottle of whisky. His face was flushed and sweaty with liquor.

'Hell Ralph. Why do you have to get yourself into this state?' Desmond took the swaying radio operator by the arm and began to steer him through the hall. 'You had better leave me to deal with him,' he said to Laura, but the girl was calmly relieving Kendricks of the jacket and whisky bottle. 'Take him through,' she said, 'I'll get the key and follow.'

Not without difficulty, for he was a heavy man, they managed to get Ralph upstairs to his room and on to his bed, where he collapsed into a stupor at once. Desmond removed his shoes and left him covered with a blanket. 'Thanks,' he said to Laura as they returned to their own floor. 'You were a great help.'

'Oh, it was nothing. I'm used to all that, I've had to do it hundreds of times.' Her words and the way she said them made Desmond glance at her sharply.

'My husband,' she answered his unspoken question in a flat tired voice. 'He was an alcoholic. I did this for him again and again and again.'

'I'm sorry,' Desmond said gently, 'I didn't realize that. It must have made dealing with Ralph a lot worse for you.'

'I'm used to it now,' she shook her head sadly. 'At first I used to cry every time. That was how he was killed in the end. He started going down into the mine when he was drunk, he got careless and there was an accident. Snap! No husband,' she made an empty gesture with her hands. 'All over in a second, just like that.'

'What will you do about Ralph?' she asked as they reached the door of Stewart Curtis' suite. Desmond shrugged his shoulders, 'I'm not sure yet,' he answered, 'I'll have to think about it and decide tomorrow. Right now all I want to do is get some sleep,' and kissing her gently goodnight he returned to his room.

VI

FROM THE EGYPTIAN GAZETTE. Sunday 12th
March 1939.

'H.M. King Farouk will today honour the Cairo
Motoring Club by starting the Club's annual race to
Fayoum at 3.30 p.m. in the Abdin Palace Square. His
Majesty will be accompanied by H.H. The Crown
Prince of Iran and members of their suites will also
be present, together with H.E. the British Ambassa-
dor and members of the diplomatic corps.'

IN the big house on the point at Warren Lake, Pat Jarrett
woke to the sound of his alarm just as the sun was climbing
above the rim of the surrounding hills. Instantly he leapt out of
bed, as he had done every day of his life since he went away to
the war. Rising at dawn, never lying in for a moment once he
was awake, were important parts of the rigorous code of self-
discipline which he imposed on himself.

Scanning the lake from the window, he checked to see that
all was as it had been the previous evening. The sky was clear
apart from a few streaks of cirrus cloud at a very great height,
and the surface of the water unruffled by wind. If the weather
would only stay like this for another five days, he thought,
everything would be perfect.

Grabbing a towel and a pair of shorts, he hurried out of the
house and down to the pier. Usually he began the day with a
cold shower or splashdown but since his arival at the lake he
had taken advantage of the opportunity to have a proper swim.

After his swim in the icy waters he set off for his daily run,
another item in his routine; five miles regardless of weather
conditions and, except when snow was lying, barefooted to
keep the soles hardened.

The fresh mountain air was doing him good; his body felt renewed and invigorated as he bounded over the grass, splashing through patches of boggy ground left by the vanished snow. Not only did he feel in peak condition but the knowledge that his long training, the years of denial and self-discipline were at last being put to use, had brought a sense of purpose and excitement back into his life.

Returning to the house he showered and rubbed himself down once more before putting on a clean shirt and set of starched white overalls from the supply which he kept washed and ironed daily. Pride in appearance was the hallmark of the good soldier, he reminded himself, as he shaved carefully and trimmed his hair in front of the mirror. Today he would begin to fit the radio transmitter. Everything was going according to plan.

The race out to Fayoum and back was not due to begin until half past three, largely to suit the convenience of the King who had announced his intention of starting the cars off and presenting the winner with his prize. The drivers on the whole, were in favour of an afternoon contest since this meant they would miss the hottest part of the day. The first cars were expected to cross the finishing line in the Palace Square at about six o'clock, just as dusk was falling, with the last of the drivers home by half past six. The final leg of the race was to be the most spectacular with the cars roaring through streets packed with spectators, their headlamps blazing in the failing light.

Desmond had been working on the Hispano-Suiza since early in the morning, following a brief visit to Heliopolis to check on the work being done on *Caterina*. Despite many assurances from Charlotte Curtis and others, he was inclined to rate his chances in the race as low. Unlike the other contestants he had been unable to practise over the course during the past three weeks, and now with the collapse of Ralph Kendricks, he would have to do without a mechanic as well. Against him would be men like Baron d'Este with a brand new expensive motor and any number of chauffeurs and mechanics to call on to help him in his preparations.

The car was kept in a small garage not far from Shepherd's, in a narrow cul-de-sac off a main street which housed several small businesses, as well as a number of taxi-drivers who were among his staunch supporters and whose children's greatest joy was to be allowed to help polish the fabulous racer.

When first made in 1924 the Hispano-Suiza Boulogne had been the ultimate in luxury and performance. The breath-taking twelve foot long body was hand-built from tulip wood on a Swiss designed chassis and powered by an eight litre version of the famous wartime aero engines, representing a pinnacle of engineering and coachbuilding craftsmanship which would never be attained again.

Every leaf of the beautifully grained red brown wooden body had been shaped and fitted by hand into the car's sweeping elegant lines, studied every few inches by countless brass screws, so that the overall effect was a rich combination of deep red and gold which gleamed and sparkled in the light.

Nine months ago, on a tour of Farouk's Palace garages, Desmond had recognized the Hispano lying abandoned and decaying behind the ranks of more recent models, and had persuaded the King to let him buy her. Since then most of his spare time had been spent in hunting down spare parts and restoring the car to her original magnificence.

All things considered, however, the Hispano was in extraordinarily good condition, he told himself as he lay on his back underneath her, tightening the sump guard bolts. True, she was fifteen years old, and lacked the acceleration of today's Delahayes and Jaguars, but given a straight road and room to manoeuvre, the huge engine was capable of equalling the speed of most cars, and holding the pace tirelessly without straining for hour after hour.

On this afternoon's course reliability and strength would be as important as sheer all-out speed. Over the desert road deep ruts, pot-holes and loose stones marred the way; split tyres, broken wheels and axles could easily result, especially among drivers unused to such hazards. There was at least a chance that he might be well placed at the finish.

Sliding himself back a short distance to begin a scrutiny of the steering assembly he heard the door to the street, which he had shut firmly to keep out the children, being tugged open. Squinting round past the nearside front tyre he saw a pair of small feet in neat white tennis shoes topped by white overall trousers with the ends turned up, walk round towards him. A moment later Laura Hartman's face was peering underneath the car at him.

'I figured you'd need a helper, so here I am,' she said when Desmond had hauled himself out. 'Your Mr. Kendricks is still out cold.' In addition to the workmanlike overalls she had caught her hair neatly back in a saaft. 'I know,' she continued as he started to protest, 'but my husband, I told you, was an engineer and almost the only thing he managed to teach me about was motor cars.' She cast an appraising eye over the Hispano.

'She's beautiful,' she said with feeling, running her fingers lightly over the gleaming woodwork of the bonnet. She gave him a stern look. '1924 model Hispano-Suiza Boulogne. Six cylinder, eight litre engine with overhead valves; nicknamed the "Tulipwood Boulogne" it is the only one of its kind in existence and was built for Andre Dubonnet of the French wine family, who raced it in the Targa Floreo in 1924.'

Desmond stared at her in amazement, and then burst into laughter. The sight of her determined figure reeling off a string of technical data was too much for him. 'Did he teach you all that?' he asked. The girl shook her head. 'No, Freddy Muller, the hotel manager told me, he told me where to find you as well, but I do know what I'm talking about, so do I get to go with you?'

He looked at her waveringly for a moment. 'The race may be dangerous, it'll certainly be tiring and dusty,' he answered doubtfully. 'A lot of the track runs through the desert and the roads are pretty bad there.'

Laura's jaw tightened, 'I can handle a little dirt,' she said, 'I can also change a wheel and grease an axle, anyone else you find will only weigh more,' she added defiantly, and Desmond laughed again.

'That much I have to admit,' he agreed. 'It seems as though I have no choice, and you certainly look the part. Where did you find those clothes?'

It was Laura's turn to grin. 'Your purser, Sandy Everett, found them for me at the airline stores. He's given me this pair to work in, and another clean set to wear for the race.'

'You'll need a helmet and goggles as well,' he told her, 'I'll see about getting hold of them for you when we knock off for lunch. I just want to finish checking her over underneath, then we'll take her out for a run.' He glanced at his watch as he spoke; the time was already eleven o'clock. They had less than four hours in which to make ready.

The entire square in front of the Abdin Palace was taken up by the rows of cars, drawn up in order according to ballot. Forty-two drivers had joined the race, though less than a quarter of these were serious contenders for the prize, the rest being older cars whose owners were entering more for the fun of the drive than for an attempt at victory.

About each of the polished and gleaming machines were clustered a throng of admiring onlookers, watching the final adjustments being made to the engines and discussing their merits critically and volubly. On the King's instructions, a cordon of police held back the crowds of ordinary spectators, but they had not prevented practically the whole of Cairo society entering to watch their friends take part and see the King start the race.

Jacquetta d'Este stood beneath an awning at the edge of the square erected by the Cairo Motoring Club for its guests. The hottest part of the day was still not quite over and out on the unprotected tarmac the noise and dust and smell of exhaust fumes had been too much for her. Nearby several of her friends chattered excitedly about the prospects of the various contestants. In front of her, almost lost in a milling crowd of supporters, her husband had seated Charlotte Curtis behind the wheel of his maroon Delahaye and was explaining the controls to her with enthusiasm. Jacquetta could see the Englishwoman's wide brimmed hat nodding from time to time in answer.

Since their debut at the Paris Motor Show in 1938, and

subsequent victory in the Le Mans Twenty-Four Hour Race in the same year, the big Delahayes had attracted great attention. To Luca's satisfaction the crowd had gathered thickly, admiring the glossy maroon paint and the whitewalled tyres, and the rich luxury of the leather and walnut interior.

From Luca's temper when Jacquetta had questioned him about the ball that morning she had realized that all had not gone well for him, and later one of her gossiping friends had telephoned her with the news that Charlotte had spent the evening at the Palace running after the good-looking pilot who had flown in during the afternoon. For once also it appeared Charlotte had not had things entirely her own way and had had to face competition from her own husband's secretary. Jacquetta wondered how she had enjoyed the experience.

Luca had been allotted a favourable position in the front rank of the start, between an enormous bright yellow Isotta-Fraschini, its long bonnet crowned by an ornate silver winged emblem, and a square nosed Bugatti belonging to a Syrian. The Hispano-Suiza driven by Desmond O'Neill whom everyone was tipping as Luca's most serious rival, was on the far side of the second rank.

A stir of excitement ran through the square, and from the crowds in the road beyond the cordon there went up a loud chorus of greeting. Looking round, Jacquetta saw the Palace doors had been thrown open and a phalanx of soldiers, uniformed courtiers and distinguished personages were descending the steps. The King, and his new brother-in-law, the Crown Prince had arrived. The crowd continued to roar its approval. Farouk was a popular King unlike his miserly father who had despised his people and refused even to learn their language.

The glittering cortège began to move slowly along the rows of cars, pausing now and then to pass a few words with the occupants. Returning to the edge of the square, Charlotte joined Jacquetta under the awning.

'It's so hot out there in the sun,' she complained. 'I do pity those poor drivers. Luca let me sit in his car,' she went on proudly. 'It really is a most marvellous machine. I do hope he wins.'

'I should have thought you would be supporting Miss Hartman and Captain O'Neill,' Jacquetta replied innocently, and was gratified to see her words bring a faint flush to the other's cheeks. For all her sophistication, and grandeur she realized Charlottle Curtis was basically little more than a spoiled child; a child who enjoyed leading men on, especially married ones whose wives she could taunt, and who became angry and jealous when her advances were rejected.

The King stood forward on the podium and the noise of the spectators died away expectantly. For the space of a few seconds the cars quivered on the starting grid, a glittering array of brightly coloured metallic creatures crouched to spring. The King raised his arm; there was a sudden bright flash and a loud report and the massed cars leapt forward with a tremendous blast of sound. The colours flashed away, blurred by the speed and dust, green, blue, red, gold, silver and yellow, it was hard to separate them. Jacquetta caught one glimpse of Luca's Delahaye turning out of the square in front of the Hispano and then they were gone, the crowds racing down the road in pursuit.

The first few miles of the course, through the streets of Cairo and along the Pyramid road leading out of the City to the south were too narrow and restricted to allow the race to develop properly, with the result that the leaders were held together in a tight bunch.

Exuberant crowds cheered wildly as they swept round the tight bends along the riverside avenues, fighting grimly for position. The hamsin of the previous evening had left a considerable amount of fine dust on the roadside and in the gutters and the sudden violent passage of the cars stirred this up, adding to the hazards facing the drivers.

Desmond and Laura in the Hispano were well up among the front dozen cars and only a length or so behind the streamlined shape of Luca d'Este's Delahaye. Although the Italian had been more favourably placed at the start he had failed to make use of his advantage to get clear of the others. Already his short-comings as a driver were becoming apparent in his nervous, jerky handling and poor positioning on the corners. Despite the fact that the Delahaye was by far the newest and most expensive car in the race, Desmond felt confident that his own driving skills would give him an edge.

For the present however he was content to hold his place, striving to avoid a collision with cars whose drivers were reck-lessly trying to force their way through from behind. When the open road was reached most of these would inevitably fall back, unable to compete with the faster machines, but at the moment they were turning the road into a dangerous mêlée of cars, swerving and jinking to avoid one another in the con-fusion.

A red Daimler double-six cut in ahead of him, forcing him to brake hard and pull out to the right. As he did so he heard Laura utter a sharp cry of warning and he saw the nose of another car accelerating past him on the outside. There was a momentary glimpse of the driver's goggled face screaming at him; then the speeding menace had flashed by, its tail barely visible in the dust. If this kept up for long he saw there was going to be a serious crash, probably involving several vehicles, and he began to regret bringing Laura with him, and exposing her to such risks.

Luca was driving with increasing wildness in his anxiety to fight off the pressure from his rear. Desmond could see him swinging the big Delahaye across the track viciously to deter would-be challengers. Obviously the Italian would not sur-render his lead willingly and anyone trying to overtake could probably expect to be crowded off the road, or even risk delib-erate ramming.

Yet overtaken he must be and if not here in the city, then on the tight bends of the road through Fayoum itself. For out on the flat straights through the desert, the Delahaye's superior speed would render the task impossible and Luca knew it.

Past the tree-lined suburbs the road opened out, and the squat yellow shapes of the Giza Pyramids became visible in the distance across the desert. Here the race grew more frantic as the faster cars pulled out on to the packed sand on the edge of the road to overhaul those in front, raising great clouds of dust in their wake. Pressing his foot hard down on the Hispano's accelerator, Desmond felt an immediate thrust of response and with a deep crackle from the exhaust the red car leapt forward. The Delahaye was already pulling way ahead as Luca d'Este made full use of the tremendous power which had carried the marque to victory at Le Mans.

Crouched down behind the tiny windshield Laura felt the excitement mounting within her as one after another the leading machines were overtaken and left behind. The speedometer was touching almost one hundred miles per hour when they turned off on to the secondary road into the desert. The whole car was shaking with the strain, the thunderous howl of the engine beneath the long bonnet filling her ears. Beside her Desmond sat hunched over the wheel, using all his strength to hold them on the road. Both of them were caked in a layer of fine grey dust.

Only a handful of contestants remained ahead of them, four or five at most, she guessed, and judging by the skilful way Desmond was handling the Hispano there was a good chance that they might be out in front with only the Delahaye to beat, by the time they reached Fayoum, ninety miles away across the sands.

There, in the oasis, all drivers had to make a compulsory stop to take on fuel and give a hurried check to their vehicles before setting off for the final, high speed dash down the main road back into Cairo. At all costs she and Desmond must have wrested the lead from Luca before then.

The oasis of Fayoum, set in the desert sixty miles out from Cairo, is the vast garden and fruit orchard of Lower Egypt. Lush with every kind of vegetation, its heart is Lake Karoum, fed by water draining in from the Nile, which lies among thick groves of almond, apricot, orange, fig and lemon, intermingled with graceful acacias and eucalyptus trees, tamarisks and tall date palms. From the shores, edged with silver sands a myriad of irrigation channels and water-wheels feed fields where water-buffaloes wade through green rice paddies and gangs of fellahin slash at the high purple stalks of the sugar cane. On all sides rich acres of wheat, cotton, maize, clover and every kind of vegetable stretch endlessly to the horizon.

On the glassed-in verandah of the Pavillion de Chasse Hotel, Yousouri Pasha sat looking out over the smooth, shining surface of the Lake. With a sigh he transferred his attention back to the man in police colonel's uniform who stood anxiously by his chair. 'So you have failed in your task?' he said disdainfully. The officer cleared his throat uneasily. 'We have not failed exactly, Excellency,' he pleaded, 'but events did not quite go as we planned. There is still time.' Yousouri selected a sweetmeat from a plate on a nearby table. 'Your orders were to apprehend Sheikh Rashid so as to prevent him from trying to assassinate Baron d'Este. All you have succeded in doing is driving him into the oasis, where he will be impossible to find, and at the same time warn him that he is being hunted.'

'The Sheikh must have known already, Excellency. His Bedouin were waiting in the ruined city to the west. They had pickets out and as soon as they spotted us they retreated back to Fayoum,' the Colonel said.

'Fool,' Yousouri's voice rose angrily, 'did you expect a man like Rashid to walk into your arms of his own accord? Of course he had pickets out and of course he retreated. You should have been prepared and had men at his rear.'

'What shall we do now then Excellency?' the man asked plaintively.

'Do! Why find him of course. Call out your men, comb the orchards and cane fields, and send patrols through the woods,' Yousouri snarled. 'You have less than an hour before the cars come through. And I promise you Colonel,' he added savagely, 'if you bungle this, if Rashid slips through the net and succeeds in killing the Baron here in Egypt, you would have done better not to have been born. Do you understand?'

From a mimosa thicket deep within the oasis on the eastern end of the lake Rashid al Senussi scanned the ground about him and cursed. The spot was ideal for an ambush; less than

216

fifty yards away across the field, the road down which the racing cars must come, skirted the shore of the lake and bent sharply to the right round a clump of trees before continuing on through a series of bends, to join the main road to Cairo. Any vehicle approaching along that way would be forced to slow down.

One thing marred the plan however. Parked under the trees, right by the edge of the road was a military truck with a dozen well armed men of the Egyptian police inside. Rashid had four of his own followers with him, and in different circumstances he would have regarded the odds as acceptable.

Today however was different. The oasis was crawling with police and troops and the sound of firing would draw scores of reinforcements at once. Outnumbered and cut off, the Bedouin would be trapped with the lake at their backs and picked off one by one.

Since early morning nothing had gone right. Details of his intended attack on d'Este had evidently reached the authorities, probably through the guide he had been forced to employ, and they had all but walked into the arms of an ambush themselves. Saved by the keen eyesight of his advance riders, Rashid had been forced to withdraw in the direction of Fayoum while the troops had made a determined effort to corner them among the sands. Only by sending some of his men off to lure the pursuit aside into the desert had he been able to slip through and reach the oasis.

Now they were bottled up again. It was unlikely that they would have another chance to get so close to the road. At the other end of the lake, furthest from the river, was the refuelling stage, but that had virtually been sealed off by police, and their patrols were working steadily through the fields on both sides of the road. He would have to create a diversion.

The branches of the mimosa were yellow with pollen which fell about his head and shoulders like dust as he crawled back to his companions. Lean, desert-hardened men like himself they were waiting in a small hollow with the horses while he reconnoitred. Calling them round him he told them his plan.

A short while later from his earlier position he watched the four Arabs lead their horses quietly round behind the thicket and ride off in the direction of the river to the east. As he had expected, before they had gone far, a cry went up from the waiting Egyptians and the truck set off rapidly in pursuit.

With a smile at the ease with which the trick had worked a second time, Rashid slipped out of the bushes, across the field and into the concealment of the trees on the other side. From here he could see a long way down in the direction from which the cars would approach.

The ground was thickly overgrown with weeds and the ever present mimosa bushes, and sloped upwards to a low ridge. Once there had been an orchard of orange trees here, but it had fallen into neglect, the irrigation ditches were choked and the water-wheel which had supplied them, stood disused and broken.

To his left, beyond the field he had just crossed, lay the reed-fringed marshes bordering Lake Karoum whose blue waters stretched towards the horizon. Before him, the road skirted the orchard and bent to run beside the lake, receding into the distance a mile or two away. Down that road he knew would come the cars.

Unslinging the Manlicher rifle from his shoulder he settled himself down in a small hollow behind a fallen tamarisk branch halfway up the slope in a position from which he would be able to direct enfilading fire upon d'Este as the Baron approached down the straight and slowed to take the corner twenty yards away and a little below.

About him, now that the troops had gone, all was quiet, save for the chatter of birds among the trees, and the faint music of hundreds of water-wheels in the surrounding fields. The sun was sinking in the sky to the west; he would not have long to wait.

After the hour long drive through the desert, the sight of the trees and lush fields of green in the middle of the sands, was a welcome change to Laura, even though she knew it heralded the start of the most urgent phase of the race. Despite all their efforts three cars still remained ahead of them; a Bugatti, the red Daimler which had passed them earlier, driven by an English army officer stationed in Cairo, and Luca d'Este's Delahaye.

The Delahaye led by quarter of a mile. On the straight roads over the sand there had been little scope for skill and each driver had pushed his car to the limit.

The fifteen or so miles through the twisting lanes round Lake Karoum would be crucial. A driver who could succeed in putting a substantial distance between himself and his nearest rivals was virtually assured of victory. The road back from Fayoum, broad, straight and well-tarmacked, was one of the best in Egypt.

The flat, fertile landscape with its neat fields and luxuriant vegetation was a novelty to Laura, and it was pleasant to feel the smoothness of a well made road again after the bruising ride over the desert, and to see spectators waving to them as they flashed past.

As it happened they struck trouble immediately on entering the oasis. Taking a corner too quickly, Luca skidded hard and slithered off the road into the grass. It took him only seconds to regain control and have the Delahaye on its way once more but in that time the others had closed the gap and were on his heels. With only a few feet between them the four cars raced along the narrow track, squeezing every second of advantage out of the bends.

The pressure was telling on Luca however and very soon the driver of the Bugatti seized an opportunity to draw level with the Delahaye on the inside. Nose to nose the two hurtled on along the road while the drivers tried desperately to pull ahead; the greater power of the maroon car balanced by the superior skill of the Bugatti's driver.

Then Desmond saw d'Este put his wheel hard over in an apparent effort to force his rival off the road, repeating the tactics he had been using earlier to prevent others from passing him.

On these fast bends the manoeuvre was so insanely dangerous that instinctively he eased his foot slightly off the accelerator, opening the gap separating the Hispano from the two leaders. As he did so the Delahaye's front bumper struck the Bugatti's offside wheel.

Instantly the thin cycle wing mudguard crumpled and with a sharp pitched bang the Bugatti's wheel sheered off and went bowling crazily on ahead along the road, as though possessed of some extraordinary motive power of its own. The two cars bounced apart and for a moment the Bugatti rode upright while its driver stared transfixedly at the runaway wheel. Then with a sickening screech of metal the right hand wing dropped to the ground and slid jarringly along for fifty yards, gouging a furious track in the roadway as it went. Desmond and Laura could see the driver still trying futilely to steer as his car slid and slewed across the path of the vehicles behind him.

Then suddenly, without warning, it pitchpoled end over end, leaping high in the air, clear of the road; bounced shatteringly and crashed to rest against the bank of an irrigation ditch, scattering debris in a wide area around it.

There was no time to do anything, almost before they had realized what was happening they were speeding past, Laura was left with a confused impression of images, superimposed one upon the other; the wheel-less car still driving upright, the horrifying somersault over the road. Looking back she saw the Bugatti lying on its back like a broken toy, the first rescuers hurrying towards it through the trees.

Desmond made no comment, but drove with a fierce concentration on Luca's tail till they halted at the fuel stage, less than a mile away, in the car park of the Hotel de Chasse. Here scores of spectators and race mechanics mingled with officials in a scene not unlike the confusion which had prevailed at the start. A large crowd had driven out to the oasis to see the finish of the first leg and a field next to the car park was packed with vehicles of every description. Six large petrol wagons were drawn up on the tarmacked yard and the mechanics had begun to refill the Delahaye's tank and were checking the wheel casing for damage when Desmond drew up, and vaulting out of the Hispano's driving seat, ran over to where d'Este was talking to a group of race officials.

'You criminal idiot!' he accused him hotly, ignoring the eagerly clustering spectators. 'You caused that accident deliberately.' The Italian was in a highly nervous state already and he flared up instantly at Desmond's charge. 'The Bugatti was responsible,' he shouted. 'He cut in on the inside of the corner, I could not help what happened.'

'Damn you!' Desmond was white with anger, 'I saw you put your wheel across with my own eyes, it was deliberate ramming.'

One of the officials interrupted, 'I am sure you must be mistaken Captain,' he said, 'nobody would do such a thing.'

'Ask any of the other drivers, ask Mrs. Hartman,' Desmond told him. 'This fool's been driving like a madman all the way out here.'

'O'Neill is right,' the owner of the red Daimler joined the group, he was a big florid faced man with a moustache. 'The man ought to be banned, as clear a case of ramming as I've ever seen.'

More cars were arriving to take on fuel, their drivers and mechanics hurrying to get started again. Luca d'Este's face took on a hunted expression, he could see the race slipping from his grasp. 'It was an accident, an accident,' he repeated, 'the Bugatti's fault not mine.'

The track officials were looking doubtful and in another moment might well have decided to call off the race, or at least forbid Luca to continue, but just then another man came running over.

'They're all right!' he cried. 'The Frenchmen in the Bugatti. They were shaken up but the ditch saved them from being crushed by the car. There's hardly a scratch on them.'

Sighs of relief went round the group and a look of triumph flashed on to Luca's face. 'Now perhaps we can continue with the race,' he snarled, climbing back into the Delahaye, which stood refuelled and waiting nearby. His action was the signal for an immediate scattering of the other drivers back to their cars.

Clenching his teeth with rage, Desmond leapt back into the Hispano which Laura had refuelled and had ready for him.

Slamming it into gear, he roared off out through the hotel gates in pursuit of the Italian.

To Rashid's annoyance the area immediately around the point he had picked for his ambush was still crawling with armed police. From where he lay, twenty yards from the corner, he had so far observed three trucks similar to the one he had seen earlier, grind past, the men inside sitting upright against the sides, clutching their rifles between their knees.

More worrying than this; a section of a dozen men was combing the ground along the shores of the lake, working steadily towards him through the marshes. Whether they were aware of his presence in the vicinity or were simply taking extreme precautions, the young Sheikh had no means of telling. For the moment he was safe enough from detection, but the sound of a shot would reveal his position at once.

All he could do was lie still and pray that by the time the cars appeared along the road, the patrol would have moved far enough past to enable him to scramble away through the trees and get clear. With luck he thought, the echoes of the shot on the lake would confuse the searchers.

The sun sank steadily nearer the horizon as he crouched tensely in the hollow, watching every movement in the fields. The soldiers drew level with him and continued past; the nearest less than a hundred yards away. Their search was painstaking and methodical, co-ordinated by an N.C.O. from the centre of the line. Rashid cursed their slowness. The first cars were already overdue, and although the failing light would give him some slight assistance the soldiers were still within easy sighting distance. His hands were sweating where they gripped the rifle and he wiped them nervously.

So intent was he on watching the patrol that he did not at first hear the low hum in the distance which signalled the approach of the cars. With a jerk however he recognized the sound and switched his attention back to the road. The sun was very near the horizon now making it difficult to distinguish shapes far away, but he could just make out the rapidly nearing trail of dust thrown up by the cars.

Cuddling the Manlicher tightly into his shoulder, he made a minute adjustment to the rear sight. He would put the first shot into d'Este exactly as the Italian reached the corner. The car would be moving at its slowest then, making a perfect target. The soldiers in the field were still too near but Rashid no longer cared. Very soon his father would be avenged.

Laura had gathered that the driver of the Bugatti was uninjured, but more than that Desmond had been unable to tell her, for it required all his attention to follow the twists and turns of the road. Certainly the conversation at the stop had aroused his anger, she could see, for he was driving with an angry determination on Luca's heels, sticking relentlessly to the Delahaye round every corner and bend, and trying every device he knew to overtake the maroon racer.

For the first time since the start of the race, Laura felt frightened. The speed of the cars rocketing along the narrow roads between the sharp corners at up to one hundred miles an hour was nerve-wracking enough, but what really terrified her were the crazy tactics Luca was resorting to, in order to fight off the Hispano, and Desmond's disregard for the risks he was taking.

Coming out at last on to an open stretch running along the eastern end of the lake Luca pressed his accelerator into the floor in a furious effort to draw clear of the pursuing car. The engine note lifted to a high pitched whine as the revolutions mounted and the needle of the speedometer climbed past one hundred and ten. Beside him Luca's mechanic paled at the sight of the corner rushing closer.

Behind them in the Hispano Laura was gripping the side of the car. Unless he slowed up there was no way Luca could take the bend and the two cars were now so close that a misjudgement by the Delahaye would involve them both in an appalling crash.

Five hundred yards away Rashid snapped the Manlicher's bolt shut and sighted in on the speeding car. He heard the squeal of tyres and the sudden bellow of protest from the engine as d'Este braked desperately and changed down through the gears. Even from the ridge it was possible to see that the Italian had begun to slow too late.

Less than one hundred yards away from the corner the Delahaye's brakes locked under the fierce strain and the big car went into an ungovernable sliding skid, swinging broadside on across the road, tyres shrieking as the rubber burnt off beneath the friction. Helplessly Luca spun the steering wheel in a vain effort to regain control before the car behind smashed into him.

With a high speed collision only moments away, Desmond reacted with lightning decision. A deep ditch ran along the right hand edge of the road, the opposite side was a narrow but unobstructed strip of grass. Braking hard he swung out off the tarmac, praying that the Hispano's weight would hold her steady at this speed. There was a violent bumping and clouds of dirt and sand shot up, as with inches to spare they flashed past the Delahaye's nose into the corner.

Putting the wheel hard over Desmond felt the car's tail break free and start to slide round as they regained the road. Releasing the brakes, and dropping another gear, he spun the wheel again, correcting savagely.

There was a split second of stomach-churning fear while he thought the heavy car would refuse to obey, and then, miraculously they were round and he was accelerating out of the corner and away. At that very instant, just as the Hispano roared clear and the Delahaye's still-squealing rear wheels slid backwards into the ditch, Rashid squeezed the trigger of his rifle.

The crack of the shot echoed sharply out over the flat landscape, alerting everyone except those in the cars. From his vantage point Rashid saw the maroon car slide headlong over the partly filled ditch and lurch over the ground beyond, to fetch up on its side with a crash, among the trees, spilling its occupants out behind it.

There was no way of telling if he had hit d'Este or not and with his quarry now hidden by the car whose still spinning wheels were towards him, and the soldiers in the nearby field running in his direction, there was no chance either of a second shot. Shouldering the rifle, he scrambled to his feet and made off through the orchard.

The noise of the Hispano's engine accelerating away from the corner had completely drowned out the crack of the rifle shot so far as Desmond and Laura were concerned. Twisting round in her seat Laura witnessed the crash and overturning of the maroon car but could tell nothing of the fate of Luca and his partner.

'They must be unhurt,' Desmond yelled back when she reported what she had seen. 'The Delahaye's a big solid car, and she must have lost a lot of her speed by the time she hit.'

'Can we win now?' she cried against the wind. 'Can any of the others catch us?'

'We've a good chance, if we can just hold the lead till we reach the main road,' he shouted.

Fortunately they had only a little further to go before striking the Cairo highway, and though even in that space the red Daimler and another car crept ominously close, once they were out on the open road, Desmond gave the Hispano her head and the awesome power of the eight litre engine drew them clear again.

Hurtling along the empty road in the dusk at a thunderous speed of more than one hundred and fifteen miles an hour, the wind stinging her cheeks and her ears filled with the deep howl of the exhaust, was an experience Laura was never to forget. Their lead built up increasingly until by the time they reached the Pyramids, silhoutted fantastically against the sunset they knew they were uncatchable.

The moonlight was glittering on the Nile as they sped on into the city, the palm trees on the banks giving way to the jacarandas and flame trees of the suburban avenues, flashing past in the incandescent blaze of the headlamps. Then they were racing through cheering streets, their pavements jammed by crowds wild with excitement.

The brilliantly lit marble façade of the Abdin Palace appeared ahead of them; ranks of police and soldiers strained to keep back the swarms of delirious spectators, and suddenly they were past the flag and into the square, and it was all over.

'He is uninjured? He doesn't even realize he was shot at?' Prince Suleiman's tone was incredulous. Yousouri Pasha made an expressive gesture. 'I know, it is unbelievable but nevertheless true. The bullet broke the steering wheel, it must have missed his head only fractionally. D'Este was too worried trying to save the car to notice, but my men found it embedded in the wing, and there was a hole in the dashboard to match.' Reaching into his pocket he drew out a flattened lump of metal and placed it on the table before them.

The two men were sitting in a summer-house in the gardens of the Prince's palace. Deaf mute servants, slaves in all but name, Yousouri knew, were ministering silently to their wants. The Prince ignored the spent bullet. 'It was fortunate for us all that Rashid missed,' Yousouri continued.

'Fortunate perhaps,' the Prince agreed, 'but I cannot share in any rejoicing at d'Este's continued escape from just punishment. He has after all murdered my kinspeople.'

Yousouri recalled for a moment the stories he had heard of the beautiful Senussi girl the Prince had brought out of the desert and married more than forty years ago. She had died in her first childbirth, but for all his want of an heir, the old man had never married again.

'We are united in condemning d'Este's crimes,' he assured his host, 'but equally we must agree on the disastrous consequences which might result if he were to be slain while in Egypt. I can see to it that this attempt does not come to light and, God be praised, the man leaves the country tomorrow morning.' He paused for a moment and regarded the table thoughtfully, 'I have however been instructed,' he put a slight emphasis on the words, and hesitated for an instant to let their full weight sink in, 'I have been instructed to ask for your Highness' word that Rashid al Senussi will not be permitted to carry out any further attacks on Baron d'Este while he is still here.'

'You assume perhaps that I have greater control over the boy than may be the case?' the Prince's tone did not change.

'That may be so, nevertheless in so far as you are able, I must ask. D'Este is in any case to dine at Shepherd's and then return to the Embassy and the whole area is now under heavy guard. Tomorrow he will be escorted to the aeroplane by the police, an attempt could not possibly succeed. There must not however be any such attempt.'

Prince Suleiman leant forward and picked up the crushed bullet. 'The boy has not yet returned,' he said turning the metal over between his long fingers. 'When he does you have my word that he shall not harm d'Este.' There was a pause, 'So long as the Baron is in Egypt,' he added.

Yousouri rose and bowed low. 'Your Highness has been most understanding,' he murmured, 'I am sure His Majesty will be pleased to hear of the assistance you have given us.'

Heinz Gerdler was walking the streets of Venice with an increasing sense of frustration and despondency. Although he and Rintlen had not arrived in the town until the early hours of the morning, the SD man had permitted only a brief interval of rest before beginning their search. While he himself remained in his room, working down the list of hotels and boarding houses in the telephone directory, Gerdler had been sent out to wander round the stations and tourist venues in the hope of catching sight of the refugee couple.

That had been ten hours ago. Since then Gerdler had walked unceasingly through the crowded streets till his legs ached with weariness and his mind had grown dizzy with fatigue.

Privately he was inclined to believe they were on a hopeless mission. Venice was already starting to fill with tourists for the spring and apparently endless hordes of people streamed past him everywhere he went. At least a dozen times he must have caught sight of a figure in the distance who looked like the Jewish girl, but always, when he had struggled panting through the crowd, it had been to discover someone quite different.

A task which at first had promised adventure and excitement was proving to hold nothing but boredom and hard work. Worse still, when he had returned to their hotel at lunch-time to report, he had found Rintlen in a sour temper after a fruitless morning on the telephone. Gerdler was afraid that if their venture were to fail, his own part in the Wienzman's flight might be dragged up. This anxiety grew as the afternoon wore on into the evening with nothing to show for his efforts.

Already the failing light was making it difficult to pick out the features of people on the other side of the street. Yet he shrank from the thought of returning again to confront Rintlen empty-handed. Turning abruptly on his heels he resolved to try once more in the Piazza San Marco.

The evening was clearer and warmer than that of the previous day and in consequence there were still many tourists about, watching the sunset over the Campanile and the pigeons wheeling away to their perches. Courting couples strolled hand in hand or sat among the cafés and children ran to and fro among the chairs. In the centre of the square a handful of amateur artists were putting the finishing touches to drawings and water-colours. Among them was Siegret Wienzman.

The Wienzmans were staying only a few minutes' walk from the square in a small hotel which, since it was unlicensed, was not included in the telephone directory and had thus escaped Rintlen's attentions. Together father and daughter had spent the morning and early afternoon in Venice's museums and art galleries, gazing at the treasures until the Professor had pronounced himself exhausted, and retired to his bed to rest while Siegret had received his permission to take her sketch pad to the square.

She had just packed away her belongings and was about to stand up and return to the hotel when to her utter horror she caught sight of the figure of Heinz Gerdler walking across the square in front of her.

There could be no mistaking that heavy build and broad, close-cropped head. Siegret ducked her head down, with a sob of fear as the coarse-featured face peered in her direction. She was hardly able to believe that they could have been detected and followed in so short a time, and yet there could be no other explanation. The youth was obviously searching the square for her and the helpless terror which, for a few hours she had almost shed, returned with undiminished intensity.

Out of the corner of her eye, not daring to look at him fully, she watched Gerdler make a circuit of the square and take a seat in one of the cafés. For a while she sat, half mesmerized with fear, trying to decide what to do. Then, clutching her basket she rose slowly to her feet and began to walk off towards the far side, away from him, trying as best she could to mingle with other passers-by, though in the past few minutes these had thinned out greatly.

Every few steps she glanced back to see if she had been spotted. It was this which was her undoing. Hard by the steps down to the Canale de Marco, where the gondolas waited, bobbing and swaying in the water, Gerdler's searching eyes met hers. With instant recognition he leapt to his feet and began running towards her. Siegret looked round frantically for a way of escape, the memory of the last, terrible chase paralysing her limbs. In blind panic she ran down the steps and jumped into the nearest gondola.

She was out in mid-channel before she saw a second craft putting out in pursuit of her. At first she thought the lead they had was too great for the youth to catch up, but straightway the other boatman gave a series of loud hails, hails to which her own gondolier responded, pausing in his strokes on the oar.

'Please,' she cried in agitation, 'you must hurry, I am frightened.' In broken Italian she tried to explain, but the two men were evidently under the impression that they were taking part in a romantic chase between two lovers, and to her dismay she saw that they were gradually allowing the distance between them to close as they crept along the canal.

Growing more and more frantic by the second Siegret appealed to the boatman to go faster, but the man only grinned good-humouredly and gave her an incomprehensible answer. Gerdler was clearly visible now across the intervening thirty yards of water, an expression of fierce triumph on his face as he bore inexorably down on her. About her numerous other craft were moving up and down the canal in the warm evening, but their occupants remained seemingly unaware of her cries, too intent on their own affairs and in enjoying the beauty of the churches and palazzos which lined the waterfront.

The address she had given was a small church only a street or two from where she was staying. To get there the gondolier was forced to turn along the Grand Canal and off into one of the myriad of smaller waterways criss-crossing the city. As he did so Siegret seized on a faint chance of escape. A short way past the turning, a small flight of mildewed steps with a rusty iron railing ran down the canal wall to the water. A boat approaching from the other direction made them pass close beside this and at that instant, Siegret screwed up her courage, stood up and made a grab for the railings.

Before anyone in either of the gondolas realized what had happened she had pulled herself on to the steps and was running up them into the streets.

'You idiotic fool! Stupid, careless oaf! Above all things you were told not to let them know we were here.' Rintlen's rage vented itself upon the unfortunate Austrian. 'What good did you think it would do to chase after the girl like that?'

'I'm sorry, Standartenfuhrer,' Gerdler stammered, sweating with fear. 'I was trying to follow her to find out where she was staying. I thought that was what you wanted.'

'Yes, but not by running and yelling after her like a bull.' Rintlen snapped in exasperation. 'This isn't the Reich any more.' The anger, which had built up over the course of the long day wasted on the telephone, was boiling over and he cursed the youth savagely. To have been right in his guess at the Wienzman's plans, to have had them so nearly in his grasp only to be frustrated by this last minute clumsiness, was infuriating. Less than an hour ago, he had received an urgent message from Heydrich via the German Consulate, demanding that the mission be accomplished with the utmost speed. The crisis over Czechoslovakia was worsening hourly and war was looming.

'We must hurry. There is no time to waste,' he told the boy, putting aside his anger for the moment. 'We must get to the station at once.'

'To the station?' Gerdler's face wrinkled in perplexity, 'but why, where are we going?'

'Half-wit! What do you imagine Wienzman will do as soon

as his daughter tells him she's seen you? He'll take the first train out of the city. We must be there to follow them.'

Venice's central station was surprisingly busy for a Sunday. Loudspeakers were blaring a series of unintelligible instructions while the staff attempted to deal with the hordes of travellers clamouring for attention and help. Several trains were standing at the platforms, mostly it appeared, waiting to begin short journeys to nearby provincial towns, but two big expresses were scheduled, one running westwards to Milan and Turin and the other to Rome.

'They might take either of these,' Rintlen said, examining the destination boards. 'At a guess Rome is the more likely, but we have no way of telling. They may not even be intending to take a main line service at all, or for that matter they could have got away already. We took long enough getting here and I doubt if Wienzman will have delayed any longer than he had to.'

Sending Gerdler off to check the queues at the ticket booths and watch the people boarding the Milan train, Rintlen bought himself a paper and took a seat on a bench from where he could see anyone approaching the barrier to the platform at which the express to Rome was standing. In his pocket he had tickets for both of them to either of the destinations.

The minutes crept by and he began to suspect that he might have guessed wrongly as to Wienzman's reactions when, just as the ticket collector was about to close the gate, a pair of figures detached themselves from a party of tourists standing not far away, and made a dash for the barrier with their suitcases.

Despite the fact that he had seen only poor reproductions of their photographs before, Rintlen had no hesitation in indentifying them as the Professor and his daughter. Their pale, worried faces left him in no doubt. Mentally he cursed the old man's cunning in timing their exit so well. There was no chance at all for anyone to follow them. The train was already starting to pull out of the station as the two clambered aboard; smoke from the engine billowing up to the roof.

Hurrying over to the other platform he located Gerdler. 'Here go and get the money back on these,' he thrust the Milan tickets at him, 'and find out when the next train leaves for Rome.'

'They took the express to Rome?' Gerdler asked unnecessarily. 'What are you going to do now?'

'Idiot! You and I will go after them at once, but first I must call our office in Rome and see they are followed when they leave the train. They may think they've escaped, but they're not clear yet.'

With the passing of the week-end Stewart Curtis' anxieties over Klerksdorp, which had temporarily receded, began to trouble him again. Monday would see the investigating team starting at their work on the mine, sifting through the assay reports and production figures and checking these against actual output. How long would it be before they found what they were looking for?

According to his own estimate he had not more than a week at the outside before the banking syndicate headed by old Suttenheim broke the news to the world. He based this not so much on the length of time it would take the investigators to uncover the fraud, in all probability they knew all they needed already, or at least guessed it, but on the ease with which the financiers would be able to unload their large holdings of Klerksdorp stock on the market.

This coming week would decide one way or another whether he was going to be able to salvage anything from the wreck for himself. The Southampton–New York flight was due to touch down on the East River at three p.m. on Friday, and Curtis had a meeting scheduled with the American group who were purchasing his land options, scheduled for five p.m. the same evening. Desmond O'Neill's decision to cut out the normal stop-over at Athens meant he could still just make it, but the margin was very slim indeed.

Sitting in the long bar he read through the reports in the *Financial Times*. The steady selling of Klerksdorp shares which had been recorded for the last fortnight in both London and Johannesburg causing the price to drift downwards had eased on Friday and there had actually been a slight gain on the day.

Probably Stuttenheim was being careful not to frighten off potential buyers. Until he had managed to put the American deal through Curtis didn't dare try and sell his own stock, for the same reason.

'Good evening Mr. Curtis, I see you too, did not go to witness the finish of the race?' Looking up Curtis recognized the figure of Frazer, the *Caterina*'s first officer standing beside him at the bar.

'I'm due at this dinner the Motor Club's giving your captain in a minute, though at the moment I have rather more important matters to worry about than motor races,' he answered sourly, 'such as wondering how long it will be before we make New York.'

'Then I have good news for you sir, I was down at the moorings earlier while the captain was out winning races,' Frazer said virtuously, '*Caterina* has been given a clean bill of health. We shall be leaving on time first thing tomorrow.'

'Then there was nothing wrong with the plane at all you mean?' Curtis asked.

'Practically nothing. The chap in Shambe had done a pretty good job it seems. Our people here replaced a couple of fuel leads and cleaned the air filters and that was it.'

'This is excellent news,' Curtis nodded approvingly, 'I am glad to note that at least one member of the crew still retains some concern for the passengers' convenience.'

Signalling the barman to bring Frazer a drink, he put the newspaper aside. 'What continues to annoy me,' he went on, 'is the fact that we have another delay when we reach England before we can fly on to New York.'

'I suppose they could run the flight a day earlier,' Frazer said thoughtfully, 'particularly since as far as I know no extra passengers are joining us for the Atlantic crossing. With the three of you, Baron d'Este and his wife, Dr. Van Smit and some Turk or other who's booked to join us at Alexandria, we shall be almost up to our limit. We can't carry more than ten or eleven passengers over such a long distance,' he explained.

'So in that case we could fly straight on the next morning,' Curtis exclaimed.

'Yes indeed,' Frazer agreed, as a new thought entered his head, 'you could be in New York by Thursday afternoon. There's just one problem though.'

'And what's that?' Curtis demanded.

'You'd need to persuade Imperial Airways to put on a new crew. You see Captain O'Neill is due to fly this crossing, and he will certainly refuse to take off until he's had thirty-six hours rest. Exactly as he has done here,' Frazer said pointedly.

It was Curtis' turn to look thoughtful. 'So it's O'Neill who's holding us up yet again. Well I might just be able to do something about it this time.' He gave Frazer a shrewd, speculative look. 'I'm grateful to you for your help, very grateful,' he said as he drained his glass. 'Keep me informed if you have any more ideas.'

Ken Frazer watched him go with a smile of satisfaction. The net round Desmond was closing in.

It was late before Rashid finally returned to Prince Suleiman's palace.

After his shot at Luca d'Este, Yousouri's police and soldiers had hunted him for three hours through the oasis, among the rice paddies and sugar cane fields. They had set up road blocks at strategic points and in the end he had been forced to escape hiding in a truckload of vegetables.

The Prince was in his study, having left word that Rashid was to be brought to him on his return. As soon as he had washed and changed his clothes, the young sheikh joined him. He found the old man seated at the ornate ottoman desk he used when dealing with his business affairs.

'So?' the Prince raised a quizzical eyebrow, 'you have decided to favour me with your presence at last.'

'I have been at Fayoum,' Rashid told him, 'd'Este was there and I wished to avenge the deaths of my father and sister.'

'And Yousouri Pasha has been here to tell me what you have been doing, or perhaps trying to do would be more correct.' The Prince replied, 'I presume you are aware that you missed?' he added with a touch of asperity.

'I know,' Rashid flung up his hands, 'the devil protects that man. The car overturned as I pressed the trigger; but he cannot escape for ever. Next time I will kill him, even if I must pay with my own life,' he swore. The Prince watched his bitter face, unmoved.

'That I do not doubt,' he said quietly, 'however, you will not do so in Egypt. I have given Yousouri my word on it.'

Rashid stared at him incredulously. 'You gave your word?' he cried, 'you promised to stop me bringing justice to the murderer of my own father and your cousin? I cannot believe it. No man would do such a thing, no man of honour or courage would so demean himself.'

'You forget yourself,' the Prince's tone was icy. 'I do not need a young boy to remind me of what is honourable. Nor do I forget your father. Since your own attempts have proved such signal failures I suggest you follow my advice for a change. It is only thanks to me that you are not even now in one of Yousouri's prisons.'

'I am sorry,' Rashid apologized humbly, 'truly sorry, I spoke without thinking.' He gave a sigh.

The Prince held out a small packet of papers. 'I have made arrangements for you to join d'Este's aircraft at Alexandria. If necessary you can journey all the way to New York with him. Neither he nor anyone else on board has ever seen you before so you will be safe from recognition. In here are your tickets, money and passport and papers in the name of Ahmed Yalchin Bey, a Turkish nobleman who has been visiting Egypt for the wedding ceremonies.'

Rashid took the old man's hands in his own and kissed them. 'How can I thank you?' he said with emotion. The Prince came out from behind the desk and embraced him. 'You must leave at once, a car waits to drive you to Alexandria. May God grant you success and a safe return.'

As soon as the prize ceremony at the Palace was over, and Desmond and Laura had received the huge silver-gilt cup from a beaming Farouk, delighted that his forecast had proved correct, Desmond slipped away to the moorings at Heliopolis to talk to Keith Payne and the engineers.

'I've kept the boys working round the clock,' the manager

235

told him. 'We found nothing major wrong but you were right to insist on a thorough one hundred hour overhaul and I'll back you up in my report.'

'Thanks, I suspect I can do with all the support I can get right now,' Desmond said. Payne shook his head doubtfully, 'Things may go all right for you,' he said, 'it's hard to tell. I wish you luck though. At least you'll be back on schedule again.'

'We'll launch her at first light tomorrow,' Payne added as he was about to leave, 'and put the gold on board straightaway afterwards, before the passengers or anyone else are around.' He gave a thin smile, 'and for God's sake don't have an accident with any of that or you really will be in trouble.'

The Cairo Motoring Club was giving a dinner to celebrate the race and honour the winner at Shepherd's that evening, but first Desmond wanted to find Ralph Kendricks and talk to him. Returning to the hotel he ran into Sandy on the terrace.

'I've contacted all the passengers and warned them we shall be leaving at half past seven tomorrow,' the young purser told him when he had finished congratulating his captain on his victory. 'Ken Frazer had spoken to some of them already. Mr. Curtis was very pleased, he seems in a great hurry to reach New York.'

'I know, he never misses an opportunity to tell me,' Desmond said. 'How's the passenger list. Any last minute changes?'

'There's a Turkish chap joining at Alex.,' Sandy answered. 'Oh, and Dr. Van Smit has decided to fly on all the way to New York with us.'

'I can't make him out at all,' Desmond remarked, 'have you any idea what he does?' but the boy shook his head. 'I think he's involved in mining in some way,' he hazarded. 'Certainly he always seems very interested in what Mr. Curtis is doing.'

Ralph Kendricks was not in his bedroom when Desmond called there. Searching through the bars and sitting rooms on the ground floor, he finally ran him to earth sitting alone in the garden by the open air dance floor of the night-club. The radio operator greeted him sheepishly.

'I'm sorry about last night,' he apologized, 'and for ducking out of the race. I've let you down pretty badly all round.' He was pale and careworn, Desmond noticed, but at least he was no longer drinking.

'You certainly have,' he agreed severely, 'The question is, what are you going to do about it?'

'I just don't know Skipper,' Ralph said helplessly, the misery evident in his face. 'I thought I had this Atlantic ditching fear licked. You've flown with me for the last three years and we've had our share of trouble in that time, but I've never lost my nerve before have I?' he appealed.

'No, you haven't, and speaking for myself, I still don't think you have,' Desmond told him, 'but you're frightened of doing so and it's having much the same result.'

Slowly the two men began to pace the garden, while Ralph spoke of his terrors and Desmond sought to reassure him and restore his confidence.

'Every flier has his own personal fear at the back of his mind,' he told the Radio Officer, 'but when the crunch comes somehow they always find the strength to carry on, and I know it will be the same with you. If I didn't I would never have taken you on to my crew.'

His Captain's calm words and evident trust in him went some way towards raising Ralph's morale and after another turn around the garden he was admitting that he had allowed the problem to assume an exaggerated degree of importance in his mind and had been making a fool of himself. Anxiously he begged Desmond to let him carry on as before and not to report the matter to the airline.

'Very well,' Desmond agreed, 'but for God's sake Ralph, if you find it's getting on top of you, come and talk to me about it, don't try drinking your troubles away by yourself,' and leaving the New Zealander professing his gratitude he went off to change for dinner.

He could only pray, he thought to himself as he went up in the lift, that Ralph would justify his confidence.

Entering the main dining suite, which had been specially set aside for the night, Desmond and Laura found the majority of the guests were already present. Both of them were immediately showered with congratulations and compliments from all sides.

'We've had one bit of trouble,' the senior race steward told Desmond as soon as he was able to get him alone for a moment. 'That chap d'Este's been claiming you purposely ran him off the road; accused you of driving deliberately dangerously and tried to file an objection to the result. Fortunately the judges over-ruled him. There's the fellow over there,' he pointed with his glass, 'I'm surprised he's had the gall to come.'

Following his glance Desmond saw Luca standing beside a remarkably beautiful woman in a white dress with a sad, shy air to her. 'Is that his wife?' he inquired with curiosity, and the other man nodded.

'Yes, she's the Baroness, and a pretty hard time of it she has, too, poor woman, by all accounts.' So now he had managed to alienate another of his passengers, Desmond thought to himself, just at the very time when he was most in need of supporters.

Dinner was a prolonged and wearying affair. There were over a hundred members and their guests seated in the dining-room and the atmosphere was informal and relaxed, though on the head table the scowling presence of Luca d'Este cast a slight air of awkwardness.

As his guests the Italian had invited Stewart Curtis and his wife, and whether by design or mischance, Desmond could not tell, he found Charlotte seated directly opposite him.

During the meal somewhat to his surprise, she scarcely addressed a word in his direction, but from time to time, she shot him a glance of such intensity that despite himself he felt uneasy stirrings of desire.

At long last the meal was over, and as the whole party moved through into the adjoining rooms she came up to him however, and touched his arm 'I must see you later,' she said in a low voice, 'I have something I want to give you.'

'Something for me?'

'Yes, it's a small prize for being the winner today. I thought you deserved more than just a silver cup,' and before he could reply to this she had slipped away through the throng.

Although pressed to stay on, Desmond escaped from the after-dinner drinking as soon as he decently could. Rescuing Laura from a group of admiring men, he took her for a walk in the gardens.

The night was very warm and clear, the still air scented with the smell of roses, oleander and bougainvillaea.

Putting his arms round Laura, Desmond kissed her long and hard on the mouth.

'I haven't thanked you properly yet for coming in the race with me,' he said a little while later. 'I thought you just did,' Laura smiled happily, laying her head against his chest, 'and anyway I really loved it, even if I was scared half to death.'

'You were frightened?' he stroked her hair softly, 'you didn't show it.'

'There were a couple of times,' she confessed, tightening her arms about him, 'like when the Baron hit the corner, and when the Bugatti crashed, but I trusted you to bring us out alive.'

They walked on in the dim light. 'I must go back I'm afraid,' Laura said, 'Mr. Curtis sometimes likes to give me a little work before he turns in for the night.'

They kissed again, holding each other close. He was amazed at how small and light she was, and he caressed her wonderingly. Then, letting go with reluctance, he led her back to the hotel.

Laura said goodnight and disappeared upstairs, but several of Desmond's friends dragged him off for a last nightcap, and it was some time before he was able to get away himself.

Thanks to his longstanding friendship with Freddy Muller, the hotel manager, Desmond had been booked into a large room with its own private balcony. Taking off his dinner jacket and tie he threw them down on the bed. As he did so a faint sound from the direction of the open french window made him look up. Charlotte Curtis was standing framed in the doorway.

'I've brought you your prize,' she said calmly. 'I couldn't find you downstairs so I came to wait for you up here.'

'How on earth did you manage to get in?' Desmond asked. Charlotte laughed lightly. 'I bribed one of the chambermaids. She was deliciously shocked at the idea. Aren't you going to open your prize?' She held out a small, flat, silver-wrapped box.

'I can't accept a present from you like this,' Desmond protested, 'it's impossible.'

'Nonsense, of course you can,' she told him, 'I got this long before I knew who would win the race, intending to give it to whoever came first. In fact I always thought it would be Luca. I'm much more glad it's turned out to be you,' and she thrust the box into his hands.

Undoing the wrapping, Desmond took off the lid and removed the layer of tissue paper inside. Charlotte's prize was a gold Cartier 'Tank' watch on a crocodile strap.

'No,' he said firmly, when he had seen what it was. 'I can't accept this. It's far too much.' Replacing the lid he handed the box back to her.

Charlotte looked crestfallen. 'But you must,' she said angrily, 'I so much want you to have it.'

'No, I'm sorry, it's out of the question,' he told her, 'and now I think you ought to go. Your husband will be wondering where you are.'

'Oh, him,' she said impatiently, 'he's all right, he's got Laura Hartman with him.'

Seeing Desmond stiffen slightly at the mention of her name, she stared at him hard for a second and then with another laugh shook her head sadly. 'Oh, so that's how it is, is it?' she said, 'My poor man, I thought you'd realized by now, surely you know Laura's been my husband's mistress for the last three years or more?'

'I don't believe you,'

'No,' Charlotte said in a soft spiteful voice, 'good, sweet innocent little Mrs. Hartman, fools everyone. Butter wouldn't melt in her mouth, but she likes nice jewellery and Schiaparelli dresses and travelling about the world. Why else do you think Stewart takes her off to South Africa by himself and leaves me behind up here?'

'But three years ago she was married,' Desmond said.

'Yes, and her husband was an alcoholic, and so might you have been if you had brought home a new wife and within a month of the wedding she was running around with your employer.'

She had moved in closer to him as she spoke and reaching up she stroked his cheek lightly. 'I know,' she murmured, 'it's hard; for me as well as for you, and you are not the first to be fooled like this,' Desmond pushed her hand away angrily. With a small sigh she put the box down on the table beside the bed. 'Wear the watch,' she said quietly, 'If I thought you could be bought that easily, I would never have given it to you. Maybe we have more in common, you and I, than you realize,' and with that she was gone, closing the door softly behind her.

Part Three

EUROPE

VII

By Cable: PERSONAL TO CAPT. D. O'NEILL, SHEPHERDS HOTEL, CAIRO: ESSENTIAL I SEE YOU TO DISCUSS OUR FUTURE PLANS. THIS IS IMPORTANT TO BOTH OF US. WILL STAY AT THE FARM WEDNESDAY NIGHT. LOVE PAMELA.

By Radio: IMPERIAL AIRWAYS OFFICE, LONDON TO CAPT. D. O'NEILL, COMMANDING G-ADHO CATERINA, FLIGHT IMPERIAL 109, CAIRO: ON ARRIVAL SOUTHAMPTON PREPARE TO ATTEND BOARD OF INQUIRY 5 p.m. TUESDAY, 14th MARCH INTO DEATH OF LIEUT. IAN THORNE AT SHAMBE STATION, SUDAN ON FRIDAY 10th MARCH. ENDS.

By Radio: IMPERIAL AIRWAYS CAIRO TO ALEXANDRIA AIR TRAFFIC CONTROL. 0740 HRS. IMPERIAL AIRWAYS G-ADHO CATERINA FLIGHT IMPERIAL 109 TO ALEXANDRIA, ATHENS AND ROME DEPARTED. E.T.A. ALEXANDRIA 0830 HRS. LOCAL TIME. ENDS.

THE train journey from Venice to Rome had taken more than seven hours, and it was not until after two o'clock in the morning that the Wienzmans, worn out by their anxieties and by the demands of travelling more than three hundred miles through the night across the breadth of Italy, arrived on Dr. Farenzi's doorstep and woke him from his sleep.

Throughout their time on the train neither Siegret nor her father had closed their eyes for a second. Despite the precautions they had taken on boarding they knew it was highly likely that German agents might still be following them, and they had scanned the faces of each person they saw, looking for any signs which would show that they were being pursued.

They had debated endlessly between themselves in whispers over what could possibly have given them away and brought Gerdler after them to Venice. Siegret's distress and terror on returning from her expedition had been so great that the Professor had never for an instant doubted that she had seen the Nazi youth. At first he had been inclined to think the Police chief Hans Meyer had been arrested and forced to betray them, in which case, as they both soon realized, the Nazis would have been hunting for them in Rome with Farenzi and not searching the streets of Venice.

'My belief is that they came to Venice because that is where they guessed we would be,' the Professor told his daughter, 'Gerdler must have been brought along because he would be able to recognize us, especially you,' he patted Siegret's arm reassuringly as she shivered. 'Provided we were not seen boarding this train, then we should be safe.'

'But suppose they did see us. What will we do then?' Siegret whispered back. 'They may be waiting for us at the other end.'

'Then we must take care to avoid being seen. I do not think they would dare to seize us openly here in Italy, and they do not appear to be receiving help from the authorities. At worst they will follow us to Farenzi's and we must hope he can be of some help.'

Their best plan they decided, once they reached Rome, was for them both to leave the train separately, and meet up again outside the station to take a taxi across to the Doctor's apartment. Siegret was so weak with fear when the moment came for her to descend from the carriage, that it was almost beyond her strength to walk down the platform and through the barrier at the end. The stations seemed to be full of men watching the new arrivals suspiciously. Trying to behave as inconspicuously as possible she ducked her head down and made for the exits.

Rome seemed very brightly lit and busy for so late at night. The taxi sped through the streets, while Siegret and her father peered from the rear window, trying to see if they were being followed. The glare of the lights and the general activity made it hard for them to tell however and to their tired and anxious eyes it seemed as though every car on the road was pursuing them.

They passed through the gap in the Aurelian walls into the Corso. Here, in a small side road off the main street, Dr. Farenzi lived in an apartment overlooking the Borghese Gardens.

It seemed an eternity before he answered his bell, but when he did appear, a small alert man, who somehow contrived to look dapper even in pyjamas and a dressing-gown, he grasped the situation at once and hustled them inside.

'You will be safe here tonight,' he assured them, fussing about to make up beds and heat up drinks. 'Even if you were followed as far as the building they will have no way of discovering in which apartment you are hiding before morning, and then we will find you somewhere safe until we can get you off to America.'

'America,' the Professor echoed with a deep sigh. 'How I wish we were there.'

'And so you shall be,' Farenzi answered determinedly. 'Mussolini and Hitler are not quite the allies many would like us to believe, and the Nazis are on their own here. In the morning we will see what must be done, but for the present sleep. Off to your rooms. I will lock the door and if anyone tries to break in, I have a gun and will not hesitate to use it if necessary.'

His words took away some of their fears, but as Siegret switched out her light she peered out of her window into the street below before getting into bed. There, sure enough, at the far end of the road under the trees, was parked a black car, which had not been there when they had arrived.

Although Pat Jarrett had rightly concluded that the area around Warren Lake was sparsely populated, unknown to him his activities had already attracted notice. Returning from a round of some outlying farms on Saturday afternoon, county sheriff Hal Franklin had spotted the tyre marks of the pick-up in the slush at the junction with the dirt road leading up to the lake. At the time he had been half inclined to follow them up to see which house by the water was being visited. All were locked up still after the winter and it was unusual for anyone to come down from the cities this early in the year. Even the workers hired from nearby Keene to put the houses in order for the summer were not to be expected before the beginning of May.

Stopping his car and examining the marks more carefully he had seen that the vehicle had returned down the track and taken the road towards the town. Most probably it was some local person who had been up to see if the lake was clear yet. Warren Lake was famous in that part of the country for the size and hunger of its trout, especially near the dam at the southern end. Hal himself spent much of his free time up there. Deciding that a check on the house could wait until the following morning he drove on.

The next day being Sunday however, with both his deputies off, there was no time to go out to the lake and it was not until early on Monday morning that he returned. He saw at once that the road had been used several times during his absence; the slush and mud was heavily rutted and there were marks of at least two different sets of tyres, one of them belonging to a heavy truck, judging by the width of the tracks and the way the soft ground at the edge of the road had been gouged out.

Leaving his car halfway up the road Hal made the rest of the journey on foot. He was anxious that whoever was up at the lake should receive no warning of his coming. The woods were very quiet and still and the sound of an engine would carry some way.

He was surprised to see how clear the water was, the ice had completely vanished and the brisk breeze was ruffling the surface. He paused by the edge of the trees and swept the shore with his binoculars, but apart from a few waterfowl feeding near the dam there was no sign of anything unusual. The tracks led up towards the northern end and he checked the houses there, shifting the glass from one to another, but still, as far as he could see nothing had been disturbed.

It was not until he reached the point that he saw the truck. It had been parked off the trail beneath the trees. 'Can I help you Sheriff?'

Hal spun round to face the speaker. He saw a middle-aged man, with a lean hard face, dressed in white overalls standing at the head of the path leading down to the house. The path was grass covered but even so Hal realized the man must have come up it fast and quietly.

'Sorry if I startled you Sheriff, I guess you didn't hear me coming. The name's Jarrett and I've rented the house here for a couple of months. I see you're looking at my truck.' The man gave a brief smile as he spoke, but there was no warmth in his voice.

'I was wondering what anyone was doing up here,' Hal answered, 'We don't normally get visitors this early in the year.'

'Sure,' the man nodded, 'I was going to come into town tomorrow and let you know I was here. Would you like to step down to the house and check the papers? See that everything's O.K. I mean?'

The house was the biggest on the lake, inside it was fitted out with every comfort. The kitchen had been cleaned of the accumulated dust of winter and it was there that Jarrett produced a copy of a rental agreement with the owners.

'You on vacation?' Hal asked when he returned and the man shook his head.

' 'Fraid not. I'm doing a meteorological survey in the area for a couple of the airlines and I reckoned this'd be as good a base as any. I was just unpacking my equipment when you came.'

It all sounded quite reasonable, Hal thought to himself, there was nothing he could pick out as being wrong, and yet somehow he didn't like any of it. The man Jarrett had been odd, ice-cold and hostile one minute, pressing him to come inside the next. There was something too in the way he looked and moved, something wary and alert about the eyes.

Then again why had he taken the biggest house on the lake side, just for himself? Clearly he was only using the kitchen; the living-room had scarcely been touched and there were five more unused bedrooms upstairs. The man had brought a small motor launch with him, Hal had seen it moored down below from the windows of the lounge, he must have towed that up with him behind the truck. Perhaps that was the reason for the truck's presence. Certainly Jarrett hadn't enough heavy equipment with him otherwise to warrant its use.

Mr. Jarrett, he decided, would repay having a discreet eye kept on him, until it became clear exactly what he was up to.

Dr. Van Smit pushed aside his half finished coffee in the breakfast room at Shepherd's and rose resignedly to his feet. Early morning starts, necessary in air travel to avoid the turbulence which tended to increase during the late afternoon, did not bother him, though for many passengers, he knew, they were the only inconvenience in an otherwise ideal journey.

This particular start however was one which he had been intending to avoid. Originally his plans had envisaged travelling no further than Cairo and, after a brief but extravagant holiday, returning to South Africa. The failure of his search of Stewart Curtis' suite on the night of the ball had changed everything, and mentally he damned the maid for returning so early.

Without doubt, he was sure, the suite would have yielded a small fortune in cash and jewellery, the kind of things people of wealth would never move without. True, the best pieces would have been in the hotel safe, or actually being worn by Charlotte, but there had still been a perfect opportunity to pick up some of the smaller bits, and such items were actually easier and safer to dispose of than larger and better known stones.

Van Smit had entered the world of crime almost by chance some fifteen years ago, when out of a job and heavily in debt as a result of his gambling, he had helped a drunk met in a bar in Durban back to his hotel room and in doing so had discovered the man was carrying a roll of bank-notes totalling more than seventeen thousand rands.

This windfall had prompted him to experiment in robbing other wealthy travellers, till he had reached a point where he had come to rely upon it. Always, when his fortunes at cards on the table shrank beneath his losses, he recouped them by looting the rooms of nearby hotels.

Very probably, had he not been relatively successful at his gaming during these past years, Van Smit would have been tracked down and arrested, but the comparative infrequency of his operations, as well as the skill and cunning with which he carried them out, had so far kept him from discovery. It was even possible for him to go about under his own name, merely putting out the fiction that he was still engaged in his former occupation of geologist.

When he had first learnt of Stewart Curtis' presence in the Cape, the financier had seemed a natural target for his talents. Van Smit had not in fact been over short of funds at that precise point, but the prospect of a visit to Cairo and its casinos had attracted him strongly and he had been confident of his ability to lift a large sum from the millionaire before the latter left the city. Accordingly he had booked on *Imperial 109*.

Events however had not gone his way. On the journey up through Africa, Curtis had been nervous and jumpy, scarcely ever leaving his private cabin even for meals, while the accident at Shambe had put the remainder of those on board in a similar mood. Once in Cairo he had only had the one opportunity to go over their rooms, owing to the constant presence of the maid, the hotel servants or Laura Hartman, and even this had proved abortive.

Meanwhile, his nightly forays to the casinos and gambling clubs had been disastrous, draining him of most of his reserves of cash, so that whereas a raid on the Curtis' possessions had once been merely a usefully rewarding exercise, it had now become a vital necessity. At some point between Cairo and New York he must pull off a really spectacular raid.

Perhaps during the stop-over in Rome and England he might have a chance. At least with the two d'Estes joining the flight the number of his wealthy fellow passengers had been doubled.

It was cold on the river down at Heliopolis. The great golden disc of the sun hung on the very edge of the horizon, gilding the landscape with fire as it rose, but the warmth had yet to stir the air and the morning was chilly and crisp. Wreaths of mist still lay over the fields, slowly dispersing as the new day took hold.

Caterina rode on the water once more, the light glinting from her freshly cleaned wings and hull. She was moored between the double sided Braby pontoons, tail into the bank, while a stream of porters passed back and forth loading in the coloured canvas mail bags. On the starboard wing mechanics were making final adjustments to the inboard engine. Beside *Caterina* two other 'C' class boats lay moored nearby, attached by their prows to buoys in midstream.

Desmond watched the scene from the doorway of the Airline Office at the head of the pier. He and the crew had been up since half past five to see the gold brought from the military barracks and stowed away in the holds, making sure that the cargo's weight was correctly distributed fore and aft and placed so as not to upset the aircraft's trim. Then there had followed an exhaustive inspection and check-over of every piece of equipment on board from the carburetter heaters to the rear trim tabs; an inspection which had turned up three or four minor faults which the mechanics were even now putting right.

Pulling the cable from his jacket he took another look at it, puzzling again over the meaning behind the laconic phrases. Coming so hard on her previous letter, it was difficult to know what to make of his wife's latest message. Most likely he feared, Pamela was building up to one of her periodic outbursts.

He had experienced these outbursts frequently during their married life together, and had never ceased to dread them. In her rage Pamela would lash out indiscriminately, seeking to hurt in any way she could, and all too often she succeeded. Her cruel, vindictive tongue would strike without mercy, poisoning their affection and love for one another and tearing the relationship they had laboured to construct, into shreds around them.

All this had come on top of Charlotte Curtis' allegation concerning Laura Hartman last night, with the result that he felt emotionally drained before the day had even begun. For the most part he was disinclined to believe Charlotte's story. Nevertheless, however, Charlotte's words had effectively pulled him up short and made him realize how near and how quickly he was coming to committing himself to a girl whom he scarcely knew.

For both their sakes he had decided, it would be better to take the affair more calmly, and allow themselves time to think. Like himself, Laura was still in a vulnerable state after the loss of her husband and it would be unfair to her to try and rush into a situation which might prove to be unworkable.

Usually the prospect of returning to the air after a spell on the ground was a pleasant one, to which Desmond looked forward. Today, however, the sight of the gold being loaded under the protection of rifle carrying soldiers, and the knowledge that a hostile reception awaited his arrival in England, served to depress his spirits.

The reserve in his manner towards Laura when she greeted him at the gangway, was more marked than he intended.

A look of hurt surprise passed over her face and seeing it, he felt instantly contrite. He tried clumsily to make amends, but the damage was done and his attempts only made matters worse. 'This is Mademoiselle Arlette Ducrois, Mrs. Curtis' maid,' she said icily, indicating a nondescript woman of about forty in a plain grey dress who accompanied her and, her lips compressed tightly with anger and humiliation, she turned stiffly away and disappeared into the aircraft, leaving him cursing under his breath, having to force himself to be polite to the other passengers.

The Kings, the Finlays and the Johnsons were all on board, together with Van Smit, which left only the Curtises and their friends the d'Estes to come. Protocol and civility demanded that Desmond be on hand to receive them, but the thought of doing so was more than he could stand; handing over to Sandy Everett he went back up to the flight deck.

Here the atmosphere was less strained than it had been on Saturday, Ken Frazer was whistling happily to himself as he laid out the route maps and chinagraph marking pencils. Ralph too was in a noticeably happier state of mind, now that he was facing up to his fears and no longer struggling to conceal them. Sliding into his seat, Desmond adjusted the safety belt.

'That's a nice watch,' Frazer commented as he did so, and Desmond's eyes flicked guiltily to his wrist.

'It was a prize for winning the race, donated by Mr. and Mrs. Curtis,' he explained shortly.

'A Cartier isn't it? Mind if I have a look?' Desmond unbuckled the strap and handed the watch over to Frazer without comment. He felt angry with himself for being so weak as to put it on in the morning when he dressed. Paradoxically it had been his annoyance with Charlotte for her behaviour and his exasperation with the events of the last three days which had prompted him to do so. At least he had felt he would have gained something out of the mess into which he had fallen.

Sandy stuck his head round the corner of the flight deck, 'All passengers aboard and settled down, Skipper,' he reported, 'and all cargo safely stowed. Ready to take off when you are.'

'Thanks Sandy,' Desmond reached forward and flicked on the main ignition switch. 'Cast off the prow warps Ralph,' he called, 'and let's get moving.'

The time was exactly seven thirty-five: by half past eight they should be in Alexandria.

Charlotte had invited Jacquetta and Luca to share their cabin in the stern, a suggestion which the Baron had accepted with alacrity, with the result that they were all comfortably installed, together with their personal possessions by the time the gangway was drawn up and the hatches closed.

Jacquetta had never before been in a flying-boat, and it was an exhilarating experience to her. When at last the noise and vibration ceased and the foaming track vanished beneath them, revealing the great city spread out below in the morning sun, she lay back in her seat with a sense of real enjoyment.

Andy Draper came round once level flight was in progress, serving coffee and hot bread rolls. The others chattered among themselves, but Jacquetta remained lost in her own thoughts. Luca was still fawning over Charlotte yet the spectacle no longer bothered her. Ever since the ordeal in the desert, her mind had run more and more upon the young Sheikh who had rescued her. In her fantasies she conjured up Rashid's proud, youthful face. In a way, she found she regretted not having told him her name.

Andy brought coffee up to the flight deck as soon as he had attended to the passengers. Desmond had throttled back the engines, and synchronized their timing. Now with the auto pilot on they were free to sit back and enjoy the view.

'So how are they behaving below decks Andy?' Ken Frazer asked jovially. He had been inspired to his unusual cheerfulness by the news of the radio message received by his captain. 'Any complaints so far?'

'Not yet sir,' Andy rejoined, 'but if you like I can tell them you will be bringing us in to land at Alex.' There was a snort of amusement from Kendricks at this; and even Desmond smiled. Frazer however was too full of himself at the thought of Desmond's impending downfall to care and he ignored the steward's riposte.

'Baron d'Este and Mr. Curtis were asking for you,' Andy went on, speaking to Desmond, 'they were wondering why you weren't at the hatch when they came aboard. I told 'em you'd had an urgent radio message from the British Ambassador and that shut 'em up.'

'Stewart Curtis' wife has joined him hasn't she?' remarked Kendricks from the radio desk. 'What's she like Andy? Is she as bad as the old man?' Andy shrugged. 'Seems like all the others to me. Wanting this, wanting that, why does the aeroplane fly so high? When do we stop for lunch?' The others on the flight deck laughed. 'Tell you one who is different though,' he added, 'and that's Baroness d'Este. There's a real lady now. You can have all the rest.'

'I thought Laura Harman was your favourite Andy,' Ralph Kendricks said with a wink at Desmond. 'Oh, well that's different,' Draper answered, 'I mean she's like one of us now isn't she?'

The others laughed, while at the controls Desmond stared straight ahead out of the cockpit windows.

Prince Suleiman's villa stood on the shores of the Mediterranean, amid the groves of an eucalyptus forest, on land belonging to the estate of the royal palace of Montazah. Smaller and less magnificent than his Cairo residence, it was nevertheless a beautiful and spacious building, with wide marble terraces and emerald lawns sloping down to the sea.

In the master bedroom Rashid dressed carefully. It was fortunate, he told himself, that on his arrival in Egypt he had taken the trouble to have a number of suits made for him by Cairo's leading tailors as well as a sufficient quantity of shirts in silk and finest sea island cotton.

He had chosen a very well cut pearl grey double-breasted suit, a mauve shirt and a white tie in heavy slab silk. Fortunately, to assume the part of a Turkish nobleman, it was no longer necessary, thanks to the reforming zeal of Mustafa Kemal, to wear a fez, and accordingly he chose for himself a soft, wide-brimmed hat. His years spent in Rome had made him almost more at home in modern western dress than he was in his traditional robes, and it was with a sense of pride that he stepped back and surveyed the finished result in the mirrors.

Very soon the flying-boat from Cairo would touch down on the water in the western harbour, and he would go on board, unknown to d'Este and those travelling with him. Then when the moment was right he would reveal his identity and watch the Italian's face dissolve in fear as he realized that he was about to be called upon to expiate his crimes.

Collecting his papers and the generous supply of money given him by the Prince, he wandered leisurely downstairs and out on to the terrace. There was something very satisfying he thought, as he strolled in the cool morning, listening to the waves; something very fine, in dressing with care and great elegance, in order to go out and kill a man.

A faint humming sound reached his ears from the distance in the north. The airliner was approaching the coast. Rashid drew in a deep breath of the sea air, filling his lungs; it was time for Ahmed Yalchin Bey to take the stage.

At the request of Charlotte Curtis and the others in the after saloon Desmond took *Caterina* round in a slow, low level circuit of the city, to give the passengers a good view of Alexandria and Lake Mareotis before beginning his run into the harbour.

By a window in the midship cabin Laura Hartman gazed out at the scene below and tried to match the enthusiasm of Harold King and his wife who were exclaiming in wonder at the aerial view of the glittering domes and minarettes of the gorgeous palace of Ras el Tin, the Cape of Figs, built by Mohammed Ali the Great on the site of one of the former seven wonders of the ancient world: The Pharos Lighthouse of Alexandria.

Laura herself was feeling anything but enthusiasm and interest in her surroundings. In her mind she was still trying to discover a reason for Desmond O'Neill's sudden change of attitude towards her. In the garden of the hotel the previous evening he had been loving and tender and she had gone to bed happier than she could remember being at any time since her marriage. His coldness when they had met this morning, coming in the face of her affectionate greeting, had hurt her desperately, so much so that she had had to grit her teeth and bite her lip to keep a hold on herself.

The long sweep of the Corniche facing the sea front and Alexandria's famous beaches, slid past beneath them as *Caterina* flew out over the pale pink towers of the Montazah Palace at its eastern end and swung round again to approach the harbour. It was possible, Laura supposed, that Desmond was feeling that their emotions were becoming too involved too quickly, and if so he might well be right, but if that were the case, she still could not believe he would have reacted so harshly. There had to be something more.

The possibility of Charlotte Curtis being involved occurred to her, but she dismissed the idea with scarcely a thought. On several occasions over the week-end, Desmond had been at pains to make it clear that he wanted to have nothing to do with the lady, and it was hardly likely that he would change his mind so quickly. A more probable cause she felt, might be connected in some way with his marriage, but here again it was difficult to think what could have arisen so suddenly, quite literally during the passage of the night.

The flying-boat came in low over the sea, dropping towards the western harbour as Desmond throttled back the engines. From the windows the white sails of the feluccas clustered round the shore were clearly visible and tied up at the quays could be seen several large steamers, as well as the squat grey outline of two warships.

Alexandria was also one of the most important flying-boat stations in the world, where traffic from Africa merged with that coming in from Asia, India, the Far East and Australia to link up with European routes. This was especially true for Imperial Airways, and at any one time half a dozen of the line's aircraft might be found there, slipping crews, undergoing repairs, or simply waiting to take on more fuel, cargo and passengers before taking off again to resume their long journeys.

For Sandy Everett the halt at Alexandria was always one of his busiest periods. Here there was invariably an immense amount of mail to be checked and transhipped, to destinations in the east, and yet more to be taken on board for carriage to Europe and North America. The bags which he had sorted through during the flight up to the delta and arranged carefully according to area, had now to be handed out in order through the mailroom hatch, and the incoming ones stacked ready for him to deal with as soon as they had regained the air.

There were people to be taken care of too. The Finlays were disembarking here, to continue their journey home by sea. Perhaps fulfilling an ambition as they claimed, but more likely Sandy guessed with insight, simply to put off their return to the strange and forgotten homeland where they would spend the remainder of their days.

In their place there came on board Ahmed Yalchin Bey.

Alexandria, being on this flight only a refuelling and loading stop, the passengers were permitted to disembark and stroll around on the piers in the sun, admiring the nearby palace on the tongue of land between the harbour and the sea, and the view of the city, but there was no time for them to venture further afield. The majority of the passengers, after stretching their legs for a while, resumed their seats and waited quietly for the flight to continue.

For her own part Jacquetta d'Este preferred to remain outside. It was pleasantly warm and bright on the pier side and a fresh breeze was blowing, bringing with it the scents of the sea and an interesting mixture of wood, tar, oil and smoke from the docks. On the feluccas, the fishermen were laying out their nets to dry in the sun, picking them over carefully for holes, while around them a horde of small boys clambered about, swabbing off the decks, and furling and unfurling the sails. Not far away on the foreshore a group of men squatting round a small fire were drinking hot, sweet mint tea out of tiny delicate cups.

Desmond O'Neill, she could see from where she stood, talking with the crews from some of the other aeroplanes which were tied up alongside the jetties and pontoons of the airline piers. Evidently Alexandria was a meeting place for fliers from all over the world, somewhere where they could exchange news and renew old friendships. The transfer of mail to *Caterina* was still in progress watched by a section of uniformed police. A security precaution she supposed, to prevent packets from going astray.

She did not at first notice the car which approached silently from the direction of the Corniche, and it was only when she started to walk back towards the flying-boat that she saw it had drawn up at the foot of the pier, and the driver was talking to one of the crew members, evidently asking for directions. Possibly the man was having difficulty in making himself understood, for whatever reason there was a short delay and Jacquetta was only twenty yards away when the rear door of the car opened and Rashid stepped out.

There could be no doubt as to the identity of the newcomer. She recognized him instantly, even here in the last place on earth she had expected to find him, and in the unfamiliar European dress. He was carrying his hat and as she caught sight of the clean cut, handsome face her heart gave a leap.

Competing emotions flooded through her: the thrill of seeing him again fighting with terror at the thought of what he had come to do, excitement at his presence and fear at the threat he posed.

Setting the hat firmly on his head Rashid strode down the pier towards the gangway. At its rail, the policemen moved forward to intercept him and as they did so a fresh anxiety swept over Jacquetta. Surely it was for this reason the detachment had been placed there? Not to watch the transfer of mail sacks, which in any case was taking place at the same time on a number of other aircraft. The authorities must have got wind of his plan and laid a trap for him.

Even as she watched horror struck, waiting for the moment of arrest when the police would seize him and drag him off; to her amazement, the officer in charge stood aside and saluted courteously, permitting the elegant figure to pass up the gangway and disappear through the hatch.

Jacquetta was now in a state of utter confusion, torn by opposing loyalties. She felt mesmerized by the danger of the situation which faced her, unable to think what action to take. Almost in a dream she followed Rashid's path down to the gangway.

'I'm afraid I must ask you to go aboard Baroness. We shall be leaving again very soon.' Sandy Everett was smiling at her at the foot of the steps but she scarcely realized he had spoken. Trembling with anxiety and nervous tension, with no idea of what she would say or do when confronted with Rashid, she went through into *Caterina*'s interior.

Thanks to a sleeping draught which Dr. Farenzi had surreptitiously emptied into her nightcap, Siegret slept more soundly than she would have believed possible. Awaking, she saw at once from the sunlight on the curtains that the hour was already late, and sprang hurriedly from her bed.

The knowledge that pursuit was not far away weighed on her spirits, but the warm sparkle of the Roman spring on the rooftops and on the gardens in the Park, added to the fact that the street was now virtually lined with cars making it impossible to pick out the one belonging to the watchers, lightened her depression. The very thought that they had passed the night in safety added weight to Dr. Farenzi's assertion that the Nazis would find it no easy task to snatch them back to Germany.

Throwing a dressing gown on over her nightdress she went through into the living area and found her father and the Doctor discussing their position over breakfast.

'Dr. Farenzi is of the opinion that we should take a ship or an aeroplane to the United States as soon as possible,' the Professor said when he had kissed her. 'We have been looking in the paper to see which is suitable.'

'Yes,' the Doctor agreed, pouring her coffee and setting fruit and bread rolls before her. Dressed in the black jacket and striped trousers of a consultant physician, he looked neater and smarter than ever. 'There are no sailings which you could take until the middle of the week, but there is a flight tomorrow, British Imperial Airways, going to England and New York. If we can get you seats, you would be in America by Friday.'

'But could we leave so soon? What about the visas?' Siegret asked. 'I thought we still had to wait for them.'

'A good Doctor, my dear, like a good cook, can always be sure of a welcome wherever he goes,' Farenzi replied. 'I will telegraph to friends of mine in the profession in America, eminent men who will be glad to assist and to recommend your father's admittance.'

'In the meantime however, do you believe it is safe for us to remain here?' Siegret's father asked. 'For your sake as well as our own I think we should find a place elsewhere tonight.'

'You are right,' Farenzi mused for a few moments. 'I have friends who can be trusted and might let you stay. I will see if they are willing when I got to collect the airline tickets.'

It was agreed therefore that while the doctor went off to the Imperial Airways office in the Via Nazionale, the Professor and Siegret would repack their clothes and be ready to leave with him by eleven o'clock.

Rintlen and Gerdler had not been able to reach Rome before seven o'clock that morning, after travelling all night. Already tired and angry from the long frustrating day in Venice, the SD officer's temper had not been improved by having had to share a sleeping compartment with the youth, owing to a shortage of accommodation on the train. On arrival in the capital, red eyed and unshaven, they were driven to the German Embassy.

'Well,' Rintlen demanded when the secretary who had received them had departed, leaving them alone with the head of the SS security section. 'What have you managed to do so far?'

'We picked them out at the station, Standartenfuhrer, although they tried to slip past us singly,' the man launched into a lengthy description of their success in tracking the Wienzmans to the street off the Corso.

'Unfortunately we have so far been unable to discover which of the apartments they are hiding in,' he finished. 'List of occupants,' Rintlen snapped curtly and the officer hastily held out a sheet of paper.

'I see here,' Rintlen ran his eye down the list of names, 'I see here a Dr. Augusto Farenzi living in apartment No. 12. Bring me a medical dictionary. I want to know more about him.'

'As I thought,' he was saying a moment later when the volume in question had been produced. 'Here we are: Farenzi Augusto. Consultant Physician, student – University of Milan and,' he tapped the page triumphantly, 'from 1905 until 1910, at the Faculty of Medicine in the University of Vienna. Where he would most certainly have met another student, there at the same time, by the name of David Wienzman.'

The SS officer was impressed by this display of resourcefulness. 'Shall we go in at once and grab them?' he asked. 'My men can be relied on to carry out the job.'

Rintlen eyed his watch. 'No,' he said, 'it's too early. There will be people about in the other apartments and I want as little disturbance as possible. Tell your men to continue watching the apartment and to report anything that moves. I shall have a bath and a couple of hours more sleep. Wake me at ten o'clock and then we will go and pay our errant Professor and his daughter a visit.'

Entering *Caterina*'s passenger deck through the hatchway into the promenade deck, Jacquetta found to her surprise, that Rashid was nowhere to be seen. The Johnsons and their daughter were standing by one of the windows watching the activity on board a neighbouring aircraft, and Charlotte Curtis' maid was occupying one of the corner seats at the rear. The steward, she realized must have shown him through into the midship cabin or the smoking saloon. With no clear idea of what she should do Jacquetta returned to her seat in the rear of the plane.

Luca and Stewart Curtis were discussing the merits of empire to the obvious boredom of Charlotte, who was wandering about the cabin in a desultory fashion and grumbling at the continual delay.

'I can't see why we're still waiting,' she was saying querulously as Jacquetta entered, 'they finished loading the mail twenty minutes ago.' Her anger, Jacquetta guessed, was due to Desmond's continued failure to put in an appearance with the passengers. The two men ignored her.

'Of course you will agree,' Luca remarked, lighting a cigarette, 'that Italy has every right to her territories in Africa, just as Britain and France do to theirs?'

'Certainly,' Curtis agreed, 'but at the same time it is essential to ensure that the great powers do not come to blows over the possession of some trivial strip of land, as nearly happened at Fashoda.'

His wife shot him a venomous glance. 'How a man as heavily involved in armaments as you are can say that I can't imagine,' she snapped, 'nothing would suit you better than a war.'

Curtis rounded on her, his face heavy with anger, but just then they heard the sound of the engines bursting into life again and felt the familiar trembling of the hull as the flying-boat began to taxi away from the pier and out into the main harbour. Charlotte flung herself down in her seat with a sigh of relief.

The realization that they were taking off once more woke Jacquetta abruptly from the fit of abstraction into which she had fallen. She had, she now saw, allowed the situation to go by default. Had she sought out Rashid straightaway and confronted him, the young Sheikh would have had no choice but to abandon his schemes and go back on shore. In which case his chances of catching up with them before they reached America would have been slim.

Now this was impossible and she was left with the choice of denouncing him to the crew and seeing him arrested and perhaps condemned as a would be murderer, or of standing by while he avenged the crimes committed against his family, killing Luca and perhaps herself as well.

The two men were still engaged in conversation and Charlotte was leafing idly through the pages of *Vogue* as *Caterina* climbed out over the Mediterranean in the brilliant sunshine and settled down to cruise at 4000 feet for the hour long flight to Crete. Bringing herself to a decision, Jacquetta slipped quietly out of the cabin and made her way forward to find Rashid.

Since the Johnsons had been joined on the promenade deck by Dr. Van Smit and Laura Hartman who were gazing at the view of the Egyptian coast receding behind them, and the Kings were still in their accustomed seats, she knew before she reached the smoking saloon in the aircraft's nose that she would find Rashid there alone.

He was sitting with his back to her when she entered, a cigarette in an amber holder between his long fingers. Their eyes met instantly and he leapt to his feet in surprise.

'Who are you? And what are you doing here?' he demanded.

'Please,' Jacquetta begged, 'don't be alarmed, I know who you are and why you are here. I won't give you away, but you must leave, get off this plane before they realize who you are,' Rashid's eyes fastened sternly on her. 'What is this? Who are you?' he demanded for the second time.

Jacquetta shrank back from his gaze and the words dried up in her mouth. Grasping her by the arm, Rashid shook her, repeating his question.

'I'm the woman you rescued from the desert,' she faltered, and then, unable to hold back and conceal the truth any longer, 'I am Jacquetta d'Este,' she cried.

There was silence in the room for a moment, then Rashid let out his breath in a long slow rasp. 'So you are Baron d'Este's wife.' He stared at her hard. 'What are you going to do now Baroness?' he accented the last word viciously. 'Are you going to tell your husband and the rest of them who I am?' Jacquetta shook her head, unable to speak.

'Why not?' he said derisively, plainly not believing her. Jacquetta found her voice.

'If I do, you'll be arrested,' she said, dry mouthed.

'And you care?' She nodded silently. 'Why, because I saved your life, is that it?'

'I don't know, I just care,' Jacquetta told him, 'I couldn't bear you to be taken.'

'And your husband? You know what lies between us, what I have sworn to avenge on him?' Jacquetta hung her head. That question she could not answer, even to herself.

There was a noise behind her in the passageway, the South African Dr. Van Smit was returning from the promenade deck. 'Ah, Baroness,' he remarked, seeing them both. 'Have you been introduced to the newest member of our company: Ahmed Yalchin Bey, the Baroness d'Este.'

Rashid bowed low. With a supreme effort of will Jacquetta managed to summon up the strength to appear normal. 'Thank you,' she answered faintly in English, 'we had just met. Now if you will excuse me, I was looking for the steward,' and before the others could reply, she turned and fled from the cabin.

From the windows of the flight deck the peaks and pinnacles of Crete's mountain ranges were faintly visible on the horizon, rising out of the deep, even blue of the sea whose wrinkled surface was frozen motionless by the 4000 feet of air beneath them. At intervals, minute, toy-like ships were to be seen crawling along the routes which led to Suez and the canal, or heading northwards towards the Aegean ports, and through the Hellespont to the Sea of Marmara and Istanbul.

Desmond had switched over to the autopilot, allowing *Caterina* to fly herself, while he and the others watched the peaceful scene slide past the windows, lulled into drowsiness after the early start by the steady drone of the flying-boat's engines, driving them onwards through the clear, bright air.

The memory of his behaviour towards Laura filled him with guilt. He still refused to believe in Charlotte Curtis' poisonous allegation, her reasons for making it were all too easy to see, yet each time he thought about it he felt a hot surge of jealousy and anger. More than anything he knew he wanted to talk to Laura, to explain what had happened, and apologize for the unintentional hurt he had caused her. He would have to try and get her alone in Rome that evening.

Pamela too preoccupied his thoughts. That her telegram signalled the opening of a fresh bout in the struggle between them, just when he had thought it was all over, he had no doubt and he dreaded the prospect of the emotional mangling which her bitter insecurity would put them both through. Worst of all was the possibility that she was having second thoughts about the divorce. The decree would not be finalized for another five weeks. Her reason for wanting to see him might be to persuade him to agree to a withdrawal.

The contrast with the emotions expressed in her earlier letter meant nothing. Pamela spent her life swinging from one extreme to another: hating one moment, loving the next; her fount of nervous energy forcing her to the limits of each new course she chose, sweeping aside all opposition to her decisions.

'We should be over Mirabella in a little under fifty minutes skipper,' Ralph Kendricks' voice cut in on his thoughts, 'shall I call them up and make sure they're ready for us?' Breaking out of his reverie Desmond examined the oblong, Roman figured dial of the Cartier watch. 'Yes, you had better Ralph,' he said, yawning and stretching as he spoke. 'I want to get away again to Athens as soon as we can.'

Mirabella was the landing area at Crete, from there it was an hour or so's flying time on to the Greek mainland and Athens. The time was ten-forty a.m.

A somewhat hesitant and worried embassy servant woke Rintlen at a quarter to eleven. 'You were sleeping so deeply Standartenfuhrer, I did not like to disturb you,' he apologized

266

when the SD officer had looked at the time and cursed him for his tardiness.

Still swearing, Rintlen rolled out of the bed and dragged himself off to the bathroom to shave and wash. The three hours he had spent asleep had left him feeling distinctly worse, groggy and hungover, and he regretted his weakness in succumbing to his weariness. Running a bath he began to shave, calling for the latest information on the Wienzman's movements as he did so.

'We have established that Farenzi indeed has the others in the apartment with him,' the head of the SS section shouted through to him from the bedroom. 'Voices have been heard through the door. He left the building shortly before ten o'clock and drove his car to the Via Nazionale. Judging from his behaviour he may have been aware he was being followed. He tried to shake off our man and evidently thought he had succeeded in doing so because he subsequently was seen going into the office of Imperial Airways on the ground floor of the Guirinal Hotel. Our man is fairly certain that he bought tickets there.'

'What flight and when? Did he find out any details?' Rintlen demanded.

'No, Standartenfuhrer, such information was impossible to discover. You know how secretive the British are in such matters.'

'Well, keep trying. Where is Farenzi now?' Rintlen rinsed the soap off his face.

'He went off in the direction of the Vatican City. There have been no further reports since then,' the officer told him.

'Then we will hit the apartment and grab the two Jews while he is absent,' Rintlen decided. 'That will save us having to find a way to dispose of him. Have your men ready to leave as soon as I have dressed, and in the meantime,' he called, 'bring me a glass of schnapps.'

The Doctor had promised to be back by eleven. When the hour had come and gone, signalled by the chimes of the city's numerous church bells, the fears of the two refugees grew

267

more intense with each passing minute. Peeping anxiously from a window in the sitting-room, Siegret was maintaining a watch on the street and to her dismay had discovered that at least one of the cars parked below was occupied. The heads of two men were discernible in the front seats.

Her agitation increased further when the quarter hour struck and still there was no sign of the Doctor returning. Then two men approached down the street from the direction of the Corso and got into the same car in which the other two were already sitting. She waited, praying it would now drive off, but it remained an immobile, silent menace.

'Yes, it must be them,' her father agreed when she called him over, 'I suppose they managed to follow us last night after all,' and he squeezed her hand as he spoke, to reassure her.

'What shall we do Papa?' she asked in a trembling voice, 'how shall we ever get away from here?'

'We shall find a way. When Farenzi returns he will know what to do. You will see,' he told her.

'I shall want six men for the operation, as well as drivers for the cars,' Rintlen announced when bathed and dressed and feeling slightly more alert. He summoned a conference to plan the assault on Farenzi's apartment. 'Four will be needed to break down the door and go in with myself and Gerdler here.' He indicated the youth who stood listening to the proceedings with astonishment, out of his depth in the whole affair. 'The other two will guard the stairs.'

'What about weapons sir, do we have permission to shoot if we have to?' the SS officer asked.

'Yes, but shoot only if you are fired upon. Remember, this operation is being carried out without the knowledge of the Italian authorities. We don't want to bring the police down on our heads.'

'And if the Jews try to escape Standartenfuhrer,' said another SS man, 'do we open fire rather than let them go?'

Rintlen hesitated, weighing the problem in his mind. 'Yes,' he said at length, 'but do so only if you can be sure of recovering the body. The Professor and his daughter may be carrying important Party documents which cannot be allowed to fall into the wrong hands, such as the Italian police for instance. Are there any more questions?' No-one spoke. 'Very well then,' he said, 'as soon as the men and cars are ready we will go.'

Dr. Farenzi did not arrive back at the apartment till after eleven-thirty, by which time his two guests were in a state of considerable nervousness. He sought at once to explain the reasons which had delayed him and calm their fears.

'The Nazis must suspect you are in here,' he told them, 'because I am fairly sure a man tried to follow me. Fortunately I spotted him almost at once and managed to lose him in the Via Beneto.'

'Did you get the tickets?' Siegret's father demanded urgently and the Doctor nodded, 'Yes,' he said proudly, 'I have two, booked in my name for tomorrow,' He drew a thick folder from an inside pocket of his jacket. 'See here,' he showed them, 'you leave tomorrow at eight o'clock from Lake Bracciano on board *Imperial 109*, a flying-boat, for England, and then on to Canada and the United States, on Thursday.'

Siegret and her father examined the tickets delightedly. There were thick complicated documents, containing different sections for each stage of the journey, and sets of vouchers for hotels and meals along the way. The sight of the latter, showing that lunch had been ordered for them at a restaurant in Marseilles and rooms booked for two nights at the Ritz in London, somehow went a long way towards restoring their belief in the possibility of escape.

'For your stay tonight,' Farenzi continued, 'I have had an excellent idea. My friends, whom I told you of, are away unfortunately, but the clerk who sold me the tickets told me that when the flight arrives this evening, all the passengers will be put up at Le Grande Hotel, near the Palazzo Barberini. It is the finest hotel in Rome. So I thought, why not ask the airline to book you in there with the rest of the party?'

'Don't you see?' he went on as they looked at him uncertainly. 'Once you are in the hotel this evening with the other passengers you will immediately become part of the flight. You will talk to them, get to know them, travel out to the aeroplane with them in the morning. You will have the protection of this group of people and once you are among them the Nazis will never be able to harm you. To try and do so would cause a great incident.'

'The idea sounds a good one,' Professor Wienzman agreed, 'but how are we to get to the hotel? There are at least four men watching the main door and if they see us leaving with our cases they may well try to stop us.'

The two men were pondering over this problem, when Siegret gave a cry from the window. 'Papa!' she called out, 'they are coming this way. The men from the car and some others, and oh!' she let out a cry of despair, 'Heinz Gerdler is with them! I can see him.'

The embassy had provided a reliable looking team, six hard-bitten, well-muscled men who could be counted on to take care of themselves in a fight. 'If possible,' Rintlen emphasized to them as they collected in the street, 'I want the three of them taken alive. I gather Farenzi is back in the apartment by the way?' he queried. 'Yes sir,' the leader of the group who had been keeping watch replied, 'the Italian returned about ten minutes ago. We wondered whether to stop him, but our orders were to do nothing till you arrived.'

'Quite right,' Rintlen approved, 'we can decide what to do about him when we have the two Jews.' He surveyed the build-ing. It was typical of the large grey walled, brown shuttered blocks to be found anywhere in the city. 'Farenzi's apartment is on the fourth floor,' one of the men told him 'two below the top.'

'Good. Then bring the tools for the door and let's go,' he said, and began leading the way across the road and into the building.

Siegret's words brought the Professor and Farenzi instantly to her side at the sitting-room window. Even from this height the solid build and uniformly similar dress of the half-dozen men who were crossing the street towards the main doors, were frighteningly apparent.

'They are on the stairs already!' Wienzman cried in alarm, as the men disappeared out of sight beneath the walls of the block. 'What shall we do?' He still had the Doctor's pistol in his pocket and now he drew it out and looked wildly round the apartment for some means of escape.

'It's no good, we can't fight them, there are too many of them for us,' Farenzi told him, 'quickly, bring your bags and follow me. We must try to get out on to the roof before they find us here.'

The suitcases had been packed and placed ready in the hall for their departure. Seizing the nearest of them, the Doctor flung open the door of the apartment and led them out on to the stairs. Pausing only to snatch up the remaining bags, the other two followed him hastily.

The staircase of the apartment building was a wide, imposingly constructed affair of polished stonework and glazed tiles. As Siegret began to hurry after Farenzi's vanishing figure, clutching a suitcase with one arm and her basket under the other, she could hear below the sounds of many feet climbing swiftly after them. Her father closed the door of the flat behind him, careful not to betray their movements by slamming it unguardedly.

Panting with the exertion she ran up the stairs, past the landing of the next floor, trying to make as little noise as she could, for fear of attracting attention. Behind her she could hear the laboured breathing of her father as he struggled to catch them up, laden beneath the two heaviest suitcases. At any moment she expected to hear cries of alarm from their pursuers as their escape was discovered.

At the topmost landing Farenzi halted, his eyes darting round uncertainly. As in the rest of the building, two apartments opened off it, but to Siegret's dismay there appeared to be no corresponding door or hatch giving access to the roof. The doctor hurriedly pressed the bell of the flat nearest to the staircase while the other two gathered beside him anxiously.

There was no response to Farenzi's ringing and he pressed the button urgently again. The sound of heavy blows on the door of the apartment they had just left, reached them up the stairs, and a chorus of voices. There came a loud, rending crash as of the lock being burst open, and shouts as the Nazis rushed through into the rooms. There was still no reply to the bell. 'Oh, hurry, please hurry, let us in.' Siegret heard herself whispering in agitation. At best it could take only a few seconds for the attackers downstairs to realize their quarry had flown and they would know instantly that there was only one direction they could possibly have taken.

When the door continued to remain firmly closed in the face of his frantic peals on the bell, Farenzi abandoned his efforts, and they ran to the entrance on the far side of the landing. Again, the ringing, and the agonizing suspense as they waited, praying that this time someone would answer. Cries of anger were already coming from below. The Doctor pressed his thumb on the bell and held it there.

Footsteps sounded on the other side of the door, then to their intense relief came the noise of the latch being turned. The door opened a few inches and an elderly woman's face, grey haired and spectacled, peered out at them.

'Who is it?' she inquired nervously, 'what do you want?' With no time to waste Farenzi pushed the door right open and brushed past her into the hall beyond, followed by the two Wienzmans. 'Thieves and gunmen, madam,' he tried to explain, 'we are being pursued. You must show us the way to the roof.'

At his words however, the old lady let out a loud wail of fear and began attempting to force them back out on to the landing. The Professor shut the door hastily, but he was too late. From outside on the stairs there came a cry as one of the Nazis, alerted by the noise, called to his fellows. There were answering shouts and a pounding of feet.

'The roof! How do we get out on to the roof?' Farenzi besought the old woman as the Professor locked the door and slammed home the bolt. The old woman cowered away from them. 'Through the kitchen,' she quavered pointing behind her.

All caution abandoned now they tore through the flat. Inside the kitchen, they found a back door opening on to a small flights of steps which led to the roof. Siegret had no idea of what they were going to do once they were out on the top but she followed the Doctor upwards, pulling the suitcase after her. There was nowhere else to go, and the men were battering at the old lady's door already.

The moment she stumbled out on to the roof however, she saw the sense in the route he had chosen. A wide flat area lay before them, littered with the projecting humps of stairwells and the low squat constructions housing the building's water tanks and other services. Makeshift washing lines, festooned with clothes drying in the sun, straddled across the open space. Best of all she could see clearly where there was a way over on to the roof of an adjoining building at the rear. On a less fraught occasion she might have noticed that the view over the city was magnificent.

Without wasting a second they plunged onwards, ducking under the clothes lines and dodging in and out among the huts. They had succeded in crossing over on to the farther building, from which a number of curious onlookers gaped at their behaviour in astonishment, before Rintlen and his gang burst through the flat below and appeared on the roof.

Choosing a stairway which looked as though it led down to the street level, the doctor flung himself down it. Both he and the Professor were near the end of their strength now, their faces streaming with sweat, and their breath coming in laboured gasps. Siegret pushed her father on ahead of her, worried lest he should fall behind and be lost, he had already dropped one of his cases. As she did so she heard a sharp bang from the direction in which they had come and something struck the wall of the stairs only a few inches from her head, with tremendous violence, sending up a shower of dust and fragments of stone.

The shock of the bullet sent renewed strength through them. Dragging them all through the door at the bottom of the stairs, Farenzi bolted it swiftly behind them as other shots echoed out over the rooftops. By good fortune this building was provided with a lift shaft, and the cage stood waiting before them. Piling in they set it rattling downwards and collapsed over one another, bent double, gasping for air.

There were few people in the street into which they staggered at the bottom, and no sign at all of any of the Nazi agents. A taxi came driving towards them and they waved it down. Loading in the remaining suitcases, they leapt in themselves. 'Grande Hotel' the Doctor shouted to the driver, and the cab bore them away, hardly able to believe they had escaped.

Above the steep cliffs of the Acropolis, the marble pediments and columns of the Parthenon, bathed in bright sunlight, faced out across the city which filled the bowl of stony hills. Behind, the sea formed a background of brilliant blue as Desmond circled *Caterina* low over Athens to give the passengers one of the finest views imaginable of the capital and its classical monuments. Then banking away again, he brought her gently down on the surface of Phalerian Bay and motored in among the ferries, tramp steamers and fishing vessels of the port of Piraeus.

The passengers were grateful to disembark after more than five hours aboard, with only the brief stop at Alexandria to stretch their legs. There was pleasure too, in visiting the most celebrated city of classical antiquity, as well as the good food and comfort of the Grande Bretagne Hotel to look forward to.

Much to the annoyance of the crew, these last enjoyments were denied them. The presence of the gold shipment in the flying-boat's holds meant they were under strict orders to remain on board or in the immediate vicinity of the aircraft during all daytime halts. Even at Rome, where a detachment of armed carabinieri was due to stand guard over her all night, one crew member had still to sleep in the cabins.

For Desmond these regulations were particularly frustrating since they meant a further wait before he would have an opportunity to try and make his peace with Laura. He had gone down to the lower deck as soon as they docked, to see the passengers ashore, and had attempted to say a few friendly words to her, but she had ignored his overtures and walked past him down the gangway with only the briefest acknowledgement.

A fleet of chartered taxis, driven with typical Greek disregard, whisked the passengers off to Amalias Square and deposited them at the steps of the hotel where lunch had been prepared on an elaborate scale. Stewart Curtis' first action on arriving was to send Laura off to rent him a sitting-room up-stairs and arrange for a telephone call to be put through to his stockbrokers in London. He badly needed to know what had happened to the price of Klerksdorp when the market opened for business after the week-end. On hearing this Charlotte de-manded a room of her own as well, to change in and rest, and dispatched her maid Arlette, back to the aircraft to fetch sev-eral items of luggage for her.

Laura engaged a suite for them both and a short while later reported back to Curtis that, for a variety of reasons, direct communication with London was impossible.

'Hell and damnation!' he cursed, so loudly that other people in the lounge turned and stared at him. 'Can't they organize anything properly in these bloody countries? Did you tell them it was vitally urgent I get through?'

'I did everything I could,' she told him, 'but there's no way it can be done.'

'If you were any damn use at all, you would have wired ahead and got them to arrange the call before we left Cairo. Why am I surrounded by half-witted fools?' He continued in this vein, till eventually even Charlotte was moved to complain. 'Do be quiet and leave the girl alone,' she said, 'it's hardly her fault; you should have warned her if you wanted calls booked ahead for you. You'll have to wait till we reach Rome now.'

'The offices in London will be closed then,' her husband snarled at her, 'doesn't anyone ever think except me?' Flinging down a three day old copy of *The Times* he had been reading, he rose angrily to his feet. 'I shall have lunch upstairs. I'm fed up with eating with the same people day after day. Are you going to join me?' he asked Charlotte.

'To eat upstairs by ourselves?' she looked at him in surprise. 'When there is a very pleasant dining-room down here? Cer-tainly not. I shall lunch with Laura and the d'Estes if you're going to do that.'

'Very well then, please yourself,' Curtis snapped furiously, and strode from the room.

After her recent exchange with Rashid, Jacquetta felt nervous and on edge, reacting irritably to Luca's offhand treatment of her, and his continued ogling of Charlotte. Sitting opposite him at lunch she tried to sort out her thoughts while the others talked. She had told Rashid she would not give him or his plans away, but nevertheless she retained some vestige of loyalty towards Luca; he had, after all, been her husband for over fifteen years. She felt a desperate need for a solution which would make him aware of the danger which threatened him, without at the same time betraying the young Sheikh in any way or putting him at risk.

To her amazement however, she heard Charlotte broaching the subject herself. 'Whatever happened about that young man you and Yousouri Pasha were telling me about?' she asked him, 'the one who had sworn to kill you?'

'Oh, him,' Luca shrugged, 'nothing at all, it was a fake alarm I suppose. The Embassy were told and the Government is giving me a police guard while we are in Rome. Personally though I regard it as a waste of time.'

'This is a young terrorist,' he explained to Laura who was looking inquiringly at him, 'one of a band which I was obliged to put down during my time in Cyrenaica. Apparently he wishes to avenge the death of his leaders.'

'Or to be more accurate,' Jacquetta interjected, enraged by his casual distortion of the truth, 'he wishes to pay you back for the callous murder of his father and his sister.'

'That is a lie,' Luca retorted angrily, flushing red as he spoke, 'you are referring to judicial execution carried out by law.'

'Is that how you describe taking old men up in aeroplanes and throwing them out?' Jacquetta could see the two women taking in her words wide-eyed. With a great effort Luca controlled his temper. 'Such stories are nothing but lies and propaganda put about by our enemies. There is not a shred of truth behind them.' Turning to his wife he addressed her in Italian in tones quivering with rage.

'Never dare to repeat such things again. You are obviously incapable of grasping the concepts of political expediency and loyalty to the state. In the same way,' he went on with a spiteful note creeping into his voice, 'that you will undoubtedly fail to understand why I found it necessary to leave instructions that your horse Balbo be sold to an Arab dealer on our departure from Cairo, rather than go to the unnecessary expense of having it shipped back to Italy and stabled till our return.'

His words cut Jacquetta to the heart. Staring at him in horror, she saw from his face that he was telling her the truth. He had done exactly as he had said and must have been waiting for just such a moment as this, to use it on her. Choking with emotion she sprang to her feet and ran from the dining-room.

Though a good ten degrees colder than Cairo, the weather in Athens was still pleasantly warm and spring like, and the tables of the cafés beneath the trees in the square were crowded with customers. Jacquetta wandered about in the sunshine, welling over with grief for the fate of Balbo, and a savage hatred for Luca and his cruelty.

Tiring eventually, she sat down by herself at a table having a view of the parliament buildings and its guards, parading in their national dress. A waiter appeared with a tray and she ordered coffee and fruit; she was eating a tangerine un-heedingly when a shadow fell across the table, and glancing up she saw Rashid standing beside her, very tall against the sun.

'I heard your quarrel with your husband and saw you run away,' he said quietly, 'I came to see if you were all right.'

'Yes, we quarrelled,' Jacquetta fought to keep her voice steady, 'but I didn't give you away if that's what you're worried about,' she said bitterly.

'I never doubted it,' he told her, pulling up another chair and sitting down beside her. 'Why don't you tell me what hap-pened?'

Holding back the tears which threatened to start from her eyes, Jacquetta recounted the substance of the quarrel at the lunch table and Luca's description of Balbo's fate. Rashid listened in silence, 'He was a good horse,' he said when she had finished speaking, 'and does not deserve to be sold off like a pack animal. I will send a message to Prince Suleiman, my uncle, asking him to buy him from whoever the dealer is and keep him for you.'

'Thank you, you're very kind,' she replied tonelessly, still staring at the white building in front of them. 'Oh, I'm sorry,' she said, guiltily, 'I didn't mean it like that, I really am grateful, but it doesn't solve the real problem, don't you see?' she seized his hand and squeezed it tightly. 'You'll never be able to get near my husband and if you try you'll be killed.'

Rashid shook his head, 'I've sworn to avenge my father, I cannot go back,' he said simply.

'And what kind of choice does that leave me with?' she cried in anguish, 'I can't just stand idly by and let you kill my husband, and yet if I raise a finger to save him you'll be arrested. What am I to do? You must give up your insane venture and go home,' she pleaded.

Rashid stood up, his face bore an expression of inflexible resolve. 'It is time we returned to the hotel,' he said, 'the cars will be coming for us soon,' and with a slight bow he left her.

In the bout of angry recrimination which followed the unsuccessful raid on Dr. Farenzi's apartment, Rintlen's temper, which had been seething for the past two days, finally exploded at this culmination to the frustration and inefficiencies he had endured. Back in the Embassy chancellery he downed two glasses of schnapps and proceeded to castigate savagely each and every member of his unfortunate team.

Thanks entirely to their slowness in climbing the stairs, and the inattention of the men left to guard on the landing, he told them bitterly, the Wienzmans and their Italian companion had managed to escape. 'Which makes the third time they have been assisted in this way by servants of the Reich!' He stormed at the apprehensive group.

The criminal stupidity of men who in defiance of his express orders had fired wildly with their revolvers during the rooftop chase, thereby drawing the attention of every person living nearby, was a matter he would deal with later, just as he would with those who had so glibly and mistakenly assured him there was no rear way of escape from the buildings.

'For the moment my only orders are to get out!' he barked. 'Get out and find them, search every hotel, every boarding house, search every building and house in Rome if you have to, but find them, find them at all costs!'

Abashed, the men filed hurriedly from the room. Ordering Strasser, the SS officer to remain behind, Rintlen poured himself another glass of schnapps and slumped down in a chair, forcing his tired brain to concentrate on what to do next. 'Tell me the earliest flight by which the Wienzmans can leave, assuming they do go by Imperial Airways,' he said.

Strasser consulted a sheet of notes, 'The next flight Standartenfuhrer, is *Imperial 109* for England and America, which leaves tomorrow morning at eight thirty from Lake Bracciano. We have been able to establish that this is now fully booked and that the remaining tickets were sold today, but no details are available as to the passenger list, except that the name Wienzman does not appear on it.'

'They would probably use a fake name anyway,' Rintlen remarked sourly, 'when's the next flight?'

'Wednesday Standartenfuhrer, there are daily flights to England from here, and there are still seats available.'

'But why the British Airline?' the SD man asked, half to himself, 'there are half a dozen foreign airlines flying out of Rome, any one of those would have done.'

Strasser cleared his throat obsequiously.

'If I might make a suggestion sir?' he said courteously. Seeing Rintlen nod curtly he went on, '*Imperial 109* is a through flight to New York. It stops in England only to rest the crew and leaves again to cross the Atlantic on Thursday. No other flight makes the trip this week. If the Wienzmans were intending to travel to America, that is the flight they would take.'

'Of course!' Rintlen's face lit up. 'You are right, that must be what they intend.' He gave a grim smile of satisfaction. 'Once again we have out-thought you Herr Professor Wienzman.'

'What will you do now?' Strasser asked, relieved at the reception accorded his idea.

'Try and head them off when they board of course,' Rintlen told him, 'I have orders not to ask the Italian authorities for help, but I think we may be able to persuade the airport police that our friends' departure should be delayed. Just in case that should fail however,' he remarked caustically, 'you had better book me on a flight, any flight which will get me into England on the same day. Or rather book two of us,' he added draining the remainder of his drink, 'I suppose I had better keep that little swine Gerdler with me.'

Three o'clock saw *Caterina* airborne again above the Bay of Salamis where two and a half thousand years earlier the Athenian navy had destroyed the Persian fleet of Xerxes and saved Greece from conquest. In the distance the jagged peaks of Parnassus rose above the land, streaked with snow about their bare grey summits and glinting in the brilliant sun.

The passengers peered eagerly from the panoramic observation windows of the promenande deck and focused their cameras. The Ionian islands fell away astern one by one, Cephalonia, Ithica, Levkas and the green slopes of Corfu.

Andy served tea while they flew out over the straits of Otranto. For him the day had seen a distinct change in the attitudes of the passengers in his charge. Stewart Curtis, for instance, while still as bad-tempered and disagreeable as ever, had ceased his complaints now that the schedule had been speeded up, but several of the others on board were not nearly so pleased at having to forgo a night in Athens and press on through the afternoon and early evening and Laura Hartman was noticeably less cheerful and easy going.

Brindisi came in sight on the heel of Italy, another stop-over on normal schedule, but today they passed overhead at 7000 feet and flew steadily above the snow-laden Appennines. Another hour and Naples was behind them, Vesuvius' smoke plume lost to sight and they were drawing near to Rome.

They reached the city just in time to see the dying rays of the sun glinting on the broad ribbon of the Tiber at the foot of the seven hills, and catching on the great dome of St. Peter's in a blaze of gold.

Four thousand miles to the west across Europe and the Atlantic Ocean, Pat Jarrett made a final adjustment to the radio transmitter. Satisfied he climbed out of the S4's cockpit on to the wing, stretching his stiff limbs gratefully. The job had taken him slightly less time than he had anticipated, but he had spent the entire morning since dawn cramped in the tiny awkward space, bent double to get at the rear of the control panel. Yesterday evening he had successfully positioned the accumulators behind the pilot's seat, in the fuselage. A ticklish job because he had had to avoid damaging the wooden formers and stringers which comprised the aircraft's frame.

With a last glance at the neatness of his handiwork he stepped down on to the right hand float carrying his open box of tools in one hand. The racer was firmly lashed between the walls of the boathouse, but even so, the float dipped sharply as his weight came on to it, throwing him off balance. Grasping the forward float strut with his free hand to save himself from falling, he hauled himself back upright. As he did so the tool box in his other hand tilted sharply and several pieces fell out into the water.

Climbing up on to the dock Jarrett checked the contents of the box and swore savagely in anger. The items lost included a set of files, essential to the proper fitting of the guns and the steel wing bracings to support them. They would have to be replaced at once, if he was to start work in preparing the gun bays after lunch.

He checked his watch, twelve-thirty, if he left straight away, he could drive into Keene, pick up the new files, and one or two other things he needed, and maybe have a bite to eat as well. He could do with a change from his own cooking.

Moreover he thought, as he switched out the lights and locked the door of the boathouse behind him, it might be no bad thing for him to be seen casually in the town, after this morning's incident. Jarrett had no doubts that the Sheriff had been satisfied by what he had seen, when he came round, but he was well aware that any stranger in a country district would be regarded with suspicion, and now his presence had been discovered the best course was to behave as normally as possible.

Swapping his overalls for his old flying jacket, he set off down the track towards the main road. The day was overcast and the weather colder than it had been last week, but the forecast for Friday and the week-end was good, with clear skies and temperatures around 45°. Ideal conditions for an interception, provided he had the plane ready in time.

He found what he needed without difficulty in a well-provided ironmongers on Main Street, as well as several other useful items of equipment which he purchased for good measure. Then, resisting the temptation to waste time looking around the town, he walked on up the street till he came to a small drugstore and bar. Peering through the window he saw the seven or eight tables inside were empty, save for that nearest the bar counter, at which two old men were sitting, chewing slowly through their food. Pushing open the door Jarrett went in and took a seat.

The two men paused in their meal and favoured him with long hard stares as he sat down, laying the parcel of tools on a chair next to him. He nodded briefly to them and one of them mumbled a greeting of some kind, and lifting his head called, 'Susie, customer for yer out front.'

There was an answering cry from the back of the store. Jarrett waited silently, conscious of the eyes of the two men on him, taking in his clothes and appearance, assessing him. Satisfied at length, they returned to their plates. A sound of footsteps drew near, accompanied by the noise of a radio playing dance music and the girl entered.

At the very first sight of her Jarrett felt a stir of excitement in his belly. During the past weeks he had been too busy with plans and preparations to think of a woman, and stuck out on the lake he had forgotten their existence. This one was no more than sixteen or seventeen he guessed, mature for her age and fully conscious of the power her attraction for men brought her. Slouching across the room she stood negligently in front of him, hip thrust provocatively forward in the too tight dress, eyeing him blatantly. She had a sullen, sluttish expression, and untidy brown hair caught together loosely at the back. In a few years time she would have run to seed, but just now she was desirable and she knew it.

'Want to eat?' her voice was flat and toneless, the accent clipped.

'A plate of whatever you're serving,' Jarrett told her, 'and a beer.'

Returning with a dish of what seemed to be an indifferent stew, she looked him up and down curiously. 'Haven't seen you in town before, Mister,' she said, 'you just passing through or staying a while?'

'I'm spending a couple of weeks up at Warren Lake,' he told her, 'surveying a route for the airlines.'

'For the airline?' the girl's voice quickened with interest. 'You a flyer then?' she asked and Jarrett nodded. 'That's right,' he said, 'have been ever since the war. Run my own outfit doing meteorological surveys.'

She fetched him the beer from the refrigerator behind the counter, and poured it slowly into the glass, watching the head carefully so as not to spill any. Setting the glass down she continued to question him. 'I love planes,' she said, 'never been in one though. You got a plane of your own Mister?' she asked hopefully.

Jarrett hesitated. He was reluctant to give away any details about his activities, yet at the same time he felt a strong urge to admit to a fact which he knew would raise him in the girl's eyes. Surely there was no harm in it being revealed now that the Sheriff had called. 'Yes, I've got a plane,' he said quietly. The effect was everything he would have wished. Respect dawned immediately on Susie's face. 'Your own plane,' she breathed open-mouthed, 'say now isn't that something? I never met a man with his own plane before.'

Jarrett was saved from having to make further comment by a shout from the old men at the other end of the room. The girl went off to fetch them portions of apple pie each; by the time she had done so and produced cream to go with it, he had finished his plateful and was downing the last of the beer.

'Nothing else?' she asked in surprise as he produced the money for the bill. 'I have to get back,' he explained, 'there's a lot of work to do before the sun goes in.'

'Which house you staying in up there on the lake?' she asked, ringing the till for change. 'Oh yeah, I know the one on the point,' she said when he told her. 'Well, come in and see us again Mister,' she handed him the coins with a knowing smile, 'and who knows, maybe one of these days I'll come up there an' you can give me a ride in your plane.'

Jacquetta's outburst had caused considerable embar-rassment to Luca. Although he had spent most of the rest of the meal endeavouring to deny her version of the Rashid affair, it was evident to him that neither of the two women were particularly convinced by his words. During the onward flight from Athens, his wife had pointedly gone to sit in the prom-enade cabin, and since Charlotte had wanted to have a bed made up for her in the stern cabin to rest on for the afternoon, and Stewart Curtis had still been in an evil temper, he himself had passed the trip in the smoking saloon, in conversation with Van Smit and the colonial engineer, Johnson.

Once during the afternoon the newcomer to the flight, Ahmed Yalchin, had joined them for a while, sitting by himself in a corner, taking no part in the discussion. He seemed a polite, if restrained and withdrawn, young man, who never-theless gave Luca the impression of watching him intently, so that the Italian was glad when he left them again. On landing at Lake Bracciano he was gratified to find an official car waiting for him, with the news that he was wanted immediately at the Foreign Ministry, where discussions were taking place on the crisis which had arisen in Czechoslovakia: German reservists were apparently being called up, and there were reports of troop movements in Munich and Salzburg. Setting off at once, accompanied by two armed police guards, he left Jacquetta to make her way to the Grande Hotel with the other passengers.

She and Luca in fact possessed a villa in Rome, in the aristocratically smart area of the Largo Goldini, but this was now let out to tenants for the period of Luca's appointment in Washington. Consequently they too, had been booked into a suite at the Grande. After the exhaustion and strain of the past few days, it was a relief for Jacquetta to be able to shut herself in the privacy of her room, rather than endure the greetings and fuss of the servants. She hated the house anyway with the elaborate d'Este crest over the doors and the oppressive grandeur of its rooms.

Luca would most probably not be back until late, she guessed, and after having a long relaxing bath, she put on a peach silk dressing gown and brushed out her hair. She was still no nearer finding a way out of the dilemma before her. In her heart she was sure she ought to go to Luca and warn him of his danger, yet each time she found herself with him, the words somehow froze on her lips, and instead she seemed to be led into making increasingly bitter attacks, as her husband's pomposity, his arrogance and his cruelty became ever more unbearable to her.

The other corner of the triangle, which was rapidly crowding all other considerations from her mind was Rashid. The very idea of the risk to him, dismayed her to a point where she could scarcely think. As it was, the young Sheikh filled most of her waking thoughts, and the mere fact of being near to him threw her into a ferment.

There was a soft tap at the foor and two waiters entered with a trolley. In former days she might have been amused to see the elaborate array of silver tureens, dishes and bowls with which the hotel sought to provide the 'light dish of cold meat and salad' she had requested. Selecting a plateful of what she wanted and a glass of wine, she took it back into the bedroom with her. Though she had had almost no lunch in Athens, she felt no hunger; sitting on the edge of the bed she picked at the food mechanically.

Perhaps, she thought, she ought to talk to someone. The trouble was there was no-one in Rome she really liked or trusted. All her acquaintances here had come to her through

Luca; her own friends were in the country and the problem was not something to be discussed over the telephone.

Three rooms along on the same floor of the hotel, Rashid switched out the light in his bedroom, and opened the french windows leading on to the small balcony, with which all rooms on this side of the Grande were provided. He was wearing only a shirt and trousers, and the night air struck chill after the warmth of Egypt as he closed the windows carefully behind him and gauged the gap between the next balcony to his right.

The distance was no more than five feet he judged, but up here, six floors above the street, with the lights of Rome spread out before him in a vast panorama, it required a considerable effort of will to climb up on to the narrow balustrade and, clinging on to the casement of the window, stretch out towards the adjoining balustrade. The gap was too wide to be bridged in a single step, and Rashid was forced to throw his weight across, risking losing his footing. One hundred feet below him, the traffic swirled past like a procession of brightly lit toys. There was a moment of heart stopping fear and he was across. The windows were screened by thick curtains. Drawing the service revolver from his belt, Rashid tried the door handle stealthily.

Luca d'Este left the Foreign Ministry in the Palazzo Chigi at a quarter past eight, still accompanied by the two guards, who had spent the last hour and a half waiting for him in the foyer on the first floor. They were hard, broad-shouldered toughs, schooled in the brawls and street fighting of Fascism's early days, the heavy automatics in their underarm holsters bulging beneath their suits. Their presence, he was sure, was superfluous, but they added an acceptable aura of importance to his position. At the bottom of the steps the car which had brought him, stood ready.

'Grande Hotel,' he told the driver, 'and wait for me there. I have to change and return to the Ministry for dinner.'

The sudden eruption of the Czechoslovak crisis over the week-end, had caught everyone by surprise. It was becoming obvious, he thought to himself as the car sped through the evening traffic, that the Nazis in Berlin were playing a close hand, and not letting slip to the Duce any hint of their intentions. The general concensus of opinion at the Palace was that Germany was planning to invade and occupy the country within the next two or three days. He wondered how Britain and France would react to such action, coming less than six months after the Munich Agreement.

The car drew up outside the hotel and the driver leapt out to open the passenger door. Followed by his two guards Luca went up to the suite, his mouth set in a grim determined line. He still had to deal with Jacquetta over her outburst at lunch.

The french windows rustled slightly and Jacquetta let out a quick gasp of fright as they swung open. Then, as Rashid stepped through she sprang up and ran towards him.

'How ever did you get in?' she cried in amazement, 'over the balconies? Oh, you must be mad. You might have fallen and killed yourself.'

'Not so loud,' he warned her urgently, 'where is your husband?'

'He isn't here, he went straight to the Foreign Office,' she noticed the revolver in his hand for the first time, and her eyes widened with alarm. 'Rashid, it's impossible. He has armed guards following him everywhere. Didn't you see them at the airport? They'll kill you if they find you here. You must go,' she implored.

'I cannot go back, whatever the danger I must keep my word,' he answered.

'But not here, not in Italy. What chance have you if you're caught?' she had hardly spoken the words when from the far room came the sounds of the door opening and voices in the corridor.

'Quick!' With a surprising burst of strength she pushed him back a few steps to the threshold of the windows. 'Go back, please go back, for my sake if not yours,' she whispered agonizingly, 'if they killed you I should die!'

Taken unawares by Jacquetta's intensity of feeling and the desperate pleading in her voice, Rashid allowed himself to be driven out on to the balcony. She had just closed the windows and was pulling the curtains together again when Luca appeared at the bedroom door.

She started round guiltily, uncertain of whether or not he had realized what she was doing. 'I was just drawing the curtains,' she began, 'I didn't expect you back for dinner.'

'I'm dining at the Ministry in half an hour,' Luca's tone was curt. 'I've only come back to change.' Looking over his shoulder he spoke to the two gunmen. 'Wait in the sitting-room,' he told them, 'I won't be more than a few minutes,' Shutting the door he turned back to Jacquetta.

'Now I should be grateful if you would give me some kind of explanation for the disgraceful exhibition you made of yourself in Athens.' His voice was icy but Jacquetta could see from the livid patches on his cheek bones that he was furiously angry.

'I thought the disgrace was all on your side,' she replied coolly, 'it was the details of your behaviour the other two found so shocking rather than any conduct of mine.'

'How dare you question my behaviour?' Luca burst out, abandoning the check he had been keeping on his temper. 'I've told you time and again I was obeying orders, doing my duty. Would you rather I had acted like one of the rebels myself, like a traitor?'

'I would rather you were anything than a cowardly butcher who orders innocent people to be flung out of aeroplanes,' Jacquetta retorted. 'How you can live with yourself after what you've done I don't know.'

'I am an officer and a member of the government of the Duce,' Luca stormed at her. 'I forbid you to address me in that fashion.'

'Oh, stop being so bloody pompous!' she snapped angrily, 'you know what I think so why bother to argue about it.'

'Yes I do know what you think, and in future you will keep your ridiculous ideas to yourself and not embarrass me in front of others. Otherwise I promise you I shall have to take severe measures,' Luca threatened. Jacquetta made no reply, but sat down on the bed to finish her meal, ignoring him. Her husband glared furiously at her for a moment and then with a gesture of exasperation went through into the bathroom.

When he emerged, twenty minutes later, dressed and ready to go out, his manner was once more cold and controlled. Collecting his cigarette case and wallet from the dressing-table, he paused in the doorway as he was about to leave and addressed her.

'You had better get one thing very clear in your head,' he said, 'you may believe that because you are my wife you can criticize me, and the State which I serve, with impunity. You are wrong. If it became necessary I should not hesitate to have you placed in the care of the authorities until such time as you recovered your senses. Before that, however,' he went on menacingly, 'there would be other steps I should take. Your father for instance, is widely known to hold views similar to yours. He is an old man of course, and in poor health, but a term in a desert labour camp or on one of the Lipari prison islands might bring you both to heel.' Seeing her staring at him with an expression of horrified incredulity on her face, Luca gave a smirk of vicious satisfaction and went out, calling the guards after him.

Rather than risk detection by remaining on the balcony, Rashid had climbed back into his own room and settled down to wait. Enough of the conversation in the bedroom had been audible for him to know that the Italian would be leaving again soon. Upon reflection he was forced to admit that Jacquetta was right about the foolhardiness of an attempt on Luca's life while he was in Italy, and where precautions were being taken to protect him. It would be far wiser to wait until they were in England or America. The question remained however, of how far he could trust her not to give him away, even if inadvertently.

As soon as he heard the sounds of the Baron's departure, he slipped along the corridor to her room and tapped softly on the door. Letting him in she threw herself at once into his arms with a sob. Instinctively he clasped her to him, and before they were aware of what was happening they were locked in a passionate embrace. Rashid kissed her fiercely, her mouth meeting his with an equal hunger. Under his hands he felt the softness of her body beneath the thin silk of her gown, yielding urgently to him.

Pulling the tie at the waist undone he slipped the gown down off her shoulders, letting it fall to the floor. His fingers moved over the smoothness of her shoulders and caressed her breasts, fondling the hardened nipples. Jacquetta gave a small moan of ecstasy, and her frame stiffened and trembled with longing as she clutched him violently to her, her nails raking his back.

Fire shot through Rashid; with a sudden hoarse groan he swept Jacquetta off her feet and, picking her up in his arms, carried her naked and unresisting into the bedroom.

There had been lengthy formalities for Desmond to go through at the Lake before he could get away. Principally this was due to the gold on board, for the crates had to be checked and counted individually before the carabinieri and the shore staff would accept responsibility for them. In part, however, as he well knew, the authorities had instructions from the Government to harass and delay all Imperial Airways flights, on the ground that Britain was Italy's greatest rival in the Mediterranean.

Ralph Kendricks volunteered to stay behind and spend the night on *Caterina* to keep an eye on the precious cargo, enabling Desmond to follow the passengers into the hotel in the centre of Rome. It was eight o'clock by the time he reached his room, and his first action was to speak to Laura on the telephone.

'I've been trying to call you myself,' was her reply when he told her that he wanted to see her. 'Can you come along to my room? There's something you ought to know about.'

Laura's room was on the floor above and inside he found her waiting for him in the company of an elderly, white haired man and a very young girl who looked to be his daughter. 'Professor and Siegret Wienzman,' Laura introduced them jumping up to let him in. All three of them appeared pale and worried, the girl's eyes reddened from crying. 'They're in terrible trouble,' she continued. 'You must listen to what's happened to them.'

Wearily the old man told his story for the second time.

'They've been hiding in here ever since, not even daring to leave their rooms for meals,' Laura interjected, 'Siegret's room is next door to mine and I heard her crying when I was going past.'

'Our greatest fear,' the Professor continued, 'is that the Nazis will prevent us from getting to your aeroplane tomorrow morning.'

'What I don't quite understand,' Desmond asked in a puzzled tone, 'is why the Germans should be going to such lengths to catch you, if you are no more than ordinary refugees. After all, Jewish emigration is still permitted there is it not?' Laura gave him a sharp look, the thought had evidently not occurred to her. Professor Wienzman sighed heavily. 'Yes, you are right Captain, there is another reason why the Nazis hunt us, a reason which even my daughter does not know.' He patted her hand gently as he spoke. 'Many years ago I learnt something about a person who shall be nameless but is now in a position of great power in Germany. I did not seek the knowledge, nor would I make it public and discredit him, for I believe a patient's confidence in his Doctor may not be abused. Nevertheless the Nazis will not believe this and they will not rest until I am in their hands.'

'So what are we going to do?' Laura demanded, 'how can we get the Professor and his daughter on to *Caterina* without them being stopped?'

Desmond was silent for a second or two, aware of Laura's eyes on him as he hesitated. There was no way in which he could possibly refuse such a request for help, yet he was conscious of being at last forced to take sides in a conflict he had managed to avoid for so long. 'The question is,' he said at length, 'are the Italian police involved? If they are not, if the Nazis are simply operating by themselves, then there isn't too much of a problem. In that case the best way of avoiding them is probably for you both to come down to the lake early with myself and the other crew members, and go aboard a couple of hours before the passengers arrive.'

'And if the Italians are watching for them too?' said Laura. He could see approval of his decision in her face.

'Then the problem is more difficult. You see the aircraft herself is under heavy guard,' and he told them about the gold on board. The Wienzmans' faces fell.

'But we must do something to help,' Laura said hotly. 'Surely you can think of some way of getting them on board without being seen?'

'I could lend the Professor a cap and one of my uniform jackets,' Desmond answered thoughtfully, 'they wouldn't fit, but they might do to get him past the port guards. Miss Wienzman isn't so easy to disguise though.'

'I know,' Laura exclaimed excitedly, 'my overalls, the ones I wore in the race. I had them washed and kept them as a kind of souvenir,' she explained a trifle sheepishly. 'If Siegret puts them on and some kind of cap as well, to hide her hair, she could pass for a mechanic, especially in the half light.'

'You're right,' Desmond told her, 'In fact that's a very good idea. There will be several mechanics around anyway, going over the plane.' The expressions of the two refugees began to brighten.

'You are sure this will not bring trouble for you if we are detected?' Professor Wienzman asked, and Desmond gave a shrug. 'I'm afraid my standing with the airline is so bad at the moment I doubt if even my being arrested could make it much worse.'

Laura gave him a grateful smile. 'Good, then that's settled,' she said, 'now I'm going to have the hotel send you two up some food. Siegret is going to spend the night here with me, sharing my bed,' she added to Desmond, 'I think she'll feel safer.'

'In which case,' Desmond suggested, 'I think the Professor might be wise to use the extra room which was booked for Ralph Kendricks by mistake. Meanwhile though, if the Wienzmans don't mind being left for a short while,' he said to Laura, 'do you think you could have dinner with me? I need to talk to you.'

Laura hesitated and for an instant he was afraid she would

refuse, then to his relief, she nodded, 'Yes, all right,' she agreed, 'I'll meet you downstairs in quarter of an hour.'

Downstairs in the foyer Van Smit approached the receptionist's desk with a feeling of annoyance. All through the evening so far he had been waiting in vain for a chance to make another search of Stewart Curtis' room, but at no point had he been able to find the suite unoccupied. First the maid had been in and out several times. Now it looked as though Curtis and his wife were returning for the night.

He had decided to fall back therefore on the d'Estes. True, they were nowhere near as wealthy as the Curtises, but they still had plenty of money, and he had observed the Baroness with one or two good pieces of jewellery on her. Certainly they were worth a try.

'Can you tell me if Baron d'Este is coming down to dinner?' he inquired of the clerk, 'I was hoping to have the pleasure of continuing our conversation together.'

'I am sorry sir,' the clerk answered at once, 'but you have just missed them, they left only a few minutes ago for the Foreign Ministry.'

Unaware that Luca was accompanied tonight by guards, Van Smit took the plural to refer to his wife, and thanking the man courteously, made his way back upstairs to the sixth floor. His skeleton keys were in his pocket and with most residents still at dinner the corridors were empty. Picking the lock of the sitting-room door without difficulty he slipped quietly inside the suite.

The lights were still on, although the room itself was deserted. A woman's peach coloured silk wrap lying in a heap on the floor caught his eye. Evidently the occupants had been in a hurry. He stirred the crumpled folds idly with the toe of his shoe, and as he did so there came a sound from beyond the half closed door to the bedroom.

Instantly, he froze motionless, poised for flight, ears straining to identify the noise. Again the sound came, a low and drawn out moan, and he relaxed his tense muscles, a thin smile crossing his features as recognition dawned on him. Very softly he tip-toed over the carpet towards the bedroom and stopped to peer through the crack in the door.

Within, the lights were dim, but the man and woman on the bed had thrown back the sheets so that their locked figures and slowly twining limbs were plainly visible. For several minutes Van Smit gazed at their passionate, abandoned lovemaking, feeling his own desire rising enviously as he watched Jacquetta's naked body moving sensuously beneath the young Arab's caresses and heard the small cries and gasps of pleasure breaking from her lips.

At last, tearing himself reluctantly away, he crept back across the suite and went noiselessly out into the corridor. His expression as he walked back to his own room was one of undisguised satisfaction. No longer would he have to risk the hazardous business of trying to search the Curtises luggage. Instead Baroness d'Este would have to pay him handsomely for his silence.

Laura was very much on the defensive, Desmond saw, after his behaviour towards her in the morning, and her response to his opening conversation as they sat waiting for their meal, in the Rupe Tarpea Restaurant opposite the Capuchin's church, was wary and careful. Deciding that complete frankness was the best approach, he told her of his visit from Charlotte and showed her the telegrams he had received before leaving Cairo.

'But surely you didn't believe that Mr. Curtis and I . . .?' she exclaimed and Desmond interrupted hastily. 'No, of course not,' he assured her, 'or I wouldn't be here now. It was just that coming on top of everything else,' he shrugged his shoulders expressively, 'she must be insane that woman,' he went on, 'or at the very least incredibly bitter towards you.'

'I should have known that something like this had happened.' Laura smiled and relief shot through him once more. 'No wonder you were a bit cold this morning, you were under attack from all sides. As for Charlotte Curtis,' she shook her head, 'I was going to resign the job when we got back to New York anyway. I guess maybe I should have done it sooner.'

'Well as soon as we get back to the hotel I'm going to give

her back her damned watch and tell her exactly what I think of her behaviour,' Desmond said vigorously.

'No,' Laura put a hand on his arm across the table, 'don't do that, at least not until after we reach New York. Charlotte is a dangerous enemy and you mustn't underestimate her. Mr. Curtis will do anything she asks him to, and he is a powerful man and you've got enough people against you at the moment.'

'At the moment I can't undo the thing anyway,' Desmond said, struggling with the catch. Laura was studying the telegram. 'How bad is this inquiry?' she asked, her face serious again. 'Can't I help? I mean I was actually there, I can tell them there was nothing you could have done. Lieutenant Thorne knew he shouldn't take the launch, he was just showing off.'

'They may ask you to appear as a witness,' he told her, 'even though they've already got your statement. To be honest I've no idea how it will go. Losing a passenger is not thought highly of, even when it's the passenger's own fault. I can't say I'm proud of it myself.'

'They can't blame you, even so,' Laura replied vehemently, 'it wouldn't be fair.' Desmond smiled at her. 'I'm afraid it may be more a question of settling old scores than holding a fair trial,' he said ruefully, 'about the only point in my favour is that they are short of crews at the moment, especially for the Atlantic division. Anyway, there's nothing to be done, so don't let's discuss it any more,' he added firmly.

He saw she was still glancing doubtfully at the second telegram, the one from Pamela. 'Listen,' he told her, 'my reaction to that would have been exactly the same even if I had never met you. As I told you at the Palace in Cairo, Pamela and I are better apart; put together we simply destroy one another.'

'But this,' Laura waved the yellow slip, 'she sounds as though she wants to try again.'

Patiently Desmond led her through the whole story of his marriage, in detail. Recounting the weeks of endless quarrels which had wracked them both, almost before the honeymoon was over. Telling her of his efforts to combat his wife's desperate insecurity, which made him the target for her savage aggression of the failure which had driven him further and further into the refuge of his job.

'She needs someone in whom she can trust, someone she doesn't see as a competitor all the time,' he concluded, 'we only makes matters worse for each other.'

'Yes, I can understand that,' Laura nodded slowly, 'Peter was just the same in a way. He could never really believe he was good enough; for me, for his friends, for his job, for anything. There seemed to be no way I could reach him.'

They talked together for a long time, and it was nearing midnight when they finally left the restaurant and walked back along the Via Veneto towards the street in which they were staying.

'You are sure everything will go all right tomorrow morning?' Laura asked anxiously, 'I mean what happens if you and the Wienzmans are stopped?'

'I doubt if there's much danger to me,' Desmond replied, 'I think at the most I should be expelled from Italy. I'm much more worried about the Professor and his daughter if we're caught.' For all his cheerfulness however, he felt a growing uncertainty as he spoke. Laura evidently felt the same, for she shivered and pressed her arm tightly against his as they walked on.

VIII

RADIO PRAGUE
(Broadcast 5 a.m. local time Tuesday 14th March 1939)

'The German army, infantry and aircraft are beginning the occupation of territory of the Republic at six a.m. Their advance must nowhere be resisted.'

By Radio: FLIGHT CONTROL BRACCIANO ROME TO IMPERIAL AIRWAYS SOUTHAMPTON ENGLAND. 0830 CENTRAL EUROPEAN TIME TUESDAY 14th MARCH 1939. IMPERIAL 109 FLIGHT TO MARSEILLES AND SOUTHAMPTON DELAYED ON TAKE-OFF OWING TO REFUSAL OF EMIGRATION AUTHORITIES TO GRANT PASSENGER CLEARANCE. END.

'YOU must be mad, all of you!' Frazer stormed as the car carrying *Caterina*'s crew members and the two Wienzmans, sped through Rome's deserted and still darkened streets, towards the foothills beyond the plain, among which Lake Bracciano lay. Desmond rounded on him angrily. The five of them, including Sandy Everett were squashed in the back of an ancient limousine, with the driver out of earshot behind a glass partition, but even so he was determined not to run any unnecessary risks, or put up with any opposition from his first officer. 'I've told you already,' he snapped, 'if the idea worries you, stop the car and get out. You can follow us later, that way you won't be involved, but if you're going to stay then shut up.'

Frazer's expression was invisible in the darkness but the sharp intake of his breath betrayed his rage. The others remained silent and tense. Dawn was just beginning to break behind the hills to the east and the gloom around them was taking on a tinge of grey. It might be wiser, Desmond thought to himself, as they crossed the Ponte Cavour and headed on out through the suburbs, to take the initiative and order Frazer out of the car. The trouble then would be that he was perfectly capable of telephoning ahead and informing on them to the Airline Supervisor at the Lake. The latter would then certainly have the car intercepted and the Wienzmans returned to the hotel, for fear of causing offence to the Italians. On balance Desmond decided, Frazer was probably better kept close beside them where he could be watched.

It had, in fact, already crossed Frazer's mind that here was an excellent opportunity for ridding himself of his Captain for good, and at a single stroke bringing about all the objectives he sought. A few quick words to the airport police would be all that were needed. With her Captain under arrest, command of *Caterina* would revert to him automatically, and the airline board would have little choice but to confirm the appointment. The only difficulty lay in making sure his actions went undetected by anyone connected with Imperial Airways, otherwise he would find himself branded as an informer with no crew willing to serve under him.

The journey did not take long. Fifteen miles outside the city, in the half light of early dawn, the car reached the shores of the lake, set in the crater of a long dead volcano whose walls had been ground away during aeons of erosion by wind and rain. The pale shapes of the flying-boats were just discernible in the daybreak, drifting on the surface among the thick mist rising off the water. *Caterina* lay moored against the jetty, lights showing at her portholes.

Desmond felt the girl tense beside him as the car halted at the entrance to the landing area. A policeman, swathed in a greatcoat peered in and the driver muttered briefly to him. Winding down the window Desmond held out his crew identity pass, but the man was already waving them on.

The office and maintenance hangars were open and lit, a few figures moving about between them; preparations to get the first of the morning flights away had already started. A pair of mail vans stood by the cargo shed, discharging their loads. In the front passenger seat Sandy directed the driver over to the jetty where *Caterina* lay. There were more guards here; three men with rifles, shoulders hunched against the cold breeze off the lake, stood at the head of the steps, stamping their feet to keep warm. Nearby was parked a covered military truck, it was empty Desmond saw, the remainder of the detachment were presumably sheltering inside the reception lounge.

Acting as casually as he knew how, he led the party up to the barrier. The professor and Siegret he had placed carefully in the centre of the group, screened as far as possible by the rest of them. The old man looked surprisingly authentic in the peaked cap and officer's jacket. The dim light concealed the poor fit of the clothes and disguised his age. About the girl Desmond was not so sure. Instead of a cap they had fixed her up with a flying helmet Laura had worn for the motor race in Cairo. With this and the white overalls she looked utterly out of place to anyone familiar with airline activities, and he could only pray that the carabinieri would be more easily deceived. He had given both her and her father cases to carry in the hope of lessening the chance of their being asked to produce identity cards.

The corporal on duty barred his way, in a friendly but firm manner. 'Siami il pilote, we are the crew of the aeroplane,' Desmond explained.

'Ah, si capisco,' the man nodded understanding. 'Il Capitano?' he glanced at the gold stripes on Desmond's sleeve. 'Si sonno Capitano io,' Desmond told him, 'I am the Captain.'

Drawing himself up, the man saluted and as Desmond touched his cap in reply, beckoned them to follow him down the jetty and up the gangway. At the flying-boat's forward entrance hatch he paused, put his head inside and gave a call. There was a wait for a few seconds and then Ralph Kendricks appeared at the hatchway. 'Yes it's all right,' he said to the guard seeing Desmond, and the man stepped back to let them pass inside, with no more than a cursory look at Siegret as she brushed by him.

Rintlen and Gerdler arrived at the lake towards seven

o'clock, a full hour before any of the passengers could be expected to put in an appearance. The failure to find the Wienzmans during the night had not worried the SD man unduly.
After the assault on Farenzi's apartment it was only to be anticipated that the escapers would take extreme precautions to
ensure their safety. An examination of the two rooms booked
in the doctor's name at the Grande Hotel had shown that both
had been occupied until recently and the receptionist had
confirmed that neither of the supposed guests had checked out.
These details had only served to confirm the conviction in Rintlen's mind that his quarry was planning to catch the England-
New York flight.

This being so the matter was one which required precise
handling. In his pocket Rintlen had credentials prepared for
him at the embassy, ostensibly identifying him as an officer of
Germany's criminal police. A few minutes before his arrival a
telephone call had been put through to the airport emigration
authority informing them that a Dr. Wienzman wanted in the
Reich on charges of performing illegal operations was believed
to be among the passengers on board *Imperial 109*, together
with his young mistress, travelling in the guise of his daughter.
Permission for this course had been wrung with much difficulty
from Heydrich, and an official extradition warrant was on its
way from Berlin to Rome to support the allegations.

Without the help of the Italians, Rintlen had argued, there
would be little hope of apprehending the fugitives, and if the
whole operation was kept deliberately low key then there existed a strong possibility that the Italians would simply hand
the two would-be refugees over into his keeping. A talk with the
lieutenant in charge of the airport police immediately upon
arrival served to confirm this view. In a carefully casual tone
Rintlen had assured the man that the matter was no more than
a tedious routine affair with not the slightest degree of political
interest involved. 'So far only the crew of the aeroplane have
arrived,' the officer told him in English, which was the only
language they shared in common. He was a thin, nervous-look-
ing over-smartly dressed man with a carefully trimmed

moustache. 'There is bullion, gold bullion on board today and so we are taking special care. You can see the sentries on the jetty for yourself.'

He pointed out of the window of his office, and following the direction of his finger Rintlen saw the small knot of grey uniformed carabinieri at the entrance to the ramp leading down to the white hull of the flying-boat. This was even better than he had hoped. Now the officer's anxiety was explained. It was plain that he would risk no chance of even a remotely suspect individual approaching the aircraft.

For the next hour Rintlen and Gerdler sat watching the activities on the jetty as *Caterina*'s pre-flight inspection was carried out, and the engines and wing flaps tested by the mechanics. A handcart of mail sacks was pulled up level with the freight hatch and the contents loaded board. It crossed Rintlen's mind that the Wienzmans might try and sneak through the security barrier dressed in some kind of airport uniform as a disguise, but from where they sat they had a clear view of the approach to the jetty twenty yards away and Gerdler remained positive that no one remotely resembling the two fugitives had gone by.

Shortly before eight the first of the regular passengers arrived. An English couple with a little girl, the wife complaining while the husband smoked his pipe stoically. Their name would be Johnson, Rintlen ticked them off on the list he had been given. They were followed by a car containing a large florid faced man and three women. Judging by the way the flying-boat's purser came hurrying down the gangway to meet them, and the eagerness with which the porters clustered about, these must be the Curtises, he decided. The striking looking woman in a silver fox bolero was evidently the financier's wife, while the blonde haired girl and the plain looking female with her, were secretary and maid respectively.

Laura Hartman had arrived at the lake in a state of acute nervous anticipation, alert for the first sign that their plan had misfired. To begin with the sight of the armed carabinieri standing about had alarmed her, and she had feared the worst, till she recalled Desmond's remarks about the gold on board. Losing no time she shepherded the Curtises quickly up the gangway.

From the look on Sandy Everett's face she could tell instantly that all had gone well. 'We've got them safely hidden away upstairs,' he whispered as he handed her in through the hatch. 'It all went like a dream.'

Inside, in the Promenade lounge Charlotte Curtis had found Desmond explaining some of the construction details of a German Dornier flying-boat which was moored nearby, to Mr. Johnson.

'Why! Captain what a surprise,' she greeted him stridently. 'We see so little of you nowadays I almost thought you had left us.'

'I'm afraid there's been a great deal of work to attend to in these past days Mrs. Curtis,' he answered her with all the civility he could muster, but the financier's wife did not seem to notice the coldness in his voice.

'My husband and I insist you have dinner with us tonight in London,' she told him.

'I'm not sure,' Desmond began, but Charlotte silenced his objections immediately, 'I tell you we insist,' she interrupted firmly, 'we won't take no for an answer or listen to any excuse.'

Desmond frowned. After all he had been through in the past twenty four hours, he was in no mood to put up with any more of Charlotte's intrigues, 'I am sorry Mrs. Curtis,' he replied in a tone of the most perfunctory regret, 'but unfortunately I shall not be free tonight.' He was about to explain that he would be attending the inquiry instead, but then deciding at the last moment that she deserved no such explanation, changed his mind. 'I have made other arrangements,' he said flatly.

Charlotte went white about the mouth, her eyes widened in surprise, for a moment she appeared about to say something in reply. He saw her bite her lower lip to keep it steady, then abruptly she flounced off towards the stern with a toss of her head.

Laura had been watching the exchange with interest, but more passengers were appearing at the hatchway, Mr. and

Mrs. King were coming aboard, followed by the d'Estes. There was time for only a brief word and smile between the two of them before they had to move apart. He would have to try and see her alone later; perhaps after the inquiry there would be time enough to get up to London and let her know how it had gone.

Stewart Curtis was unwilling to pay much attention to his wife's complaints over Desmond's behaviour. He was in any case in a highly worried state of mind. The B.B.C. News broadcast from London which he had managed to catch late last night, had reported that the current political crisis was seriously depressing stockmarkets around the world. Klerksdorp had already drifted substantially downwards during the day's trading in London, and with the political situation worsening hourly, further falls were inevitable. If Suttenheim, or anyone else for that matter were to unload large lines of the mine's stock at such a time the effect would be disastrous.

The financier's moroseness was matched by equally strained feelings on the part of Luca and Jacquetta. The gulf between them caused by the quarrels of the last few days had been widened incalculably by the events of the night so that communication between the two was now non-existent. While the Baron entertained Charlotte with his forced gallantries, Jacquetta for her part sat counting the hours and minutes before she could be alone with Rashid again.

'Those are the last of the passengers,' the Italian Police lieutenant informed Rintlen unnecessarily as the figures of Dr. Van Smit and Rashid disappeared into the flying boat. 'Now we must wait to see whether these Farenzis or Weinzmans of yours attempt to board.' Rintlen grunted in reply and glanced at the time; it had gone half past eight, if the Professor and his daughter intended repeating the trick they had pulled at the station in Venice, they were cutting it very fine.

A telephone on a nearby desk rang shrilly; leaving the window the Lieutenant crossed the room and lifted the receiver. For a moment or two he listened, then the two Germans heard him utter a sharp exclamation of surprise, followed by what was obviously an urgent demand for confirmation.

'I do not understand,' he said, replacing the handset and confronting the others. 'It is the Captain of the airliner, they say he is telling the flight controllers all his passengers are on board and is asking permission to begin take-off.'

'It's a mistake,' Rintlen retorted, 'it must be, we've been watching here since seven and there are still two passengers not yet arrived. You've counted them yourself.'

'I know,' the Lieutenant's face contorted unhappily, 'that is what I said but they tell me the crew are insisting they are ready to go.'

'Damnation!' Rintlen leapt to his feet, 'they've tricked us somehow. They must have managed to smuggle the two aboard disguised as crew members or workmen sometime during the night before we arrived. Quickly!' he took the startled Italian by the arm and hurried him to the door. 'You must search the plane!'

'I am sorry, Lieutenant,' Desmond O'Neill was saying a short while later, 'I would like to be of assistance to you, but I am afraid what you ask is impossible. I cannot allow my ship to be searched and my passengers upset on such a slender pretext. As far as Imperial Airways is concerned two people have failed to keep their booking and the flight must leave without them.'

The young police officer blinked in surprise at this refusal. 'But Captain, I have the permission of your Airline Manager,' he protested; Desmond shook his head firmly, 'I am the Captain and the only person whose authority matters on board *Caterina*. Until I am shown some kind of warrant informing me why these people are wanted, or proof that they may be travelling under another name, I refuse to allow a search. To do so would be to cast suspicion on myself and my crew.'

Reluctant to return empty handed to Rintlen, the Italian tried once more, 'I can assure you Captain,' he affirmed, 'a warrant, an official request for the arrest of these persons is even now on its way from the German embassy. It details charges made against them and contains full descriptions and aliases.' Desmond gave him a hard look. 'Are you quite sure this is a civil matter?' he asked. 'Or are you in reality a member of the political police?'

'I have already proved my credentials,' the Lieutenant snapped, stung by the question, 'you will serve no useful purpose by this obstruction, and if you persist the consequences for you may be extremely serious.'

Desmond's lips tightened angrily, 'I was not aware that Italy was yet part of the Third Reich,' he said crudely and was gratified to see a flush of outrage on the face of the Lieutenant. 'Produce your warrant if you can, but until then neither you nor your men set foot aboard my ship.'

Leaving the carabinieri to guard the gangway, the Lieutenant retreated back to the shore to find the Airline Manager and see what he could do to speed up the arrival of the warrant and other documents.

The senior management official on duty was a small, cheerful ex-naval commander named Donaldson. 'I don't know what you're up to old boy,' he said when he poked his head through the hatch a few minutes later, 'but I can tell you, you can't win. If you don't let these chaps look over the plane they won't let you take off. It's as simple as that. They've got half the Italian Army outside as it is, and there's a motor launch cruising off your bows into the bargain.'

'How long do you think we can hold them off?' Desmond asked him. The older man pursed his lips. 'The word is the police will receive authority from Rome to make a forced boarding within the next thirty minutes. There's a German fellow here representing the affair as a direct challenge to the Italian government. You can guess how sensitive the Duce will be on that point.'

They were standing on the flight deck by the radio desk. Desmond was uncomfortably aware of Frazer watching him with a virtuous 'I told you so' expression on his face. As yet no-one outside the crew and Laura Hartman knew of the refugees' presence. He wondered how much longer he could maintain the charade.

'I have an idea,' he told Donaldson, as he escorted the latter down to the hatchway. 'Give me ten minutes or so, and then tell the Lieutenant that as a compromise I am prepared to allow him and him alone, on board. Say to him I will show him all over the ship as a private visitor, but not as a police official. But make sure he realizes the offer applies to him only, I don't want any German Gestapo men coming with him.'

'Sounds feasible,' the manager agreed. 'I'll give it a try anyway, but I'm telling you,' he warned as he ducked his head to step outside, 'this is as far as I can go to help. If the Lieutenant won't swallow it you'll have to let the search go ahead.'

Several of the passengers had clustered round listening to this latest exchange. Fending off their questions Desmond made his way forward; at the stairway to the upper deck Laura stopped him. 'What's happening?' she asked, 'are they going to search the plane?'

'I think I may have thought of a way out,' he whispered, 'there will be a Police officer coming round in a few minutes so for God's sake act naturally.' And with no time to waste in further explanation he began to climb the stairs.

To Desmond's relief the Lieutenant presented himself at the passenger gangway some quarter of an hour later and the two men saluted one another punctiliously.

'It is most kind of you to extend your invitation Captain,' the Italian remarked in what he assumed was correct formal English. 'Not at all,' Desmond assured him, 'it is an honour to welcome you on board.'

Eyeing each other warily they began their conducted tour, starting with the after cabin. Stewart Curtis and the d'Estes regarded their intrusion with curiosity, especially when Desmond unlocked the door in the far bulkhead to allow the Lieutenant to peer through into the freight and baggage hold beyond.

'Most interesting Captain, most interesting,' he commented, betraying slight signs of embarrassment at having to carry out his task under the eyes of so distinguished a government official as the Baron. 'I understand there is a second hold on the upper level also?'

'There is a mail compartment beyond the flight deck,' Desmond agreed, leading the way out through the promenade cabin. 'A part of the bullion shipment is stored there.' The policeman glanced surreptitiously at the passengers in the two cabins they passed through, and took care Desmond noticed, to look inside the cloakrooms and galley as they continued forward. For all the man's apparent politeness he was evidently determined to make a thorough examination of the flying-boat. In the smoking saloon he paused and rapped on the forward bulkhead. 'I am told there is another compartment in the nose,' he said pointedly.

'Yes, the mooring compartment,' Desmond answered, praying inwardly that this was as far as the Lieutenant's homework went, 'it is reached from the cockpit above, we will go up there now.'

At the rear of *Caterina*'s mail room, behind a low hatch on the bulkhead, now concealed by the carefully stacked bullion crates, Siegret and her father lay prone in total darkness amid the airless confines of the narrow bedding locker. Squeezed in between the high ceilings of the promenade and midship cabins, and the flying-boat's spine, this cramped space, nowhere more than three feet high, was the storage chamber for the mattresses, pillows and linen, used when the lower deck cabins were converted into bedrooms for sleeping.

It was into here, screened by the hastily shifted crates that Desmond and Sandy had bundled the pair during the few minutes before the Lieutenant's search. Afraid almost to breathe, they lay still and silent beneath a layer of blankets, listening to the faint sounds of the other passengers below.

Up on the flight deck Sandy Everett was waiting for them; at a slight nod from Desmond he directed the Italian right into the mailroom. 'This, as you see Lieutenant, is the second hold you were inquiring about. Normally it is used exclusively for mail.' Together they watched uneasily while their visitor poked among the piled mail bags. At length he straightened up and gave a look at the stacked crates at the rear. 'Ah, the gold,' he exclaimed with a trace of awe in his voice, 'there is really two million American dollars in these boxes?'

'Here and in the after hold yes, very nearly that amount,' Desmond replied, 'and now if you would like to see the cockpit and the mooring compartment, I'll take you forward.'

Frazer was in his seat contriving to maintain his expression of outraged contempt. Ralph pulled open the floor hatch, and they all waited while the Lieutenant bumped and fumbled about below. When at length he emerged his appearance was dishevelled and his attitude crestfallen.

'Is there anything else you would care to see?' Desmond offered, but the Italian shook his head. 'Thank you no,' he said brushing dust off his uniform, 'you have been very helpful. It seems the gentlemen from Berlin have made a mistake.'

Concealing his relief beneath a mask of indifference, Desmond conducted the Lieutenant down to the entrance hatch once more. The two bid each other farewell courteously. No sooner was the hatch closed again than Desmond leapt back up to the flight deck. 'Cast off the bow warps, Sandy,' he told the young purser who was still standing in the cockpit. 'Ken, start doping up the motors. We're pulling out of here right away. Ralph, get on to flight control and tell them we've been cleared by the police and are taking off. Don't ask permission, just tell 'em we're doing it and then cut the contact.'

The crew sprang to his orders with alacrity. Down below the startled passengers heard the sudden thump of the hatch doors being slammed shut and the burst of sound from the engines as the four motors snarled into life one after the other in rapid succession. As they hastily sought their seats, Rintlen was screaming at the Lieutenant in the terminal building. 'You must stop them, they are getting away.'

'There is nothing we can do,' the officer shook his head. 'Your man is not on board. I searched the whole aircraft from end to end.'

'Fool! You half blind idiotic fool!' The German was beside himself with rage, the others in the room regarded him with amazement. 'They tricked you, the Wienzmans were hidden somewhere and you missed them, why else do you think they are leaving in such a hurry?' The Lieutenant hesitated for a second, 'Call them on the radio,' he ordered, 'tell the Captain he does not have permission to take off yet.'

'Control are trying to get through to us skipper,' Kendricks shouted above the roar of the engines running up under full power, 'Ignore them,' Desmond called back. *Catrina* was already out into the open lake. 'Can anyone see that blasted launch?'

'She's off the starboard bow, about a half mile down wind,' Frazer told him, 'she looks to be hove to.'

'The plane does not reply, we cannot contact her,' an anguished operator told the Lieutenant. Rintlen was plucking at his sleeve. 'The launch, you must radio the launch. Tell it to move across the plane's path and force her to stop.'

On the desk the telephone rang again. 'It's Rome sir.' A clerk held out the receiver. 'They are saying if the aeroplane has not gone you are to hold it.'

If the precise words escaped Rintlen, the man's meaning was only too clear to him. As the Lieutenant stood gaping at the news, unable to decide what to do, the SD officer galvanized him into action. 'Send a radio message to the launch out there at once,' he instructed, 'tell them they are to intercept the flying-boat. They still have time. See the plane is turning into the wind, she has not yet started her take-off.'

'The launch has started moving towards us Skipper, she's picking up speed, you can see the wash kicked up behind her.' With his presence at the radio desk no longer necessary, Ralph Kendricks was maintaining a watch from the windows with the binoculars. Bringing *Caterina*'s nose round into the wind, Desmond eased the throttle momentarily to steady her. 'She's moving to cut across our path,' Ken Frazer said in alarm, 'they're going to head us off.'

'Not while I'm flying this ship they're not,' Desmond snapped, slamming the throttle levers open viciously. 'Give me full boost.' Engines roaring, the great aircraft surged forward over the surface of the lake.

'They have begun their take-off run, they are not slowing down yet,' the Police Lieutenant commented, as he and the two Germans, together with a small crowd of interested spectators, watched the drama being acted out on the water. Like clock-work toys, the craft in the distance began closing in on one another.

'He must be aiming to pass right in front of the aircraft,' the Lieutenant exclaimed in wonderment as he watched the launch's commander altering course slightly, bringing the craft up on to a heading which pointed her bow directly at the terminal. 'He is trying to force the pilot to turn away and abandon his take off.'

'Haven't they got guns? Why don't they shoot?' Rintlen demanded. The Lieutenant and his men were shocked. 'Shoot at an unarmed passenger plane? Impossible. Even in war we could not do such a thing.'

Rintlen took the rebuke in silence. In fact it seemed certain he thought as he looked out at the converging white tracks in the water, that the suggestion was in any case unnecessary. Even from where he was standing the launch commander's action appeared impossibly suicidal. The combined closing speed of the two vessels had to be over one hundred and twenty-five knots, a devastating collision was only seconds away.

There had been no time to release the Wienzmans from their hiding-place.

The noise of the four engines starting up only feet away half-deafened them, the thunderous roar echoing through the tiny unprotected space, drowning out all other sound, till their bodies shook and their ears hurt. As the power built up and the flying-boat raced across the lake, they clung to one another in the dark, with relief. Incredible as it seemed their plan had worked, they had slipped free from the Nazis' grasp again.

'Flaps one quarter,' Desmond called out. The servomotors whined as Frazer's hand adjusted the levers. The motor launch was now less than two hundred feet ahead, 'Seventy knots Skipper,' he yelled, 'lift-off speed.' In point of fact the aircraft was travelling barely fast enough to break loose from the water's grip, but they had no time to wait longer, easing the control stick back Desmond waited for her to come away.

'She's not going to make it,' Frazer's voice rose, high pitched, in a cry of sheer terror. 'We're going to crash.' From the windscreen they could see the appalled faces of the launch crew as her commander slewed his wheel hard round in a desperate attempt to escape the bellowing leviathan which was racing down upon them.

With a savage curse, Desmond pushed the stick hard forward and as quickly dragged it fiercely back again, rocking the plane sharply in a last ditch effort to jerk them free. For an instant he thought he had failed and braced himself for the crash. Then, even as the boat loomed to fill the windscreen, he felt *Caterina* lift her nose and almost unbelievably they were in the air.

So close overhead did they pass that at first the stunned observers on the shore thought the two craft had actually collided in some way. As *Caterina* rose off the surface, the launch disappeared in a tremendous froth of spray which reached above her stubby masthead and blotted her out completely for several seconds. Only her subsequent reappearance and the sight of the flying-boat winging its way unharmed above the hills, convinced them that a catastrophe had been averted.

Both Bracciano and Rome air-traffic controls made repeated efforts to contact *Caterina*, and order an immediate return to the Lake, but obedient to Desmond's instructions, Ralph Kendricks switched off his equipment, simulating radio malfunction and assisted Sandy to extract the Wienzmans from the bedding locker.

Seemingly none the worse for their ordeal, father and daughter were taken down to the lower deck cloakrooms to make themselves presentable before being introduced to the other passengers. With the exception of Laura these had been unaware till now of their presence, and the two fugitives were received with interest and curiosity.

Mr. and Mrs. King were both delighted at the adventure. 'But you should have let us in on your secret,' they remonstrated when Laura brought the Jewish girl and her father in to meet them. 'Why, we would have considered it our privilege to be allowed to help you all.' Only Luca d'Este and the Curtises remained aloof in the seclusion of the after cabin.

Jacquetta herself had forsaken their company to go and sit in the smoking saloon with Rashid. Though the presence of Mrs. Johnson's husband and the enigmatically friendly Dr. Van Smit acted as a restraint, both felt a need to be close to one another.

The Doctor himself was temporarily in something of a quandary. His original intention had been to demand money from the couple under threat of revealing their affair. When he had found himself sharing a taxi out to the lake with the young Arab, he had welcomed it as a perfect opportunity to open negotiations. Something in Rashid's manner however, in the pride with which he disdainfully regarded his surroundings, had prompted Van Smit to hold his tongue. It might be wiser, he decided to approach the Baroness alone, rather than risk the unpredictable reactions of her lover.

On the flight deck Frazer and Ralph Kendricks were plotting a route for Marseilles which would take them out of Italian territorial waters in the shortest possible time. 'We should see Mt. Rotondo in Corsica in approximately half an hour, Skipper,' Frazer said. Desmond had withdrawn the engine boost and the noise level in the cockpit had dropped to normal. They were flying at 7000 feet in a clear sky, the mainland coast line was almost out of sight astern. 'Do you think they'll send fighters after us?' he said. Desmond shook his head. 'We've got a good lead and by the time anything could catch us we will be in French airspace. It was close but I reckon we made it back there.'

Unknown to him, Paul Rintlen had arrived at the identical conclusion. The Italians, he had discovered to his chagrin, were inclined to think the flying-boat Captain had distinguished himself by his determined exploit and any kind of pursuit was obviously not being considered. The entire operation had turned into the kind of fiasco he had wanted to avoid. The Wienzmans, and he had no doubt at all in his mind that they had both been on board, would be safe in England by the afternoon, leaving him with the alternative of either following them, or returning to confront Heydrich with his tail between his legs, and the last course he did not relish at all.

'What shall we do now Standartenfuhrer?' Gerdler asked foolishly, and goaded beyond endurance, Rintlen lashed out savagely at the youth. 'We follow them of course,' he snarled with a string of abuse.

'To England?' Gerdler cringed away at the blow, his voice registering his astonishment.

'Yes, to England, where else did you think we'd go?' At least, Rintlen told himself as they sat in the car on the way back to the embassy, by continuing the pursuit to England, he was postponing the day when he would have to face Heydrich's wrath.

Charlotte Curtis was bored again. 'I want a drink,' she answered when the steward appeared in response to her summons. 'A dry martini.' Her husband glared at her. 'Well, I'm bored,' she said with a toss of the head, 'what else is there to do, for heaven's sake?'

'Can't you wait a bit?' Stewart Curtis grumbled. 'It's only a short flight. We'll be in Marseilles soon.'

'No, I can't wait, I want a drink now,' Charlotte replied petulantly. 'Very good Madam,' Andy answered, concealing his distaste for women who started on spirits before eleven o'clock. 'Will the gentleman be requiring anything?'

'Coffee for me,' Curtis grunted without bothering to look up. 'And I too, shall have a cocktail,' Luca decided and was rewarded with an approving look from Charlotte.

'And hurry it up damn you,' Curtis snapped suddenly and unnecessarily as the steward prepared to leave, 'last time my coffee was ice cold.'

'I'll do my best sir,' swallowing his anger at such treatment, Andy returned to the galley where he found Laura mixing a glass of barley water for the Johnson child. 'I hope you didn't mind,' she said a little guiltily, 'I thought it would be a help if you were busy.'

Andy smiled. 'Mrs. Hartman, it's a pleasure to fly with you,' he assured her, 'which is more than I can say for your boss.'

'Oh dear,' Laura made a wry face, 'Is he being rude again? I'm afraid he doesn't seem to be in a very good temper today.'

'You never said a truer word Ma'am,' Andy agreed, setting to work to brew up coffee and mix the cocktails, Laura watched him. 'Tell me something Andy?' she asked. 'Yes Ma'am?' he looked up from the stove. 'Your trips, are they always as . . .' she groped for a word, 'as eventful as this one? I mean things have never stopped happening from the moment I got on the plane it seems. First the crocodile, then the race in the desert, and now the narrow escape with those poor Jewish refugees.'

'Well,' Andy considered for a moment or two, 'things do 'appen on these long flights. The public, passengers and the rest, they don't mind at all, but the bosses hate it.'

A few moments later Laura came out of the galley and returned to her seat looking thoughtful. The steward's words had put an idea in her head.

Hurrying in through the imposing double doors of the German Embassy in Rome, Rintlen stormed along to the office he had been allocated and flung himself down in a chair. The journey back into the centre of Rome had coincided with the city's morning rush hour and more than an hour had been wasted sitting in the traffic-locked car. He and Gerdler were booked on the K.L.M. flight to London leaving shortly after 12 noon, but before they left Rintlen needed to telephone ahead.

'Go and find Strasser,' he said brusquely to Gerdler, 'and send him to me here. Then you can pack up our things.'

'Yes Standartenfuhrer, at once,' the youth turned to go, 'and find someone to send me some schnapps,' Rintlen yelled after him. Christ, but he needed a drink now. The job had gone wrong, badly wrong and news of that was probably on its way to Heydrich already. Unless Rintlen could reach England and achieve some kind of success his outlook was bleak indeed.

An orderly entered with a bottle of liquor and a glass, but the minutes ticked by and failed to produce any sign of the SS officer. Fuming with impatience at the delay, Rintlen rang the bell for the orderly again and was bawling out his demands when Strasser appeared in the doorway, behind him stood two uniformed men. 'Where the hell have you been?' Rintlen snapped, 'I've been waiting here twenty minutes.'

Motioning to the orderly to leave Strasser approached the desk. His former attitude of subservience and even fear seemed to have been shed, and he now addressed the SD man coldly. 'I

have been on the telephone to Berlin,' he replied, 'before your
return the Ambassador had begun to receive complaints about
your actions out at Lake Bracciano. You have caused considerable embarrassment; naturally I felt compelled to report
this to the proper authorities, to Obergruppenfuhrer Heydrich
to be exact.'

For the first time in his life Rintlen felt the beginnings of the
fear which he had so often seen in his victims. A curious numb-
ness seemed to spread through him, his mouth became so dry
he could speak only with difficulty. 'Heydrich?' he croaked.
'You called Heydrich?'

'Yes, I spoke with Heydrich,' Strasser said with satisfaction.
'He was most grateful for what I had to tell him. He also gave
me orders concerning you.' His voice grew abruptly harsh.
'You are to be returned to Berlin forthwith under escort.' He
held out a hand. 'You will now surrender your pistol.'

There was nothing to do but obey. At a curt order the two
SS guards took up station on either side of the door. Pocketing
the weapon, Strasser stalked out without another word. Behind
him Paul Rintlen reached for the schnapps bottle with trembling hands.

Ken Frazer had taken over the controls from Desmond to
enable the latter to write up the flying-boat's log. Normally the
task was left till after they arrived at Southampton, but on this
occasion Desmond had little doubt that the records would be
required of him as soon as *Caterina* landed. He wrote slowly,
choosing his words with care. In the matter of the Wienzmans'
escape, he had decided to adhere strictly to the truth, reporting
the facts exactly as they had occurred and leaving the inquiry
panel to make their own judgement.

As regards Ralph Kendricks he was still not sure in his own
mind whether he had taken the right decision in not revealing
the radio officer's near breakdown at Cairo. Though he had
been pleased to see that Ralph had borne up well during the
tense last seconds of their brush with the police launch, and it
seemed likely that by talking about his fears to his Captain, he
had largely overcome them, Desmond was aware there were

commanders who would have insisted on the man's removal.

The B.B.C. news broadcast which had come on the air shortly after they passed over Corsica was still at the back of his mind. The threat of another war in Europe appeared to be growing with depressing speed. The point in time where the ever increasing appetite of the Nazis would have to be stopped by force could not be far distant. Soon, Desmond thought heavily, he would be exchanging *Caterina*'s flight deck for the cramped cockpit of a carrier-borne torpedo bomber and the world he knew now would have been swept away for ever, just as the world of his boyhood had vanished in another war twenty-five years ago.

At least now he had no family left to receive a black edged telegram of regret from the War Office, like the one that his parents had received on Mark's death. They had both survived only another three years themselves, before the great post-war influenza epidemic had claimed them.

In the right hand cockpit seat Frazer idly observed the small movements made by the control yoke in response to the auto pilot. He was in no doubt that Desmond O'Neill was about to suffer severely at the hands of the airline management, and that he himself was morally justified in taking the action he had. It was his duty, no less, he told himself afresh, to place the full facts of the trip before the inquiry; and a man should be proud of doing his duty. Already he was turning over in his mind the phrases he would use when revealing his Captain's incredible behaviour at Rome.

Paul Rintlen was being sent back to his death. There could be no room for doubts or illusions on that score. He had too good a knowledge of the mind of his master 'hangman Heydrich' to allow himself the luxury of thinking otherwise. Failure of any kind was punishable always; failure coupled with the knowledge of secrets which threatened the state could result in only one penalty. Rintlen shivered as he recalled a night in 1934. June the 30th, 'the night of the long knives' when Hitler and the SS had settled accounts with Ernst Rohm's storm troopers, and over four hundred top figures had perished in the slaughter.

Rintlen had been a junior officer then, an Untersturmfuhrer newly assigned to Heydrich's Sicherheitsdienst. It had been Heydrich who had masterminded the arrests and decided who should die and who merely disappear into the shroud of a concentration camp. To demonstrate proof of his total dedication to the service of the state, Untersturmfuhrer Rintlen had been required to participate in the executions. He had been placed in command of an eight man SD firing squad at the Stadelheim Prison in Munich.

They had stood in the prison's sombre, high walled courtyard in the chill, grey light of early dawn, as one by one, thirty-seven frightened men were led out from the cellars by black uniformed guards who tore open their shirts and drew a charcoal circle round each one's left nipple, before tying them against a wall twenty feet away.

With an effort he brought himself back to the present. He was sitting in the rear of one of the embassy's Mercedes, between Strasser and an SS sergeant. In front of him Gerdler slumped next to the driver. Rintlen speculated briefly on what fate held in store for the Nazi youth; probably nothing worse than a spell in a forced labour battalion working on the new autobahns or on the border fortifications.

The car turned right into the Corso Vittorio Emannuele heading for the Tiber bridges. The plane was due to take-off at midday; ironically only a quarter of an hour before the K.L.M. flight for Paris and London on which he and Gerdler had been booked. The tickets were still in his inside pocket.

Strasser leant forward suddenly and rapped the driver sharply on the shoulder. 'Where do you think you're taking us?' he said. The driver half turned his head. 'I thought you said to go to the Lake,' he answered.

'Fool, I said the aerodrome, not the marine airport,' Strasser snarled at him. 'Turn the car round and be quick about it, we haven't much time.' Muttering apologies the driver put the wheel over and attempted to swing across the traffic. Within seconds they were in collision with a car travelling in the opposite direction.

The damage was not serious, no more than a slightly scraped wing on the driver's side, but the owner of the other vehicle leapt out instantly and proceeded to attack the occupants of the Mercedes with loud abuse.

'Tell him we will pay for the damage. Tell him to call at the embassy.' Strasser wound down his window and began trying to pacify the Italian. Almost without thinking Rintlen saw his opportunity for escape and grasped it. Reaching quickly across the sergeant on his right he wrenched open the door handle at the same time pushing with all the strength he could muster. Before the others in the car realized what was happening the force of his shove had sent Rintlen and the SS man spilling out into the road.

Picking himself up in the same instant, Rintlen was on his feet and dodging away through the traffic amid squeaking brakes and the angry shouts and horn blasts of nearby motorists, while his captors were still staring round in bewilderment.

A quarter to twelve saw *Caterina* gliding quietly in to touch down at Marignane, the civil airport for Marseilles, amid the crisp brightness of a spring day. Here again taxis were waiting to carry the passengers off to their hotel, the Noallies at the top of the Canebiere, while the crew waited at the dockside berth, and cursed the crated bullion which fettered them to their plane.

For Siegret and her father the air of France was intoxicating with its freedom and their happiness communicated itself to the rest of the passengers, with the result that lunch was a cheerful affair in spite of the seriousness of the political crisis. Even Jacquetta momentarily forgot the dilemma of her position with the thought that soon she would be able to snatch a few hours alone with Rashid while Luca was off on diplomatic business in England.

Only Stewart Curtis remained unmoved by the atmosphere. As at Athens, his first action had been to call through to his brokers in London, and though he had been successful this time, the news he had received had been unrelievedly bad; worse even than he had expected. In the wake of the general collapse of the market, Klerksdorp had fallen sharply as news of the German invasion of Czechoslovakia had been received. More alarming still, the broker reported several large lines of stock had been offered for sale during the past thirty-six hours. These had found buyers, but only at prices well below current market levels, and this had weakened the stock further. There could be little doubt, Curtis reckoned, with an increasing sense of hopelessness, that in his rear, the South African bankers had begun to unload their holdings. It was now only a question of time before the news broke on the world, leaving him ruined unless he could reach New York first.

With this thought in mind he told Laura to place another call for him; this time to one of the directors of Imperial Airways, a business acquaintance of some standing.

'I'll certainly do what I can to help Stewart,' the director was telling him a short while later, 'as a matter of fact I've just been reading a report on your flight. The problem is, these schedules depend on three factors. The first is the weather; the Atlantic is a tricky crossing at the best of times, the second is crew availability, and the third is the convenience of the passengers. Right now I can tell you we are very short on experienced crews in the Atlantic division. What the passenger position is at the moment I don't know.'

Thanking his friend and hanging up, Curtis sent Laura off to settle the bill with the hotel and went in to lunch. Laura Hartman made a call of her own to London. She spoke for almost twenty minutes from the phone booth in the foyer of the hotel and when she came out she paid the bill with her personal money. Then she went off to talk to the Wienzmans.

By a quarter to two the flight was under way again and *Caterina* was heading northward, climbing steadily to cross the mountains which lay between her and the coast of Britain, three and a half hours away.

As she did so, some two hundred miles to the east a Junkers 52 of K.L.M. Airlines was approaching the Swiss Italian border. Among the passengers, secure in the cover of his false passport which proclaimed him to be a citizen of Switzerland, was Paul Rintlen. Now that the immediate danger had receded, he had begun to plan once more. If only he could reach England undetected he might still find a way of carrying out his mission and eliminating the Wienzmans even if he could no longer recapture them for Germany. In which case Heydrich might well be suitably impressed. If not . . . Rintlen tried not to think of the future if he failed. His wife and two young children were still in Germany. Even if he himself were to remain abroad, they would be at the mercy of the SD – sippenhaft – collective responsibility. Visions of the police smashing in the doors of the trim little house in the Wansee suburb of Berlin and dragging away his family, swam before his eyes. At all costs he had to finish off the Wienzmans for good.

The five hours time difference between Europe and the New England seaboard meant that in the boathouse on Warren Lake, Pat Jarrett was still only halfway through the morning. Now he was actually engaged in fitting the Colts into the wings of the Supermarine, his task had taken on a new immediacy; the previous evening he had worked on until past midnight, only to be up again as soon as it was light.

Standing back for a moment he wiped a sleeve over his face and surveyed his progress so far. On the portside wing a section of the aluminium plating had been carefully removed, to reveal the twin machine guns lying snugly in their bay, held in position by diagonal steel bracing struts attached to the main spars. On the wing's leading edge a pair of neat holes had been cut to admit the mouths of the spring loaded blast tubes. To the right of the gun-breeches lay the ammunition trays, with their carefully packed contents of eight-hundred and fifty rounds of .50 ammunition; enough for a full half minute's firing at each gun's rate of fourteen rounds per second, and certainly adequate for the purpose. Running away behind were the leads to the fire control system, wired up to the firing button on the joystick, and the gunbay heating tube from the radiator, necessary to prevent the Colts from freezing up and jamming in the icy slip-stream at several thousand feet of altitude.

The starboard wing was less well advanced, but here too, Jarrett had made better progress than he had anticipated. The bay had been opened up and the bracings attached, but the guns themselves had yet to be placed in position. Mentally he checked off the list of things still to be done: installation of the second pair of Colts and their ammunition; connecting up of the fire control system and fixing up of the gunsight. Modern fighters were using sophisticated reflector sights, but Jarrett had been unable to obtain one of these and was having to make do with the old metal ring and bead model, unchanged since his former combat days. Then the guns themselves would have to be rest fired and adjusted, and finally the S4's engine would need a last careful tuning.

Even allowing for unforeseen difficulties he was well ahead of schedule. Indeed the only real factor which remained to worry him was the weather. Today for the first time the sky was heavily overcast and rain had been falling for the past hour, turning to sleet at times. Comforting himself with the knowledge that he still had three days to go before the bullion flight was due, he returned to his labours. The thought had come to him that with everything going so well he could afford the time off to drive into Keene for lunch again. The memory of the girl Susie had proved surprisingly difficult to throw off.

Fifty miles inland from the Mediterranean coast the cloud cover began. Layers of stratocumulus stretching out on either hand to the horizon, burying the fields and villages of Languedoc beneath an impenetrable white blanket and building up ahead over the Cevennes Mountains into threatening peaks.

'We should be safe at 10,000 feet according to the forecasters; we'll set the autopilot at that altitude for the present and keep a careful watch on the engine temperatures,' Desmond instructed.

'Aye, aye, Skipper,' Frazer lined up the indices for speed, course and altitude on the sperry autopilot control and clicked it into engagement. 'I've turned on the carburettor heat too,' he added flicking down the switches and watching the slight drop on the engine rev. counters as they registered the move.

Ice forming on the carburettor inlets was the Empire class boats only vice. In severe weather conditions they could be forced to 20,000 feet or more without oxygen, to the considerable discomfort of those on board, in an effort to climb above the clouds. The introduction of the exhaust heat system had gone some way toward solving the problem, but at such times, all crews listened carefully to the forecasts for the weather ahead of them.

On this occasion however, the forecasters were correct and *Caterina* soared on untroubled in a bright afternoon sunlight reflected back brilliantly off the surface of the cloud below. Full and sleepy after their excellent luncheon, the passengers drowsed in their comfortable armchairs, occasionally scanning the papers and listening to one another's small talk. In the smoking saloon the bridge game had restarted and at half past three Draper began serving tea and hot buttered toast.

In his office in Piccadilly the Public Relations Manager of Imperial Airways had just been telephoned by a big London newspaper. 'We've had a report that one of your airliners has rescued two Jewish refugees from under the noses of the Nazis and Italians,' the reporter was saying, 'an old man and his daughter. Apparently the passengers and crew smuggled them on board at Rome and then the Captain took off with the Italian secret police in hot pursui.'

'I've heard nothing of this,' the Manager protested in surprise, 'are you sure? What flight is it supposed to have happened on?'

'Flight 109 from Cairo through to New York,' the journalist consulted his notes. 'We have definite confirmation our end anyway. The plane's due in at Southampton at half past four and the two escapers have agreed to give their interviews. It should make a good story, apparently the Captain's quite a hero; on this trip he saved a girl's life when her companion was attacked by a crocodile, outflew a storm in the desert, won a motor race while they were in Cairo and now he's finishing up with a Scarlet Pimpernel stunt. Chap named O'Neill, you must be pretty proud of him.'

'We do have an officer of that name,' the Manager admitted cautiously, 'and there may be an element of truth in some of your statements, but I can't confirm anything at this stage.'

'Don't worry about that,' his caller brushed the words aside, 'we've sent someone down to meet the plane. It'll make a nice lead, what with all the news of Hitler invading Czechoslovakia, "the human side to Nazi expansion", "victims flee German terror in British plane", the readers will love it.'

Caterina sunk slowly through the wet grey fog of the clouds. From the windows the passengers stared out gloomily at the swirling mist flying past beyond the glass. Then abruptly the flying-boat dropped clear and the white capped sea of the channel was visible beneath them, cold and inhospitable. A shoreline came in sight and drew swiftly near and soon they were passing over the Isle of Wight; peering down as they descended steadily they could distinguish the features of individual ships in the Solent, while at Spithead, and in the harbour of Portsmouth off the starboard wing, lay the sleek, grey outlines and white decks of the warships of the Channel Fleet.

On schedule almost to the second the flying-boat was made fast between the pontoons of berth 108, alongside the towering superstructure of Orient Line's *Oronsay*. Immediately the aircraft was surrounded by an eager throng of reporters and photographers.

IX

From. FLIGHT CONTROLLER'S LOG. IMPERIAL AIRWAYS (MARINE DIVISION) HYTHE SOUTH-AMPTON TUESDAY 14th MARCH 1939.

16.30 hrs. DURBAN–NEW YORK FLIGHT 109 CATERINA IN BOUND FROM MARSEILLES ON SCHEDULE, WITH GOLD BULLION TO VALUE OF $U.S. 1,980,000 CONSIGNED TO CARE OF FEDERAL RESERVE BANK WASHINGTON FOR ONWARD CARRIAGE. FIFTEEN PASSENGERS, THREE DISEMBARKING, REMAINDER IN TRANSIT FOR NEW YORK.
ON ARRIVAL CAPTAIN AND CREW ORDERED TO ATTEND INQUIRY INTO DEATH OF PASS-ENGER AT SHAMBE STATION, EQUATORIAL SUDAN.

THE inquiry by the Imperial Airways Management into Ian Thorne's death at Shambe was turning out to be everything Ken Frazer could have wished for. To begin with it was plain that the panel, composed of three of the company's senior Managers, all he was glad to note, appointed before the Government amalgamation and nationalization, were extremely annoyed at the degree of popular support being whipped up by the Press for Desmond O'Neill. Probably as a direct result, the chairman had announced in his opening remarks that the scope of the investigation had been widened to include the incidents at Lake Bracciano, and Desmond's general behaviour over the whole period of the flight from Durban.

Given all this to occupy them, Frazer felt it was going to be highly unlikely the panel would concern themselves overmuch with the possible causes of the fuel leak which had led to the landing at Shambe in the first place.

At the moment they were listening while a clerk read out passages from the log, dealing with the actual touchdown and the decision to send the passengers ashore. Besides the panel and the clerks and shorthand secretary, there were present Desmond and the crew of *Caterina*, including Andy Draper the steward, and one other of the Airline's Captains, Phil Harris, representing B.A.L.P.A. the Pilots Association, as well as a representative from the Foreign Office, and a Naval Commander sent by the Admiralty. Jack Priestly, the Operations manager was conspicuously absent. The proceedings were taking place in a long, bare and rather shabby office, normally used only for lectures and special briefings. The three panel members sat behind a table at the end furthest from the door, with the secretary and clerks at a desk on their left, and everybody else sitting on folding wooden chairs in front of them. Each time anyone moved in their seat these gave off a strident squeaking which made the chairman, a sour, cadaverous man close to retirement age, glare irritably at the culprit.

The clerk finished his reading and immediately Phil Harris rose to his feet. 'Mr. Chairman,' he began, 'may I ask why this committee has not invited any of the passengers from Flight 109 to attend this inquiry? Surely their evidence would be of some help?' He was an older man than Desmond and thicker set with a gingery moustache, Frazer regarded him with hostility. So too did the Chairman. 'I have already referred to this point Captain Harris,' he answered, 'the only passenger who witnessed any part of the incident was Mrs. Hartman and we already have her statement.'

Seemingly satisfied with this Harris resumed his seat whispering a few words to Desmond next to him as he did so. There then followed a lengthy cross-examination by the panel of the entire crew who were led step by step through each stage of the tragedy from the moment the first passengers reached the shore to the point where the search for Thorne's body was finally abandoned. Interspersed with this were more readings from the log, and quotations from Airline Regulations.

Frazer's part, like that of Ralph Kendricks, was limited to affirming that he had remained on board the aircraft and had been too far away to observe what had taken place on the jetty. It was clearly evident however, that the panel were seeking to show Desmond had been negligent in failing to warn the passengers of the danger from crocodiles.

'Looking back now, I suppose I should have done,' he conceded, when pressed on the point, 'but on the other hand I can't see that my doing so would have stopped Thorne from trying to take the launch out. He knew perfectly well he shouldn't be doing it, Laura, Mrs. Hartman has already said so.'

The chairman sniffed disapprovingly, 'Mrs. Hartman seems to say a lot of helpful things, but then her own part in this sorry affair is less than creditable in the opinion of many.'

'I can't accept that statement,' Desmond leapt to Laura's defence, 'Mrs. Hartman cannot be held responsible for the behaviour of an idiotic boy who insisted on showing off; any more than I can,' he added bitterly. The chairman smiled nastily, 'Mrs. Hartman is not under investigation,' he said, 'you, on the other hand, are and your degree of responsibility is just what we are attempting to ascertain.'

Here Captain Harris entered the fray once more, standing up he addressed the panel 'Are you aware Mr. Chairman,' he asked, 'that Mrs. Hartman has made an additional statement before a number of witnesses, a statement which is to be published in several national newspapers, to the effect that only Captain O'Neill's prompt action prevented her from falling into the river and very possibly being seized by a crocodile herself?'

'I have told you once we have Mrs. Hartman's statement before us made at the time of the incident,' the chairman replied sharply, 'any further evidence on her part is inadmissible.'

'This young lady certainly seems to be playing a most energetic role in the affair,' one of the other panel members, a stout, smartly dressed man with an unhealthy, pallid face remarked sardonically, 'is Captain O'Neill usually on such excellent terms with all his passengers?'

Before Desmond could reply to this insinuation however, Phil Harris interposed again, offering to produce a copy of Laura's statement to the press. This too was rejected, though with a noticeable hesitation on the part of the panel's third member. 'All the fuss in the papers is putting pressure on them,' Ralph Kendricks murmured to Frazer in a low voice, 'I wonder how the Board are taking it?'

It was just possible, Frazer realized with a jolt, that if the publicity being given to the flight were sufficiently favourable, the Airline board would feel unable to take disciplinary action against Desmond for diplomatic reasons unless the evidence against him were so strong, and the recommendation of the inquiry so severe, as to be incapable of being ignored. The incident at Shambe alone would be insufficient, therefore Frazer himself would have to provide the evidence when the turn came for him to speak on the events at Bracciano.

The investigation of this topic began quietly enough with Desmond outlining the circumstances of his introduction to the Wienzmans and his decision to help them. There were some snide remarks when he revealed that it had been through Laura he had first met the Professor and his daughter, but for the most part the three investigators contented themselves with taking notes and asking an occasional question.

'I decided to smuggle them on board,' he said in response to one of the latter, 'because it was plain they would be in extreme danger if they remained in Rome. I think any person would feel the same way, and make the same decision when faced with such a choice.'

'We are not here to listen to your speculations about the rest of the world's attitudes Captain,' the chairman told him dryly, 'kindly proceed with your story.'

It was the take-off drama however which was the crucial issue and it was here that the panel pressed hardest. When had Desmond realized the launch was trying to stop them? At what point did the launch begin to constitute a danger to the aircraft? Why had he taken no avoiding action? Why in the first place had he ever tried to leave against the wishes of the Italian authorities?

Desmond parried as best he could. When it was Frazer's turn he replied to the panel's questions carefully, 'Yes,' he admitted, he had been in the cockpit when Desmond began the take-off manoeuvres. How soon had the launch begun to interfere? Well, quite soon. Soon enough for the take-off run to be aborted? Perhaps, Frazer hesitated, feigning inner conflict between his loyalty to his Captain and desire to tell the truth, yes, perhaps in his view the aircraft could have been stopped. Had he suggested this to the Captain? Here again Frazer hesitated and cast an anguished sidelong glance at Desmond; well as a matter of fact yes, he had urged that they stop the run and turn away but the Captain had disagreed. Finally had there, in his professional opinion as a pilot, been a serious risk to the flying-boat and its passengers? At this Frazer's acting rose to new heights, swallowing hard, in an almost inaudible voice, he replied, 'Yes.'

Nodding their heads in grim approval at his testimony, the Panel ordered him to step down. Thereafter the remainder of the inquiry was a formality. A statement was heard from Ralph Kendricks who stoutly defended his Captain, but as Radio Officer he carried nothing of the weight of Frazer's damning evidence. The chairman spent a few minutes summing up, then he and his two colleagues withdrew to consider their verdict

'You bloody idiot!' Ralph Kendricks rounded on Frazer. 'What the hell did you want to go and say all that for? They can find against him on your story alone now!'

'What else could I do? You saw how they were pressing me.' Frazer protested, 'it was easy for you, you weren't asked any tough questions.' Behind his pretence of dismay there was a degree of real anxiety. If it should come to be believed in the airline that he had deliberately betrayed his Captain then he would find himself ostracized and refused a berth on any plane in the Imperial fleet, or in the whole of the British Isles quite possibly. 'I tried to do what I could,' he went on. There was none of the hoped for response in Kendricks' manner; with a look of contempt he turned away.

Desmond and the B.A.L.P.A. Captain, Phil Harris, had retired to a corner of the room and were talking together in low
voices. Once or twice Frazer saw them glance in his direction,
and the knowledge that he was under discussion made him
uncomfortable. None of the rest of the crew spoke to him.

After less than a quarter of an hour the three managers
returned and everyone resumed their seats and waited expectantly for the verdict. Dusk was beginning to fall outside and
the lights had been switched on, casting a harsh yellow glare on
the spartan furnishings. *Caterina*'s crew shifted uneasily in
their chairs while the panel shuffled their papers and held a last
minute whispered colloquoy. Then the chairman cleared his
throat and waited for the noise of squeaking wood to cease.

'This inquiry was called to investigate the death at Shambe
station, Sudan, of Lieutenant Ian Thorne and the responsibility of Captain O'Neill for this and other incidents
later in the journey, notably those at the Lake Bracciano
Marine Terminal, Rome,' he began. 'Although with regard to
the former we are of the opinion that little could have been
done to forestall the tragedy, the panel is critical of the way in
which the transport launches were left unattended and the
movements of the passengers inadequately supervised.' (God,
thought Frazer, they're not going to let him get away with
anything.) 'With regard to the extraordinary events at Rome,'
the chairman continued, and here there was complete stillness
in the room as his audience concentrated on every word. 'With
regard to these, the panel is under no doubt that Captain
O'Neill grossly exceeded his authority in aiding Professor
Wienzman and his daughter to evade the Italian Police and
Emigration Control. The Government of Signor Mussolini has
made strong representations on this subject. We also find the
Captain responsible for hazarding his aircraft, the lives of his
crew and passengers and a highly valuable cargo unnecessarily,
by performing a take-off which had not first been properly
cleared by Bracciano Flight Control.'

He paused to sip from a glass of water on the table and the
crew exchanged worried glances. Their Skipper was clearly
about to have the book thrown at him. 'Furthermore,' the

chairman went on, reading from his notes, 'we have received several complaints concerning the high-handed way in which passengers on board Captain O'Neill's commands, are sometimes treated.' There was an outburst of surprised gasps from the assembled crew at this statement, and the chairman gave them a severe look over the tops of his glasses, 'Silence please,' he ordered, 'the management wish to make it clear that such behaviour will never be tolerated in Imperial Airways.'

So his mother had done her stuff after all, Frazer thought to himself concealing his satisfaction.

The chairman laid down his notes and surveyed the room coldly. 'Normally,' he intoned 'the next step would be for the panel to impose disciplinary sanctions. In this instance, however, we have decided to reserve our recommendations, and report them, together with our findings, to the board of directors who will communicate them to those concerned in due course.'

Silence greeted this last sentence as his listeners attempted to work out the significance of it.

With a brief word of thanks to his crew, and a promise to let them know the moment he heard anything further, Desmond escaped into the corridor. The inquiry's result had come as no shock to him, indeed Phil Harris had correctly forecast the reserved sentence. Even Frazer's treachery had failed to surprise him greatly. Instead he had sat through most of the trial in a state of curious detachment as though watching the enactment of an unreal stage play in which he was supposed to be taking an interest.

Hurrying down the corridor, he set off towards the other end of the administration block. He was due to call on Jack Priestly, the flying-boats Operations chief, in his office, immediately after the inquiry was over, but first he wanted to sort through the mail which had accumulated for him during his absence. Often on these occasions he would find a great bundle of letters and packets waiting his attention, but today the haul amounted to no more than a few bills and a flying periodical, a curt note from the Admiralty requesting acknowledgement of their previous letter, and a letter from his wife's solicitors informing him that in accordance with instructions received they had arranged for a valuation to be carried out on the farm and the results were enclosed for his consideration.

Leaving the magazine in the post rack Desmond stuffed the letters in his pocket and went off to keep his appointment with Jack Priestly.

The flying-boats Operations manager had been an enemy for almost as long as Desmond had been with the airline. In some ways Desmond considered, he bore an extraordinary resemblance to Stewart Curtis being large, ugly and domineering, with a fondness for terrorizing his subordinates. Unfortunately, however, Priestly's voice failed to match up to the rest of him; he invariably spoke in a sharp, high pitched key, which, when his temper grew frayed, would rise to a near hysterical scream. This afternoon it was apparent he was very angry indeed.

'Would you like to explain to me just what the devil you think you've been up to?' he demanded, his tone so obviously at variance with the hectoring nature of his words that Desmond was hard put not to laugh. 'I've already told everything to the inquiry,' he answered sitting down, 'you must have heard the finding by now.'

'I certainly have,' Priestly snapped back. 'You and your escapades have caused me a great deal of trouble. The Government is furious about the risk you took with the gold and, Mr. Curtis has been raising hell over your rudeness to him, and the fact that you've been running around Cairo and Rome with his secretary.' It's just as well he doesn't know how his wife's been behaving then, Desmond thought to himself; to Priestly he said, 'Mr. Curtis is lying, he has bullied my crew and the other passengers throughout the trip, and seems to think his wealth entitles him to do as he pleases. I told him if his manners didn't improve I'd throw him off my plane. A promise which still stands.'

'Well you had better not,' the operations manager retorted, 'because at Mr. Curtis' request the board have ordered you to fly *Caterina* across the Atlantic to New York starting tomorrow instead of the next day. You leave at three p.m.'

Desmond gazed at him in astonishment. 'What is it that scares everyone so about this man that they'll sack pilots and switch flight schedules for him?' he said bitterly. 'Ignoring as I assume you will, any thoughts of rest for myself and the crew after eight days of flying, what about the other passengers? I mean,' he went on, 'Why doesn't Curtis try a Pan American flight if he's in such a hurry, or even hire his own aeroplane? He takes up a third of our list as it is.'

'You know damn well the next Pan Am flight doesn't arrive till Thursday,' said Priestly, 'and as it happens the remaining passengers have been consulted and have raised no objections.' Holding up a sheet of paper he read from it, 'besides Mr. Curtis and his party, the d'Estes will be staying at the Italian Embassy in Washington, an earlier arrival will cause no problem to them, indeed the Baron would welcome it. The same applies to Mr. and Mrs. King who are staying with friends in New York. Your proteges the Wienzmans, have not yet booked rooms anyway. Which leaves only the Turkish fellow and Dr. Van Smit, Mr. Curtis has agreed to reimburse the airline for the cost of their additional accommodation.'

'I suppose it's up to him if he can afford to pay,' Desmond shrugged, 'personally I don't mind one way or the other. The forecasters say there's a depression moving east from Labrador but its travelling slowly, so the weather might be clearer tomorrow than on Thursday. Is there anything else?'

'Yes, there is,' Priestly answered quickly, clasping his hand together on the desk top, he looked Desmond squarely in the eye. 'I've had reports of your radio officer drinking heavily, behaviour which is of course totally unacceptable to the airline. I shall not at this juncture go into your failure to report the matter; suffice it to say I intend to replace him at once.'

'The hell you will.' Fury at the Manager's pompous vindictiveness seized Desmond. Not content with destroying himself they were out to get at his crew also. 'Right now you can't touch me Priestly, more than that you actually need me. The inquiry hasn't been able to order disciplinary action because the board is too worried about the newspaper publicity, and if I refuse to captain the flight which you've promised Curtis,

332

you're in real trouble because we both know mine is the only available Atlantic Division crew at the moment. So Kendricks stays and you wait till I'm gone before you start on my crew.'

Jack Priestly's face suffused with rage, 'How dare you O'Neill?' he spluttered, his voice a falsetto scream. 'How dare you dictate to me?'

Standing up to leave Desmond eyed him with contempt. 'Just remember what I said,' he told him, pausing in the doorway, 'and one other thing since I'm here, I know very well who's been feeding you with information and tales behind my back, so when I return from New York next week you can have a new first officer waiting for me if you want me to fly again. I've had as much as I'm taking of Frazer. He's bloody useless as a pilot when he's not repeating lies and gossip to you.' Leaving the manager staring at him open mouthed, Desmond walked out, slamming the door behind him.

As he walked away he realized he would have to call Pamela and either postpone or re-arrange their meeting. An action which, he told himself resignedly, she was sure to misinterpret.

The remainder of *Caterina*'s travellers were already on the outskirts of London. Since Southampton was England's greatest passenger port, they had had literally only to cross to the other side of the pier, where, at the boat train railway terminus an express was waiting. Normally, had there been only a single day's wait before the flight resumed, rooms would have been booked at the South Western Hotel in Southampton itself. As it was however, the decision to advance the departure had been taken too late, and the passengers were being taken to the Ritz in Piccadilly where it had originally been assumed they would prefer to pass a two day stop-over.

Charlotte and Luca d'Este were in the dining car sitting over a second cup of tea. Though the day was overcast and chilly after the sun and warmth of the Mediterranean, the way led through some of the most beautiful country in England, where the first green of spring was just beginning to restore colour to the landscape, and Charlotte was watching the view with enjoyment.

'So you will understand, my dear Charlotte, these stories my wife repeats could not possibly hold a word of truth,' Luca's words broke in upon her thoughts and she turned back to him with a trace of irritation. The Italian was beginning to bore her with his fawning attentions and pompousness. 'Luca, you might as well save your breath,' she said witheringly, 'I don't believe you, and neither does Laura.' Taking a last draw at her cigarette she stubbed the end out in the ash tray on the table and stood up to go. 'For your sake,' she added as she left, 'I hope that Sheikh never does catch up with you. I should imagine he's got something rather special stored up.'

Jacquetta had known she and Luca were due to dine with the Italian Ambassador in London that night, and it was a simple matter for her to plead a headache after the flight and remain behind. Luca indeed had been in such an unbearable temper she doubted whether she would have gone with him, even had the attraction of Rashid not existed. She lay on her bed while he washed and put on his evening clothes, simulating travel sickness, and the moment she was sure he was safely out of the way, leapt up and hurried eagerly along the corridor to Rashid's room.

Downstairs Van Smit had been waiting in the ornate cream and gold palm court cocktail lounge where fashionable Londoners held rendezvous before going on to their dinner engagements. Raised up several steps on a dias the lounge held a commanding view of the main entrance into Piccadilly; from one of the gilded chairs beneath the palms Van Smit watched to see who came and went.

The problem of how and when to open negotiations with the Baroness still posed itself. The more he thought about it, the more convinced he was he must take the initial approach when she was alone. The Arab, her lover, was far too uncertain a factor, to be included at such a delicate stage. Ideally Van Smit would have liked to wait until they had all reached the United States, but there was no telling how the situation might have changed by then, and he dared not leave it so long.

The sight of Luca, in white tie and evening tails, leaving the hotel on his own, made up his mind for him. Tossing down a handful of change for his drinks, he went quickly upstairs.

He reached the d'Estes suite just in time to see Jacquetta disappearing round the corner of the far end of the passage in the direction of Rashid's room and though he hurried after her, she vanished from sight before he could catch up; leaving him with nothing to do but return angry and frustrated to the lounge. One thing was sure, he told himself vindictively as he went, Baroness d'Este was going to pay heavily, pay very heavily indeed, for his trouble.

The consternation caused by Rintlen's precipitate escape had been considerable. Being at first unaware that his quarry was in possession of both a ticket to London and a passport, as well as an ample quantity of foreign currency, and anxious to try and avoid any unnecessary confessions of their failure to Heydrich, Strasser then proceeded to call up every available man to mount a search of railway stations, airports and hotels in the hope of recapturing the prisoner. This operation continued until five o'clock in the afternoon when an underling had the thought to suggest Rintlen might indeed have got away with his air ticket and worse still might have used it. After which there was nothing to be done but to contact Berlin again.

This was necessary anyway since by this time Rintlen was due to have been delivered to the SD Headquarters in the Prinzalbertstrasse. Owing to the pressure of events in Czechoslovakia however, (Heinrich Himmler was due in Prague on Thursday and the first of five thousand arrests necessary to ensure his safety was being carried out), Heydrich was not immediately available and it was a quarter to six before he was informed of the escape. When this did finally happen his fury was without precedent.

Pausing only to order Strasser's immediate arrest, he gave instructions to his Adjutant Lindeman to contact the SS sections at the German Embassies in Paris and London and have Rintlen eliminated forthwith, should he show up in either capital. 'Only our own people are to know mind, and tell them to make sure there are no blunders this time unless they want to join him.' An hour later however Lindeman was reporting back that the SD officer had already passed through London airport and was nowhere to be found. 'These fools in Rome waited till he had almost got there before telling us,' he informed his master. 'Well they will most certainly regret doing so,' Heydrich answered with icy determination. 'Tell London to keep looking for him, he shouldn't be that hard to find, and if he should murder those two Jews openly there will be hell to pay. What plans have you managed to come up with for dealing with him?'

'My staff are co-ordinating action to find and eliminate him,' the Adjutant replied calmly as though discussing a day's outing in the country. 'Using agents from the embassy. I hope to have the results ready to put before you shortly.'

'Very good,' Heydrich nodded approval, 'inform me as soon as you have news,' he rubbed his long hands together thoughtfully for a moment. 'and now, let's see where we are with those list of Czech undesirables.'

Rintlen had been reasonably confident of being able to outwit an attempt by Heydrich to have him intercepted at London's Croydon airport. With his Dutch passport and good English he felt certain of the protection of the authorities while in a public place, and German agents he knew would be under strict orders to avoid any kind of embarrassing incident.

The absence of any reception committee however, puzzled him for a while. He had at least expected to be followed and watched. It took him some time to conclude that either London had not yet been notified of his arrival, or more probably he thought, no-one, not even Heydrich believed he would be so crazy as to continue his hunt of the Wienzmans alone and unaided. They most likely supposed he had gone to ground somewhere in Paris.

Walking through the terminal building, he was struck by an Imperial Airways sign over a ticket booth, and on an impulse went up and inquired of the girl on the desk about the trans-Atlantic flight.

'Yes, there's one tomorrow at three o'clock, not from here,

from Southampton,' she told him, 'it reaches New York at four the next afternoon.'

'No, no,' Rintlen told her, 'there is one the next day, Thursday.' With an effort he recalled the Wienzmans' flight number, 'Imperial 109 via Montreal.' The girl smiled, she was pretty he noticed with blue eyes and curly blonde hair. 'Yes,' she said, 'that's the one, Imperial 109, the departure date's been put forward twenty-four hours though. Did you want to make a reservation sir? I can see if there are still berths available for you.'

She paused, looking at him expectantly, hand poised over a telephone, and Rintlen, who had not so far given any real thought as to the exact means by which he was to accomplish his objective, and who had been thrown out of his stride by the discovery that he had less than a day in which to do so, nodded.

There was a wait of some time while the girl telephoned through to the head office in Piccadilly, during which Rintlen stared round the booking hall anxiously for any sign of German agents. Eventually the girl laid down the receiver for a moment and said, 'we do have just the one berth left sir. Do you wish me to reserve it for you?'

By now Rintlen had come to the conclusion that he might as well take the flight since to do so would not only extend his opportunities for doing away with the Wienzman father and daughter, but in the event of failure, would at least leave him on the other side of the world from Heydrich. Again he nodded.

'Thank you sir, then if I could have your name please.' Rintlen pushed across his passport and the girl repeated the name on the cover into the telephone. Hanging up she smiled at him again. 'Very good sir, I have secured you a reservation,' she said, 'I am afraid I can't issue you with the ticket here, you will have to collect it from the Piccadilly office before midday tomorrow.'

She handed him a slip of paper with the address on it and the times of the flight's departure and also that of the train connection from Waterloo. Thanking her mechanically Rintlen went off to find a taxi to take him into the city. It was not likely he thought, there would be much he would be able to do before morning. He had yet to find where the flying-boat's passengers were staying, he had been afraid to ask the girl on the desk for fear of causing suspicions. As it was he felt desperately tired and in need of a drink. Moreover he still had to find himself a room for the night, collect and pay for his ticket and buy a suitcase and some fresh clothing for the journey. Perhaps during the night a plan would come to him.

The taxi was pulling out of the terminal entrance when there occurred an incident which served to bring home the danger which still surrounded him. A large black car of a British make unknown to him swept into the forecourt and squealed to a halt in front of the main passenger building. Three men in rain-coats and trilby hats leapt out and ran swiftly inside. To an ordinary observer they might have seemed no more than travellers in a hurry, but Rintlen had caught a glimpse of the face of one, and recognized him as a man he had trained with during his first months in the SS. The hunt was on for him in London.

There was a cold wind blowing straight down the main street of Keene. The sleet had ceased falling but the sidewalks and roadway were wet with slush and there were few people about. Pat Jarrett parked the truck opposite the cafe where he had eaten on Monday and hurried inside out of the cold.

The look of interest which brightened her face immediately on seeing him wiped away any doubts he had had about the wisdom of coming. She was wearing the same dress as before and its provocative tightness sent a quiver of excitement through him. Hips swinging she strolled across the room to where he sat. 'Didn't expect to see you back so soon,' she said casually, 'specially not on a day like this.' The sleet had begun to fall again Jarrett saw through the window, white specks pouring out of the sky to melt the instant they touched the ground. 'I like your food,' he said clumsily and the girl gave a laugh. 'Well, that's good 'cause you got the same again as yes-terday.' She produced a knife and fork from her apron pocket, wiped them half-heartedly and leaned over to lay them in front of him. Her skin was very smooth and clear, Jarrett had a fleeting impression of the swell of her bosom as the neck of her dress dipped open.

'Want a beer as well?' She straightened up and he nodded. 'Like one too?' he offered when she returned with a glass, but Susie shook her head. 'Uh, uh, no thanks, not allowed to drink with customers. I'll have a coffee though.'

She brought the coffee together with his plate of stew. Sitting opposite she regarded him carefully over the rim of the cup. Feeling embarrassed by her scrutiny, Jarrett tried to find some small talk. 'Long winter you have up here,' he began and the girl snorted derisively. 'Sure, nine months winter and three months damn poor sledin', that's what my step-pa says and I guess he's not far wrong.'

They both laughed. 'You still got your plane mister?' she asked him, 'when you going to let me see it?'

'The name's Pat, Pat Jarrett,' he told her, 'and you can see the plane anytime.'

'An' you'll take me up in it?' She had put down the cup and was leaning forward eagerly, lips parted and eyes rounded in pleading.

'She's a single seater,' Jarrett said, adding hastily to lessen her disappointment, 'you can sit inside though, even start the engine if you want.'

'Can I really? You could teach me to fly maybe?' Susie giggled. 'When can I come?'

'Like I said anytime, not this afternoon though. I've work to do.' He would certainly have to have the gun bays in the wings finished and closed up before she arrived.

'Tomorrow then, after lunch? I get the afternoon off and the evening on Wednesday.'

'You work here in the evenings?' Jarret asked in surprise. The establishment hardly looked as though it would do much business after dark.

'It's the bar,' Susie explained resignedly. 'We get a few customers in at night. Can't think why.' She gazed round the room, her lip curling with contempt at the flaked paint and cheap furniture. 'Lousy joint. I keep telling them I'm going to walk out 'n leave 'em to it. Guess maybe I will one day.'

'Do your people own the place?' Jarrett pushed away his plate and the girl gave another sniff of amusement. 'Not a chance,' she told him, 'my pa was a farmer up beyond Bellows Falls, I came down here to get away. Imagine that.'

Another customer came in at that moment and she left the table to wait on him. Jarrett finished his beer and stood up to pay the bill. 'Tomorrow then?' she said, giving him his change. 'Yes, tomorrow after lunch,' he agreed.

'I'll be ready.' She shot him a sudden knowing glance, as she opened the door for him. 'Bye, Pat, see you soon.'

Jarrett drove back to the lake, his mind heady with anticipatory excitement. It had been a long time since he had had a girl, a real young girl. Not since the war.

Stewart Curtis was not the only one among *Caterina*'s passengers to be interested in the performance of Klerksdorp shares. Laura Hartman, too, had been studying the financial reports in the evening papers. Much as she disliked her employer, she respected his commercial judgement and what little money she had was largely invested in the mining company's stock.

Over the past few weeks however she had begun to notice that his behaviour was growing steadily more erratic. He was prone to bouts of deep depression, during which he would appear more morose and withdrawn. These would alternate with sudden, savage bits of temper which all around him had come to dread. In business affairs also, he seemed to have lost the dispassionate, even callous approach which had once marked him; instead he now reacted fiercely to the slightest setback or suggestion of criticism.

He had become increasingly secretive too, where many of his activities were concerned, reserving far more of the details to himself only, than had previously been his habit. Frequently nowadays he sent her out of the room when he was making telephone calls, especially when these were to his bankers or stockbrokers. Each morning there would be three or four letters left out of her post, handwritten and sealed by him, another departure from the normal.

To begin with Laura had been inclined to attribute these aberrations to the general pressure of work and strain brought about by the tales of his wife's affairs. Charlotte had become very nearly notorious during her stay in Cairo, and Curtis, Laura knew, felt this deeply.

Since their return from Durban however, the financier seemed less and less interested in his wife's behaviour. For long periods while the aircraft was in flight he ignored her altogether, and though there were moments when he displayed irritation at her flirting with men like Luca d'Este and her pursuit of Desmond O'Neill, these were becoming less frequent. Certainly he no longer appeared to regard the Baron as any kind of serious threat, and tolerated his presence in the after cabin. Privately Laura guessed, he realized Luca had ceased to rate at all highly in Charlotte's estimation, and was merely useful as a source of amusement for her.

Charlotte, Laura still believed, was less vicious and depraved, than simply bored. Born into a comfortable, protected background, her beauty and intelligence had smoothed life before her till she had met and married Stewart Curtis. Though considerably her senior in age, he was already an immensely successful man and well known figure in society. Charlotte was widely admitted to have made a brilliant match, and their wedding had been one of the events of the season. Now, ten years later, sated with every luxury and indulgence her husband's money could procure for her, she was finding life beginning to pall.

Laura had grown fairly accustomed to seeing Charlotte manipulating the people around her but it had come as something of a shock to find herself caught up in one of the lady's intrigues. Her first instinct had been to confront both of the Curtises and hand in her notice forthwith. Only the worry and confusion over Siegret and her father had prevented her doing so at once, and later, on the flight to Marseilles she had begun to have doubts. In his present mood Curtis was unpredictable, and she did not want to draw any more trouble down on Desmond's head. She still had to reach America and the journey across the Atlantic would be vastly easier without a quarrel. All things considered she decided it would be far wiser to wait until she reached New York.

The gist of these feelings she repeated to Mr. and Mrs. King over dinner that evening. Harold King had pronounced himself fed up with eating in big hotels. 'I want a quiet, old fashioned place, serving good plain food,' he said, and Laura, who knew London well, took them off to a small restaurant off the Strand where they were served with roast beef and Yorkshire pudding which it would have been hard to fault.

'I've thought all along you shouldn't be working for that man,' Mr. King remarked when she had finished telling her story, 'it's not a fit job for a young lady.'

'I know, and you're so right,' Laura admitted, 'I should never have taken it in the first place,' she sighed, 'you know how it is though. I needed the money, and there wasn't a big choice of jobs back in South Africa. I wanted to travel and meet interesting people and I've done quite a lot of both. In many ways I've had a marvellous time.'

'Well, it's got to stop now,' Mrs. King said decisively. 'You can't go on with Mrs. Curtis spreading lies about you to everyone. I've a good mind to speak to her myself. I'd soon let her know what I think of such behaviour. Millionaire's wife or not.'

'Now, take it easy, Sarah,' Harold King took a drink from the silver tankard of beer which had been brought for him. 'I'm sure Laura is very capable of looking after herself, there's no cause for us to interfere.'

'I still think it's disgraceful,' his wife replied, 'as for you my dear,' she turned to Laura, 'if you want any help, or a place to stay in New York, well we have friends who will be glad to oblige I know. Isn't that so Harold?'

'It certainly is,' he agreed, 'and you can be sure there'll be no trouble about finding a job. People will jump at the chance of employing someone with your experience.'

'You're both very kind,' Laura was touched by the genuine concern in their manner. 'To be honest I'm more worried about the trouble I may have brought on Captain O'Neill. Mr. Curtis has it in for him already, I know, and he's facing enough just now, with the inquiry, and the trouble at Rome.'

In believing the major part of Charlotte's behaviour stemmed from boredom Laura was correct. Unfortunately she had underestimated the degree to which the lady's pride had been wounded and the lengths to which she was prepared to go to obtain revenge. The knowledge that Desmond had somehow seen through her attempt to discredit the American girl and had spurned all her advances, had aroused her passionate anger. To lose a man to one's husband's own secretary was a humiliation not to be borne.

So it was that when Laura and the Kings got back from their dinner at the comparatively early hour of ten o'clock, the clerk at reception informed her that her employer wished to see her and had left instructions she was to be sent along to his suite the moment she returned.

She bid goodnight to the Kings and hurried upstairs.

Less than a quarter of an hour later she was back in her own room, close to tears, and frantically trying over the telephone, to persuade a reluctant night staff at the Head office of Imperial Airways to divulge a number or address at which Desmond could be reached.

Desmond was in London. He was in fact sitting in the Grill Room of the Savoy Hotel having dinner with his wife.

The evening had started badly. Leaving Jack Priestly's office Desmond had put a call through to the farm only to receive no reply. Surprised, for Pamela's telegram had stated specifically that she would be there on Tuesday night, he had then tried the magazine in London, where she had been working since their separation.

'I thought we were going to meet down at the farm this evening,' were his opening words, and instantly regretted them, for Pamela took them as criticism and came back aggressively.

'I understood from the airline you were likely to be too busy to have time for me tonight so I stayed up here,' she answered,

'I suppose I should be flattered you've been able to tear yourself away from the newspaper men. You've certainly managed to attract plenty of publicity.'

'I know,' Desmond agreed tiredly, 'and besides which I've had to spend the evening being interrogated by an airline management trying to take my job away from me. So forgive me if I sound a little short. What I really rang to say anyway was that we shan't be able to meet tomorrow unless we do so first thing in the morning. They've moved the schedule up, I'm leaving for New York at three in the afternoon.'

'Oh really Desmond, this is too much,' Pamela's voice snapped back over the line. 'You and your damned job. Why is it you could never find time to see me, but apparently have plenty to go off winning motor races in Cairo with pretty blonde Americans?'

'If you're going to begin slanging someone you've never met, or had even heard of until today, I'll hang up,' Desmond warned her. 'If you really want to see me that urgently I suppose I can come up to London tonight for dinner, but it will have to be quite late I'm afraid.'

'Well, yes, perhaps that might be a solution.' With her customary abruptness Pamela calmed down and became briskly efficient. 'Let's see now, the time has just gone seven o'clock. I'll order a table for ten o'clock. You should be able to manage that easily.'

'Thanks a lot,' Desmond told her, 'I'm glad you think so. Just tell me where it is I'm supposed to be meeting you for God's sake.'

'There's no need to get irritable,' Pamela rebuked him. 'The Savoy Grill. You had better hurry if you're not going to be late. I'll meet you in the bar.'

The prospect of a two hour drive in his open MG on top of a day's flying was not an attractive one, but it was worth the effort, he knew to clear up whatever it was Pamela had on her mind. At least, to judge from her tone she was not thinking of calling off the divorce; most likely it was some problem to do with selling the house. And if he stayed in London overnight there was a chance he might be able to see Laura for a while the next morning. Phil Harris and his wife would always give him a bed for the night he knew.

The second surprise of the evening had been to find Pamela was not alone.

His immediate reaction had been one of relief. There had been more traffic on the roads than he had bargained for and despite all his efforts he was nearly a quarter of an hour late, and Pamela kept waiting by herself invariably developed sufficient ill temper to poison an entire evening.

'Desmond, this is a friend of mine, Simon Collier, he's a barrister.' Pamela's companion was a slimly built man of about his own age, with a thin intelligent face and carefully brushed hair. He was dressed with immaculate care, and Desmond guessed expensive elegance, although in a curiously old fashioned and conservative style, normally favoured by men a good deal older. Barristers, he recalled, that peculiarly British breed of lawyer whose work consisted almost exclusively of court appearances, with little or no contact with their clients, lived a rarified and anachronistic existence in many respects.

There were two empty cocktail glasses on the table, dry martinis to judge from the olives lying in the bottoms. Collier signalled a waiter to bring three more and sitting down Desmond took stock of his wife.

At first glance she seemed unchanged, the same sculptured face beneath the glossy blue-black hair, the same electrifying vitality, the impression she gave of restless, questing interest in the world around her, the strikingly fashionable clothes. Looking more deeply, however, there appeared to Desmond's eyes, to be something frenetic about the nervous speed of her conversation, her sudden changes of subject and the impatience with any failure to follow the mercurial workings of her mind. There were signs of strain in the intensity of her expression, an almost feverish quality to her stare, which told him she was building up to an emotional crisis, which would soon explode upon her. He prayed fervently that they would get through the meal without a drama.

'I don't understand why they should want you to fly to America for them at the same time as they are trying to give you

345

the sack,' she remarked, referring to Imperial Airways. 'And surely the airline can't be so stupid they don't see what the public reaction would be if you were thrown out. Why you're a hero at the moment, of sorts anyway,' she added disparagingly.

'They're short of crews,' Desmond told her. 'Eugene's still on his way back from the Far East, Kelly Rogers is on leave. *Champion*'s Captain and First Officer are both down with 'flu. The choice was between using me or cancelling and leaving the field open for Pam Am. The publicity certainly helped though I admit.'

'Farouk let you buy the car I see,' Pamela extracted a cigarette from a case on the table in front of her. Collier leant forward at once with his lighter. 'Thanks.' She inhaled deeply and blew a long stream of smoke into the room. 'I'm amazed he still likes you after you refused to become his personal pilot.' Desmond shrugged. 'He has hundreds of cars, one less meant nothing to him. He was pleased when it won the race though.'

The Martinis arrived. Pamela took a swift gulp and began again on a new topic. 'I've asked Simon to be here because he's a lawyer and has been very good to me,' she said. Her words were ambiguous and left Desmond and Collier regarding one another with a slight degree of embarrassment. Pamela however was clearly enjoying the situation, with a quick smile of satisfaction she went on, 'we, you and I that is, Desmond, still have to resolve the question of the farm. I thought it would be useful to have Simon here to clear up any legal points.'

'Purely as a friend of course,' Collier put in hastily. 'Pamela hasn't retained my services professionally.' He cleared his throat, 'but I'd be happy to give you any advice if you should want it.'

'I don't see there's really any problem,' Desmond said quietly. 'We bought the farm together, now we're getting divorced and you want your money out; it's obvious the farm has to be sold. I've seen the estate agent's valuation and it seems fair enough. So let's go ahead and put it on the market.'

'Just like that, no fuss or arguments?' Pamela answered, rather taken aback. 'I thought you were desperately anxious to hold on to the place? Why the sudden change of heart?'

'I don't want to sell the farm, I would like to keep it very much if I could afford to, but since I can't there's no point in digging my heels in against the inevitable. You can force me to sell legally and anyway you have a perfect right to your money.'

'Are you sure you've thought this out?' Pamela asked doubtfully. 'I don't want you changing your mind back again tomorrow and then disappearing off abroad for a month where we can't contact you.'

'Listen,' Desmond told her, 'I made it perfectly clear all along I wouldn't sell until we were divorced. By the time the solicitor gets moving that will be through, so go ahead and put the farm up for sale.'

'Have you considered what you will do then?' she wanted to know.

Her question irritated Desmond, 'No I haven't yet,' he answered, 'there's no particular urgency for me to look around for somewhere else to live. I am away most of the time.'

'You don't have to tell me that,' she retorted, 'your being away all the time was what caused all the trouble to begin with.'

There was no point in trying to reply to this. Fortunately however, the lawyer Simon Collier interrupted diplomatically. 'I rather think our table is ready,' he announced, 'shall we go in, it's getting quite late?'

The restaurant was crowded. The three followed a waiter to a table near the centre of the room and heads turned inquisitively as they passed.

'Those pictures of you in the evening papers were better than I'd expected.' Pamela remarked, 'you are quite a little celebrity. Several people have recognized you.'

The attention he was receiving was evidently annoying her and Desmond knew from bitter experience she would spend the remainder of the meal competing with him. Sure enough she began to monopolize the conversation, talking about herself and her work on the magazine, stressing the importance of her job as fashion editor. She was at pains too, to emphasize the success which her companion was enjoying at the criminal bar and the heights to which he was expected to rise.

347

For himself Desmond was surprised by the detachment he felt. Though Collier was the first of his wife's new friends he had met, and it had become fairly obvious the two were having an affair, he discovered somewhat to his surprise that he felt no jealously, nor even very much interest. The barrister struck him as ineffectual and totally dominated by Pamela. If he was able and willing to tolerate her moods, that was his business.

The menus were passed round and Desmond, bracing himself for yet another heavy meal, ordered smoked salmon to be followed by carre d'agneau. The salmon had barely arrived when the maitre d'hotel approached to inform them Captain O'Neill was required on the telephone.

'I'll bet it's only the press,' said Pamela, 'tell them to go away.' Excusing himself, Desmond went out to take the call.

'Desmond?' It was with a shock that he recognized Laura's voice. For all his wife's sarcasm he had been expecting either a journalist at the other end of the line, or else someone from the airline office.

'I called Imperial,' she explained, 'and the girl on the switchboard gave me Captain Harris' number and he said to try you at the Savoy. I'm sorry to interrupt your meal.'

'Don't worry about it, it couldn't matter less,' he assured her, 'but tell me what's happened? What's gone wrong?' From the sound of her voice he could sense her distress.

'Oh Desmond, you won't believe this, I'm still not sure I do myself. It's the Curtises and your watch, they're accusing me of having stolen it from them and given it to you.'

'They're what?' he exclaimed, unable to credit his ears with what he had heard. 'They can't be; they must be insane. Charlotte gave me the watch herself.'

'I know, I know, but that's not what she's saying now. Desmond, I've no idea what to do. Mr. Curtis wants the watch back first thing tomorrow.'

'To hell with tomorrow. I'll come over right away and ram it down his throat.' Demond told her furiously. 'After which I shall break his wife's neck for her.'

'No Desmond, for God's sake don't do anything,' Laura beseeched him. 'Look could we meet for a few minutes? I need to talk.'

'I'll be over in ten minutes,' he told her. 'Are you at the Ritz with the other passengers?'

'Yes, I'll wait for you downstairs,' and thanking him gratefully she rang off.

Pamela was less than pleased when Desmond returned and announced his intention of leaving them at once.

'My God you've got a nerve,' she said indignantly. 'This is the first time in months I've managed to make you sit down for a serious talk and you want to run off halfway through. Why on earth can't you have a sensible job like other people instead of this ridiculous chasing around all the time?'

'I'm sure Desmond wouldn't be leaving unless it was essential,' Collier said tactfully. 'Is there anything we can do to help,' he asked.

'No thank you.' Desmond shook his head. 'It's something I'll have to attend to myself.' The barrister was clearly relieved at his going; the meeting had been a strain for both of them. 'I'm glad we've settled about the farm,' he said to his wife. 'I may drop by there on my way past tomorrow morning for a last look. I'm sorry to have to go now but I'll give you a call as soon as I get back from New York next week.'

For a moment Pamela seemed about to speak, her face took on an expression of almost desperate intensity as she stared at him. Then apparently changing her mind, her shoulders drooped and with a sigh of indifference she nodded goodbye.

The Ritz was every bit as crowded as the Savoy had been with late night diners. Desmond found them a quiet corner in the cocktail lounge and sat Laura down beside him. She was looking pale and anxious, her eyes round with worry. Glancing about at the fashionably dressed occupants, she shivered. 'You know it frightens me,' she whispered, 'seeing all these people here, enjoying themselves, eating and drinking and party-going as though nothing was wrong with the world, while all the time their enemies are preparing for war. Don't they know what's happening in Germany and Austria and Italy? Haven't they heard that the Nazi's occupied Prague only this morning?

349

Surely they must realize they are going to have to face them themselves one day soon?'

'They realize it,' Desmond answered quietly, thinking of the letter from the Admiralty he had found waiting for him. 'We all do, and at long last we're beginning to prepare. These people,' he indicated the rest of the room with his hand, 'are simply trying to forget for a few hours.'

'I suppose you're right,' she agreed abstractedly. Then abruptly she broke into the account of her interview with Stewart Curtis. 'He sent for me after dinner, like he often does and I thought nothing of it till I was in the sitting-room of his suite. He was there sitting behind the desk wearing a silk dressing gown in place of his dinner jacket I knew he was angry because he addressed me as "Mrs. Hartman". Normally I'm Laura to them both.'

She sat silent for a second or two, reliving the scene, then she continued. 'He said his wife had noticed you wearing the watch during the flight up from Marseilles. When they reached the hotel they had checked through the cases and found the one she had bought from Cartier was missing!

'At this point he grew very solemn and started telling me how they had considered every possibility before coming to the inevitable conclusion as he put it, that I must have taken it from their rooms at some time and given it to you.'

'But didn't you tell him his own wife had given it to me when we were in Cairo?' Desmond demanded.

'Yes, of course I did,' her voice trembled, 'I told him the whole story, but he didn't believe me. He said I had taken the watch without permission and could be prosecuted for stealing.'

'Well that's a lie for a start,' he said angrily, 'because I shall make sure the truth comes out.'

'Don't you see though?' Laura said hopelessly, 'we've no proof. It's your word against hers and you know how she can twist things. Anyway it doesn't matter really. He said he was going to do me the kindness of assuming I had only borrowed the watch and had meant to return it. Provided I return the watch at once no action will be taken. I get the sack at the end of the month of course, but since I was going to leave anyway as soon as we reached New York that's no handicap.'

'I'm not standing by and seeing you accused because of Charlotte Curtis' lies,' Desmond said hotly, 'I shall go straight up to their suite now and have the whole business out with them. If she thinks she can get away with a stunt like this she's made the biggest mistake of her life.'

'No, Desmond please!' Laura clutched his arm. 'Don't you see? Stewart Curtis can never admit his wife tried to . . .' she fumbled for the word, 'tried to buy another man. If you make an issue out of it he will have to bring charges. And we haven't enough proof. I don't want to be accused of theft, which is what will happen if you try telling him the truth. Just let me take the watch back and forget about the whole business. It's my fault partly, I should never have persuaded you to hang on to it in Rome.'

Desmond thought for a moment. 'I'll certainly return the watch,' he said unbuckling the strap. The clasp had left a curious mark on the skin of his wrist, shaped like the little D. He gave a rueful smile. 'What's so annoying about the blasted woman is I like the watch very much,' he confessed. 'I should have been a great deal more strong minded and thrown it back at her originally.'

He passed the thing over to her and she shut it hastily away inside her small evening bag. 'Tomorrow morning however,' he said, 'after you've seen him, I shall have a few words with him myself. Don't worry,' he held up his hand as Laura began to protest afresh, 'once the watch is in his possession again he will have no grounds for accusing you. All he can do is accuse me direct, and the threat doesn't frighten me. I very much doubt if he would ever actually dare to bring charges. The publicity would make him look ridiculous.'

'But Desmond you can't be sure. Why take the risk?' Laura begged. 'The Curtises aren't worth it. Let them go, out of our lives. It was stupid ever to have let myself become mixed up with them.' Desmond shook his head, 'No,' he said firmly, 'The Curtises get away with too many things and have bullied enough people already. I mean to see they're stood up to for once. Besides,' he added, 'Curtis is not in a very strong position where I'm concerned; he needs me to fly him across the Atlantic.'

'Well, if you're sure,' Laura said doubtfully, 'but I do wish you'd let it all alone.'

Desmond smiled at her reassuringly. 'You'll see, I'll even make them offer you your job back,' he said, 'and afterwards how would you like to leave London early and have lunch in the country? I want to drive down and have a last look at the farm before we fly off.'

This time there was no hesitation in her voice, 'I'd love to come,' she said, smiling back, 'so whatever you do don't get me my job again or I won't be able to.'

'Good, then that's settled. I'll pick you up at ten, after I've dealt with the Curtises.'

Leaving the lounge they made their way out into the foyer. 'Desmond, I am sorry,' she said, putting a hand on his sleeve as he was about to go. 'I've been so wrapped up in my own problems I forgot to ask you how it went at the inquiry.'

'The outcome was pretty much as I expected,' he said, giving her a brief outline of what had taken place at Southampton, 'but for the publicity in the papers and the fact that they need a crew to fly tomorrow, I think it might have been a good deal worse.'

Laura looked relieved. 'I'm glad,' she said, 'I was a bit worried the publicity might only make things more difficult for you.' Desmond laughed, 'so it was you who spread the story? I guessed it was your idea. I suppose perhaps I should be angry, but to tell the truth I'm very grateful; but for you I might now be without a command.'

Bidding goodnight to her in the foyer, Desmond went out into Piccadilly, declining the doorman's offer of a taxi. He had left the MG in Jermyn Street, parked behind Fortnum and Mason. The clouds which had obscured the sky during the afternoon, had disappeared and the night was clear and cold, the stars glittering brightly. With luck, he thought, tomorrow would be a fine day, a good start for the long ocean flight. As he walked he passed a newspaper placard, 'British pilot in daring rescue' the black letters proclaimed, and underneath in smaller print, 'German troops parade in Prague'.

At about the time Desmond started his car and began driving back towards Phil Harris' home in Kensington, Jacquetta d'Este propped herself up on her elbows in Rashid's bed and kissed him on the shoulder. 'I must go back soon,' she said, 'Luca will be returning.' Rashid was lying on his back, one arm around her waist, stroking her flanks gently. Reaching out with his other hand he felt for his watch on the table beside the bed. 'Eleven o'clock,' he said glancing at the dial, 'when do you expect him back?'

'He said not before midnight. The Slovak business will keep them late at the Embassy, but he might be tired after the journey and leave early.'

'Wait a little longer,' he pulled her across to rest on his chest, her dark hair brushing silkily against his face. 'No, I must go,' she protested half heartedly, but he drew her head down and kissed her lingeringly on the mouth. 'There is time,' he murmured. 'Again, before you go,' and his hands began moving over her body, caressing and arousing. 'Again, once more,' he repeated more insistently.

Under his touch her belly and thighs responded, growing heavy with desire. 'Rashid, no, no,' she cried softly, but her pleadings were already giving way to quick moans of pleasure. Passion swept over her in a wave, and she abandoned herself to it, hugging him fiercely to her as he rolled her over beneath him.

Later, when they were lying spent and exhausted in each other's arms, she lifted her head from his shoulder and said, 'Rashid, I must talk to you for a minute.'

'About your husband?' he replied, his fingers toying idly with her hair.

'Yes, about Luca,' she answered.

'What is there to say? You know what I have to do.'

'Yes, but,' Jacquetta insisted, 'you must see our being together makes a difference? I mean,' she continued, speaking plainly, 'I can't be the lover of my husband's murderer.'

'And how can I forsake my word to avenge the killer of my father and my sister?' he asked.

'Luca did not do the actual killing though. He was with the Governor's office, why don't you take your revenge on the unit involved?' she demanded. Rashid let his hand drop from her hair, 'We did,' he answered, in a flat, hard voice, 'my men and I, we laid an ambush on the edge of the sands last year. We killed many of the men and all the officers.'

'Then surely you have had your revenge a dozen times over?' Jacquetta urged. 'At worst Luca was only one link in the chain. If you have to kill those responsible, try the Generals, or the Duce himself. They're the guilty ones.'

'And my sister, what of her?' he said bitterly, 'she was only fifteen when the soldiers carried her away to the Governor's palace, where she killed herself because of the things they did to her.'

Jacquetta's eyes filled with tears, 'Rashid, look at me,' she commanded. For a second they gazed at one another intently. 'Rashid do I matter? Am I important to you?' His hand stroked her cheek and wiped a teardrop from the corner of her eye. 'You are more than any other person to me,' he told her gravely, 'and will always be so.' Jacquetta clasped his hand in her own and held it tight. 'Then listen,' she said, 'the Fascists have murdered your father and your sister, and enslaved your country. Are you going to let them destroy us as well? Because that is what will happen if you kill Luca. Is he worth that: Will his death help your people, or will it only mean more misery and pointless waste of life? You alive and leading your men are a far greater threat to the tyrants in Rome than the killing of Luca. He's not worth sacrificing yourself for; better to avenge your family by freeing their land.'

Rashid sighed deeply. 'There may be some truth in what you tell me. I must think,' he said at length, staring up at the ceiling. 'As you say, I must consider not only myself, but my people as well.'

'Oh, my love.' Jacquetta felt a surge of hope within her at his words, 'I know I'm right.' She sat up and kissed him tenderly, 'and now I must go or I'll be missed. I'll come and see you in the morning after breakfast.'

In his apartment at the Abdin Palace in Cairo, Yousouri Pasha lay back against the embroidered cushions of a divan and sucked a sweet thoughtfully. Though forty-eight hours had passed without incident since his conversation with Prince Suleiman on the subject of Rashid and Baron d'Este, he nevertheless felt a faint unease. Intensive investigation by his spies had not so far come up with any clue as to the young Senussi Sheikh's whereabouts, and Yousouri was an instinctively fastidious person who preferred to gather up the loose ends to his plots.

A second interview with the Prince had failed to elicit any further information, and had ended with the old man querulously threatening to go to the King and demand a stop be put to this 'insolent detective work' as he had so contemptuously phrased it.

The question was; if, as seemed highly probable, Rashid was no longer in the country, where else had he gone? There were only two logical possibilities, Libya or Italy. The latter would seem an almost suicidal destruction, yet Yousouri was reasonably sure Rashid had not so far passed westward over the land border between Egypt and Libya. There was a chance, to be sure, that he might have made the journey by sea, but to have done so would have been both dangerous and time consuming for him.

If Rashid had on the other hand, returned to Italy; perhaps abandoning his pursuit of d'Este to wreak his vengeance on some other important figure, the consequences if he succeeded and were found to have entered the country from Egypt would be extremely serious.

The risk might be non-existent, but a discreet warning to the Italians could do no harm, and might even prove useful in the light of current, and covert, approaches being made by the Palace, with a view to providing a counter to British influence.

Clapping his hands, Yousouri ordered a secretary to be summoned. A friendly note to the Italian Ambassador would be sufficient. No direct or definite knowledge need be claimed, simply a passing on of chanceheard rumour which might possibly be of benefit to an ally.

The Court, he thought, would be pleased at this delicate solution.

The security round-up in the Czech capital, and elsewhere in the newly occupied territories was proceeding sufficiently smoothly for Heydrich to have taken time off to attend a gala dinner at the Italian Embassy in Berlin and it was here his Adjutant Lindeman came to report on the progress of the Rintlen affair.

The building, in the most elegant and exclusive part of the city, had been bought from a Jewish banker in 1935 and restored by the previous ambassador Vittorio Cerutti, and was imposing even by the standards of Fascist magnificence. Approached up an awe-inspiring ramp, flanked by columns with lanterns adorned with Italy's golden crest, the portals were guarded by exquisitely beautiful, heavy bronze trellis-work.

Once inside the hall, the illusion was created of being in Venice, in one of the fabulous, sunlit palaces of the Doges. Flowers were everywhere among the vast expanse of marble, light glittered from the countless facets of Venetian chandeliers reflected back in tall mirrors.

Dinner was over and the guests had spilled out of the dining-room, separating into different groups. Some were seated in the reception hall on Renaissance pews taken from Italian churches. Others had gathered in the library and salons furnished with antique wooden panelling and dungeon gates where the curtains were woven in pure gold thread, with priceless paintings of the old Italian masters adorning the walls.

Footmen in blue silk tail coats and white wigs moved silently among the groups of gossiping, flirting guests, bearing trays of coffee and liqueurs. Lindeman went from room to room in search of his chief. The cream of Berlin society, both diplomatic and social, were present, as well as nearly all the most high ranking Party politicians. At one of the marble fireplaces he saw Herman Goering and the former heir to the German throne, Prince Wilhelm, standing with arms linked, telling one another jokes, the slenderness of the Crown Prince emphasizing the enormous fatness of the bemedalled Luftwaffe Overlord.

Lindeman finally ran Heydrich down in a small salon off the library in conversation with the President of the Reichsbank, Dr. Schacht, an anxious, colourless man who seized the Adjutant's arrival as a pretext for slipping away. 'The good Doctor,' Heydrich remarked sarcastically regarding the banker's retreating figure, 'has been most unwise. He has recently presented the Fuhrer with evidence that Ribbentrop, Goering and several other other high officials had been illegally purchasing foreign currency. Now he wonders why he has enemies.'

Together they wandered back in the direction of the hall. Lindeman noted with amusement the alarm caused by the presence of the black uniformed security chief. Heydrich inspired greater fear in Germany than any other single man, with reason. The mere sight of the merciless unsmiling features of 'Himmler's Black Ghost', as he was widely named, was sufficient to halt conversations and drive away the more nervous guests. On the way out they passed Magda Goebels sitting, sour and angry with Count Ciano. 'Her husband's lechery has become a scandal,' Heydrich observed in an undertone, 'I am told this evening he was dancing with a pretty Jewish girl from one of the embassies. "You should go to the Anthropological Institute for consultation" he said to her. "I think it is absurd that you should be Jewish. Your skull has the perfect Aryan formation."'

Lindeman smiled, Heydrich's contempt for the Party's leaders was well known. Their self-indulgence served only to highlight his own ruthless efficiency. Small wonder he was feared and hated by everyone from Goering and Himmler downwards.

'Goebels,' Heydrich continued when they were in the car and on their way back to PrinzAlbertstrasse, 'Goebels,' he mouthed the Propanganda Minister's name with distaste, 'saw fit to complain to me about British press reports concerning the Wienzmans' escape from Rome. Fortunately I silenced him by saying the matter was proceeding under the Fuhrer's personal supervision. Which, in a sense, it is. However you had better see to it that Rintlen is got out of the way and quickly. What news of our plans?'

'Our people in London are still looking for Rintlen,' Lindeman answered. 'They are checking hotels and boarding houses where he might be staying. Unfortunately there are a great many such places. London is a big city.'

'I know London is big, curse you. I don't need you to tell me that,' Heydrich's voice lashed back, 'What I want is Rintlen found and in the shortest possible time.'

'It will be done Obergruppenfuhrer, have no doubt,' Lindeman assured him hastily. 'There is one point which has arisen however,' he cleared his throat nervously. 'Well?' Heydrich demanded coldly. 'It seems,' Lindeman went on, 'Rintlen has booked a seat on the flight taking the Wienzmans to America. It is possible he may still be intending action of some kind against them.'

'You mean he plans to kill them?' Heydrich exclaimed in disbelief, 'after the publicity given to their escape. He must be insane!'

'I agree Obergruppenfuhrer,' Lindeman replied unhappily, 'but that, it seems, may be the case.' The car swayed as it rounded a corner. Heydrich gripped the armrest to steady himself. 'Mark this Lindeman,' he said in a low, savage voice, 'if Rintlen succeeds and brings down any more unfavourable publicity on the Reich, it will go ill with you and everyone concerned with this operation. He is to be found and dealt with at once. This whole damned business has been mishandled from the start. Wienzman alive and in our hands would have been of some value. His death serves no useful purpose whatever, except to rid the world of another Jew.'

'Rintlen will be found and eliminated Obergruppenfuhrer,' Lindeman promised him. 'I expect confirmation hourly.'

'It had better come soon,' Heydrich told him, 'and let his

punishment serve as a warning to the rest of you of the penalty for failure.'

In his battle for survival against the agents searching for him, Rintlen was using all the skills and tricks picked up during scores of similar operations in which he had been the hunter, tacking down enemies and stratagems which he had learned to anticipate and watch for were ironically now enabling him to stay ahead of his pursuers.

To begin with he knew better than to use a hotel or lodging house for the night. Any place which could be checked was a potential trap. True, London had far too many addresses to be covered by Heydrich's agents working alone, but there was no telling whether the British police might not have been persuaded to assist on some pretext, just as he himself had used the Italians in Rome.

Instead therefore, after collecting his ticket, he spent the evening in a West End cinema near Leicester Square. The film was an indifferent thriller starring Rita Hayworth, which he found difficult to follow and he dozed for much of the time. Emerging towards ten o'clock he ate a meal alone in a nearby Italian restaurant, and after a much needed drink set out to organize his accommodation for the night. It did not take him long; by Piccadilly Circus he found what he was seeking. From out of the shadows under the wall a woman stepped forward to accost him. 'You on your own mister?' The invitation was casual, but unmistakable.

'Do you have a room?' he asked and the woman nodded. 'Five minutes in a cab,' she said briefly.

'For the whole night, until morning?' At this she shrugged, 'Sure, if that's what you want. Cost you though.'

Other people were passing by and he moved aside out of their way. The woman looked at him intently, 'Twenty quid,' she said, 'for the whole night, anything you like.' Rintlen hesitated for a second, mentally converting pounds into Reichsmarks. 'It's a nice room,' she assured him, 'quiet, an' there's a bath. It's not far. Anything you like,' she repeated.

Rintlen inclined his head curtly, 'Very well,' he agreed, 'twenty pounds for the night.' It was a small price to pay, he reflected as he hailed a taxi, for immunity till morning from Heydrich's killers, and his new companion was attractive enough to make the experience promise to be an interesting one.

Only a few hundred yards away, in the Ritz Hotel, Siegret kissed her father goodnight and went quietly back to her own room. The events of the past four days had left the Professor utterly exhausted, and the strain of conducting interviews with the horde of reporters who had met them at the dockside, had almost been too much for him. An evening spent in bed however, and a good night's sleep without worry, would see him greatly recovered, she did not doubt, and tomorrow they would start the final stretch of their travels.

After the setbacks and disasters which had overtaken them at earlier stages in their escape, whenever they had thought themselves free at last, Siegret was determined not to raise any false hopes again. Though it was true she felt immeasurably happier and more secure in England than at any previous point in their journey, she was refusing to count herself safe until she actually set foot upon the soil of the United States. In England as in Austria and Italy and France she had seen everywhere the preparations for approaching war: the recruiting posters on the hordings, the air raid warning notices; the newspapers with their pictures of battlefleets and troop reviews. The news from Czechoslovakia had frightened her further; yet another country fallen beneath the domination of the Nazis. How long would it be before the whole of Europe followed, and perhaps England too?

The completion of the second gun bay kept Jarrett up late, but by the time he returned to the house he was feeling thoroughly pleased with the day's work. Not only had he installed all four machine guns in position together with their ammunition trays, and replaced the wing panels, but the task of connecting up the gun bay heating tubes, and the fire control system, had gone so well that another hour or two put in after supper, before he turned in, would see the Supermarine armed and operational.

With only a few remaining items to be completed the engine would require a thorough check over. The gun sights needed aligning and he wanted to raise the pilot's seat to improve forward vision, Jarrett estimated he was running more than a day in advance of his allotted schedule: a most satisfactory state of affairs.

In the kitchen he set a tin of canned stew on the stove to heat. To give himself something to do while waiting, he went down into the cellar and returned with another cloth-wrapped bundle. Opening this up on the kitchen table, he drew out a carefully oiled Thompson sub-machine gun and began examining it under the light. Once the flying-boat had been forced down to land on the lake, a personal weapon of some kind would be necessary and he had chosen the Thompson as being the most easily obtainable and well proven design available. Cleaning off the surplus oil he snapped the fifty round drum magazine in place and cocked the bolt. The gun had a solid, dependable feel about it, and at the same time was sufficiently formidable in appearance to deter all but the most suicidal from attempting resistance. Satisfied with his purchase, he took it upstairs and stowed it away in the cupboard in his bedroom with the rest of his flying gear.

Tomorrow, he told himself as he sat down to his meal, he would take the afternoon off and with luck the evening as well, to enjoy himself with Susie from the town. He would taxi the aeroplane out on to the water for her, maybe even let her sit inside like she had asked. His pulse quickened at the thought of what he might expect from her in return.

Which, he reflected as he eyed his place with disgust, would not be before time; he was getting fed up with stew.

Ralph Kendricks' scream of fear woke him from his dream. For a moment he lay, exhausted and trembling in the darkness, uncertain of where he was. Then there was a click as his wife Anne, switched on the lamp and light flooded the room.

'You've been having that nightmare again?' she said, peering anxiously at him. 'Yes, I know. I'm sorry I woke you.' He felt drained of energy, unable almost to speak, as the fear ebbed slowly from him. The bedclothes were drenched with sweat. 'Was it the same one?' she asked and Ralph nodded wearily, 'yes, the same as before, the fire and the plane going down into the sea.'

Morning had come at last to the three fliers aboard the Junkers, but it had brought no comfort with it. Beneath them stretched only the bitter North Atlantic, an endless vista of white capped grey waves, frequently obscured by drifting banks of mist. According to Ralph's calculations the coast of Newfoundland was less than two hundred miles away, but the already erratic performance of the compass had deteriorated further during the night and they could only guess at their true position. It was easily possible they were hundreds of miles to the north of their intended course; the weather they were experiencing made this seem all too likely.

The icing on the wings and fuselage had grown more serious too, affecting the aircraft's handling and the temperature inside the cabin had dropped noticeably. 'What's our altitude now?' Bell demanded. Carl Huisson scanned the altimeter, '800 feet skipper,' he answered. 'Do you think we ought to to take her a bit higher?'

'I've been trying, but it's all I can do to hold her at this level,' Bell told him. Sudden squalls of rain were forcing the plane down towards the sea all the time. In the rear of the cramped cabin, Ralph worked with numbed fingers, vainly seeking a way to make radio contact through the constant static, without which, he knew, they would have little chance of making land.

'What's that ahead?' Carl pointed to a greyish-white cloud which loomed ominously in their path, 'more mist or is it a thunder storm?'

'Worse than either of those,' Bell answered, 'it's snow.' Snow would affect the weight of the plane even more than ice, and with the constant squalls driving her ever downwards, there was no hope of rising above it. All three men's eyes remained

locked on the flickering needle of the altimeter as the Junkers plunged into the cloud and their view from the windows was blotted out by the swirling whiteness. Back and forth the needle oscillated, swinging right down to zero and then up again, and at any moment they expected to feel waves thrashing against the fuselage.

On and on they flew amid what proved to be a blizzard of arctic intensity. Occasionally they would strike a clear patch and their hearts would lift, but inevitably the snow would close in around them once more within a short while. Bell and Huisson struggled desperately with the controls but it was all too obvious they were being forced inexorably lower by the crippling weight of ice and frozen snow.

It was Carl who first drew attention to the red warning light on the engine temperature gauge. 'I know,' Bell said tersely, 'she's way over the limit, but there's nothing I can do. It's taking every scrap of power we can get just to keep us out of the water. I daren't ease up.' Ralph peered over his shoulder at the altimeter again, 400 feet was now the upper limit of the needle's travel and for much of the time it was registering less than half that figure.

Through the snow and cloud vapour the angry surface of the ocean was visible, the crests of the waves being torn into ragged streaks of foam by the wind. Ralph thought of the small escape dingy they carried in the rear of the plane. How long would they survive in it in such a sea?

'We must gain height. We're being forced into the water,' Bell shouted to him. 'Throw out everything you can to save weight, spare nothing, not even the radio; it's no use anyway.'

Hastily Ralph unlatched the door in the rear of the cabin and pushed it open. A freezing wind shrieked in through the opening, lashing the interior with stinging particles of flying snow. Half-blinded and numb with the cold he worked frantically, manhandling the heavy radio set across the floor and tipping it out. It was followed by tool boxes, spare parts and their supplies of food and extra clothing. The two large drums of oil they carried for emergencies in case of a leak were jettisoned too, as were the gauges and recording devices of the meteorological equipment, ironically the reason behind the whole flight. Ralph even unscrewed his seat and chart table from the floor and threw them out into the sea. When everything moveable had been stripped out he tugged the door shut again and returned to the others.

'What about the dinghy?' he asked. Whether because of a slackening of the squalls or from the loss of weight, they had gained a little height and were now at between four and five hundred feet but the red warning light remained on. 'Yes, get rid of that too,' Bell told him, but Carl Huisson protested. 'No, the dinghy is our only hope if we do crash in the sea. It weighs nothing. Leave it on.' They were still arguing when the engine gave a sudden cough and started to run with an unnaturally loud roaring. 'Christ, what's the matter?' Bell exclaimed, throttling back. The nose dipped with the loss of power and as it did so a long plume of black smoke spurted from the nacelle. A series of more sharp coughs sounded from the engine, followed by a terrible clattering vibration. 'We're going to ditch,' he cried as the plane went into a dive, and he pulled desperately back on the control column in an effort to straighten her out.

Then suddenly the entire nose of the Junkers was enveloped in flames, streaming back over the windscreen the roar and crackle of the blaze engulfing the front of the cabin. Ralph could hear the screams of the two pilots above the howl of the slipstream as the aircraft plunged towards the sea.

They struck the surface with a terrific jarring, bouncing smash which seemed to go on and on, shaking and hammering as though the aircraft were being broken into pieces. Water and spray poured in through the broken windscreen and a dozen other places and steam mingled with the smoke and fumes from the fire. Stunned and dizzy, Ralph picked himself up from the floor where he had been thrown by the impact. Now that the noise of the engines had ceased, the slap of the waves against the fuselage and the whistle of the wind outside were audible but they seemed unnaturally quiet after the shattering ordeal of the crash.

Still amazed to find himself uninjured, he dragged the dinghy out from the recess in the tail and prepared to launch it. The door had jammed shut and required all his strength to force it open. At once a rush of water swept in, submerging the floor knee deep. Through the hatch he glimpsed a terrifying prospect of heavy seas and spray breaking over the hull.

Carl came stumbling up from the nose, half carrying Bell with him. The German was badly burnt about the face, neck and hands, and his flying jacket was smouldering in patches. The Skipper too had burns, though these were less serious. He appeared to be unconscious and there was blood in his mouth. 'The stick crushed his chest,' Carl said, speaking with difficulty through blistered lips, 'I had to cut him free. Help me get him into the boat.'

The aeroplane was sinking fast. Hampered by the seas bursting through the opening, they scrambled aboard the dinghy, dragging Bell's limp form in after them, and pushed off from the wreck. Minutes later, from a short distance away, they watched the Junkers' tail lift high into the air and then slide slowly from view beneath the waves, leaving them alone in the rubber boat.

Fortunately the memory of those terrible days in the boat had been blurred by the delirium he had endured towards the end. Bell had died during the first morning without regaining consciousness. Carl Huisson, in intense pain from his burns had followed him two days later, after suffering the agony caused by the salt spray on his skin with great courage. Only the thick, furlined flying clothes he had been wearing had kept Ralph alive till a sharp eyed look-out on a freighter had spotted the dinghy and its lone survivor. It had taken two months in hospital for his injuries to heal.

Sitting up Ralph pushed back the bedclothes and swung his legs on to the floor. 'What are you doing?' Anne asked as he parted the curtains and stood staring out into the night. 'Looking to see what the weather will be like for tomorrow,' he said. The sky over Southampton and the estuary was clear with not a whisp of cloud to be seen. With a sigh he drew the curtains closed again and climbed back into bed. 'Don't go on the flight tomorrow,' Anne pleaded with him. 'Stay behind, say you're sick. You'll only make it worse for yourself.'

'I have to go,' he told her. 'And I shall be fine once I've made the flight again. Now go back to sleep.' His words seemed to reassure her, for she switched out the light and settled down among the pillows, but Ralph lay awake for a long time in the darkness, his mind filled with foreboding.

Part Four

TRANSATLANTIC

X

By Radio: IMPERIAL AIRWAYS SOUTHAMPTON
ENGLAND TO BRANCH OFFICE, LA GUARDIA
MARINE TERMINAL, NEW YORK. 0800 hrs. GMT.
WEDNESDAY MARCH 15th. IMPERIAL 109 TO
BOTWOOD, MONTREAL AND NEW YORK
DEPARTS SOUTHAMPTON 1500 hrs. GMT
TODAY. E.T.A. NEW YORK 1600 hrs. EASTERN
STANDARD TIME THURSDAY MARCH 16th
ENDS.

By Radio: (Trans from Italian Diplomatic Code)
URGENT AND SECRET. TO MINISTER BARON
LUCA D'ESTE ITALIAN EMBASSY LONDON.
FROM FOREIGN MINISTRY ROME. INFOR-
MATION RECENTLY RECEIVED RASHID AL
SENUSSI NOW IN EUROPE, POSSIBLY AT-
TEMPTING TO REACH ENGLAND. URGENTLY
RECOMMEND EXTREME CAUTION ENDS.

UNITED PRESS INTERNATIONAL – WALL
STREET MARKET REPORT OPENING TRADING
MINING: FURTHER FALLS. KLERKSDORP GOLD.
$135: down 4½.

As he drove round in the car to the Ritz, Desmond was
aware of a tension growing within him at the thought of the
flight he was due to make. The most difficult and dangerous
journey in the world. He had said as much to Charlotte at
Cairo and he had been speaking the truth; eighteen-hundred
miles of ocean, through the worst weather conditions anywhere
on earth. On a flight of this nature the smallest error, or breakdown in equipment, unimportant on an ordinary trip, could

result in catastrophe. *Caterina* was immensely reliable, and he himself had made the crossing in perfect safety half a dozen times before but even so it was only twelve years since Charles Lindbergh's epoch making flight, and he still felt keyed up with anticipation.

Laura was waiting for him in the foyer where they had parted the night before, well prepared for the car journey in a warm, fur-trimmed coat. 'I've some bad news for you I'm afraid,' she said jumping up as he came through the door from the street. 'What's that?' he asked with a grin. From the smile on her face he could see nothing serious had gone wrong. 'It's Stewart Curtis, he's not here,' she told him. 'He went off first thing. Where I've no idea, but I guess it's something important, normally he doesn't start work so early. I won't say I'm not relieved,' she admitted buttoning up her coat, 'but honestly maybe it is as well if you don't see him.'

'I shall see him all right,' Desmond replied, 'I've no intention of letting either him or his wife get away with treating you in the way they have. If I can't talk to him now, I'll catch him at Southampton before we take off.'

The M.G. was parked outside the Arlington Street entrance. Laura gave a cry of delight when she saw the porter loading in her suitcase. 'Desmond,' she turned to him, 'I can only come with you today on one condition.'

'Which is what?' he asked with a laugh. Laura held out her hand, 'The keys,' she demanded, 'I let you drive me in the race to Fayoum, now you're going to sit beside me while I drive you down to Hampshire.'

Desmond looked at her suspiciously. 'Are you sure you can handle her?' he asked doubtfully, 'I mean a sports car isn't the easiest machine in the world to drive.'

'Can I handle her?' Laura responded with outrage. 'I've been driving since I was fourteen. Just you get in the left hand seat Desmond O'Neill and I'll show you what real motoring is like!'

Moments later they were roaring off down Piccadilly and she was cutting through the traffic, displaying a verve and dexterity which surprised him.

'At least I've done one thing you'll approve of,' she cried as they flashed past the fountains in Trafalgar Square beneath Nelson's column and headed down towards the Thames. 'Before you arrived, I sent a telegram to my stockbroker in New York asking him to sell all my Klerksdorp shares and put my savings into something else. I've so few it's no more than a gesture, but it's given me a lot of satisfaction.'

The two had much to talk about as they drove happily on in the crisp spring morning, and neither paid any particular attention to her words. However, Laura had underestimated the effects of her action.

Stewart Curtis had left the Ritz early to keep an appointment with his stockbrokers. Until recently he had maintained an office here himself to manage his British and European business, but since his interests had become virtually exclusively concentrated in Africa and the United States, he now divided the majority of his time between these two continents.

Klerksdorp, however, was quoted on both the London and Wall Street exchanges, and the considerable shares held by British investors, combined with the City's close links with South Africa, had prompted him to retain advisors here as well as in New York.

Curtis' relationship with his brokers was ambivalent. Raikes Saumarez and Company were an old established, immensely prestigious firm, with a well deserved reputation for scrupulous honesty. His acceptance by them as a client shortly after his marriage to Charlotte, and partly as a result of her social connections, had seemed to him to put the seal upon his acceptance in the British world of finance. Satisfaction at this, however, was mixed with annoyance at the condescending, and frequently arrogant tone which many of the partners adopted in dealing with him. Curtis, they made it plain, might be a very rich man, he might even be a business genius, but he was also a jumped-up parvenu and the City had seen them before. Up until now their behaviour, though irritating had not upset him greatly since, with the continued prosperity of his affairs, he had been able to dominate any meetings between them with little difficulty. Today the situation was entirely different.

The high-ceilinged, dark panelled office of the senior partner, looking out over Threadneedle Street to the Bank of England opposite and the building of the Stock Exchange itself, was furnished with a quiet, dignified elegance which spoke of generations of inherited wealth and social position. Gervaise Raikes too mirrored the qualities of his room. Tall, silver haired and soldierly, dressed in the formality of morning tails, grey waistcoat and striped trousers, he regarded Curtis across the wide Georgian desk with disfavour.

'The fact is Curtis,' he was saying in cold tones, 'there is very little we can do unless you are prepared to contribute something for us to work on. When someone starts selling stock in a market as weak as this one then it is bound to affect the price. If you won't release more details about Klerksdorp's progress, my only suggestion is to begin buying on your own behalf and try to drive the price up.'

'I've already said once I'm doing so at this very minute on Wall Street,' Curtis snapped, 'you can't expect me to support the price in every country single handed.' Raikes consulted a note on the desk. 'Then I'm afraid it doesn't seem to be reflected in the share price,' he remarked dryly. 'What do you think Giles? Wall Street is more your pigeon.'

Giles Raikes was a slimmer, darker version of his uncle and some twenty years his junior. Though dressed with the same courtly distinction, he was not lacking, Curtis knew, in either initiative or intelligence, and his urbane manner hid a shrewd business insight. Just now he was sitting cross-legged opposite Curtis, to one side of the desk.

'I don't know quite on what scale your purchases in America have been, Mr. Curtis,' he said quietly in response to his uncle's question, 'nor exactly at what point they were made. Since the time in New York at this present moment is approximately five o'clock in the morning, I assume your statement is not to be taken literally. The price of Klerksdorp however has moved downwards steadily over the past ten days, just as it has in London. Kimber, Crossfield, Smith, the company's broker

372

on Wall Street report a similar pattern to the one we find: sizeable lines of stock are being offered for sale at regular intervals, and bargains being struck at ten to fifteen per cent beneath the current bidding. Incidentally,' he added, 'their report yesterday made no mention of recent buying of any significance.'

Curtis frowned. The inference behind the polite phrases was perfectly clear. The man was accusing him of being a bare-faced liar. Accustomed to behaving as though he was a financial wizard whose statements were not to be disputed, he was finding the Raikes' attitude an unpleasant surprise. Previously they had been content to sit passively while he dictated a series of instructions he wished carried out, even if their manner in doing so had been one of fastidious distaste. This new tough-ness was wholly unexpected.

Gervaise Raikes was speaking again. 'Can you shed any light at all on who is behind this persistent selling?' he asked. 'Cer-tainly some of it appears to be originating in South Africa and since you yourself have so recently returned . . .?' he left the sentence uncompleted, but Curtis shook his head, 'I've not the slightest idea,' he retorted angrily, 'which is why I'm here asking you.'

The two brokers exchanged glances. This time it was Giles who spoke. 'Of course during the past twelve months,' he said casually, 'our firm has put more than one million pounds worth of Klerksdorp stock through the London market, on your per-sonal behalf.' He paused and Curtis interrupted. 'You know damn well those sales were made as part of a world wide rationalization of my business interests,' he said hotly. 'And the money used to finance further exploration at the mine. Are you suggesting I've been selling my own stock short?'

'No, of course not Curtis, everyone knows how ridiculous such an idea would be,' the senior partner responded smoothly. 'Nevertheless, I'm sure you can see that in the face of all this confusion some form of positive action on your part is highly desirable if not vital.'

'Dammit, I've told you once, I can't support the price here and in New York,' Curtis swore angrily, 'why don't you put some more of your clients' money in? A bit of outside buying is all it needs.'

Gervaise Raikes gave him a long, hard look. 'I'm afraid we should find that impossible at this present juncture,' he said, clearly and with emphasis, 'in fact we are having to do the very opposite.'

Curtis stared at him in amazement. 'You mean you're advising your clients to sell? My God I won't stand for that! You're brokers to the company, it's unethical. I'll go to the courts.' Giles stood up and began gazing out of the window, watching the figures streaming in and out of the Stock Exchange; turning back to the room, he cut through Curtis' frothing complaints. 'What my uncle means,' he said crisply, 'is that we no longer consider Klerksdorp is an acceptable risk, and nothing you've said to us today has done anything to change our minds. You don't seem to realize the market is in a dangerously weak state and your company is now on a knife edge. Unless you can come up with some way to stop the slide in your share price then the quotation may have to be suspended. As it is rumours are beginning to go round. The slightest thing could cause a run on the stock which might bring bankruptcy.'

It was only too easy to read what was in their minds Curtis saw – uncle and nephew both believed he had sold stock earlier in the year because he had known then the company was insolvent. Ironically the money raised had genuinely been loaned to Klerksdorp in a desperate attempt to stave off disaster for a few more months, in the hope new ore loads could be discovered in the meantime.

There was no point in trying to argue the matter further; the meeting was clearly at an end. The Raikes' were regarding him with inflexible determination. He had failed to allay their suspicions and their intentions were obvious. They would continue the process they had already initiated; clearing out the Klerksdorp stock from their clients' portfolios and feeding them on to the market. The effects would gather momentum, until within forty-eight hours, the steady selling of the past fortnight would have become a wave, touching off a chain reaction across the Atlantic.

Unless he could reach New York before the news broke and complete the option sale he was ruined.

Paul Rintlen was shaving with considerable difficulty in the whore's room in Covent Garden. The mirror above the basin was placed so low he was forced to stoop at an uncomfortable angle in order to see his reflection in the glass, and added to this, since he had omittted to buy a razor the previous evening, he was having to make do with a miniature one belonging to the woman.

He swore as he scraped awkwardly around his chin and a trickle of blood appeared among the lather; he had cut himself for the second time. Dabbing at it irritably, he continued with short painful strokes. At least, he reflected, he had managed to secure a sound night's sleep, undisturbed by fears of Heydrich's killers. The woman too had displayed considerable talent and expertise at her profession, and Rintlen had been able to respond with an enthusiasm which had surprised him, considering the exhaustion he had felt.

He had completed shaving and was rinsing off his face in the basin, when the door opened and she appeared, bearing several brown wrapped parcels. 'I bought everything you wanted,' she said, setting them down on the bed. 'Socks, underwear, three white shirts and collars, the same size as the one you had on, pyjamas and a dressing gown.' Reaching into the pocket of her coat she pulled out a handful of bills and loose change. 'I kept the receipts like you said, only I'll need a bit more for the suitcase though, if it's got to be a good one.'

Rintlen's suit had been hung tidily on the back of a chair. Taking out his wallet he extracted another note. 'I want a bath,' he told her, handing it over, 'and breakfast as soon as you get back.' The woman nodded. 'I'll run it now, it takes a while.' She showed no curiosity in the purchases she had been sent to make. In the daylight without the heavy make-up she had been wearing when they met, she appeared younger and more attractive. Her room too, though cheap, was clean and pleasant, its colours and furnishings unexpectedly imaginative.

Soaping himself in the bath, he directed his mind to the task ahead. On the whole he was inclined to think it would be safe for him to take the train down to Southampton with the other passengers. There was no reason to suppose Heydrich's men had guessed that he was still intending to fulfil his mission, and even if they had, there would be little they could do in public to prevent him. The flight to New York took more than twenty-four hours and involved two stops in Canada on the way. At some point on the journey there would be the opportunity he needed to finish with Wienzman and his daughter.

Back in the bedroom he found the woman packing his new belongings neatly inside a smart brown suitcase. 'I'll start your breakfast,' she said standing up. Seen in such a domestic setting, and with the plain jersey and skirt she had on in place of her flashy evening clothes, she gave more the impression of a young housewife than of a prostitute. There was an oddly innocent air about her which brought a reassuringly commonplace touch to their relationship. Under normal conditions Rintlen would probably have felt contempt, even revulsion by now, as it was however, hunted and an outcast himself, with the life he was used to slipping even further from his grasp, he felt a bond of sympathy. It occurred to him he did not even know her name.

'Not yet,' he said firmly and taking another five pound bank note from his wallet, he laid it on the mantelpiece. His train after all did not leave till one o'clock.

The girl laughed good naturedly. 'You're keen I must say,' she said, and stepping over towards the bed she began undoing her skirt.

The journey through the spring countryside of Surrey and Hampshire in the open car, on such a glorious day, had thoroughly restored the spirits of Desmond and Laura after their troubles of the previous evening. Laura in particular was delighted at the chance of showing off her skill at the wheel. The MG's firm handling and quick response made it a joy to drive and they sped along the twisting roads, the wind blowing through her hair and bringing the colour to her cheeks.

Past the ancient town of Winchester, Desmond directed her

off the main road and through the narrow lanes in the valley of the Itchen river. 'One of the finest trout streams in the whole of England,' he told her proudly. They passed by small villages set among water meadows and rolling fields whose earth lay freshly turned by the spring ploughing. Then, turning down a track which wound for a quarter of a mile between high banked hedges, they came upon the farm, in a fold among the downland, gazing back up the valley to the south.

On the way down Desmond had described the house and its surroundings to her, but even so she was struck by its beauty. 'Do you like it?' Desmond asked, smiling.

'Do I like it? It's the loveliest house I've ever seen! I can't believe you really live here.' The drive opened out into a wide square of gravel, bordered by a lawn. 'I'm afraid the place hasn't been very well looked after these last few months,' he apologized, glancing at the weeds pushing up through the stones and the unkempt grass.

Scrambling out Laura filled her lungs with deep breaths of the invigorating air. In the distance she could see the river sparkling in the sunshine and the rust red roofs of a village amid the green and brown patchwork of the fields. 'What a magnificent place,' she turned to him her face flushed with happiness, 'no wonder you wanted to live here.' The sunlight glinting gold on her hair made a bright splash of colour against the pale hues around.

Desmond laughed. 'I'm glad you approve,' he said, searching for the key in his pocket. 'Come on and I'll show you round inside.' The heavy studded oak door opened with some reluctance to allow them into a lofty hall over whose stone flagged floor the dim light from the leaded windows threw dappled patterns. Directly opposite stood a great open fireplace. 'It's a pity Pamela had all the furniture put into store,' he said as he led her on through another door. 'This is the sitting-room. It was in a terrible state when we first arrived. The last owner was a farmer who used to store hay in the ground floor rooms. The beams you can see had all been covered over with plaster which we had to strip off by hand.'

'It's incredible,' Laura answered in an awed voice. The light here was brighter, giving the room a rich warm glow despite being bare of furnishings. 'You were lucky to have made such a find. How old is it by the way?'

'The majority was built in 1520,' Desmond answered, 'but parts, like these flag stones and the kitchen are much older, probably a hundred years or so earlier. And there's been a house of some kind here since before the days of the Conqueror. There's certainly one mentioned as existing in the Domesday Book. The site is near perfect you see, sheltered by the ground around, yet with marvellous views, and of course plenty of water. We've a small well of our own in the courtyard at the back.'

Upstairs he showed her the bedrooms; small, cheerful rooms with crooked floors and sloping ceilings; telling her of the further plans they had once had. From the windows he pointed out the land which had once gone with the farm and the two paddocks which were all that remained. Returning to the ground floor once again he led her out into the paved courtyard, between the rear of the house and the old stables and barn.

'In the summer, it gets so hot we used to bring out a table and have dinner here on fine nights,' he told her, recalling the memories of the early days of his marriage. Laura was interested in the well in the middle of the yard, with its stone surround and wooden canopy, and Desmond obligingly hauled up a bucketful of clear water for her to taste. 'It's delicious,' she gasped, 'but so cold.' They both laughed, their eyes met and moving together they kissed happily.

They were still embracing when a hard, bitter voice broke suddenly in upon their private world. 'Well, this is a charming spectacle to find in my own house, I must say.' Springing guiltily apart they looked round to see Pamela standing by the kitchen door watching them. She must have driven up unnoticed, Desmond realized, and seeing their car, had walked through to find them. 'I came down in the hope of having a talk with my husband alone, and what do I discover?' she said, coming across the yard, 'but him and his girlfriend making love in the stables.' She was wearing a loose brown coat hanging open to reveal a bright red jersey and skirt beneath, her face was very pale, accentuating the crimson of her mouth, her dark eyes glittering dangerously, and the vivid blackness of her hair. 'This, I suppose, is the celebrated Mrs. Hartman.' She gave Laura a venomous glance. Desmond pulled himself together with an effort, 'Laura, I am sorry,' he apologized, 'this is my wife. I wasn't expecting you,' he went on to Pamela. 'Why didn't you tell me you were coming down?'

'I only decided this morning, it never occurred to me you'd bring your airline pick-ups here,' she answered.

'Pamela, that's enough,' Desmond warned her sharply. 'If you want to quarrel then do so with me, but leave Laura out of it.'

Laura meanwhile had recovered her composure. 'I had better leave you two alone to talk,' she said to Desmond, 'I'll wait for you by the car.'

'Running out on us already?' Pamela sneered, stepping forward to bar the American girl's way. 'Afraid you might have to listen to a few home truths?' Laura, however, faced up to her defiantly. 'Did you really come here because you wanted to speak to your husband Mrs. O'Neill?' she asked witheringly. 'Or do you simply want to pick a fight with me? Because I've been pushed around for most of this past week and I'd just love a chance to hit back for once.' The two women faced each other angrily for a moment till Pamela abruptly dropped her gaze and with a contemptuous sniff stood aside allowing Laura to pass.

Desmond waited until the sound of her footsteps had died away inside the house before speaking. 'Well?' he said shortly, 'here we are alone. Now why did you want to see me?'

'Why the hell shouldn't I want to see you? You're my husband still aren't you?' Pamela stormed at him, 'or does it mean nothing to you that we are about to be divorced after only four years of marriage? Do you imagine it's very pleasant for me to come down to try for a last attempt to reason things out with you, only to find you in the arms of another woman?'

'Almost as pleasant as for me to find you with Simon Collier last night,' he answered. In truth he couldn't have cared less if

Pamela were having an affair with him, but her talk of wanting 'to reason things out' had worried him. Fortunately she was in too much of a rage to pass up a chance for an argument. 'Simon, he's just a friend,' she dismissed the barrister with a toss of her head, 'and even if he weren't I certainly would not go bringing him down here. This was our home, or had you forgotten?'

'Of course I hadn't, and I'm not likely to either,' he retorted 'and in any case you seem to forget it's you who has been so keen to sell the place recently.'

'I know, which is why I'm here,' Pamela had been standing facing him, hands thrust into the pockets of her coat, now she began pacing up and down. 'I want to be quite certain you're aware of what you're doing.'

'Of course I know what I'm doing,' Desmond said irritably. 'I've been perfectly sure all along. We made a mistake, you and I, in believing we could ever live together. The only sensible thing to do is to cut ourselves loose.'

'And suppose I said I was willing to have one last try. What then?' she demanded, checking her stride and looking at him intently. Desmond shrugged his shoulders wearily. 'We have been through this before. You've no more wish to stay married than I have, you'll be much better off with some other man, someone like Simon Collier, who isn't always disappearing abroad for weeks at a time.'

'Leave Simon out of it,' Pamela snapped. 'The truth is you can't wait to be free so you can marry your new girlfriend. Nice fools you'd both look if I called off the divorce.'

Desmond had had enough. 'Pamela,' he said to his wife quietly, 'If you really want to believe I would jump straight from one marriage into another, I can't help you, and I'm certainly not staying here to argue over it. You must do what seems best for you, but as far as I am concerned, we're finished. I'm not standing for any more emotional indulgences, these scenes are pointless, they do neither of us any good, and we just end up hurting each other more. Now we have agreed to sell the farm I don't want to see you again.'

He had spoken more brutally than he had intended, and felt

a momentary pang as he saw the effect of his words. Pamela stared at him in astonishment, her mouth working soundlessly, the shock of rejection seemed to have left her speechless.

'You bastard!' she said at last, between tightly clenched teeth, her voice shaking with hatred. 'You unutterable bastard! I'll make you regret you ever said that. I swear if it's the last thing I ever do. I'll never give you a divorce, do you hear? Never. I'll make you beg me first.'

Her voice rose to a pitch of hysteria as the emotional storm to which she had been building up burst out into the open. Overwhelmed by rage and fury, she screamed savage denunciations at him in a blind unreasoning flood. There was no point in staying to listen, Desmond knew from his experience of the past, or in attempting to calm her; his very presence was the cause of her bitterness. Turning on his heel, he fled back through the house.

'Do you think she meant what she said?' Laura asked as they drove back down the valley. Desmond had taken the wheel this time, and was giving her the gist of his confrontation with Pamela. 'I don't know,' he said with a shake of his head. 'Maybe not. I doubt if she really knew what she was saying most of the time. When one of these nervous crises breaks on her, she simply strikes without thinking. I'm only sorry you had to be there when it happened.'

'Oh, that doesn't matter,' Laura smiled, 'I've had much worse things thrown at me before. I feel sorry for her.'

'Well, it had to be faced sooner or later,' Desmond said. 'I always knew I'd probably have to have it out with her once more before we finally cut ourselves free. Poor Pamela doesn't know any other way.' He drove on thoughtfully, running back in his mind over the scene which had taken place in the courtyard. Above them in the sky a formation of planes etched white vapour trails with unerring precision. Fighters, he guessed, Hurricanes, or Spitfires from the nearby base at Tangmere. How long would it be he wondered before they were patrolling in earnest?

Towards half past eleven Jacquetta d'Este returned to her room at the Ritz from a walk in the Park with Rashid.

There were no doubt that Rashid had very nearly been persuaded to switch the target of his revenge from Luca to some other more prominent figure. Not that this was without its dangers, Jacquetta shuddered at the idea of the risks he might run. At the back of both their minds though so far unvoiced, was the hope they might one day be able to return together to Egypt and live there under the protection of Prince Suleiman and the King. Such a course would be impossible though if Rashid were to be in serious trouble with the Italian government.

Against all this was the disturbing news that the Italians suspected Rashid's presence in London. The telegram to the embassy from Cairo had been relayed to Luca at breakfast and had instantly thrown them both into a state of confusion. Luca had hurried off to the embassy to consult with the authorities while Jacquetta, with equal anxiety had hastened down the corridor to Rashid.

At first she had believed all was lost, and it was only when he had calmed her down and made her repeat to him everything her husband had told her, that she realized she had been exaggerating the dangers. The Italians, it was clear, had only learnt Rashid had disappeared from Cairo. The rest was pure conjecture. Besides, Jacquetta knew, her husband's mental conception of Rashid was as a vengeful figure in Arab robes, mounted on a horse. A far cry from the elegantly western Turkish nobleman travelling aboard *Imperial 109*.

A soft tap at the door interrupted her thoughts. Springing up to open it she was surprised to find Dr. Van Smit standing outside. 'Are you certain it is me you want to see?' she asked when she had let him in. 'My husband will be back before we go to the station, but I am not sure at exactly what time.'

'Thank you Baroness, but it is you to whom I wish to speak,' Van Smit answered in his clipped accent, 'I have a matter of great delicacy to discuss.'

'A matter of great delicacy?' Jacquetta repeated in amazement. 'Whatever can you mean?' Even as she spoke though, a terrible suspicion shot through her. The South African was eyeing her intently, here in England his deep tan was even more noticeable as was the tightly stretched skin of his face and head, making him seem to her eyes grotesquely out of place in the luxurious comfort of the room.

'I am sure you are already aware of my meaning Baroness,' Van Smit answered, observing the sudden draining of colour from her features, 'but since you ask I will make it clear. The night before last, while we were in Rome, I had occasion to come to your suite during the evening. I wished to see if your husband would be interested in a game of cards. The door to your suite was not quite fastened,' he continued, 'nor was the door to your bedroom. In there I saw . . .'

'Very well, you need not go on. We both know what you saw.' Jacquetta interrupted sharply. 'What is it you want of me?' The Doctor's thin lips twitched briefly in amusement, he was clearly enjoying the situation. 'I should have thought that was obvious,' he replied, 'I want money, and a great deal of it. We will start with twenty-five thousand dollars payable as soon as you reach America.'

'Twenty-five thousand dollars!' Jacquetta echoed in astonishment. 'You can't possibly be serious. How do you imagine I can obtain such a sum? It is out of the question. We are not rich.'

'Not in comparison with Mr. Curtis, I agree,' Van Smit said calmly, 'But you must certainly have money. Also jewellery,' he added, 'like the nice diamond brooch you're wearing now.' Jacquetta's hand leapt instinctively to the hooped clasp pinned to the shoulders of her green silk dress. The piece was one of her favourites, left to her by her mother, and the thought of losing it to this loathsome man enraged her.

'Get out!' she cried furiously, 'get out, and go to my husband with your tales. Do you think I care? It is all finished between us long ago. And when you do I shall go to the police. In both England and America, the penalty for what you are doing, for blackmail is severe. Then we shall see who is the loser after all.'

Van Smit was taken aback by her spirited attack. 'You had better think again,' he said menacingly. 'Imagine the reaction of your family and friends if they were to hear about your affair. How would you feel then?' Jacquetta however, was not to be beaten so easily. 'It is you who should think again Doctor,' she said with contempt. 'Among my friends are men of honour who will know what to do to prevent my disgrace.'

'Don't threaten me Baroness,' Van Smit spat back, 'I took the precaution before coming to see you, of leaving a letter with lawyers explaining everything, to be sent to your husband in the event of my death or disappearance. So tell that to your lover, Baroness and you can also tell him for me, he may be able to fool everyone else in this flight that he's Turkish but I've met his kind before. He's a desert Arab from out of the deep sands, you can see it in his eyes and face.' Seeing Jacquetta's look of alarm he chuckled briefly. 'Yes, I thought maybe there would be people interested in knowing we have an impostor among us. So find the money between you, twenty-five thousand dollars. I'll give you forty-eight hours from the moment we land in New York.'

Jacquetta could only stare at him in fear, paralysed by the thought of what would follow were Luca to learn of Rashid's true identity. 'Good day Baroness.' Satisfied with the outcome of the interview, Van Smit took his leave of her. 'Remember,' he said with one hand on the door, 'Twenty-five thousand dollars by Saturday afternoon or your husband will learn everything.'

Dawn at Warren Lake was breaking on another day of mists and dull overcast sky, as Pat Jarrett edged the Supermarine carefully out from the boathouse for the first time since his arrival. According to the most recent weather forecasts the cold front was moving away eastwards; by tomorrow in all probability the skies would be clear with the fine weather expected to last through the week-end.

Jarrett listened with a glow of satisfaction to the familiar roar of the 700 horse power beneath the long cowling. A quick check of his instruments and he was away racing across the lake into the wind. At 3000 revs he lifted off and hurtled over the tree covered slopes of the opposite shore. The little racer was handling as sweetly as he could wish for, the extra weight of the guns made only a fractional difference to her performance. Relieved, he shot up over the dam wall, pressed hard down on the starboard rudder bar to bring her round in another tight turn and dived low over the lake's surface.

Levelling off he flicked the firing buttons into the ON position and sighted in on his target. A quarter of a mile along the eastern shoreline from the house, and close to the water's edge lay the decaying remains of a small cabin cruiser broken and beached some years in the past. Rocketing in at 50 feet Jarrett opened fire at a range of 400 yards, holding the burst for three seconds.

Even above the slipstream he could hear the tremendous blast from the gunposts as the whole aircraft trembled with the recoils. A swift moving line of red dots arced up into the sighting ring from the guns below, to zero in on the hill side. He had loaded with ball and tracer for the practice, one tracer for every three rounds.

The boat disappeared in a sudden violent cloud of dust and smoke. Jarrett had a fleeting glimpse of timber and panelling bursting explosively apart before he dragged the stick back into the pit of his stomach pulling the aircraft up to scrape clear of the trees. A fierce joy swept through him as all his old war memories came surging back with the sensation of the attack. Swinging back in to touch down by the jetty again he found his whole body quivering with excitement, thrilling at the sound and feel of the guns and at the sharp smell of the cordite in his nostrils.

When he reached the scene minutes later, he stared amazed at the effect of his handiwork. There could certainly be no doubt as to either the alignment of his sights or the efficiency of his guns. The cabin cruiser was scarcely recognizable as a boat any longer. The entire midship section had been torn out and smashed into fragments, the heavy spars pulverized by the blast of the fire which had literally blown the vessel into pieces, leaving only the bow and a portion of the stern as identifiable sections.

Here was proof Jarrett thought, picking through the

scattered wreckage of the error the British R.A.F. had made in fitting eight .303 calibre Brownings in place of half that number of the .5 inch Colts to their Spitfires and Hurricanes. Although the lighter weapons had a fifty per cent higher rate of fire, the vastly greater size and velocity of the Colt bullets actually delivered more than double the hitting power to the target, in the same time.

Back in the boathouse he cleaned out and re-oiled the guns and fed in fresh ammunition, lapping the long belts carefully into the feed chutes. Resisting the temptation to go up for a second practice shoot, he replaced the doped on fabric patches over the muzzles of the blast tubes as a protection against dirt and spray and returned to the house for breakfast. By conducting his firing test this early, and with the added advantage of the low cloud to muffle the noise within the valley, it was unlikely in the extreme he thought that the gunfire would have attracted attention.

His plans were now virtually complete, he had only to await the arrival of *Imperial 109* and her cargo of bullion.

A quarter to one saw *Caterina*'s passengers boarding the Southampton express at London's Waterloo station having been conducted from the Ritz Hotel under the watchful eyes of two Imperial Airways staff, delegated to make sure nobody went astray and thus delay the flight. Installing their charges in the Pullman compartments which had been reserved, and reminding them that luncheon would be served in the first class dining car as soon as the train started, they then retired to check the passengers' luggage aboard and to await the arrival of Mr. Ernst Perler, of Berne, Switzerland, the identity under which Paul Rintlen was travelling.

Rintlen himself was already in the station. For the past half hour he had been watching the approaches to the platform from the corner of a nearby buffet. So far he had observed nothing to alarm him but he was still apprehensive. The station was very crowded, numerous men in uniform, both naval and military, were passing through part, no doubt, of Britain's recently introduced armed forces call-up, making it difficult for him to detect if anyone suspicious was lurking in the vicinity. Several times he thought he had spotted one or more of Heydrich's men, but on each occasion they had shown themselves to be perfectly innocent travellers, merely waiting for family or friends to join them. Perhaps after all, he had managed to slip his pursuers successfully.

Feeling at length he could leave it no longer, he picked up his case and slinging his raincoat over his arm, approached the ticket barrier. The two airline staff waiting there he had noticed earlier, and revealing himself to them he was led away at once to join the remainder of the flying-boat's passengers. There was just time for him to be found a seat in a compartment with Rashid, Dr. Van Smit and Charlotte Curtis' maid Arlette, before, with a shriek of its whistle, and a blast of white smoke, the train began to move.

Jacquetta was sitting two doors along in the window seat of a compartment occupied by her husband and the two Curtises. The men were discussing the latest developments in the Czechoslovakian crises and their significance for Europe and the world at large. Jacquetta listened with half an ear to their conversation while at the same time keeping up a chatter with Charlotte about the clothes she had bought. Most of all however, her mind was occupied in trying to think of a way to break Dr. Van Smit's hold upon her. So far she had been unable to speak to Rashid and tell him what had occurred. Luca had returned to the hotel moments after the Doctor's departure from the room, though fortunately he had ascribed his wife's nervousness and distress to the effects of the telegram received at breakfast.

To no small degree her worries were caused by fear as to what Rashid's reaction would be. His pride would be outraged, she knew, and in his fury he might easily take violent steps against Van Smit, the results of which might be calamitous. If the South African were to vanish or be found dead, having indeed done as he said and left a letter with lawyers, to be sent to Luca, she and Rashid would most certainly be indicted for murder.

Rintlen ate only a light lunch and left the dining car early as the train steamed out of Winchester. He was fortified by a bottle of wine shared with the Doctor. The latter had proved an interesting companion full of gossip about his fellow travellers and providing considerable information on the flight which lay ahead.

He wandered back down the train. After the drink at lunch he needed to use the lavatory; the first two he came to were locked and displaying engaged signs in the slot above the door handles. Continuing on down the corridor he passed through the second class section towards the rear. The train was emptier here, and there were few passengers to be met with He had reached the end of the last carriage but one when, looking back he saw two men at the far end, coming towards him.

Instantly, without the need for a second glance, he recognized them for what they were. Tall, athletic-looking men both in their late twenties or early thirties, fairheaded and smartly but unobtrusively dressed in sports jackets and grey flannel trousers; individually they would have passed unnoticed as Englishmen in any group, which was how they must have escaped his attention on the way through. Seen together however, as they approached, methodically checking every compartment they came to, there could be no room for doubt as to their true identity and purpose. They were an execution team sent by Heydrich to kill him.

Immediately to Rintlen's right was an outside exit and hard by this stood the door to another lavatory. Reacting instantly, he seized hold of the handle, praying that it too would not be occupied. To his relief it opened and he slipped inside, turning the lock at once behind him.

Tense with fear and expecting any moment to hear the rattle of the handle as the door was tried, he waited, ear pressed close to the woodwork, straining to catch the sounds in the corridor outside, above the noise of the wheels on the track. He hoped desperately that the two men had not seen him duck round the corner. If they had ... he looked around the small cramped cubicle. There was no way out from here; above the window his eyes fell on a red emergency chain. If the worst came to the worst he would have to pull that and trust to the resulting confusion to save him.

He was still listening when all at once, without warning, the door was smashed violently inwards, tearing the lock bodily from the frame, striking him a savage blow on the side of the face and hurling him on to the floor against the toilet bowl. In the same moment the two men burst through and flung themselves upon him. Dazed by the suddenness of the attack, Rintlen lashed out fiercely, kicking and punching blindly but in the confined space his opponents were too much for him. Blows rained down on his head and body, his arms were pinned and he was hauled struggling to his feet.

Pushing the door shut again, his captors faced him grimly. All three of them were panting hard, their clothes disarranged by the fight. Producing a small calibre automatic from an inside holster, the leader of the two pointed it at Rintlen's chest, 'Foolish to try and escape from us Standartenfuhrer,' he said, breathing heavily. 'You only make things worse for yourself.' He had gingery fair hair, grey eyes and a freckled skin. Rintlen's head was still singing from the effects of the beating he had received, and his body ached. 'What are you going to do with me?' he gasped, knowing it was pointless to dispute his identity. The man behind him gripping his arms twisted them viciously and Rintlen let out a cry of pain. The other agent smiled thinly, 'In approximately six minutes,' he said, looking at the time on his wrist watch, 'this train enters a long tunnel. When that happens, we take you into the passage, open the door,' he jerked his head, 'a little push and out you go. We are travelling at one hundred and twenty kilometres per hour. At a guess the authorities will have some difficulty in identifying your remains. In the meantime,' he went on as Rintlen stared at him in dumb horror, 'we will wait quietly here together.'

Jacquetta d'Este had at last managed to snatch a few moments alone with Rashid. Luca and Curtis were lingering in the dining car over coffee and brandy, while Charlotte had returned to her seat in the Pullman coach. Pouring out her story to him in the passageway, she told him of the Doctor's visit to her hotel room after their walk in the Park, and of the demands he had made. His reaction was just as she had feared and it was only with the greatest of difficulty that she was able to prevent him from seeking out and confronting Van Smit there and then.

'It is useless to try and buy off such a man,' he told her, 'he will demand more and more until you are bled dry, and in the end he will still go to your husband.'

'Not so loud,' she begged him, terrified lest someone should overhear them. 'I know, but what else is there to be done?'

'What should have been done long before now,' Rashid whispered back fiercely, 'your husband must die and this Van Smit must die with him.'

'Please, Rashid, for God's sake,' Jacquetta pleaded with him frantically, 'Couldn't we just go away together, you and I, back to Egypt and forget about them both? Then none of this would matter.'

'No, it is impossible,' Rashid shook his head decisively. 'I should never have listened to your advice and allowed myself to forget my duty.' In vain she tried to reason with him, but he remained adamant. 'Afterwards, yes, perhaps we can go away,' he said to her, 'but first, I must do what I set out to do.'

Before Jacquetta could reply to this, the sound of voices down the corridor warned them Luca and Stewart Curtis were returning. Shooting a last anguished look of pleading at her lover, she fled away in the direction of their compartment.

In the lavatory at the rear of the train, the leader of Rintlen's two captors looked at his watch again. 'About two more minutes,' he said. 'We had better bring him out into the passageway.' Changing the gun over into his left hand he opened the door a fraction and checked to see that all was clear. Then backing out, he motioned to his companion to push Rintlen after him.

Out in the corridor they took up positions on either side of the exit, holding the SD officer firmly between them. The leader squinted through the glass of the window at the ground ahead, speeding towards them at over one hundred feet per second. 'Here it comes,' he said, 'get ready with the handle.'

Letting go his grip on Rintlen's arm with one hand, the other man reached down and fumbled with the latch of the door. As he did so, with a sudden deafening shriek, the train plunged into the mouth of the tunnel. Taken unaware the man allowed the door to be jerked from his grasp, caught in the slipstream it flew open and slammed back against the side of the carriage.

Seeing the agent stretching between himself and the roaring black void before him, Rintlen seized the only chance he was likely to get. Lunging forward with all his weight he drove his shoulder and hip into the man's left side. His action took his assailants totally unprepared, both had been bracing themselves to prevent Rintlen from trying to break backwards, away from the yawning exit. Caught off balance the man was pitched headlong through the doorway. With a terrible cry, he clawed desperately at Rintlen's arm with his other hand, trying to maintain his grip, but the momentum of his fall and the pull of the slipstream were too much for him. His fingers tore loose, and he was whirled away into the darkness of the tunnel behind them, his scream cutting off abruptly as his body thudded sickeningly against the rear carriage.

The force of Rintlen's lunge had sent both him and the remaining agent crashing to the floor, in a furious struggle for possession of the gun. Though Rintlen had the advantage of surprise, the other man was stronger and fought back savagely, endeavouring to twist the weapon free from his grip and at the same time using his superior strength to heave his opponent half out of the open door.

Choking and half blinded in the smoke and soot-laden blast of air, with his head and shoulders hanging out over the track as the train thundered through the tunnel, Rintlen tightened his grip frantically on the other's gun hand attempting to pull himself back inside. Panic rose within him as he fancied himself slipping and he thrashed convulsively, striking out with his feet. All of a sudden there was a sharp report, he felt a stinging, burning sensation in the fingers of one hand, then the body on top of him relaxed and went limp.

Rintlen's one thought was still only to save himself from falling under the wheels. Grasping the edge of the door-frame he jerked himself back into the carriage and squirmed out from under his attacker. The agent was either dead or seriously wounded, and Rintlen did not stop to find out which. Snatching up the pistol, he seized the man's legs and tipped him out through the exit, dragging the door shut behind him just as the express flashed out into the sunlight again.

Twenty minutes later, and shortly before the train pulled into Southampton, Rintlen emerged from the lavatory and set off back to his seat. During the intervening period he had successfully removed the traces of dirt and damage suffered in the struggle, with the exception of a bruise on one cheek and a powder burn on the fingers of his right hand, neither of which would attract particular attention. Though the fight for his life had left him weak and shaky, he felt elated at the thought that he had defeated the attempt to kill him. No-one else on the train seemed to have heard the gunshot above the noise of the tunnel, and there was a good chance that the bodies of the two men would not be discovered for some while. Even when they were, there was nothing to link him with their deaths, so far as the British were concerned; the German Embassy would certainly maintain silence in the affair. And on the credit side he himself was now armed once again.

Meanwhile on the other side of the Atlantic Pat Jarrett had switched on the big shortwave wireless receiver set which he had installed in the kitchen up at the house, and was listening in, over his breakfast, to the early morning radio traffic between Botwood in Newfoundland and New York's La Guardia Airport. In doing so he overheard the Botwood operator acknowledging the prior receipt of the overnight message from England concerning the re-scheduling of *Imperial 109*.

A momentary anxiety passed over him at the realization that he had only another thirty hours to go before the plane was due and for an instant he even considered calling off his afternoon date with Susie. On reflection however, he told himself there was ample time for him to complete the last few minor jobs on the Supermarine. The engine had been running so smoothly during the firing test he anticipated little trouble over the final tuning; he had small worries of not being ready in time.

Going over to the window he looked out across the lake. A fresh breeze had sprung up, ruffling the surface of the water. Overhead the leaden cloud base was starting to thin and patches of blue sky and sunlight were showing through; the fine weather was on its way. He would be sorry to leave the lake; he had enjoyed working in this lonely, beautiful valley with its clear waters and hills of dark trees and fresh clean air. The life had suited him, perhaps one day, when it was all over, he would find another place like this.

Right now though, he had to work to finish before setting off to Keene. Clearing away the table and switching off the radio, he hurried back down to the boathouse.

A pleasant lunch in a small restaurant outside Southampton had done much to dispel the gloom Desmond felt after his meeting with Pamela. By skilfully manipulating the conversation Laura had contrived to turn it to other and more cheerful topics: of his boyhood in Ireland, in the Wicklow Mountains south of Dublin, of learning to fly after the war, and of his early days with Imperial Airways. 'Those were marvellous times,' he said nostalgically as they drove on into the city, 'Aviation was very new and exciting and each journey was a tremendous challenge. New routes were being pioneered and opened up everywhere; people were performing incredible, unheard of feats; night flights, flying over deserts and mountain ranges; men like Lindbergh crossing the Atlantic alone.'

Parking inside the dock they made their way down to *Caterina*'s berth. 'There's a fine sight,' Desmond exclaimed as they went. 'It's one of the Cunarders, the *Queen Mary*, leaving harbour.' Laura gazed in awe as the enormous blue liner slid slowly out towards the open sea to the accompaniment of a chorus of whistle blasts and sirens from the other ships. 'Come on,' he said, taking her arm, 'and I'll show you round over the flight deck before the others arrive.'

In the main passenger terminal of the Port, Junior Immigration Officer Ian Smallpage awaited the arrival of the contingent travelling on *Imperial 109* with impatience.

Twenty-four years old he was a skinny, gangling young man, whose thick glasses and generally studious air had earned him the nickname of 'Professor' among his colleagues. Conscientious and meticulous at his work, off duty he was quiet and un-adventurous, living with his parents in the city's northern suburbs, and spending most of his evenings studying for pro-motion to a higher grade. Today however was especially im-portant for him, he was about to become engaged.

Ian Smallpage and Helen Rowe had been walking out together since Ian's sixteenth birthday and during that time it had never occurred to either of them that they would not one day marry each other. Their parents had been near neighbours all their lives and the match was as much a foregone conclusion as it was possible to be. Ian was well aware of this; all the same he felt on edge and in a hurry to be away. His shift was due to finish at three o'clock and he was meeting Helen outside the terminal. Then he would take her up for a cream tea in the centre of the town and over the tea he would tell her the pro-motion he had been waiting for had finally been confirmed for the end of the month, and would ask her to marry him.

The passengers appeared through the doors of the departure lounge at last and advanced towards him in a straggling bunch. With one eye on the clock opposite his desk, Ian began flicking through the proffered passports, cancelling the entry stamps of the foreigners among them and, out of long habit, auto-matically checking the photographs and descriptions for errors. Emigration procedure was largely a formality, he knew, but an ingrained sense of duty forced him to go through them without skipping.

Of a sudden he paused frowning; something in one of the passports in front of him had struck a jarring note. 'Mr. Perler?' he looked up inquiringly. 'Yes?' The man before him was of medium height, slimly built dark with a narrow face, he wore a brown double-breasted suit of continental cut and somewhat crumpled. 'Is there anything wrong?' His English was good, the accent that of a German speaker, reasonable enough in a Swiss. His left cheek bore the mark of a recent bruise.

Ian wavered. Over the past three years he had acquired a

certain instinct for sniffing out frauds and forgeries. A re-touched photograph, blurred lettering, a smear or the faint stains of chemicals on a page; he had learnt to spot the small signs which betrayed the impostor. This time there was nothing obvious he could pin down. There was merely a feeling which warned him something was not quite right. 'You are travelling through to New York?' he asked as he turned the pages again, seeking a clue which would shake the passport's authenticity, but if anything it was too perfect. 'Yes, from Rome via Paris and London,' the man answered.

Other passengers were queuing up at the desk now, beginning to look impatient. Ian handed the passport back and moved on to the next. After all, he consoled himself, what did it matter? The man was leaving the country anyway.

Although *Caterina* had had a thorough one-hundred-hour service at Cairo, the engineers had been over her again in preparation for the Atlantic crossing. There was still much preliminary work for Desmond and the crew. The flying-boat would take off, lightly loaded with fuel, and two hours later they would rendezvous with a tanker aircraft over Foynes on the mouth of the river Shannon in Ireland. After a midair refuelling, they would head out over the North Atlantic. It would take approximately twelve hours to cover the one thousand eight hundred miles to Botwood, Newfoundland, though it might be longer if strong head winds were encountered. For part of the trip, the cabins would be converted into bedrooms equipped with comfortable bunks to enable those who wished to do so to rest.

Landing at Botwood, the local time would be only three or four a.m., owing to the three and a half hour difference between London and North America, and the next morning would see them in Montreal in time for a leisurely lunch before the final two-hour stage over the Adirondaks and Catskill Mountains to New York, touching down on the East River at four o'clock on Thursday.

Ralph Kendricks was already on board checking his wireless equipment and radio direction finding sets; the rest of the crew turned up shortly afterwards, including Ken Frazer, who had spent the previous evening and morning pleading with Jack Priestly for a transfer to another flight, and whose colleagues were now punishing him for his betrayal of their Captain. They refused to speak to him except on technical matters.

Laura was interested to look round the flight deck, but she saw that the men were busy; moreover, that there was an awkwardness in the atmosphere, caused by the first officer's presence. Retreating tactfully into the mailroom, she passed the time until the other passengers arrived helping Sandy Everett sort the mail.

The three officers completed their checks and retired back up to the airline meteorological officer for a comprehensive briefing on the conditions likely to be encountered on the crossing.

'The only weather system we really have to worry about,' the senior met. officer told them as they examined a wall-chart of the North Atlantic, 'is here.' He indicated an area in the extreme north-east of Canada. 'There is a deep depression moving eastward out of Labrador towards Greenland. We've been watching it for a couple of days now and by all accounts it's pretty bad; storm force winds, snow blizzards, severe electrical interference – the lot. Fortunately, however, it is merging on a track that will take it well to the north of your course, so you shouldn't experience any difficulties, apart perhaps from slightly increased head winds.

'Otherwise, the reports we've been getting in from Canada and from shipping indicate that you will have very little to worry about,' he went on. 'The skies should remain fairly clear until you are about five hundred miles or so out into the Atlantic. From then on it will probably begin to cloud over and you'll meet fairly continuous cover up to eight to ten thousand feet, I'd say, with winds mainly easterly, force four to five at maximum. Temperatures about average for the period.'

'What about isolated thunderstorms or rain squalls?' Desmond inquired.

'No reports of any,' the met. officer answered. 'As I said, provided that the storm over Labrador holds to its present course and speed, the bad weather will all pass to the north of you.'

Cheered by this optimistic view, the three men returned to *Catarina* in time to greet the returning passengers.

The approach of Laura's travelling companions was signalled by the appearance of a number of photographers and journalists intent on obtaining a follow-up to last night's story. They were accompanied by an irate Jack Priestly who was equally determined to ensure that Desmond at least received no further publicity. 'No interviews! You're to give absolutely no interviews to anyone. I forbid it categorically,' he said, hurrying up the gangway to where Desmond stood greeting the arrivals.

'I've not the slightest intention of doing so,' the Irishman told him coldly, shaking hands with the Kings as they climbed aboard. Priestly looked relieved, but his anger returned when Laura stepped out of the plane and, standing on the side of the pontoon, conducted a lengthy conversation with the reporters, in the course of which she was deliberately loud in Desmond's praises.

Jack Priestly was infuriated, but there was nothing he could do, and Desmond slipped back inside the hatch. He had quite a different matter on his mind altogether. He made his way to the after cabin. Entering without knocking, Desmond found Curtis slumped in a chair, with a copy of the *Wall Street Journal*. 'What the devil do you want?' he scowled at the interruption. 'I've got something to say to you about the allegations you made last night concerning Mrs. Hartman and the Cartier watch,' Desmond said with icy calm.

'Well, I've no wish to hear it,' Curtis retorted rudely. 'As far as I am concerned the matter is closed,' and he resumed his study of the paper. 'You'll listen,' Desmond told him, 'because unless you do you're not going to reach America tomorrow.'

Curtis glanced up sharply at his words. 'What exactly do you mean by that?' he demanded.

'It's quite simple,' Desmond answered, 'the watch was given to me by your wife last Sunday as a prize for winning the motor race in Cairo. I didn't want to accept, but she pressed it on me. I've no wish to have it back. What I will have though is a signed admission from you that the watch was a gift freely given by Mrs. Curtis and equally freely returned by me, and furthermore that Laura Hartman played no part in the affair.'

Stewart Curtis flushed angrily. 'If you think I'm going to sit here and listen to you insult my wife and myself,' he growled, 'you're mad. I shall see what your superiors have to say about this. You wouldn't dare to refuse to take the flight out.'

'I don't have to refuse outright,' Desmond replied coolly. 'It's too simple. We haven't finished the pre-flight checks yet. I only have to say I'm dissatisfied with the functioning of one of the instruments for a complete test to be ordered. By the time that's been completed, or by the time you've made your complaint, it would be too late in the day when we reached Ireland, for there to be light enough to refuel by. They'll have no alternative but to postpone the flight by twenty-four hours.'

'I'll see you fired for this,' Curtis began, rising to his feet, when the door behind them opened and Charlotte entered. 'I just want to get my camera,' she said, then seeing Desmond, she stopped abruptly, alarm registering in her expression. Her reaction was not lost on Curtis. 'Welcome, my dear,' he went on tight-lipped, 'Perhaps you can clear up this argument? Captain O'Neill here,' he nodded contemptuously in Desmond's direction, 'has the effrontery to contend that you actually gave him the watch as a present when we were in Cairo.' Charlotte shot Desmond a single searching glance. Meeting his steadfast, hostile gaze she dropped her eyes and looked away. 'Yes, it's true,' she answered shortly.

'It's what?' her husband shouted in astonished anger. 'You mean you lied to me last night?'

'That's right' Charlotte leant over the back of a chair to get her camera, affording Desmond a display of her silk stockinged legs as she did so. 'Yes, I lied.' She straightened up, her voice hard and bitter. 'People lie all the time. I did it last night. I know,' she continued to Desmond as he started to speak, 'it was inexcusable and wrong and I'm sorry.'

'Laura's the one who deserves an apology not me,' he told

398

her curtly. Charlotte's eyes flashed. 'Damn Laura! and damn you!' she snapped and made for the door again.

'Charlotte, where are you going. I demand an explanation for this,' Stewart Curtis cried.

'Oh go to hell both of you!' she yelled and ran out slamming the door behind her.

The two men stared at one another in silence. Without a word the financier crossed to a table against the bulkhead. Pulling a sheet of paper from his briefcase he began writing.

To Ian Smallpage's annoyance the feeling of disquiet aroused by the passenger from Switzerland, persisted at the back of his mind. As he handed in his record sheet, he mentioned the matter to his supervisor. 'There was nothing definite, more of a hunch I suppose than anything else. He just didn't seem quite right for what he claimed to be.' The supervisor had enough respect for Ian's judgement to listen to him.

'A refugee of some kind?' he hazarded.

'No sir,' Ian was definite. 'It was too good a job for that and the man was too sure of himself to be a refugee. If it was a fake then it was a professional one.' The supervisor thought for a moment. 'It's not worth taking action over,' he said at length, 'as you say the man was only passing through and he'll have to face a much tougher screening anyway when he arrives in New York. Make a note of the incident on your report and we'll pass it on to Police Special Branch later.'

Relieved to have the responsibility removed from his shoulders, Ian hurried away to do as he was told. He left the terminal building just in time to see *Caterina* lift off from Southampton water in the direction of Ireland and the rendezvous with the refuelling tanker.

Unluckily for Paul Rintlen the body of the agent he had shot on the train had fallen just at the mouth of the tunnel and consequently was spotted from the cab of another train passing through shortly after three o'clock. It was thus nearly four o'clock before the body was finally located by a maintenance unit sent to investigate. A search was then made of the tunnel's entire length and the corpse of the second agent discovered. A murder inquiry was straightaway instituted and Chief Inspector Bill Moyers of the Hampshire Constabulary placed in control.

By the time Moyers reached the scene, the bodies had been removed from the tunnel and were lying beside the track on the grass bank of the cutting. 'We had to shift them as soon as possible I'm afraid sir,' he was told apologetically by the Detective Sergeant who had been in charge of the situation until then. 'It's a busy line and we couldn't keep it blocked. I had a complete search made through on both sides of the track and we brought out everything we found.'

'I may as well have a look at them first,' Moyers answered. He was a large, slow-speaking Westcountryman looking more like a farmer than a policeman, with his broad weatherbeaten face and ill fitting suit, who possessed nevertheless a formidable reputation. 'Then you can send them off to the mortuary for a post mortem.'

Climbing over the wire fence at the top of the cutting, they scrambled heavily down the steep bank to where the bodies lay, covered by sheets. Other police were still engaged in scouring the track beyond the tunnel mouth and a little distance away three railway signalmen equipped with red flags and a portable field telephone stood ready to give warning of approaching trains.

'This was the one found first sir,' the Sergeant lifted back the canvas sheet and exposed the corpse beneath. 'As you can see he's been shot once in the chest, otherwise he's not in too bad condition, a bit battered but that's all. The other one's a right mess, he must have fallen under the wheels, he was properly chewed up.'

'Any sign of the weapon?' Moyers asked.

'No sir,' the detective told him. 'But see this,' stooping down he turned back the left side of the dead man's jacket, 'he's wearing a shoulder holster. We've searched the whole tunnel and both sides of the track for five hundred yards beyond but so far we've found no trace of a pistol to fit it. The Railway Police are checking the coaches of every train passing through in the previous six hours, so it may turn up in one of them.'

'What about identification?' Moyers said, pulling the sheet back over the body.

'Both German nationals, living and working in this country as far as we can tell. Names of Keller and Scherf.'

'You had better contact the German Consulate in London and ask them for any information they have on these two.' Leaving the bodies to be taken away in a police van, Moyers stepped down on to the track. 'Is it all right to go into the tunnel?' he called to the signalman.

'Aye, there's nothing due for another ten minutes.' One of them shouted back. 'We'll hold everything till you come out again,' and lifting the telephone receiver beside him he began cranking the handle vigorously.

As the Sergeant said, there was little enough to be seen in the tunnel. The search his men had conducted had been exhaustive. Only a few dark splashes of blood on the sleepers and gravel two thirds of the way along marked the spot where the second man had been found. After examining them by the light of torches, Moyers returned to the entrance once more and began trying to piece together the sequence of events.

'The bodies were both found on the left hand side of the track leading away from the tunnel,' he said, 'which means therefore they either fell or were pushed from a train proceeding in the direction of Southampton. They were first spotted at around ten past three. Have we established yet whether anyone else thinks they might have seen them before then?'

'No sir,' the Detective shook his head. 'So far we've only been able to trace the drivers of the preceding train. The one p.m. express from London. They are fairly sure the body wasn't by the tunnel mouth when they came through. They think they would have noticed it. I must say I'm inclined to believe them,' he added grimly, 'I think I'd have noticed it myself.'

'In which case,' Moyers continued slowly, 'it would not be an unreasonable assumption for the moment to suggest both men might have been on that train.' He paused for a moment then went on. 'Two German nationals on the Southampton bound express? What does that suggest to you Sergeant?'

'They were on their way to catch a boat, I should think Sir,' the policeman answered brightly.

'Yes, or an aeroplane,' Moyers agreed, 'So perhaps whoever was responsible for their deaths were doing the same. We'll start by obtaining lists of all passengers passing through Southampton today.'

Climbing back up to the top of the cutting he had another thought. 'What kind of man goes around carrying a pistol in a shoulder holster?' he remarked. 'We'll get on to Special Branch as soon as we get back Sergeant. Maybe they'll have some ideas about this business.'

'Tanker coming up astern now Skipper,' Ralph Kendricks called out from the radio desk. 'The Captain is starting to make his approach.'

'Very good,' Desmond acknowledged. 'Tell him I will maintain my present height, course and speed.' 3000 feet above the lush Irish countryside and the wide mouth of the Shannon River, *Caterina* and her crew were about to engage in one of the most complicated of all aerial manoeuvres. In a few moments a tanker aircraft, a converted R.A.F. twin-engined Harrow bomber would endeavour to pass a hose across to the flying-boat and transfer some eight hundred to one thousand gallons of aviation fuel into her tanks. It was an operation calling for strong nerves on the part of all concerned, as well as supreme flying ability and fine judgement.

Desmond and Ralph were alone in the cockpit. Ken Frazer had left his seat and was now in the rear hold on the lower deck, in the extreme tail of the aircraft behind the piles of baggage and the stacked crates of bullion in their wired cage, crouched beside an open hatch in the floor, through which the refuelling hose would be passed. Sandy Everett meanwhile had unclipped the door of the mailroom freight hatch and was maintaining a running commentary as the heavily laden tanker closed in towards them.

'Looks like she's just about right,' he shouted, straining to make himself heard above the noise of the engines. He was shivering in the freezing draught of the slipstream, clinging to the side of the door to prevent himself being sucked out. 'She's about fifty feet above us, and a length behind on the starboard quarter and coming up slowly.' Turning his head a fraction Desmond could just catch a glimpse out of the side windows of the bomber's black nose creeping into view. Behind him there was a crackle from the radio 'Tanker's ready to start the pick up Skipper,' Ralph told him.

'Right, stand by everybody,' Desmond ordered, gripping the control yoke firmly. Though a few patches of cloud had appeared in the sky as the afternoon had worn on, the air was still calm and free from any trace of turbulence. Pressing the intercom button he called through to Frazer in the tail. 'You can begin letting out the line now Ken.'

'Aye, aye Skipper,' Frazer's voice came back, distorted by the earphones. There was a short pause, then the radio crackled again. 'The tanker's spotted our line, it's trailing out nicely,' Kendricks told him. 'They're preparing to lower their grapnel.' Seconds later there came a confirming shout from Sandy.

Down on the lower deck, while the passengers were watching the performance excitedly through the starboard windows, Ken Frazer peered out through the small opening in the tail at the two thousand feel of weighted line which he had paid out from the power winch behind him, and which was now streaming back near horizontal in the flying-boat's wake. As he watched a second line appeared in his field of vision, dropping down from above like a black thread. Suspended on its end was a small grapnel, the steel barbs glinting in the sun as it twisted and jerked.

Frazer observed its progress carefully, reporting back over the intercom to the flight deck. For the crew of the tanker this was the trickiest part of the operation. Manoeuvring so close in to the huge flying-boat, in danger of being buffeted by its slipstream, while attempting with their grapnel to hook and fish up the line being trailed from *Caterina*'s stern. It was extraordinarily difficult to judge the distance separating the two cables, and to anticipate their behaviour in the aircraft's wake.

'They've got her Skipper!' From his vantage point Frazer had seen the tanker's grapnel snag against his own line. Slowly and painstakingly the men in the bomber reeled it in. In *Caterina*'s hold, Frazer released the brake on his winch, ready to pay out more cable if necessary. Then the intercom came alive again with Desmond's voice. 'The tanker has attached the hose to the cable Ken, you can start winching her back in.' Throwing the switch on the machine behind him Frazer set the drum in motion again, watching carefully to be sure the line was running smoothly. Over the intercom Desmond relayed observations from Sandy in the mailroom, and messages passed on by Ralph Kendricks from the tanker's commander.

The winch wound away steadily, hauling in on the cable; a thicker line appeared in the air attached to its end, curving down in a wide arc from the second aircraft, the tanker's hose. Fifty feet above him, Frazer knew, the other crew were paying out on their winch. The hose swam nearer; a heavy metal nozzle at its end became visible. Then all at once it was bumping and grating at the entrance to the hatch. Reaching down, Frazer gave it a tug to help it through and into the mouth of the auxiliary fuel inlet, hearing the union click home solidly as he did so. 'Fuel hose engaged,' he called over the intercom. There was a brief acknowledgement from Desmond, a short pause, then the hose began to pulsate, there was a sound of fuel gushing through into the tank, and a stench of petrol filled the hold.

For Desmond this was a tense period in the manoeuvre. From the gauges in front of him he knew he had to take on board very nearly nine hundred gallons and the tanker's pumps were capable of transferring at a rate of one hundred and twenty gallons a minute. For the next seven or eight minutes therefore he must maintain *Caterina* in exactly her present position in relation to the other aircraft. Any sudden deviation, any widening of the gap separating them and the hose would be ripped away.

The problem was made more difficult still by the extra weight now being pumped aboard, nearly two and a quarter tons in all, altering the trim of the flying-boat, and equally upsetting to that of the tanker's above. Five minutes into the transfer they hit a small patch of turbulence; but Desmond was alert for the faintest sign of trouble and he eased *Caterina* through, catching her smartly before her nose could drop.

'Cease pumping,' he ordered as the gauge needles reached their limits. 'You can release the hose now Frazer,' he told his first officer as soon as the tanker had acknowledged his signal. 'Secure the hatch and return to the flight deck.'

'You should have told him to jump out after it,' Kendricks muttered from the radio desk. 'No-one would miss the bastard.' From the rear there came a thump and a bang as Sandy slammed the mailroom door shut again. 'O.K. everyone,' Desmond called, 'Stand down and resume normal flying routine. Give me a course for Newfoundland will you Ralph?' he asked the Radio Operator, and bringing *Caterina* round towards the red disc of the slowly sinking sun, he headed out over the ocean.

XI

By Radio: IMPERIAL AIRWAYS SOUTHAMPTON
ENGLAND TO G-ADHO CATERINA. FLIGHT IM-
PERIAL 109 TO BOTWOOD NEWFOUNDLAND,
MONTREAL AND NEW YORK. 1900 hrs G.MT.
WEDNESDAY MARCH 15th. CANADIAN
WEATHER BUREAU REPORTS MAJOR DE-
PRESSION MOVING EASTWARDS INTO CEN-
TRAL NORTH ATLANTIC FROM LABRADOR.
SEVERE STORM CONDITIONS NOW PRE-
VAILING OVER DAVIS STRAIT AND SOUTH-
ERN GREENLAND. WINDS FORCE NINE RISING
TEN. SEVERE ICING AND SNOW. CLOUD BASE
3000 FEET. RECOMMEND ALTERATION TO
PROPOSED COURSE TO ALLOW DEVIATION
SOUTHWARD. ADVISE INTENTIONS. ENDS.

DESMOND studied the contents of the radio message which
Kendrick had passed him with a sense of mounting anger. The
weather picture ahead of them had changed radically during
the hours since the last forecast from Canada had been received. The depression which had been first noticed two days
ago over the Beaufort Sea, had moved across Franklin District,
north of Hudson's Bay and over Baffin Island, to link up with a
second pressure trough near the coast of Greenland, deepening
as it went until it had developed into a storm front of major
proportions.

Of this Desmond had been aware when they took off from
Southampton, but at that time in had seemed that the track of
the storm centre would take it well to the north of the flight's
proposed route, leaving them with little to fear beyond some
slight turbulence, and poor visibility should they be brushed by
the system's fringe. Now it appeared that the entire front had

altered its direction and was veering southwards on a course which would bring it perilously close to *Caterina*'s.

With luck they should be able to dog-leg round the threatened area, making a wide detour out towards the south into mid-Atlantic. Unless the speed of the storm increased markedly during the intervening period that should see them through. Even so there was a strong suspicion in Desmond's mind that back at Southampton Jack Priestly had deliberately held over this late report until the flying-boat was well out to sea. Had he relayed it when they were still within sight of the Irish Coast, it was conceivable Desmond might have decided to abort the flight altogether.

It was probably also true, he guessed, that Priestly himself was under strong pressure from the Government in London to whom the urgency of the gold delivery appeared to be all important. For a moment he was tempted to send a sharply worded riposte to those responsible, pointing out that by their actions they were endangering the entire plane, the cargo as well as the people on board.

It would be an empty gesture though, he knew, nothing more. They could only crack on with all possible speed and hope to avoid the worst of the weather ahead. Resignedly he ordered Ralph Kendricks to prepared the necessary alterations to the flight plan. It was beginning to look as though the Radio Operator would have to face a worse ordeal than even he had expected.

In *Caterina*'s galley Andy Draper prepared for the evening ahead with care. Although of the flying-boat's crew only Desmond had actually made the crossing before, he knew from previous experience of long distance flights as well as from his days as a Cunard steward, the importance of forecasting the passengers' morale correctly. At the moment they were in a relaxed and cheerful frame of mind. There was still an element of adventure and romance about the trans-Atlantic flight. This was after all only the sixth such regular crossing, not counting those made by the ill fated 'Hindenberg' whose catastrophic loss at Lakehurst, New Jersey two years ago had put a stop to airship development.

For the past hour and a half, as *Caterina* headed out across the hazy purple surface of the great ocean towards the unchanging sunset, he had been kept busy with his cocktail shaker, serving round after round of drinks, as his charges celebrated the start of their journey. The clear weather conditions prevailing at this stage had enabled Desmond to desert the upper deck and play host at the cocktail party in the promenade lounge, organized by Sandy on company instructions. Even the Curtises had consented to put in an appearance and after some initial strain the atmosphere had become unexpectedly good-natured.

Despite this, Andy could see, there would come a point when the enjoyment would begin to wear thin. There were still another twelve or thirteen hours to go before they reached the Newfoundland coast, and thanks to the flying-boat's constant westward progress, the evening would seem a long one. It was his job therefore to anticipate correctly the moment when boredom would start to set in, and be ready with a thoroughly excellent dinner. The meal, he was determined, would be memorable. The time by the wall clock was only seven p.m. Already he had some of the cold dishes prepared and the chicken cooking. It would be another hour before the passengers were ready to eat; with luck though, he could then prolong the meal through till ten, by which time they would be ready to start thinking of their beds.

The galley door clicked open and Sandy's head appeared in the entrance.

'Pass me out another bottle of champagne will you Andy?' he said. 'Mrs. Curtis and the Baroness are fairly mopping the stuff up. I reckon you'd better get round with your shaker again soon too, some of the others look as though they'll want another cocktail in a couple of minutes.'

'I'll be out in a moment,' Andy told him, opening the refrigerator and removing a bottle from the stock of wine he had placed there to chill. 'Just as soon as I finish setting out this salmon. I don't mind 'em drinking a lot before dinner, it'll mean they'll sleep better afterwards. Less trouble for you an' me if there's bad weather.'

'Do you think we'll have some?' Sandy asked with concern as he uncorked the champagne. The Steward pursed his lips, 'You saw the forecast, storms are normal on these trips. Don't worry about that lot though,' he nodded in the direction of the promenade lounge, 'they'll be all right once they're tucked up in bed.'

The cork came away with a loud pop and Sandy caught the spurting wine neatly in a glass. 'The Skipper was telling me you want to turn the Curtises out of the after cabin for the night,' he said. 'Isn't that going to make them furious?'

'Their hard luck,' Andy replied with indifference, 'we can make up all the beds in the first three cabins and leave the after cabin for those who don't want to sleep. It's better for everyone that way.'

'I suppose you're right,' Sandy agreed, 'it's the furthest from the wash rooms too. We can put the Curtises and the D'Estes in the smoking saloon together. They'll be out of the way of the others then ... How do you think we should divide up the rest?'

'The Kings and the Professor and his daughter in the midships cabin,' Andy began.

'Won't Laura want to be in with the Kings though?' the Purser objected. It was a measure of the American girl's popularity with the crew that among themselves they referred to her by her Christian name. 'No, I've already spoken to her,' Andy replied. 'She says the Wienzmans will be happier in the smaller room with the Kings. They've got to know each other now.'

'And the remaining five in the promenade lounge,' Sandy nodded thoughtfully, 'I agree it's a good plan if the Curtises will wear it. Someone's bound not to want to turn in with everybody else.' Closing the door again he returned to the party with his champagne. Behind him the Steward chuckled to himself. The plan was a good one and all the more so for inconveniencing Stewart Curtis; up in the bedding loft there was one particularly uncomfortable mattress normally kept only as a spare which Andy had earmarked specially for him. The financier was due for a disturbed night.

Given the tensions existing between the various groups and

personalities on board, it was surprising that the party before dinner was such a success. Desmond certainly had had his doubts as to the wisdom of holding the affair, but company policy had ordained that the passengers be entertained in this fashion weather permitting; and he had faced up to it as best he could. It proved to be far less of a strain than he had expected.

The two Wienzmans for instance were bubbling with good humour and gratitude. 'We owe everything to you Captain O'Neill,' the Professor assured him repeatedly. 'Our lives, our freedom, all the kindness we have been shown since leaving Rome.' Desmond made a deprecating answer. 'Mrs. Hartman and the rest of the passengers and crew helped every bit as much as I did,' he said with some embarrassment. 'But I understand there has been trouble for you on our account?' the Professor continued, a worried expression on his face, and Desmond hastened to reassure him. 'I think the airline was a little surprised, but nothing more really. To be honest I believe the Board was quite pleased with the publicity.' The Professor looked relieved. 'That is good, I am glad. We are both glad, my daughter and I.'

At the mention of her name the girl smiled. She still seemed wary and uncertain, Desmond thought, but the fear had begun to fade from her eyes slowly. She had put on a smart new dress for the flight and he complimented her on it. 'Yes, we bought it this morning to celebrate our escape. It makes her look pretty don't you think?' her father said proudly while his daughter blushed. She certainly did look very pretty indeed, Desmond thought; Sandy Everett was standing nearby unable to keep his eyes off her. 'And for myself I bought a complete new set of instruments for my profession,' Wienzman continued happily, 'everything a doctor needs to have with him. My own I was forced to leave behind in Austria,' he explained, 'the Nazis would not have allowed me to bring them out with me. This morning too I obtained this.' From an inside pocket he produced a heavily embossed and sealed document, held together by a tassled cord. 'Our American visas for Siegret and myself. The officials at the Consulate were also very kind. I had worried we might have to wait many days for it.'

'Do you hope to be able to return to Austria some day?' It was Harold King who spoke, 'I mean do you believe the persecution of your people will cease?' The Professor shook his head sadly, 'I hope so, I hope so. Vienna is my home and I would like to return one day. I cannot believe this evil will last. There are still many good people in Austria. Men like Herr Meyer who helped us to get away; and in Italy too, my old friend Farenzi, I pray no harm will come to them. At least now though Siegret and I will be able to live in peace again.'

Paul Rintlen had been following the exchange closely, though pretending all the while to listen to a conversation between Mrs. King, Laura and Luca d'Este in which the latter was explaining how he would have won the race to Fayoum had he not been forced off the road. So far Rintlen had been deliberately avoiding the two Austrians. Though neither they nor anyone else on board had seen him before, and he had no reason to believe his cover story would be suspected, he intended taking no unnecessary risks. The Wienzmans were still plainly on their guard, the girl very much so, and with his German accent and obviously continental origins he was afraid of causing them to take fright unwittingly.

Even so he could not help but be drawn to the mention of Meyer's name. So he had been right all along in holding the police chief responsible for the escape. If he did finally succeed in bringing the mission to a successful conclusion there was going to be a score to settle there. He strained to catch more of the old Professor's words, and in doing so he heard him describing how the research notes and case histories had been smuggled past the border guards disguised as Siegret's schoolbooks. Instantly there flashed back into his mind the words of Heydrich when the arrest of the Wienzmans had first been ordered: 'Bring away unread all personal documents you find.'

In the chase to catch the fleeing couple, those words had seemed unimportant, now they suddenly assumed special significance. Suppose the Professor was in possession of some vital secret? It would have to be political of course, Heydrich had hinted as much. Secret information on a person of high standing in the Reich. That was exactly the kind of scandal the SD chief was always most eager for. If as well as eliminating the two Jews he could recover those notes, then indeed he would have no fears about returning to Berlin.

While Rintlen was speculating in this fashion Desmond had been observing the behaviour of the Curtises. He had not originally expected either of these two to put in an appearance, and now he was struck with the cordiality which they were displaying towards their fellow travellers. Charlotte certainly had been avoiding meeting his eyes, and there was a forced quality to the gaiety with which she was chatting to Jacquetta d'Este and the quiet young Turk from Alexandria. She was also getting through the champagne he noticed, Sandy Everett was refilling her glass for the fourth time.

Her husband was meanwhile engaged in a discussion with Van Smit, close beside him. Glancing at the two of them his attention was claimed by the South African. 'Captain,' he wanted to know, 'do the Boeing of Pan American Airways use this technique of mid-air refuelling also, for their Atlantic flights?'

Desmond smiled politely as he answered. 'No they don't,' he said, 'the Boeings are bigger and more modern aircraft with the range to make the journey unassisted. Very fine planes they are too,' he added.

Like his wife, Curtis seemed to be making an effort to be pleasant and was behaving as though the angry scene between Desmond and himself in the after cabin before take-off had not occurred. Perhaps the financier's anxieties were diminishing now they were actually on their way across to America, or perhaps the exposure of his wife's lies had brought about the change. Whichever it was, Desmond wondered if it would stand up to the pressure of being made to give up his private cabin when night fell. For the sake of preserving peace for a while longer it might be diplomatic to wait before springing the news on him.

Andy Draper appeared on the edge of the throng with a fresh tray of cocktails. The guests seemed to be enjoying themselves and it looked as though he might safely return to the upper deck. Flicking back his cuff he checked the time on his wrist watch, seven fifteen, *Caterina* was two hours and three hundred miles out into the Atlantic, with another twelve hours and seventeen hundred miles to go before the lights of the landing area at Botwood became visible.

'There's a report due in from the ocean weather ship about now,' he said to Laura.

'Are you expecting to run into bad weather Captain?' Van Smit inquired in his direct way as he turned to go. 'Not at all,' Desmond answered him, there was no point in causing unnecessary alarm among the passengers and as yet it was by no means certain the storm ahead of them would cross their path, 'but it's important for navigational purposes for us to have as much information as possible on the strength and direction of the winds we're encountering because they can greatly affect our speed. It's possible for strong head winds to delay us seriously, and on an east-west flight they are not uncommon.' Stewart Curtis, who had been staring out of the window, ostentatiously ignoring the conversation broke in again, 'Delayed!' he snapped, 'by how much delayed?'

'I only said delays were possible,' Desmond replied, 'and any time lost on the actual crossing can nearly always be made up on the following day. We should still arrive in New York tomorrow afternoon whatever happens.'

Leaving the financier mollified by this, he excused himself. It was time to check *Caterina*'s progress and see how Ralph Kendricks was standing up to the demands being placed on him.

As it happened Ralph had so far been kept too busy since leaving Ireland to give overmuch thought to the fears which had been troubling him earlier in the week. Although both Desmond and Frazer held Master's Certificates in Navigation, it was on Ralph that the bulk of the work on the trip lay. Spread out in front of him on the table was a chart for the North Atlantic, the immense void of the ocean fringed along either side by the shore of the two continents which it separated. Projecting from the right hand edge a red line struck out to follow the start of the great circle route between Ireland and Newfoundland. All around lay scattered other instruments and paraphernalia employed in plotting the flying-boat's course. A Byrd bubble sextant, drift bearing plates, a stopwatch, parallel rulers, dividers, books of astronomical tables, and scraps of paper covered with intricate calculations.

As they were at the moment, some three hundred and ten miles from the coast of Ireland, Ralph was still relying primarily on the Marconi radio direction finder to enable him to establish their position, and only using the technique of Dead Reckoning and Astronomical Observation as a safety check, and as a means of discovering such details as rate of wind drift. Further on, however, when either the range became too great for radio fixes to be made accurately, or if weather conditions should interfere, then he must be ready to fall back on the older methods.

Taking a straightedge and a crayon in his hands he bent over the chart and with infinite precision extended the red line of *Caterina*'s track fractionally, to meet the tiny pencilled cross representing her latest position. Navigation was demanding work, requiring considerable skill in the handling of instruments and the use of the equipment, as well as mathematical ability and meticulous neatness. All the same Ralph found it immensely satisfying. To guide an aeroplane across two thousand miles of featureless ocean, much of the time in darkness or poor visibility and in the face of constantly varying winds, would be no mean achievement and one he could be proud of. Moreover by occupying his mind in this way he hoped to crowd out the gnawing images from his dreams.

Reaching over the table he drew towards him *Caterina*'s pre-flight plan showing her proposed course worked out at Southampton using information available to them before take-off and a sheet of transparent film on to which he had traced a summary of the details passed on by the *Jacques Cartier* out in the ocean ahead and the Canadian Weather Bureau. Comparing the three it was possible to see that the storm centre from Labador was moving south-east more swiftly than they had originally anticipated, and at its current progress would intercept the flying-boat's projected course in approximately six hundred miles. The detour they had originally proposed would clearly have to be extended southwards to enable the aircraft to skirt round the now widened danger zone. Bending over the chart again Ralph began to calculate the course alteration required. 'Hell!' Frazer exclaimed in disgust when he was shown the proposed change. 'That'll add another two hours to our time at least, we're bending far enough out of our way as it is.'

'I know,' Ralph agreed, 'and I've cut us in as far as I dare, but the whole front is moving across our path. I reckon we'll have a tough passage even so.'

'I don't see what you're getting in such a panic about,' Ken remarked maliciously. 'It's only a thunder storm and we've flown through plenty of those before.'

'They weren't over the North Atlantic though; and they didn't consist of sixty knot winds driving snow from the Arctic,' Ralph replied. 'There's cloud up to 20,000 feet, severe icing and storm force winds covering a two hundred thousand square mile area between the Hudson Strait and the coast of Greenland, and the whole lot moving out into mid ocean right into our path. If we make the course alteration I suggest, we can still skate round the worst of it.'

'You mean you want us to steer an additional three hundred and fifty miles off our course because you're afraid to fly through a storm?' The jeer in the First Officer's voice was unmistakable, but Ralph ignored the insult. 'It's the Skipper's decision anyway,' he said tersely, 'And you know bloody well what he'll order so what's the point in arguing?'

'Lucky for you, no other Captain would carry a radio officer who had lost his nerve,' Ken sneered, 'must make it a lot easier for you.'

This time the barb sunk home, Ralph's jaw tightened angrily. 'You treacherous little bastard,' he grated. 'Wait till I get you on the ground. Then we'll see who's scared.' Frazer sniffed contemptuously. 'Better see if you've got the guts to make it first hadn't you?' he responded. 'Only two hours out from Ireland and you're cracking up already.'

Shaking with rage Ralph sat down again at his table. He tried to resume his work on the charts, but the lines and figures

415

swam across the page and his mind refused to hold the calculations. Staring at the storm track he had sketched in on the map, and at the weather reports which he had completed he knew Frazer was right. He was afraid, deeply and terribly afraid. Afraid of the empty waste of the endless ocean beneath them, and of the cold, hungry waves waiting for him.

Desmond noticed the change in the Radio Officer's manner immediately he returned, and though he made no comment, he could not help but be worried. However, he backed up Ralph's judgement on the need for a change of course, and after a brief glance at the charts, ordered Frazer to make the alternations necessary to deepen the flying-boat's sweep round to the south.

Even this would not enable them to escape all the effects of the storm, he knew, and slipping into his seat again he ran his eyes over the instrument panel, taking stock of the situation. *Caterina* was flying at a height of three thousand feet, and the air speed indicator was reading one hundred and sixty miles per hour, though Ralph's navigation indicated that head winds were reducing this to one hundred and forty. Outside the sky was starting to cloud over with patches of drifting cumulus, merging into a solid line on the horizon. The air temperature was forty-two degrees, no danger of icing yet.

Switching off the autopilot, he flew manually for a while, testing the flying-boat's response to the controls. The heavy load of fuel was unevenly distributed at present, making her handle a trifle sluggishly, but by the time the storm reached them much of the excess would have been consumed. With luck too, the passengers would be comfortably in bed by then.

Ahead of them the sun was sliding slowly into the sea, casting a yellow glare on the white-capped waves of the heavy swell and on the great rack of clouds building up the west, staining them with a lurid, unhealthy glow.

Laura Hartman had observed the steady fall in Klerksdorp's share prices over the past fortnight, but she had ascribed its cause to no more than market nervousness in the wake of the unstable political climate. Certainly she would have been surprised, to have learnt that the company's difficulties were as serious as they were, and even more so, had she known the telegram to the firm of Wall Street brokers, she had sent, was the subject of intense debate among the partners.

These were the senior members of the firm of Kimber Crossfield Smith and Company, to which Gervaise Raikes had referred only that morning. The general attitude of those present was much the same as that of their English counterparts six hours previously. Like the Raikes, they had during the past weeks seen large blocks of stock being offered for sale at below the ruling prices, with no clues as to who the sellers might be or the reason behind the disposals.

The financier had, it was true, telegrammed himself that morning to the head of the firm, but the message had contained little beyond a string of meaningless and unsubstantiated assertions about the vast, though admittedly so far unproven reserves of ore within the mine and the intrinsic asset backing to the shares which these implied.

At the moment the firm's senior Vice-President held the floor and was summing up his argument. 'Mrs. Hartman is Curtis' personal secretary so she probably knows as much as anyone of what's happening,' he ticked the points off on his fingers as he spoke, 'we also know she's been with him in South Africa and is travelling back with him at this moment; in fact, she's the only person who has been continuously in touch with him for the whole of the last fortnight. She is due back here in New York tomorrow afternoon, yet all of a sudden she seems to think it necessary to cable across the Atlantic, only a day before she arrives. Finally her instructions are quite specific, she asks for no advice, she makes no suggestions. "Sell all stock held by me in Klerksdorp, immediately, at best possible price." '

'Maybe she's only panicking because of the slide she's seen in the price?' someone else suggested.

'The price has slipped back before, and she hasn't run to the nearest 'phone,' the Vice-President countered. 'I say the stock is in danger of collapsing and Mrs. Hartman knows it. She's getting out and so should we. What do you say Harvey?'

All eyes in the room swung to the lean, patrician features of the old man who sat very erect behind the desk. For more than a quarter of a century Harvey Tilset Kimber had run the firm with an iron discipline, and a totally rigid adherence to the principles of the proud and conservative New England background from which he sprang. Now at the age of seventy, his grasp of affairs was as firm as ever, and the gaze from beneath the thick white eyebrows still keen and penetrating. 'If anyone has panicked, it is Curtis,' he remarked in dry, cold tones. 'Racing about the world in this fashion and trying to hoodwink us with fairy-stories. Something is badly wrong and he's running scared. Never liked the man,' he said with contempt, 'never trusted him either, no more does Raikes in London. If he's going down, none of our clients are going to be caught in the crash. I want the firm's books cleared of Klerksdorp stock by four o'clock this afternoon.' There was a short pause, then the old man permitted himself an instant's cold humour, 'and that includes Mrs. Hartman, gentleman. We'll put her first in the queue, she deserves a decent price for her pains.'

As the men in the room filed out to put his orders into effect he was struck by another thought. Motioning the Vice-President who had spoken earlier, to stay for a moment, he told him 'I want you to get a cable off to the people in South Africa. Let them know what we intend doing. Maybe then they'll start letting us in on what's wrong with Curtis and Klerksdorp.'

At Southampton Police Headquarters, Bill Moyers was making progress with his investigation. An examination of the one o'clock express from London had revealed blood splashes on the wheel-bogies of the rear carriage and also a bullet, embedded in the panelling inside the corridor, eighteen inches up from the floor and close to one of the doors. 'Nine millimetre,' the ballistics expert told him, 'if you say the gun belongs to a German then it's most probably a Walther, or a Luger. The former is more likely, the P38 replaced the Luger as standard military issue last year.'

In addition, although the German Consulate had been unhelpful, and seemingly embarrassed when contacted about the incident, a call to the Metropolitan Police Special Branch concerned with political offences, had yielded the information that the man Keller, who had been found at the tunnel mouth with the bullet wound in his chest, was a known agent. 'More of a secret police thug really,' the officer on duty told Moyers. 'We think they used him as a frightener to keep their countrymen over here in line. He was supposed to be under surveillance, he must have slipped away somehow and joined the train. We've no idea why at the moment but we're doing what we can to find out.'

'They're sending men down to liaise.' The Chief Inspector informed Dewhurst, the Detective Sergeant working with him on the case, as the latter entered the room with a sheaf of papers in his hand. 'Did you get those passenger lists I asked for?'

'Here they are sir,' Dewhurst handed the papers across the desk. 'Being able to establish definitely which train the victims were on has been a big help. It let us rule out the *Queen Mary* for a start and she was carrying more than a thousand passengers. As it is there's a big Italian liner left for Geneva at four p.m., we've got a complete list on her, the P & O's *Oriana* departed around the same time, and half an hour before that there was a Swedish ship headed for Copenhagen and Stockholm. The names for all those are there in front of you.'

'*Oriana* was on the Australia run I suppose,' Moyers replied, sifting through the lists. 'Is this the lot?'

'I'm afraid not sir,' the Sergeant told him. 'Several cargo vessels and coasters left during the period in question and I'm still trying to get details of those, and of course there were the ferries, they don't keep lists for those. Also there were two aeroplanes: *Imperial 109*, a trans-Atlantic flight to Canada and New York, and a Pan American on its way to Lisbon.'

Moyers examined one of the lists thoughtfully. 'Which of all these people would have been most likely to travel down on the one o'clock do we know?' he asked.

'We have some idea sir,' the Detective Sergeant answered, 'but not a list. Any of the passengers on the channel ferries might have been aboard, it's a very good connection. Some of those for the *Oriana* and the Italian ship might have done so too, but the majority would probably have taken an earlier train. One thing we do know for certain, though, Imperial

Airways reserved a coach for the passengers boarding their flight over the Atlantic; but they're only thirteen out of nearly six hundred.'

'Well we had better start getting down to it,' Moyers said heavily. 'I'm issuing an appeal for anyone locally who was on the train and heard or saw anything suspicious to contact us. In the meantime we'll start checking through these lists for German citizens, and just hope the Special Branch can come up with something in the way of motive. They should be here by nine.'

Settling down at their desks the two men began working steadily down the columns of names.

The same winds which were driving the storm out into the northern Atlantic had cleared the skies over New England, and the warm afternoon sun was melting the snow on the hills around Warren Lake. Susie had not been in the café when Jarrett arrived for lunch to keep their appointment. Instead a sour-faced, slatternly old woman was serving behind the bar, who scowled when he asked after the girl. 'She's gone, sent 'er packing myself. Dirty mouthed little hussy. "I'll teach you to speak proper to me" I says, "you can take your money due an' git out," an' she did. Left this mornin.'

Put out by this unexpected disappointment, Jarrett finished his meal in moody silence and returned to the truck. He was just starting up when the door on the passenger side was jerked open and he saw Susie standing there in a dirty black coat and clutching a much battered suitcase. 'Thought you had run out on me.' He grinned, as he helped her up beside him. 'The woman back there said you had left for good.'

'The old rat,' Susie said vindictively, 'she wanted me to stay in this afternoon an' clean out her filthy kitchen. I told her she could clean her own damn floor so she threw me out.' She sighed resignedly, 'I was goin' to leave soon anyway, figured maybe you'd give me a run over to Bellows Falls when we've been out to the lake?'

'Sure, glad to. You going back to your step-father's place?' Jarrett pushed the truck into gear and began driving up the street. 'Maybe, I'll see.' Susie shrugged, 'He don't like me stayin' around for long. Might find a job near there though,' she said listlessly.

Little by little as they drove up to the lake she told him about herself. Her father had spent a lifetime of backbreaking labour in clearing his small farm in the woods of Vermont. He had married late and Susie had been only ten years old when he had died one winter, prematurely worn out by the harsh struggle for survival. Less than a year later her mother had married again, to a hard man with an evil temper, who allowed the land to fall into decay while he spent the time drinking and hunting with his cronies. She had never liked her stepfather and he, for his part, had resented the little girl and begrudged the money spent on her keep. At the age of fifteen she had left home when he had started forcing his way into her room at night.

Now three years later her mother was dead too, and the farm would soon be sold to pay off her stepfather's debts. There was nothing to go back to any more. Instead she could only look for another menial job like the one she had just lost. She told the tale philosophically enough but behind her words Jarrett could sense the bitterness and frustration she felt. Life had never held out a great deal for her, but what it once had, it had taken away.

Up at the lake, however, her spirits brightened. The Supermarine racer was a brilliant success. Jarrett sat her in the cockpit and explained the controls while she fiddled delightedly with the steering yoke, and worked the rudder bar with her feet. Then, sitting her on the jetty, he put the silver plane through its paces in the air; flying a series of aerobatics over the water for her, ending with a shallow loop out in mid lake and a low level swoop across the head of the jetty which had her flattening herself against the planking.

'Some more, do some more,' she pleaded when he set the seaplane down on the surface again and taxied in. 'I never had my own stunt show before.'

'Later,' he promised, scrambling ashore and making fast. 'If you're good and behave yourself.' The warmth of her approval sent a glow of pleasure through him. The girl giggled. 'Do you really promise, if I'm very good?' she said in a deliberately provocative voice. Reaching out, he pulled her to him, and for an instant he felt her greedy little mouth hard against his own and the firmness of her body beneath his hands. Then giggling again, she slipped free, wriggling from his grasp like an eel, and with a shriek of laughter, fled up the path towards the house.

He caught up with her as she burst through the door into the kitchen and they tussled briefly inside, before he pinned her back against the wall, forcing his lips on hers once more and working his hands hungrily over her body. For a moment or two she continued to struggle, twisting her head from side to side, straining to break away. Then slowly she relaxed and her mouth sought his again.

Dinner on board *Caterina* was not the success Andy had hoped it would be. This was not in any way due to the quality of the meal he had served, or the care he had taken in his preparation. Indeed, it would have been hard to have faulted a single detail from the outset. Against a background of crisp, white linen and fresh daffodils picked during the morning, polished silver and glass gleamed in the soft lighting of the cabins. Night had fallen at last and the curtain had been drawn on the darkness outside, where the moon shone fitfully between banks of scudding clouds, scattering an uneasy tracery of silver on the restless waves below.

Much of the passengers' earlier gaiety had vanished however, and even the excellence of Andy's cooking was not sufficient to restore their good humour. They were for the first time beginning to experience the full import of the voyage they had undertaken.

While the flying-boat had droned on across the seemingly limitless ocean they had stared out from the windows at the never-changing sea three thousand feet beneath them, gripped by a consciousness of their own frailty and insignificance in the face of such emptiness and immensity. England had already been left behind, America lay yet further ahead; two-thirds of the journey was still before them: fourteen hundred miles without a sight of land. All sense of time and movement had vanished, leaving them cocooned in a tiny bubble of warmth and light, suspended above a darkening, lifeless world.

Jacquetta had dined in the after cabin with her husband and the two Curtises, in an atmosphere of unrelieved gloom, despite Luca's attempts to maintain a flow of conversation. The champagne had left Charlotte in a mood of sour depression, which alone had been sufficient to put a blight across the meal, while her husband sat, morose and withdrawn, scarcely bothering to reply when addressed.

Jacquetta herself could only long for the meal to be over. Rashid, she knew, was having dinner next door; ironically in the same cabin as Van Smit, and she was in a fever of anxiety lest the façade of indifference between them should break down. Added to this was the constant fear which seized her each time the young Sheikh entered a room in which her husband was present. Like Rashid, Luca was now armed, having provided himself with a pistol from the Embassy, on receipt of the telegram from Rome, thus turning the situation into a powder-keg that a single out of place word could explode.

There was a soft tap at the door and the steward entered with a tray and began clearing away the remains of the dessert and coffee. 'I suppose you're wanting us to hurry up and make way for the rest of them?' Charlotte observed, with distaste. Andy smiled back politely, he was perfectly aware that the Curtises had been deliberately prolonging their meal so as to delay the moment when they would have to admit the rest of the passengers. 'There's no need for you to worry, just yet Ma'am,' he said condescendingly. 'We've made up the beds ready for you in the smoking saloon and we'll be starting on the mid-ship cabin shortly, but we'll probably leave the promenade lounge for a while yet until more people are wanting to go to bed. Of course,' he added casually as he backed towards the door again with the loaded tray, 'the Purser and I will be having to pass through here a lot to get the passengers' cases out from the rear hold for them to use tonight. You might be more comfortable in your own cabin up for'ard.'

'Blasted insolence,' Stewart Curtis complained as soon as he was gone. 'He's going out of his way to make life as difficult for us as possible.'

'It is all the doing of the Captain,' agreed Luca, for whom Desmond had been an established enemy ever since Cairo, 'he has taken a dislike to the four of us, and permits his crew to treat us rudely.'

'Not without reason where some of us are concerned,' Charlotte remarked dryly, reaching out to press the bell push on the wall of the cabin as she spoke, and Jacquetta hid a smile at the flush which rose to her husband's cheeks at the rebuke. 'Personally,' Charlotte continued, 'I'm feeling quite tired myself already, and so too I should imagine is Jacquetta. When the maid comes I shall tell her to start getting our night cases out and laying out our things. Ah, there you are Arlette,' she said as the French woman appeared silently in the doorway. 'Bien, ecoutez. Madame la Baronesse et moi. . . .'

Charlotte and Jacquetta were not the only ones on board to feel like turning in early. The majority of the passengers were beginning to feel sleepy, following the heavy meal on top of the seven hours they had already spent in the air. The sight of the comfortable twin-tier beds, complete with fresh linen sheets, blankets and down pillows, each cunningly designed to have its own window, reading lamp and individual curtain, which the steward and purser were erecting with practised efficiency, was sufficient to start them making preparations to retire.

Rintlen, in particular, observed the change-over with interest. No sooner had the Curtises and d'Estes been dispatched forward out of the way, than Andy Draper fastened back the door through from the after cabin into the tail of the aircraft and began bringing out the rest of the passengers' baggage needed for the night. Out in mid-Atlantic the safety of the bullion secured behind its locked metal grills at the rear end of the hold was less of a worry, and a number of passengers were allowed through into the echoing, cavernous hold, to assist in identifying their luggage.

It might be, Rintlen reasoned, as he waited his turn to use the washroom, that whatever documents or papers the Professor had escaped with he would be careful to keep in his possession. On the other hand a surreptitious watch on the couple, had revealed that one case at least of theirs, remained untouched in the hold; and he was determined to attempt a search of this once the rest of the aeroplane was asleep. Very probably those notebooks held the key to what he wanted.

Preoccupied with the business of changing and getting themselves ready for bed, and distracted by the novelty of the new arrangements few of those on the lower deck were especially aware of the growing turbulence through which the flying-boat had begun to pass.

Up above however the crew were finding themselves under increasing strain. *Caterina* was flying between banks of dense cloud while Desmond struggled to hold her steady in the face of the eddying winds whose strong cross currents were causing her to pitch and yaw uncomfortably. Ominously, the outside air temperature had dropped to only thirty-four degrees fahrenheit. Ever since leaving Ireland he had had the carburettor heat full on, but all three of them knew that it could be only a matter of time before they were driven to descent to a lower altitude to avoid the danger of icing.

At the portside navigation window, Ralph Kendricks levelled his sextant, and peered through the eyepiece at the reflected image of a star, fleetingly visible through a gap in the clouds. For the past half hour he had been trying unsuccessfully to obtain a fix on Rigel, now in desperation he had switched to Aldebaran in the constellation of Taurus. Adjusting the arm of the instrument he managed to read off the angle, before the pinprick of light in his mirror faded out again.

Resuming his position at the table, he forced himself to concentrate while he plotted the fix against his own dead reckoning. There could be no doubt *Caterina* was already brushing against the storm's leading edge. The front itself, four hundred miles or more in breadth was still an hour away. Behind it, blizzards of hurricane intensity raged over a quarter of a million square miles of ocean. His fingers shook as he drew in the converging paths of aircraft and storm. The margin of safety was being cut frighteningly narrow.

The team of investigators from the Special Branch arrived at ten o'clock headed by a sharply dressed Superintendent some years Moyers' junior, who gave his name as MacLain, and announced that he had now been placed in charge of the case. 'Of course,' he added patronizingly, 'we shall be glad to accept any help you local chaps can give us.' Moyers eyed the man's elegant city suit doubtfully, the appearance of the others with him was in equal contrast with his own loose tweeds, and it was clear he himself had been relegated to a subordinate role; nevertheless he felt policemen should look like policemen and not like stockbrokers.

'So far sir the only fact we've discovered which might have a bearing,' he said to the Superintendent when the latter returned from a protracted inspection of the bodies, and an examination of the dead men's clothes and other possessions, 'is that this flight *Imperial 109* ...' for the visitor's benefit, he extracted the sheet of paper containing the details from amongst the pile on the desk, 'is carrying the two refugees who escaped from Rome. You know, the ones who have been in all the papers. They're called Wienzman. As well as which the plane was also carrying a large sum in gold bullion.' He spoke with a slight edge to his voice. Owing to the poor communication between the various units of the force, this last item of information had only a short while ago been passed on to him.

'I'm sure that will be most helpful,' the Superintendent replied loftily. 'Though I rather doubt if one old man and a girl would have accounted for two trained agents; and whatever else we may be dealing with here, it is certainly not a case of simple theft. Don't worry though, we'll keep you informed of anything we come up with, naturally.'

Concealing their anger at this cavalier treatment, Moyers and the Sergeant returned to their efforts to reconstruct a list of the train's passengers from the information they had on those who had passed through the port. Their revenge came towards eleven o'clock when, as they were about to pack in their work, depressed with their lack of progress, one of the Superintendent's men came into the office. 'It seems you may have been right after all about that Imperial Airways flight,

426

Chief Inspector,' he said with a trace of embarrassment. 'The fact is, the Yard has called through with a report sent in by one of the Immigration people down at the terminal. One of the passengers on board may have had a suspect passport. A man by the name of Perler, Ernst Perler.'

'Then why on earth did they let him on?' Moyers asked. 'It was a bullion flight. Wasn't that reason enough to pull in whoever it was?'

'Apparently no-one had told them about the gold,' the officer replied, 'there was too much secrecy. The point is that it looks now as though there may be a connection between these Austrian refugees on their way to America, the dead agents and whoever this man Perler is who's boarded the plane under an assumed name. We need to get hold of the Immigration fellow who spotted him, in a hurry.'

Ian Smallpage arrived at Southampton Police Headquarters in a state of near shock. A few minutes previously he had been round at Helen's parents' home, happily celebrating the formal announcement of his engagement by allowing himself to become as near drunk as he ever had in his life. Then the bell of a police car had sounded outside in the street, there had been a loud knocking at the door, and the party had been brought to a rude halt by the entry of several policemen who demanded that he return immediately with them to the station.

Pandemonium had followed, with Helen bursting into tears and both sets of parents angrily seeking to know what offence Ian was being accused of. To this the men in the patrol car could only reply that they had been ordered to bring him in urgently at the request of the Special Branch, but knew nothing further. As an answer it left much to be desired and only served to increase the dismay of the assembled relatives and friends.

So it was that the now rapidly sobering Smallpage had been accompanied back to the station by his new and tearful fiancee as well as both sets of parents. Their arrival *en masse* created instant chaos at the reception desk, with everyone trying to talk at once to the bewildered Sergeant on duty; which lasted until Moyers appeared. Explaining that Ian was only required in order to help identify a traveller, he calmed the situation and led the young man away for questioning.

Fortunately Smallpage was gifted with a retentive memory and was able to supply not only an accurate description of the man calling himself Ernst Perler, but also such details as his rumpled clothes and bruised face, and the information that he had originated from Rome.

'Sounds as though he's the chap we want all right,' Superintendent MacLain agreed when he had listened to the story. 'What exactly is behind it all I don't know, but it seems clear this man Perler followed the Wienzmans from Rome, and is himself an agent. Why he should have killed his two colleagues I don't know, but one thing is sure, we had better get a message out to that plane fast.' Moyers' gaze flicked to the clock on the wall of the office. The time was eleven fifteen. The flying-boat had been airborne for eight hours, and would be getting on for a thousand miles out into the Atlantic.

Imperial Airways night staff were contacted immediately by telephone and the position explained to them. 'At least the crew are armed thanks to the bullion they're carrying.' MacLain murmured as they waited for news while the airline endeavoured to communicate with *Imperial 109* by radio.

A little after midnight however a worried Jack Priestly came on the line, having been summoned from his bed by the emergency. 'I have to tell you,' he said, 'we can't raise the plane, and neither can the Canadians. We've completely lost contact with her. She's flying through an area of bad storm at the moment which must be blocking our transmissions.'

'Either that,' someone in the room remarked when Moyers repeated the message, 'or else she's gone down.'

'You're going to hold up a plane? I don't believe you, you're crazy!' Jarrett and Susie had been lying in one another's arms in the pilot's narrow bed, exchanging lovers' confidences, when his sudden confession jerked her bolt upright and drew the exclamation of disbelief from her. 'I don't believe you,' she repeated frowning down at him. 'You're just teasing me.' Jarrett smiled up at her. In her amazement she had allowed the bed clothes to slip from her back, and he ran his hand up from her hip, over her rib cage, to the firm high breast. 'It's true,' he said gently, 'tomorrow afternoon at three o'clock I am going to hold up a plane and take off it two million dollars in gold.'

The girl pressed his hand tightly against her breasts as though afraid of losing him, her eyes serious and troubled as she sensed the purpose behind his words. 'Tell me,' she commanded, 'tell me it all.' And lying there beneath her gaze Jarrett revealed every detail of his plan and its long preparation.

If anyone had ever asked him why he had chosen to unburden himself in this way to a young chit of a girl whom he had met for only the third time, he would probably have been quite unable to reply. He had spoken almost without conscious thought; certainly it had never crossed his mind that in doing so he might be putting himself in danger. He had simply taken it for granted that the girl would understand when he explained it all to her.

'And when we've got the money,' he concluded, 'We'll go away, together you and me, and start a decent life somewhere.' For a moment they stared at one another gravely, in silence; studying each other's expressions intently for confirmation of their feelings. Jarrett saw conviction and hope gradually replacing the incredulity in her features and knew his instinct had not played him false. Like himself, Susie had experienced the sour disappointment of a world which seemed to promise much yet delivered only bitterness and humiliation.

He waited for her questions; ready to dispel her last lingering uncertainties, but with surprising fatalism she accepted every word of his proposals without hesitation. There was only one thing she wanted to know. 'Where'd we go to?' she asked, wrinkling her brow. 'The boat takes us south to Mexico,' he answered, 'But afterwards we can go anywhere you like. We could go to Europe maybe, see England or France.'

'France!' Suzie's face lit up and her eyes sparkled at the name. 'France, could we really go there, to Paris even? You were there, before in the war. Tell me about it.' And diving back down into the bed again, she snuggled up against him, drawing the clothes round them.

For a space he let her rest there while he recalled for her the images of the wartime city he had known years before when he had been a dashing young fighter ace on leave from the front. 'Go on,' she urged him when at length he stopped, but Jarrett shook his head. 'Come on,' he patted her gently on the bottom, 'there'll be time enough for that later, and there's work to be done if we're to be ready tomorrow.'

Out in mid-Atlantic weather conditions had worsened considerably during the hour before midnight. The first sign of the deterioration had been the rapid build up of dense banks of low-lying cloud to a point where *Caterina*'s crew found themselves flying blind, completely hemmed in by opaque drifts of vapour. At first Desmond had attempted to climb above the cloud layers. The temperature outside was still dropping ominously and in these wet-fog conditions the ice danger was very real. Gunning the motors he had taken the flying-boat up to 12,000 feet, and for a short while they had found relatively clear air.

Then in the light from the distorted ball of the moon, showing through the patchy cover above, they had seen an enormous bank of black clouds, as solid as a range of mountains looking ahead of them, the menacing thunder heads rearing up to 20,000 feet or more. The moment they entered these they encountered severe rain squalls, and strong gusts of wind with considerable air turbulence. Before long too the temperature had dropped well below zero and the wings became covered in a crusting of frozen sleet. There was nothing for it but to descend.

Downwards they plunged through a blackness so intense, the wing tips and even the outer engines were at times obscured. The turbulence increased, with buffeting and air pockets rocking the plane. Desmond was relying totally on his instruments; unable to distinguish either sea or sky, it was only by keeping a close watch on the artificial horizon and the turn and bank indicator that he could tell what was happening to the flying-boat. Without such guidance it had been discovered in the past, the effect on the augean canals in a man's ears of the centrifugal force developed by a turn in cloud caused such a complete loss of dimensional equilibrium, that he was inclined to believe his aircraft was level even when it was actually at a steep angle with the horizontal. The horizontal in fact, seemed to him to be inside the plane. If he went into a spiral or a spin he would have no way of telling how to pull out.

Lightning flickered momentarily off the starboard bow, the cold radiance revealing a scene of boiling, storm-rent clouds, churning beneath the force of giant vortices, through which the pilots strained for a glimpse of the ocean. Already the altimeter showed they had less than 1200 feet between them and the surface and in such conditions Desmond dared not continue the descent for much longer unless the visibility improved.

The lightning flashed again, this time almost dead ahead. A searing double pulse so near that their retinas were dazzled painfully for several seconds and *Caterina* bucked wildly in the savage inrush of air. The rain squalls turned to hail mixed with snow, blasting at them from out of the darkness with malevolent fury. The temperature outside was now only twenty-two degrees and through the window at his side, Desmond could see patches of ice on the leading surface of the wing and on the cowling of the inboard engine, gleaming dully in the light from the cockpit.

More lightning crackled around them, and *Caterina* shook so violently he was sure she must have been struck. Caught in the grip of a monstrous down draught the aircraft dropped horrifyingly while before his eyes the needle of the altimeter wound back through five hundred-foot revolutions in as many seconds. Engines racing, the propellers clutched at the flailing air as Desmond dragged the stick back and opened the throttles, to pull her out of the dive. The port wing dipped sharply, threatening to put them into a spin and he stamped down on the rudder bar to level her up again, feeling the aircraft shaking beneath the strain as he did so.

Then, almost miraculously it seemed, they broke through the bottom of the cloud layer and the storm-whitened surface of the sea was faintly visible below. 'Jesus! What on earth's that?'

Frazer exclaimed in awe, peering down through the flying sleet at the waves now only 400 feet beneath the flying-boat's keel. The other two followed the direction of his gaze, Ralph Kendricks leaning over his Captain's shoulder to see out of the windscreen.

A scant quarter of a mile ahead a huge whitish mass was distinguishable against the darker background of the ocean, nearing rapidly as *Caterina* hurtled low over the heaving plain. Reaching down on the left hand side of the instrument panel Desmond flicked on a pair of switches, and at once, from the nose and starboard wing, twin searchlights stabbed out into the night. In the murk even their 10,000 candle power brilliance was pitifully inadequate to piece the near solid sheets of rain and sleet, but still their beams enabled the stunned fliers to pick out the glinting, perpendicular cliffs and sweeping hump-backed crest of the giant iceberg in their path. 'We're going to hit it!' Frazer cried, and for an instant Desmond was of the same opinion as the mountain of grey-streaked ice seemed to fill the windows.

Jerking the stick back he felt the flying-boat lift and they soared overhead, scraping above the drifting menace by feet, or so it seemed.

'Jesus!' Frazer repeated, in the glow of the cabin light his face was green with fear, 'I didn't think bergs that big came this far south?'

'Ever heard of the *Titanic*?' Desmond replied shortly, with little breath to spare from the effort demanded by controlling the plane. A shiver ran through him as he spoke, at the memory of the White Star liner and her fifteen hundred passengers lost in this very area on a night in April twenty-seven years before. If the weather grew any worse *Caterina* too might succumb to the freezing waters of the Atlantic.

Surprisingly, down on the lower deck, a number of the passengers were managing to sleep through the storm, despite the terrific buffeting which the aircraft was taking. Those who could not lay, largely unworried by the noise and erratic motion, in the warmth and comfort of their beds, fortunately unaware of the gravity of the position the flying-boat was now in.

Paul Rintlen was among this latter group. The promenade lounge in which he was lying had been made up with five beds; the two nearest the forward door being occupied by Laura Hartman and Charlotte Curtis' maid Arlette, while the rest had been allocated to Rashid al Senussi, Van Smit and Rintlen himself. In the rear of the plane, and screened off from the other cabin by a thick curtain, the after cabin remained light and untouched for the use of those who might find themselves unable to sleep and unwilling to stay in their beds. At present it was unoccupied.

On the far side of the cabin Rintlen could distinguish the huddled form of Rashid in the dim light, turning restlessly in his berth. Later, when the aircraft was riding more smoothly and there was a better chance of everyone else on board being soundly asleep the SD officer intended making his way through into the lighted cabin and on into the hold beyond. With reasonable luck he should be able to carry out a thorough search of the Wienzmans' luggage undetected.

Meanwhile in England, attempts to contact the flying-boat were still being made, but anxiety for her safety was growing at the continued failure to elicit any reponse. Reports coming in from weather ships and other vessels near the area hit by the storm, drew a bleak picture of the conditions a thousand miles out in the Atlantic. The storm had moved directly across the path *Caterina* had intended to follow, and even allowing for the detour she was to have made in her efforts to avoid it, there could be little doubt that the aircraft must be in serious difficulties.

At the police station Moyers and the other officers waited for news. The air in the room was thick with the smoke from cigarettes, the tables littered with heaped ash-trays and half-finished cups of black coffee. Conversation was desultory, but exhausted as they were, no one was willing to leave before hearing some positive indication of the flying-boat's fate. From time to time one of the telephones on Moyers' desk would ring, startling the room awake, but always the message was the same. 'Still no news'.

By two o'clock in the morning, when in normal circumstances, with fair winds *Caterina* would be nearing the Newfoundland coast and with no word from her, the Government was informed. Instructions were then beamed to two Royal Naval Aurora class light cruisers which were riding out the storm in heavy seas, some four hundred miles south of her projected track, to close the distance and try to raise her through the storm's interference on their own wireless. In addition ships of the United States Coastguard were asked to keep a watch for the missing plane.

But still there was no reply from *Imperial 109*.

The strength of the storm was increasing. Indeed Desmond had begun to fear their course was taking them right into its very heart. They were still travelling at less than a thousand feet, amongst sleet and snow squalls of unremitting ferocity, the aircraft being shaken by violent, quartering winds which threatened at every moment to dash her into the seas below. The temperature outside had fallen further to twenty degrees, and the weight of the ice build-up on the wings and fuselage was beginning to create a noticeable drag. Much of this was due to the thick banks of freezing fog they were encountering.

Most of all Desmond was worried by their inability to fix their navigational position. Ralph's last accurate plot had been more than three hours ago and at the time this had indicated they were drifting south much faster than they had expected. Desmond had endeavoured to compensate for this tendency in the subsequent period, but the result was they were left with only a poor idea of their actual course, calculated by dead reckoning without check by any other means.

At frequent intervals they were still trying to make contact over the radio either with Newfoundland or with some passing ship, but static from the electrical discharges in the storm made it impossible to tell if their transmissions were being answered; equally it ruled out any hope of their being able to use the radio direction finding equipment.

Until he could be more sure of their position Desmond was unwilling to risk heading any further south and trying to run

before the storm, or at least skate through its fringes. They had
been flying now for almost ten hours during which time they
had maintained an average speed of 160 mph according to their
air-speed indicator. Actually he was sure their true ground
speed had been considerably less for most of that period,
thanks to the effect of the wind: 130, perhaps even as low as
120 mph, leaving them still seven or eight hundred miles short
of their destination.

If such were the case the situation was by no means critical.
Caterina had taken off with an adequate margin of fuel to
allow for extra consumption due to head winds; but from early
on in the voyage they had been forced to amend their original
route so as to try and dog-leg round the storm, adding a
further two or three hundred miles to the total length of the
trip. This figure was being increased by the impetus of the
winds, carrying them constantly southward, and it was possible
that they might now have reached a point where the flying-
boat no longer carried sufficient fuel to permit another, and
still wider sweep out into the middle reaches of the ocean.

Another fog bank loomed before them. It was virtually impossible to tell where the sea ended and the cloud vapour
began. Already ice crystals might be forming in the slender
intakes of the carburettor; Desmond had been listening ever
since they had entered the storm for the dreaded stutter and
misfire which would indicate a blocked fuel jet. Once that occurred, out here in mid ocean, the end would be very near.

The fog belt was a narrow one, but no sooner did they
emerge on the other side, than they struck a squall so violent
and twisting it made the plane tremble along her entire length
and through the windows the wings could be seen bending and
flexing in an alarming fashion, while hail rattled against the
glass and drummed noisily on the metal plating. An ice floe was
slipping past below, the jagged blocks smaller in size than the
giant berg they had seen earlier, but more numerous, an indication of the bitterly cold temperature of the seas. Then a
further patch of wet mist enveloped them, blotting out the
way ahead for several minutes while the moisture laden air
condensed on the aircraft's exposed metal skin.

Abruptly Desmond came to a decision; to remain as they were for very much longer was impossible. The danger of icing had grown acute, and moreover the flying-boat was taking a terrible hammering. The passengers too, Sandy had warned him, were beginning to grow upset and frightened, and though their comfort was not a major consideration when weighing the safety of the plane, it was nevertheless an added factor to be taken into account.

'I'm taking another shot at climbing out of the cloud,' he announced, 'if we stay on the deck much longer we'll soon be carrying so much ice we'll fall out of the sky. Ralph!' he half turned his head to call out to the radio operator. 'I want you to have that sextant of yours ready, and to be standing by to try and make a star fix the moment there is any kind of break in the cover overhead, I must have an idea of our position.' The engine note deepened as the plane used increased power to lift her through the cloud layers, Desmond watched the rev. counters carefully. 'Did you hear me Ralph?' he called out more loudly. 'Aye, aye, Skipper. I heard you.' The radio officer's voice came back faintly. He sounded tired and old but Desmond was staking everything on his belief in Kendricks' ability to overcome his fear. They were all relying on him to find them a way out of the storm.

Ever since the weather had closed in on them, from the time of the last navigational fix he had taken, Ralph had been sitting at his desk, working at the radio sets with an inner conviction of hopelessness. *Caterina* carried a Marconi telegraphy transmitter working on the short and medium wave bands as well as a medium wave telephony transmitter and a loop aerial direction finder. In addition, transmitter, receiver and direction finder were duplicated by Hermes aircraft trans-receiver auxiliary apparatus, designed to provide a fall-back should the main system fail; but the appalling atmospherics were drowning out all sound in a wash of static, rendering this array of complex equipment useless.

As their course had taken them deeper into the depression, Ralph's fears had deepened with it, rising over him like a slow, cold tide, numbing his limbs and dulling his mind. He felt as though he were being sucked down into a bottomless dark morass of despair which was enveloping him in its freezing embrace, slowly stifling the life out of him. Locked and immobile he stared at the useless, flickering dials of the wireless in front of him. For him, for all of them on board, death was only a short while away he knew. He was almost resigned to it.

Desmond's words reached him through his lethargy as though from a vast distance, like a voice echoing in his sleep. With a great effort he managed to force a reply. Stretching out a hand he reached towards the sextant lying on top of the pile of charts. His movements appeared to him to be slow and distorted, like the actions of a sleep-walker. Dimly he was aware of Frazer watching him, his expression a mixture of vindicated revenge and dismay. What did it matter? He thought; there was so little time left; nothing mattered any more.

The flying-boat droned on through the darkness, with only the slowly winding arm of the altimeter to show the men in the cabin they were ascending. All sense of speed and altitude, even of motion itself, save for the unwavering vibration of the engines had vanished. They felt the concussion of thunder near at hand occasionally but no lightning penetrated the obscurity. Between six and eight thousand feet the turbulence increased sharply, a series of air pockets jolted the aircraft's frame; but gradually they rose through and the bumping died away.

They were climbing at 600 feet a minute, the air around them growing colder with every second that passed, multiplying the ice threat to the carburettor and adding to the burden the flying-boat was hoisting aloft. Despite the heating in the cockpit, the temperature had fallen noticeably, setting the two pilots shivering in their seats. Sandy Everett came through from the mail room with a pair of sheepskin flying-jackets and joined them in scanning the windows for a sign of the hoped for thinning of the clouds. Outside the temperature had fallen to below zero, the altimeter indicated a height of more than 13000 feet, and Desmond was forced to open the engine throttles to their maximum extent to maintain their climbing altitude. 14000 feet ... 15000. The engines were labouring, and now a new hazard was being added to those

437

already facing them. The engine temperature gauges were moving over towards the red danger zone, there was a serious risk of fire or of seizure within the engine blocks themselves as well as the continued fear of ice build-up in the air inlets. Tension on the flight deck mounted as he held his course.

Frazer's nerve was the first to give way. 'It's no good!' he burst out, 'we're taking on too much ice, she's overheating, there could be another ten thousand feet of cloud above us easily.' Desmond made no answer. He could sense the nerves of the others were also stretched to breaking point, but he was determined to press on. Rather than turn back he would jettison some of the cargo; better to lose that than the lives of everyone on board. The needle of the altimeter had slowed, they were scarcely rising at all now. 16000 feet, 16200 feet, and 300: the needle steadied quivering. The engines were straining to their limit. The temperature gauges firmly into the red; their speed was falling off and at any second the flying-boat would stall. The controls were growing sluggish already.

'We're going to stall! You must ease off, she can't make it!' Frazer cried out again. 'Shut up and give me full boost,' Desmond snarled at him, holding the stick tight back. The First Officer gaped at him. 'You're mad! She won't take it I tell you. Do you want to kill us all? If she goes into a spin we'll never pull her out in these conditions.'

'Give me full boost I said,' Desmond repeated savagely, and seeing Frazer making no move to obey the leant across the other's seat and yanked the switches open himself. Instantly the engines roared out as the superchargers cut in and the needle of the altimeter began to climb again. Shaking under full power the aircraft rose while Frazer watched the overloaded gauges aghast.

Then, unbelievably, just as even Desmond was about to abandon hope they saw a streak of light ahead and for a single instant, the moon shone through a rent in the black pall above them. 'Ralph!' he called out, 'Get ready, here it comes.'

Ralph Kendricks was unable to move. The desperate climb through the rain and clouds had brought his fear to a pitch of intensity where he could only sit paralysed and bereft of will.

Now that the moment had come for him to perform his duty he seemed bound in place, rigid and transfixed. He knew their only hope of survival depended on his making a star fix. He was aware of how vital it was and how little time there was left to them. Indeed he wanted to act, but his limbs refused to obey the commands of his brain. He heard Desmond's cry, saw the sextant lying on the table before him beside his hand, but his fingers refused to move across the intervening inches. Again he heard Desmond's voice 'Ralph get to the window!' followed by Frazer's panic-stricken cry 'Can't you see he's too bloody scared?'

Scared! Were they going to die because he was scared? Desmond and Sandy, Andy Draper, Frazer even; the passengers below: Laura Hartman, the Wienzmans with their escape so near? Was he about to let all of them down? Anne too, she had begged him not to go on this flight, was he going to fail her now? Very slowly, so slowly it seemed to him he could measure the time in minutes, the finger of his right hand flexed, moved and gripped the sextant. Somewhere deep inside him a small residue of will was fighting back against the overpowering fear which was trying to choke him.

With an immense effort, Ralph pressed down on the table and heaved himself to his feet to gaze out of the window by his head. As he did so the spell broke and the spark of resistance within him was fanned into a blaze which swept through him. High above them the winds had torn the cloud veil open and in the gap a triple group of stars glittered, the brightest very clear and brilliant with a faint bluish tinge to its light.

'Ralph, can you see anything?' Desmond was calling from the front. A wave of exultation passed over Kendricks at the knowledge that he had faced and conquered his fear at last. He had experienced the awful, the appalling naked terror of the certainty of death, and he knew he would never be afraid of it again.

Lifting the sextant he caught the image of the bright star in its mirror. 'Just hold on a moment Skipper,' he called out, in calm tones once more, 'I've got a sighting on Vega for you.'

Minutes later Ralph had taken three separate fixes on the

439

star, had calculated their position and worked out the fuel range. Though they were some one hundred and fifty miles farther south than they should have been, there was still sufficient reserves in the tanks for them to try and break away from the storm track. Withdrawing the boost, Desmond banked away to port, relieving the straining engines as the aircraft descended.

That his decision had been a wise one was shown less than half an hour later when they found themselves cruising easily above the cloud layers at 8000 feet in bright moonlight, still experiencing headwinds, but out of reach of the worst effects of the storm, and with the danger of icing receding.

There was a mood of elation and satisfaction in the cockpit, with the exception of Frazer who sat sullen and dispirited at the Radio Officer's resilience by comparison with his own weakness. Desmond was feeling exhausted by his long struggle, and handed over the controls to him, while he himself took to the mail room bunk for two or three hours rest.

'Any luck with the radio?' he inquired of Ralph as he squeezed past the wireless desk. Kendricks shook his head, ''Fraid not Skipper. There must still be too much electrical interference below. It should be clearer in another hour or so. I'll keep trying.'

'Fine, let me know if there's anything important.' There was no need for either of them to mention what had taken place earlier. Ralph had fully justified his confidence in him. Stretching out on the bunk among the canvas mail bags, Desmond fell instantly asleep.

The resumption of normal flight was also a considerable relief to the passengers, several of whom had felt worried and unwell during the flying-boat's long fight through the storm. Reassured by the steady beat of the engines in the calm air, and by the moonlight gleaming silver on the backs of the clouds below, they drifted comfortably off to sleep again.

One exception was Professor Wienzman. He had slept well during the early part of the night, waking only as the aeroplane began its climb up through the cloud. For a while he lay talking quietly with his daughter in the berth above, and with the

Kings on the opposite side of the room, but gradually they had grown drowsier and fallen silent, as sleep overcame them. Unable to follow their example, the Professor sat up and reached for his dressing gown. If he could not sleep he might as well read. His case notes were still in his bag in the hold, perhaps if he could get those out they might send him off.

Quietly, so as not to disturb the others, he rose from his bed and crept out of the room. The overhead bulbs had been turned down to their lowest extent and there was barely enough light for him to see where he was going. The long promenade lounge was full of sleeping forms, none of them stirring. Entering the after cabin the professor found it empty, and the strong light here made his eyes blink after the dimness of the forward cabins. Opening the door in the far bulkhead he went through into the hold beyond.

The light was on here too, somewhat to his surprise, and the figure of a man was bending over one of the suitcases. Thinking it must be the steward or purser, the Professor started to explain his presence, and what he had come for. Then he saw that the suitcase which lay open on the floor was his own, and that the man who was straightening up and turning towards him was neither of these two. He was the Swiss, Ernst Perler, and in his hand he held a gun.

'Come in Professor Wienzman,' he said softly in German, 'and shut the door. You have led me a long chase from Vienna.'

It seemed to Desmond he had barely fallen asleep before Sandy was shaking him awake again. 'Skipper, we've managed to get through on the wireless to St. Johns. They've an urgent message for you. They've been trying to contact us for the last four hours.' Cursing sleepily Desmond followed him through into the cockpit, pulling on his flying-jacket as he went.

'It sounds serious.' Ralph handed him a copy of the message he had taken down. 'England seem to think we may have a killer on board with us.' Desmond studied the form. 'Ernst Perler, travelling on a Swiss passport believed to be a forgery, boarded at Southampton.' He read out the official phrases. 'Urgently wanted for questioning in connection with killing of two men. Almost certainly armed and dangerous, to be approached with extreme caution'. 'Who the hell do they think we are?' he exclaimed in exasperation. 'The U.S. marines?'

'What do you reckon we ought to do?' Kendricks asked.

'I don't know,' Desmond stared at the paper again. 'I suppose the best course is for two of us to go down now and grab him while there's a chance he's still asleep. We can lock him in with the gold behind the grill in the mail room.'

'Couldn't we leave him and let the Mounties handle it when we reach Botwood?' Sandy suggested, but Desmond dismissed the idea. 'No,' he said firmly, 'the authorities wouldn't have been so anxious to get through to us, if they didn't think this man was a threat. If he has a gun and realized we were on to him, or that the police were waiting God knows what might happen. It'll be safer if we act at once.' He turned to where Ken Frazer sat at the controls. 'How's she handling?' he asked.

'Fine,' the First Officer told him without looking up. 'Steady as a rock.'

'I reckon you're right Skipper,' Ralph agreed, 'how do you want to play it? Sandy here says Perler's berthed down at the after end of the Promenade lounge.'

'Starboard side, far end, lower berth,' the Purser interjected. 'With Dr. Van Smit above, and the Turkish chap opposite.'

'Anyone else in there?' Desmond opened the locker by his seat and took out the two pistols.

'Laura, Mrs. Hartman, and Mrs. Curtis' maid,' Sandy told him, 'one on each side at the forward end.'

'We'll still have to risk it, there'll never be a time when he'll be totally alone.' Desmond handed one of the revolvers to Ralph, 'I'll go down, you follow behind and we'll take him between us. You're quite sure which is his bed?' he looked inquiringly at the young boy.

'Positive Skipper,' Sandy affirmed. 'I checked all the cabins a few minutes before the message came over the radio, and he was there. He seemed to be asleep too.'

'Right then.' Desmond spun the chambers of his revolver, checking the action. 'Call up St. Johns again on the wireless

Ralph, and tell them what we intend doing; then we'll go down.'

The words were hardly out of his mouth, when the sound of a shot shattered the stillness of the lower deck.

Horror and amazement dawned slowly on the Professor at the realization of what was taking place. 'You are a German?' he blurted incredulously, unwilling to believe the evidence before him.

'Standartenfuhrer Rintlen of the Sicherheitsdeinst,' the man smiled tightly. 'Do you really think you could ever escape from us Professor?'

'But please, what is it you want of me? Why can you not leave us alone?' the Professor begged. 'We have done no harm, my daughter and I.'

'Yes, you have done immeasurable harm, as you are well aware,' Rintlen snapped. 'Why else did you flee secretly from the Reich and try so hard to evade our attempts to recapture you in Italy?'

'We were frightened. My daughter was frightened, that lout Gerdler was with you.' The Professor tried to explain, but Rintlen waved him to silence. 'Enough of this, there is no time for talking. You have papers, important papers with you. I want them, at once.'

'My notes you mean? They are in the suitcase, labelled as school books. If they are all you want take them. I would have given them to you gladly. Believe me it was never my intention to publish the names of my patients. Take them by all means and let me go.'

The SD officer gave a chuckle. 'Let you go,' he mimicked. 'Oh no, Professor, it is not as simple as that. We have come too far to let you go. You are a threat to me personally now, as well as an enemy of the Reich.'

'But you cannot touch me here, in the plane!' The Professor's voice rose in anguish as the words sank home. 'They could find out. There would be an investigation, you would be arrested!'

Rintlen laughed again. 'They will find nothing, my dear Pro-

443

fessor, for the simple reason that there will be nothing to find, only the evidence of a most unfortunate accident.' Stepping round the baggage on the floor he moved over to the massive door of the freight hatch, set in the side of the hold. 'You are about to take a walk Professor, a very long walk, straight down.'

Reaching up, he snapped back the first of the four heavy latches securing the hatch. 'Come over this way,' he ordered, motioning with his gun. As if in a dream the Professor obeyed, mesmerized by the gun and the harsh stare of the SD man. He took a couple of faltering steps and then stopped. 'Come on more.' Rintlen had unclipped two more latches and was stooping to reach the bottom one, still keeping the pistol trained on Wienzman's chest. 'And don't worry,' he said cruelly, 'your daughter will soon be joining you. I will attend to her when we reach America.' With a grunt of effort, he snapped open the last of the four latches.

All his life David Wienzman had been a man of peace, a man who believed that wars, and clashes and violence could be avoided, if people would only come together and talk reasonably to each other. He had never raised his hand against any one or threatened to do so. But now as he heard the gloating promise to destroy his daughter, from the thug who had persecuted and pursued them for so many days, a furious hatred welled up within him.

The German had begun to wrench open the handle of the door lock. Close by Wienzman's side, on top of a leather cabin trunk, stood a lizard skin hat-box belonging to Charlotte Curtis. With a surge of defiant courage the Professor seized it and flung it at the Nazi's head.

Taken by surprise at the sudden movement Rintlen's fingers tightened instinctively on the trigger. In the confined space of the hold, the crash of the shot was deafening. Flinging himself down, Wienzman felt the bullet part the air inches from his head, as he dived for cover among the baggage strewn on the floor. At the same instant there came a terrible cry from Rintlen and with a terrific roaring noise, a violent blast of air swept through the hold.

Jerking his head up, an appalling vision met the Professor's gaze. The great metal door of the freight hatch had swung open; dangling from it, clawing on the handle, was the figure of the Nazi agent, his head hanging back, his mouth open in a scream which was torn soundlessly away by the slipstream.

Even as Wienzman stared, transfixed by the sight, he saw the man's fingers slip, break loose, and his body drop away to vanish into the freezing darkness outside.

He was still staring in horror at the empty hatchway when seconds later Desmond and Ralph Kendricks burst through into the hold.

'He must be tougher than I thought, the old man,' Ralph remarked later when he and Desmond were back in their seats on the flight deck. 'It took a lot of guts to do what he did.' The Professor certainly was tough, Desmond thought. When the two of them had secured the freight hatch, and helped him through into the after cabin, dismissing the other passengers who had crowded in also, having been woken by the sound of the shot, he had been able to give a lucid and clear headed account of what had happened in the hold, as well as comforting his daughter's renewed anxieties.

Taking a statement from him Desmond had dispatched this over the air to the authorities, and on receiving a lengthy reply had been able to dispel the refugees' fears of further pursuit. 'London are pretty certain this was one man acting on his own without orders, and it seems likely also apparently that agents from his own country had actually been trying to prevent him from getting near you,' he had told them. 'So it looks as though you should both be safe from now on.'

Explanations to the excited passengers, and dealing with the stream of messages which continued to pour in from the Canadian wireless stations took longer, and it was five o'clock before he was at last able to take the controls once more.

The clouds had vanished during his time on the lower deck, and light was starting to creep up into the sky from the bright line on the horizon. Dawn was not far off. Below them, a swell was still running in the sea, but the angry white-caps of the

445

night had vanished. From time to time they flew over thick belts of sea fog hanging low above the water, sure proof that they were in the area of the Grand Banks fishing grounds, where the cold Labrador current coming down from the Arctic met a branch of the warmer Gulf stream.

Next to him Ken Frazer was scanning the way ahead through binoculars. Adjusting the focus he let out a sharp cry of excitement, 'There it is! Five degrees to starboard,' he sang out jubilantly. 'Land, we've made it across!'

XII

By Radio: 1400 hrs. local time Thursday 16th March, 1939. AIR TRAFFIC CONTROL MONTREAL CANADA TO LA GUARDIA MARINE TERMINAL NEW YORK. TRANS ATLANTIC MAIL PLANE IMPERIAL AIRWAYS FLIGHT 109 REGISTRATION G-ADHO CATERINA LEFT HERE E.T.A. NEW YORK 1600 hrs. EASTERN STANDARD TIME. END.

THE afternoon sun was shining brilliantly on the waters of Champlain Lake as *Caterina* climbed away from the St. Laurence and flew over the Canadian border into Vermont. They were flying at seven thousand feet following the line of the lake, between the long ridges of high ground on either side. The air was clear, with only a few patches of drifting white cumulus and free of turbulence.

Desmond yawned; with the aircraft on the auto pilot there was little for him and Frazer to do, but check the instruments occasionally and watch the snow-streaked terrain unfolding beneath them.

Fighting off his tiredness, Desmond turned his attention to the log and began filling in the remaining details of the flight from Europe. They had arrived at Botwood amid the bleak, stony Newfoundland landscape at a quarter past six in the morning, just as the sun rose above the horizon, thankful to be able to rest and stretch their limbs. Much of the time on the ground had been taken up with inspecting the outside hull of the flying-boat, which fortunately had suffered no damage in the storm; and in making reports to the police on the events of the night and the death of the Nazi agent. Apparently an inquest was necessary though there was doubt as to whether this would have to be held in England or Canada. At least at Botwood there had been no newspaper men.

At Montreal where they had landed at midday, their reception had been tumultuous. Flying in over New Brunswick and Maine, and the Notre Dame Mountains of Quebec Province, they had touched down on the river below the city, to be besieged by journalists and photographers with flash-bulbs from the moment they drew alongside the dock. Everything about *Caterina* it seemed, was news. Her glamorous passengers, her journey through the storm and overdue arrival; the attack on Professor Wienzman, and before that in Europe, the couple's escape at Rome; even poor Ian Thorne's death on the river at Shambe was dragged up again.

Desmond had been one of the newsmen's prime targets. He had been thankful when the airline management had come to his rescue, and hurried all the crew off. With the weather reports fair for the final leg of the trip everyone was anxious to be away and by two o'clock the last of the passengers were back on board and *Caterina* was nosing out into midstream while a crowd of waving spectators lined the river bank to watch her take off.

Glancing down out of the window again, Desmond saw they had reached the middle of the lake and were passing over Burlington. The time was half past three, in another ninety minutes they would be arriving at La Guardia.

Seventy-five miles to the south west Pat Jarrett and Susie were making their final preparations. They too had been up since dawn monitoring the radio traffic between Botwood, Montreal and New York, which had marked the safe arrival of the bullion flight from England in Canadian territory and its subsequent passage up the St. Lawrence to Montreal. From these, and from the news broadcasts, they had gathered something of the dramatic adventures of the night crossing, and of the intense interest which had been generated in *Imperial 109*, around the world.

The publicity the flight was receiving had caused Jarrett some moments of anxiety and at one time he had even considered whether the attack ought not to be abandoned. A thorough re-examination of his plans however had convinced him that the new development would in practice have a minimal effect as far as they were concerned. It was possible that because of the press reports, the flying-boat would eventually be located rather sooner than he had anticipated originally but even allowing for this, he and the girl would still have plenty of time to cover the tracks of their escape effectively.

So together they had manoeuvred the sea-plane out from the boat-house and moored her fast to the jetty, where he had made a final inspection of the Napier engine, and Susie, dressed in one of his overalls, had worked away with a soft cloth, polishing the duralumin plating on the nose and wing surfaces, and wiping down the white paint of the fuselage and tail. Then, the inspection finished, and minute adjustments made to the setting of the carburettor and ignition timing, the two of them had man-handled the drums of aviation fuel down to the end of the jetty and replenished the tanks in her twin floats.

'That will give me enough for three hundred miles provided I'm careful,' he told Susie as he screwed back the caps. 'Why do you need so much?' she asked, 'I thought the plane was coming close by.'

'She is, reasonably close,' he replied, 'I shall make the interception about forty miles from here, between Hudson Falls and Saratoga Springs, but I want to have plenty of fuel in hand in case I don't spot her right away. It shouldn't be too difficult, I know her height and course and the speed she's making; all the same I want to have the extra just in case I have to go looking.'

'How long will you be gone for?' They began rolling the empty drums back up the jetty to the rear of the boathouse.

'Not more than three quarters of an hour if it all pans out as I intend,' he answered, 'but don't get worried if I happen to take longer.'

Returning to the house Jarrett went through the painstaking ritual of preparing himself for the action he was about to undertake. He washed and shaved himself again, put on fresh underclothes and shirt, and donned his old uniform from the Army Air Corps. Then the girl helped him into the fur lined boots and heavy leather greatcoat he had last worn in combat over the Western Front, twenty-one years ago. Even with these and his gauntlets and leather flying helmet, he knew he would be freezing cold seven thousand feet up in the open cockpit travelling at two hundred and forty miles an hour.

Taking out the Thompson sub-machine gun, he showed Susie how to work the action and change the magazine. 'Are you sure you know what to do?' he asked, handing it to her. The girl gripped the weapon tightly in her hands. 'As soon as the flying-boat lands on the water, I go down to the jetty and cover the crew with the gun while they tie up,' she slapped the butt of the Thompson as she spoke. 'That's right.' Jarrett nodded approvingly. 'The jetty is very low and the airliner will be able to get her starboard wing and props over the top, and nose right in alongside, with the pier fitting easily between her hull and the starboard wing float, like a pontoon mooring. So make sure you keep well back out of the way until the Captain has switched off the engines. Then what do you do?'

'Then you'll tell them over the radio to get out, and I'll line them up and keep covering them while you come in on the water in your plane, and tie up on the other side between them and the shore.' Susie repeated the briefing she had been given. 'Yes, I've measured it out, there should be plenty of room. The flying-boat can't come all the way up because the boat-house is in the way,' Jarrett affirmed, 'as soon as I'm out of the cockpit, I'll take over and we'll set them to work unloading the gold.'

'Couldn't we leave the gold on the plane and just fly off with it?' Susie suggested. 'I mean you know how and we could go anywhere then? It'd be quicker too.'

'No, it's the plane they'll be searching for,' Jarrett told her, 'until they find her they won't have a clue of what's happened to the flight, and you and I will be safe until they do. Their best guess will probably be that she's gone down somewhere in the Adirondacks, I reckon. No, we'll stick to our plans.'

Going out through the kitchen he stopped momentarily to

switch on the main wireless set. Holding the headphones up to his ear, he listened for a while. 'Can you hear the flying-boat?' Susie asked, watching him tune the dial delicately along the wave bands. 'Nothing but ordinary traffic between the ground stations,' he answered laying down the headphones and switching off again. 'The Captain made his last report as he turned south down the valley of the Champlain soon after he crossed the border. It's unlikely he'll come on the air again until he's drawing near to New York.'

For the hundredth time that day he looked at his watch. 'It's nearly half past two, time I was getting down to the plane.' Taking his arm she walked down the path with him to the pier, and stood holding his navigating pad while he put on the helmet and glasses. 'This is it. If you want to back out, now's the time to say so?' By way of answer Susie put her arms round him and kissed him. 'I'll be ready,' she promised, 'don't worry about me.'

Once in the cockpit he made a quick check of the cockpit fittings; all seemed well. He switched on the master ignition, feeling the excitement surge back afresh as the dials and gauges flickered into life. Meticulously he scanned each one: fuel indicators, oil and petrol pressures, rev. counter, compass, altimeter, temperature gauges for the engine oil and radiator coolant, air speed indicator; all were functioning as they should. He pressed the black starter button.

Without a moment's hesitation the engine burst into life with a roar, puffs of blue-grey smoke spouting from the exhaust cowls. He let her run for a few seconds, working the throttle as she warmed up. As she settled down to run smoothly, he lifted his hand to the girl signalling her to unleash the stern lines, and the little plane began to taxi forward across the water.

Pulling down his protective goggles over his eyes, he steered out into the middle of the lake, watching the power build up. The wind was light, hardly more than three or four knots from the south. With a final wave to Susie, he let the silver racer have her head. The roar of the engine deepened as he opened the throttle wide and she bounded forward to streak along the surface with spray flying up over the rim of the cockpit and streaming out behind.

As the airspeed indicator reached ninety at two thousand revs, Jarrett pulled the stick firmly back and felt the Supermarine lift off like a bird. A fierce wave of elation swept through him as the potent, thoroughbred machine responded to his touch on the controls and soared up over the dark trees which crowded the hill-side. A light press down on the rudder pedals and he was banking round to the north-west; looking down, five hundred feet below him he could see the deep blue expanse of the lake, the house on the point and the tiny figure on the end of the jetty which was the girl, all dwindling rapidly as he climbed away out of the valley.

Now he was about to show the world what he could do. This was what he had been working for so long; the moment when the years of frustration and poverty, the rejection and indifference, were to be repaid. He was back where he belonged once more, in the seat of a high performance fighter, fuelled and armed. His mouth fixed in a hard, grim line, he set a course to intercept *Imperial 109.*

While *Caterina* was still cruising peacefully high over the New England countryside, oblivious of the assailant closing in on her from forty miles away; and while in New York's financial district people were settling down to the afternoon's work after lunch, Harvey Tilset Kimber left his office in the thirty-nine storey Bankers Trust Company building opposite the pseudo-Greek façade of the New York Stock Exchange, with its six huge columns of white Georgia marble and instructed the chauffeur of his limousine to drive him north along Fifth Avenue to the St. Regis Hotel on the junction with Fifty-Fifth Street.

Smaller and more exclusive than the twin-towered, two thousand bed Waldorf-Astoria nearby, its decorative, turn-of-the-century style appealed to Harvey's discriminating taste, and he was accustomed to dining frequently at its celebrated La Boite restaurant. It also made an admirably discreet venue for the meeting which was about to take place, of those parties who held a financial interest in the affairs of Stewart Curtis and Klerksdorp.

In the beautifully panelled double drawing-room, over-looking Fifth Avenue, Harvey found half a dozen men waiting for him. They rose from their chairs as he entered and one of them came forward to meet him with an outstretched hand. 'Harvey, it was good of you to come.' Edgar Mathers was a big, genial man who, like Harvey, lived in a baroque brownstone mansion on Murray Hill and was a member of the influential and prestigious University Club opposite. 'Gentlemen,' he announced to the others, 'I'm sure I don't need to introduce Harvey Kimber, President of Kimber Crossfields Smith, brokers to Klerksdorp Gold.'

One by one the men shook hands. Harvey knew them all, by sight and reputation if not by actual acquaintance. Like Edgar Mathers, they were bankers and investment barons. The formalities over, they took their seats facing one another round the centre of the room. 'We are meeting here this afternoon to discuss,' Mathers began to say, when he was interrupted by a small dried up husk of a man in a tight black suit and wing collar; this was Statten, President of First Financial Trust Company, one of the nation's premier institutions. 'No need for all that,' he snapped petulantly, 'there's only one thing we want to know: is Klerksdorp sound?' His colleagues echoed his remarks and everyone in the room looked expectantly at the stockbroker.

Sitting bolt upright in his chair, Harvey marshalled his facts in his mind before replying. 'No Kerksdorp is not sound,' he said clearly. 'I received confirmation of this from Stuttenheim in South Africa only a short time before I left to come here. The Securities Exchange Commission is being informed and the share quotation will be suspended in a few minutes.' From the resigned way in which his news was received, he could tell the verdict was not unexpected. 'A survey of the mine carried out over the past fortnight,' he continued, 'has shown the reserves were grossly overstated. It is doubtful whether it would be viable at all, and certainly not on the scale which it is being operated at the moment.'

'And the options on the surrounding mineral rights and real estate?' Mathers inquired with a worried frown.

'Worthless,' Harvey told him laconically, seeing no point in mincing his words.

This time the murmurs of discontent were louder and it was Statten who summed up the general feeling once more. 'That crook Curtis,' he spat the words out vindictively, 'has taken four million dollars off us as a down payment on those options, and three hours from now he'll be in the city demanding the balance of sixteen million. He won't see any of that, but I want to get back what we've already paid him.'

'I agree of course,' Mathers supported him, 'but Curtis is a slippery bastard. The contract for the sale was with him personally, it wasn't linked specifically to the fortunes of Klerksdorp, the mine isn't even mentioned in the wording. A court might say we still had to pay up even though the mine had failed.'

'I won't hand over another cent, whatever the courts say,' Statten retorted vigorously. 'Everyone knows these options were only of value because of Klerksdorp's gold strike.'

'Curtis will argue though that mining is always a gamble and we knew what we were doing,' interjected another.

'It might be cheaper to buy him off in the long run,' suggested Mather.

'Never, I won't hear of it,' the old man snapped back shrilly.

'There may be another way,' Harvey interposed quietly, and the conversation ceased at once as his audience turned to listen. 'Since in part this whole affair may be said to have originated from an introduction I gave Curtis to Edgar Mathers,' he nodded in the direction of his friend, 'some years ago. I have felt all along that I have a duty to do what I can to help you. Whether we can recover the money already paid is hard to say, personally, knowing Curtis I would doubt it.

'As far as preventing him from trying to enforce the contract however, I think there is more hope. In their telegrams to me our South African friends informed me that charges of fraud will be brought against Curtis in the Union. On my suggestion they are contacting the Department of Justice even as we sit here now, with a view to having an extradition order made against him. I am glad to say there is every possibility that Stewart Curtis will be arrested the moment he steps off the aeroplane at La Guardia.'

Fortunately for Stewart Curtis' peace of mind, he was as yet unaware of the moves which were being made to bring about his downfall. With the flying-boat's arrival in American airspace, his former confidence had returned, and with it the arrogance and contempt for his inferiors which had been so marked earlier on in the trip. Not many men, he told himself, would have been able to keep up the façade of Klerksdorp's prosperity sufficiently well to persuade a syndicate of bankers to part with twenty million dollars simply for the right to mine nearby.

Already he had been highly abusive towards Andy Draper, about the discomfort of the bed with which he had been provided during the night. 'Your captain may be able to protect you while you're on this plane,' he had stormed at the steward, 'but I can promise you that when we reach New York I shall make personal representations to the airline management. After all,' he remarked with crude self-satisfaction, 'if I can have one of their flights rescheduled, I should be able to have a miserable steward sacked.'

With Draper thus dispensed with, Curtis had next turned his attention to Laura. Summoning her to the after cabin, which had been returned to his private use, and in the presence of Luca d'Este, he subjected her to a long harangue, accusing her of treachery and theft, while the Baron looked on, smiling at her discomfiture. He had not forgiven Laura for taking his wife's part against him during lunch at Athens.

'But Mr. Curtis, I thought Captain O'Neill had explained to you?' Laura tried to protest.

'Captain O'Neill has explained nothing.' Curtis cut her short, 'he came to me with a pack of lies which he demanded I accept or else he would delay the flight. Well, he can't hold that threat against me any more and I have no hesitation in repudiating my agreement. You're sacked as from last Sunday when

455

you committed the theft, and as soon as we reach New York I intend to have you both arrested by the police and charged.'

'I think you are quite right Curtis.' Luca egged him on approvingly. 'One has after all a moral duty in these matters.'

Laura had been taken aback initially by the attack; when Curtis had called her in she had been expecting to receive an apology. Now however she reacted fiercely. 'Don't waste your time trying to frighten me with talk about police,' she said contemptuously. 'We both know perfectly well all you're saying is lies, and the admission you signed proves it. Don't think you can sack me either because as far as I'm concerned I've already resigned. I've had enough of your boasting and bullying. You two make a fine pair.' She included Luca in a scornful glance. 'An international swindler who ought to be in jail himself and a common murderer.'

Curtis turned puce at her description of him; by contrast the face of the Italian took on a sickly grey appearance. Laura gave them no chance to respond. 'You're both very fine at ill-treating servants and people who have to depend on you,' she continued hotly, 'but it's easy to see that the moment you do come up against someone your own size, then you're shown up for the cowards you are. Well from now on I don't have to worry about being polite to either of you any more, so mind how you speak to me because otherwise I'm likely to let fly in a way you won't be forgetting in a hurry.'

The vehemence of her words took the two men by surprise. Leaving them gaping, Laura made for the door before they could begin to splutter in reply; as she did so however it opened suddenly and Charlotte entered, wearing the white satin suit she had put on to board the flying-boat in England. 'Oh hallo Laura,' she said pleasantly, then peering more closely at the girl's face she asked, 'you look rather upset, are you alright?'

'If I am upset Mrs. Curtis,' Laura replied freezingly, 'it is only because the people in this cabin seem to think they can treat everybody as though they own them, and as I've just told your husband, I am one person he doesn't own any more,' and without waiting for an answer, she strode past her, through into the promenade lounge.

Behind her in the cabin, Charlotte rounded on Luca and her husband. 'What the hell have you two been saying to her?' she demanded, 'Have you been going on about that watch again?'

'There's no need for you to concern yourself,' Curtis attempted to dismiss the matter. 'I simply told the girl she was being sacked for theft and that I was putting the matter in the hands of the police.'

'My God, you've got a nerve!' his wife exploded at him, 'I suppose you realize that after what you've been saying about her she could well sue for slander. I told you I took the watch and that Laura never had anything to do with it. You'll have to apologize to her at once.'

'Don't start telling me what to do,' Curtis rebuked her angrily. 'None of this would have arisen in the first place if you hadn't made such a fool of yourself over that bloody pilot. I can't possibly keep the girl on now.'

At this point Luca d'Este made the mistake of interrupting on Curtis' behalf. 'Your husband is right you know Charlotte, one must be able to have absolute confidence in one's employees.' His words drew the full weight of Charlotte's wrath down upon him. 'Be quiet, you sycophantic little man, it has got nothing to do with you. Why don't you get out of here anyway?' she snapped savagely, 'I'm fed up with you always hanging around.'

Astonished by this, Luca could only stammer with embarrassment. Rising hastily to his feet, he scuttled out of the cabin muttering apologies. 'Ridiculous little toad,' Charlotte snorted contemptuously as the door closed behind him. 'I can't think why you have him in here.'

'You found the Baron amusing enough in Cairo while I was away,' her husband observed acidly, 'and until Captain O'Neill came on the scene and you decided he was a more attractive prospect to run after.'

'For Christ's sake stop going on about him will you,' Charlotte answered, growing suddenly weary, 'the affair is ended, let's leave it at that.'

After being driven out so abruptly into the main body of the aeroplane, Luca's first thought was that he badly needed a cigarette, and he made his way forward to the smoking saloon. Dr. Van Smit and the two Wienzmans were standing looking out of the promenade lounge windows at the scenery below but he passed them by without a word. Next door in the midship cabin he found Laura Hartman obviously engaged in recounting what had just happened to the Kings. All three glared at him as he entered and he hurried on through into the passageway beyond.

In the smoking saloon Jacquetta and Rashid had found themselves alone together for the first time since leaving London on the train on Wednesday afternoon. Up until a few moments ago the presence of Harold King had forced them to maintain their apparent indifference to one another's company, then to their relief, he had been summoned aft by his wife to hear Laura's tale of the Curtises' latest crime.

At once Jacquetta ran into the young Sheikh's arms and they embraced, tense and afraid at the thought of being discovered, yet unwilling to relax their hold. 'Rashid,' she whispered, 'what are we to do? In a little while we land in New York and in two days Van Smit will go to Luca.'

'If he does that the Italians will make a demand for me to be returned to them in Rome,' he answered. 'To stand trial for rebellion.' He spoke matter of factly but his words struck a chill into Jacquetta.

'They wouldn't do that, the Americans? It would mean sending you to your death.' She tightened her arms about him in terror. 'Perhaps. Who can tell?' Rashid shrugged. 'I do not intend to take the risk.' He did not elaborate, but the unexpressed threat was only too clear to Jacquetta. 'Rashid, please,' she begged him, 'for my sake, forget both of them and let us go back to Egypt. You can do more good there.'

'Listen,' he said grimly, 'there is no other way. Would you really have me break my word, forget my father and my sister? My oath means more to me than the fear of what might follow.'

With a sob of despair Jacquetta buried her face in his chest,

hugging him fiercely to her, as though trying to force the resolve from him with her own strength. They were still holding
one another in this fashion when Luca entered the saloon.

Jacquetta had been right in thinking her husband was aware
of the strained atmosphere which existed between himself and
the young Turkish nobleman who had joined *Caterina* at Alexandria. Several times on the flight, he had spotted the man
watching him with a peculiarly disquieting intensity. It had
never crossed his mind for a moment, though, that his wife was
carrying on an affair on the aeroplane itself, right under his
very nose; still less that his rival was in reality the Senussi
Prince whose retribution he so feared.

Startled by the sudden appearance of the one man they
wished to avoid, the couple sprang apart, while Luca, incensed
with fury and outraged pride, seized his wife by the arm and
jerked her roughly across the room, throwing her against the
chairs by the door. As she stumbled and fell to the floor she let
out a cry of pain.

For Rashid this was all the excuse he needed. Springing
forward he struck the Italian a terrific blow on the side of the
head, sending him crashing against the bulkhead. Dazed Luca
slid to the floor, and Jacquetta, looking up from where she had
fallen, and seeing him lying at the Arab's feet, let out a frantic
cry, 'No Rashid!' she screamed, thinking in the confusion that
the Arab was about to carry out his threat to kill Luca. 'Don't
harm him.'

At her words both men froze. The Italian had been picking
himself up, but at the mention of Rashid's name, he stiffened
and stared up at the man standing over him, his face white and
sweating with fear. 'Rashid,' he croaked, dry mouthed, 'Rashid
al Senussi?' he repeated slowly, as if unable to believe what he
had heard.

'Yes, that is my name,' Rashid nodded tersely, 'I am the man
whose father and whose sister you murdered and whose people
you enslaved,' he said in a voice of hate, 'I have trekked half
across the world to find you and avenge your crimes.'

Luca continued to stare open-mouthed at the figure above
him, then suddenly as though coming out of a trance, he

fumbled beneath his jacket for his pistol. Seeing Rashid going for his own gun, Jacquetta flung herself between them with another desperate cry.

Pat Jarrett had a more difficult task than he had anticipated in locating *Caterina* in the air above Vermont and New Hampshire. When he first arrived in the area where he expected to see the airliner he could find nothing but empty skies, and began to fear he must have made a miscalculation in his navigation. Desperately he scanned on all sides, searching between the scattered clouds for the glint of sunlight on metal. Though he was carrying fuel enough to enable him to loiter for a considerable period, his greatest worry was that the airliner might have increased her speed and placed herself well to the south of his present position, thereby forcing him into a long stern chase perhaps carrying him too near the populated areas where the attack might be witnessed from the ground.

Increasing his height to eight thousand feet he turned southward and began following the line of the Hudson River towards Albany, and almost at once he spotted his quarry a thousand feet or so below him, cruising majestically out from the cover of a puffy white drift of cumulus. She was about half a mile ahead of him he estimated and some ten miles beyond her expected position. Probably she had met with following winds on her flight down the valley.

A sharp current of excitement ran through him at the sight of the huge, sleek white target, flying all unsuspecting below. For a moment he was tempted to roar down on her in a power dive, attacking from the classic 'up sun' position, then collecting himself, he resolved to stick to the plan he had so carefully worked out in the weeks past.

Pushing the stick gently forward, and easing off the throttle slightly, he put the Supermarine into a shallow swoop, taking her down behind and a little below his victim. Levelling off about a hundred feet beneath her he increased power to bring himself up till he was only a length behind. This was another classic attack position, against the undefended belly. Tucked up forward on the flight deck the crew would be totally unaware of his presence as yet. He was close enough to make out every detail of the enormous white hull. From where he was he could even distinguish the scratches on the step of the flying-boat's planing bottom.

Seen from this distance there was something awe-inspiring about the great aircraft. Jarrett felt dwarfed in the tiny racer beside the lumbering giant which cruised on blissfully ignorant of her danger, and for the first time he was struck by a sense of the enormity of what he was about to do, and of the colossal odds against him. Could he really succeed? Could he really force this great aeroplane to surrender to his own puny machine? Taking a deep breath, he gripped the stick tightly in his gloved hands. This was it, this was the moment he had been preparing for. With a flick of his right thumb he switched the firing button to 'ON'.

Giving a light touch of the starboard rudder and a small increase of throttle he eased the racer out from behind the flying-boat and brought her up till the two were almost level. Very deliberately he sighted in on the extreme tip of the starboard wing. He did not want to cause any real damage with his first burst, merely to prove to the crew that he had guns and was prepared to use them. With a second intake of breath he pressed the firing button.

He held it down for the merest fraction of time, about a half second, no more, and deliberately aimed so as to miss the important wing flap. The Supermarine shuddered with the recoil and a brief scatter of red dots appeared in the sighting ring. Instantly it seemed the flying-boat's wing tip shredded like cardboard under buckshot, pieces of debris splintering off in a burst of metallic fragments, as some thirty of the heavy calibre bullets smashed through it.

Now that he was committed to his operation, Jarrett hesitated no longer. In front of him he saw the stricken plane buck wildly and then dip as the pilot on the flight deck banked frantically away from the attacker. Matching their manoeuvre he tucked the racer tight in beside them and switched down the transmit button of his radio, preset to the flying-boat's normal communication frequency.

'*Caterina, Imperial Airways Caterina*. Do not use your radio. I repeat do not use your radio,' he intoned, praying the transmission was getting through, and that the airliner's Captain would obey. 'I say again, do not use your radio.' His own equipment was specially low powered to reduce as far as possible the chances of ground stations overhearing. 'Steer course 273 degrees. Repeat 273 degrees. Maintain current height and speed. Do not use your radio.'

For what seemed to the anxious flyer like several minutes but in reality was a period of only some thirty seconds, the airliner continued in her banking descent, sliding earthwards against the tilted horizon. Then at last, to Jarrett's exultant relief, he saw the flying-boat's wings level up as she began straightening up and coming round on to the new course. He had done it. The Captain was obeying. The bullion flight *Imperial 109* was now under his command. In the open seat of the tiny Supermarine Pat Jarrett crowed aloud in triumph.

'Passengers are all O.K. Skipper,' Ken Frazer reported to Desmond on the flight deck. 'We've got them packed into the galley passageway like you ordered. They're frightened and nervous but so far under control.'

'Good. They'll be safest there with the mail room above and the extra walls of the galley and washrooms to protect them,' Desmond said. 'Just in case that bastard decides to start firing at us again. You had better get up to the mail room windows and keep an eye on him for me.'

'What do you reckon he intends doing?' Ralph Kendricks asked. He was sitting at the radio ready to receive further instructions from their assailant. Already they had been told to drop to one thousand feet and had been given two course alterations.

'My guess is that he and his friends are going to make us land somewhere,' Desmond answered. 'Where they can remove the gold.' He glanced out of the window at his side at the heavily wooded country they were flying over. 'This is a pretty remote area by the look of it. Ideal for the job.'

'And what about us and the passengers?' said Kendricks.

Desmond shook his head, 'I've no idea what they'll do once they get us ashore,' he said. 'But I know one thing I'd rather face it out on the ground than start taking chances up here with that fighter. He made a hell of a mess of our starboard wing. Whatever he's using carries a hefty punch and he's a good shot.'

'It's definitely a Supermarine type,' Ken shouted back from the mail room. 'I can't tell what model though and I think I can see the two gun-ports in his nearside wing.'

The Supermarine had been the prototype for the new Spitfire Desmond recalled, which flew at more than three hundred and fifty miles per hour.

He doubted very much whether the sea-plane would be able to manage more than three hundred with the extra drag of the floats and probably not even that. All the same it would still have speed enough to overhaul and destroy the slow, unarmed *Caterina* in any chase.

He felt a deep hatred within him, for the dark, helmeted figure in the cockpit of their attacker; a sense of personal outrage that anyone should dare shoot at *Caterina*, which far outweighed his fears for the moment. If only they had some means of firing back, of defending themselves.

'He's calling again Skipper,' Ralph said suddenly. 'He says you should be able to see a small lake about two miles ahead and ten degrees to starboard.'

'I have it,' Desmond answered. 'Is that the place he wants us to come down.'

'Yes. You're to land from the southern end, without circling round. He says the water is clear and deep.'

'It's going to be a bloody steep descent,' Desmond growled back, 'if I'm not allowed to circle and lose height. Those hills are closer than I like too. You had better tell Frazer to get below and send the passengers back to their seats for the touch down, they'll be safe there.' Reaching out to adjust the settings of the wing flaps, and to ease off the throttle levers, he started to take the flying-boat down on to Warren Lake.

Susie had never seen a big airliner before. Indeed the Supermarine was the only plane she had ever been close to. Consequently she was unprepared for the sheer size of the great flying-boat, appearing suddenly over the rim of the hills to the south and swooping steeply down towards the lake.

Amazement that they had actually achieved their objective was coupled with fear and a degree of awe, at the enormous, ponderous bulk which came roaring in, the noise of its descent echoing off the hillside. Compared with the light touchdown of the silver plane, the flying-boat alighted on the water with a splashing burst of spray which it flung so high and wide that Susie thought at first it had crashed and was about to sink. Then as she watched she saw the airliner breasting smoothly over the lake's surface, uninjured and, evidently in obedience to instructions from the sea-plane wheeling low overhead, turn in towards the point and begin to taxi shorewards. Taking a firm grip on the sub-machine gun, she prepared to receive it.

'Christ the man's bloody crazy!' Desmond swore as Ralph passed on to him the latest of the fighter's commands. 'How the hell does he think I can manoeuvre an eighteen ton aircraft on to a tiny little jetty like that without the help of a boat? Call him up and tell him it can't be done without damaging the aeroplane.'

'He's just coming down on to the water behind us now,' Frazer called out, 'he must have been waiting for our wash to die away.'

There was a wait of a moment or two, then Ralph turned back to his Captain with a helpless gesture, 'He says to do what he orders or he'll start shooting again.'

'Hell!' Desmond swore again. 'If he makes me damage *Caterina* I'll take him apart with my bare hands if I have to.' Gritting his teeth he began to line the flying-boat up for the attempt. 'Cut the power to the outer engines, will you Ken,' he asked. 'We'll go in as slowly as we can.'

Downstairs on the lower deck, the passengers huddled together in the narrow passage between the smoking saloon and the midship cabin, where Sandy Everett and Andy Draper had made them return the moment the flying-boat had touched down on the lake. No one had argued with the order, though they knew the thin partition walls would, in practice, give them

464

little extra protection against machine-gun bullets. The illusion of safety was there, and besides that there was an added sense of security in being close together rather than scattered throughout the separate cabins.

The initial panic which had gripped them when the Supermarine opened fire had been swiftly checked by the two cabin crew aided by Frazer. Now they stood pressed against one another, sometimes whispering nervously, but for the most part in frightened silence. Unable to see what was happening, they strained to catch every sound around them; the water slapping against the hull outside, the slow beat of the two inboard engines as Desmond steered cautiously in towards the pier, and the occasional muted exchange of voices from the flight deck above. To each of these their imaginations ascribed innumerable and ominous meanings, fear of the unknown magnifying their anxiety.

Near the after end of the passage Laura stood squeezed in between Charlotte Curtis and Siegret Wienzman, trying vainly to still the tense quivering of her limbs. Beside her she could feel Siegret trembling also; the girl's head was buried against her father, and Laura could see her shoulders shaking as the old man held her tightly. Turning to look the other way she found herself face to face with Charlotte. Pale and plainly terrified as she was, the older woman forced a brief smile; reaching out she gripped Laura's hand in her own and the two stood holding on to each other for comfort.

At the end of the passage Rashid held his arms protectively round Jacquetta, his quarrel with the Baron abandoned for the present, as he concentrated on the fresh threat to their lives. In the pandemonium which had followed the fighter's attack, he and Luca had barely had time to struggle to their feet before Sandy Everett had come running in, shouting at them all to take cover in the corridor.

Rashid felt trapped and helpless inside the plane, unable to see his opponents and forced to rely on the judgement of the men in the cockpit. If only they could get out on to the shore, then perhaps they could begin fighting back.

'Two of us here, the Baron and myself have guns,' he whispered over Jacquetta's head at Sandy who stood at the entrance to the saloon, peering round the corner through the windows, trying to make out where they were. 'Tell the Captain he can count on my help.'

'We have some pistols on the flight deck ourselves,' the Purser whispered back, 'but the Captain's afraid of what will happen if anyone starts shooting. We're a sitting duck for the machine-guns of that fighter.'

'What can you see outside?' Rashid asked him. Sandy put his head round the corner again. 'We're coming in at a small pier,' he said turning back again, 'there's at least one person on it carrying what looks like a Tommy gun.'

Rashid's heart sank. It was obvious that their enemies outgunned them overwhelmingly. Even at close range their revolvers would be useless against the concentrated fire of a single such weapon. With one sustained burst the rawest shot could cut down every person on board; and with the heavy armament of the fighter at their backs . . . Rashid could visualize the bullet-riddled aircraft, shattered and in flames, drifting out in mid lake, her interior a bloody shambles of dead and injured.

'You had better get down into the mooring compartment and open the hatch,' Desmond told Ken as, engines idling, *Caterina* closed in on the jetty. 'I'll need you to tell me how to steer. I can't see well enough from up here.' The first officer hesitated, visibly dismayed by the prospect. 'Come on, hurry up,' Desmond said tersely. 'Can I have a pistol with me?' Frazer asked, getting slowly out from his seat. 'If it'll make you feel braver,' Desmond answered. 'But hurry it up. We're practically on the jetty now.' Sticking the weapon in the waistband of his trousers, Frazer lifted the trap in the cockpit floor and lowered himself through. Moments later they heard the sound of the hatch opening below.

Susie backed slowly off from the foot of the pier as the airliner crept across the last few feet of water. At this distance the noise from the two engines was so loud it drowned out even the sound of the Supermarine approaching from the side, circling in towards the shoreward end of the jetty, on her left, and she could feel the vibration through the planking under her feet. Seen so near the enormous size of the flying boat was overwhelming, making her feel small and scared. She clutched the Tommy gun tightly, wishing Jarrett would leave his plane and come down to help her. Glancing nervously behind she saw he had reached the jetty and was preparing to switch off and tie up.

The sudden opening of the hatch caught her by surprise. Seeing a man's figure emerging she jerked the muzzle of the gun up towards him. The sequence of events which followed came so swiftly it was impossible to be definite as to their correct order. Whether Frazer saw the submachine gun swinging up and panicked, or whether instead he saw the girl was alone and decided on a mad attempt at heroics will never be known. All that is certain is that he drew his pistol and fired.

His aim from the unsteady platform of the aircraft was poor, and the round struck the water on the far side of the jetty without passing closer than two feet to the girl. For Susie however it was sufficient to know she was being shot at. Tightening her finger on the trigger she sent a burst of fire towards him.

Her reaction was instinctive and unaimed, and the thundering blast from the heavy weapon almost deafened her. A cone of bullets screamed over the man's head and smashed into the side of the cockpit. The thin duralumin plating was little hindrance to the big slugs at such a range and they tore through into the flight deck. By some miracle all missed Desmond, though the side windscreen by his left shoulder disintegrated in a shower of glass and one bullet ripped into the padding of his seat back. Ralph Kendricks however was less lucky. Both radio sets in front of him took several hits, and a jagged lump of metal ricocheted off one of the casings and slammed into his chest.

Instantly Desmond jerked open the throttles on the inboard engines and pushed hard down on the rudder bar, slewing the flying boat across to port in a desperate attempt to scrape clear of the jetty. He heard Ralph's cry of pain behind him, but there was no time to consider what might have happened to him. Their only chance now lay in getting away from the shore and out into mid lake again where the aircraft could manoeuvre.

Another burst of shots echoed out and again he felt the shock of bullets striking the aircraft, lower down on the fuselage this time. He punched the starter buttons of the two outer engines. *Caterina* was coming round but not nearly fast enough, they were going to hit the wooden piling at the end of the jetty. Directly in front of him he could see the pilot of the Supermarine trying to swing the nose of his plane round so that his guns could bear; any moment now he would be pouring fire into the helpless airliner.

With the huge prow of the flying-boat now bearing down upon her, turning in on a path which must bring it crashing into the jetty; with the sudden roar of the two idle propellors starting up again, and with Frazer in the nose hatch still firing shots at her, Susie lost her head completely. Holding down the Thompson's trigger she blazed away the entire contents of the fifty round magazine, spraying the aircraft with bullets. The fierce recoil of the sub-machine gun made it impossible for her to aim with any pretence at accuracy, but *Caterina* was far too big a target to miss. She saw the figure of the man with the pistol tossed suddenly backwards beneath the impact of the heavy shells, then slump down to tumble out of the hatch into the water beneath the aircraft, but in her terror she could only keep firing. Round after round pumped into the white hull, punching through the metal skin.

Too late she realized the danger she was in. Before she had time to turn and run the airliner's raked prow crashed into the jetty. The worn old timbering stood no chance against the eighteen ton weight of the flying-boat. *Caterina*'s nose rose up for an instant and then burst through the obstruction, disintegrating some thirty feet of the jetty, into a welter of broken logs and debris surging in the foaming wake thrown up by her passage. The harsh stutter of the gun was choked off abruptly as, caught in the devastating collision, Susie vanished into the boiling maelstrom.

Up in the cockpit Desmond felt the jarring shock of the crash shake the entire aircraft, but he had no time to worry about the probable damage it had caused. All four engines were biting at the air with increased power and they were beginning to pick up speed. The starboard wing came round and there was another heavy shock as the wing float rammed into the stump of the jetty. Glancing out he saw it buckle beneath the impact and scrape over. The Supermarine fighter was turning too but *Caterina*'s wing swept on past and, as her tail followed, the tiny plane began to buck and wallow in her wash. Desmond saw the sparkles from her gun ports, but the fire went wide and the next instant the airliner's tremendous slipstream was driving the fighter shorewards, spinning her nose round again so her armament no longer pointed at them.

Knowing the aircraft had suffered heavy punishment Desmond could only pray the damage had left her still flyable. The starboard wing float was trailing uselessly, threatening to dip the wing on to the surface at any moment, but the controls at least seemed unaffected. Running the engine up on to maximum boost, and setting half flaps, he streaked across the width of the lake, desperate to get airborne and away before the pilot in the fighter could regain control of his craft and come after them. There was barely sufficient distance for a take-off but he had no time to alter course and take a longer run. He waited until the last moment he dared before pulling back the stick hard and, almost unbelievably, felt *Caterina* lift off, scrape above the trees and skim over the crest of the surrounding hillside.

'Ralph, how badly are you hit?' They were streaking away southward with Desmond hugging them close to the ground, navigating by instinct. He had forced the throttle levers as far open against the stops as they would go, holding the engine straining at maximum power, heedless of the rapidly rising needles of the temperature gauges. Amazing as it seemed, *Caterina* appeared to have suffered no major damage to either airframe or engines, and they were making nearly two hundred miles per hour. If they could hold this speed for another twenty minutes they would reach New York and safety.

To his relief he heard the Radio Officer answering back, 'I'm all right I think skipper. I seem to have stopped one in the ribs but it doesn't feel serious. I'm trying to call up some help on the radio; the main set's had it, but the auxiliary sounds as though it may be repairable.' Sandy came leaping up the stairs from below, followed by Professor Wienzman carrying his black doctor's bag, and Laura. 'We've lost one passenger,' he reported quickly while the other man set to work at once on Ralph's injury, assisted by Laura. 'Van Smit was killed outright by a bullet in the head. Andy's been hit in the leg but it's not bad according to the Professor, and Baroness d'Este has a grazed shoulder. Everyone else is fine except for a few bruises. We've taken a lot of holes but so far we seem to be in one piece apart from the starboard float, and the hull seems to have survived the smash through the pier.'

'Frazer's gone,' Desmond told him in reply. 'I saw him fall into the lake just before we hit the jetty. Otherwise we seem to have got away more lightly than I'd have thought possible. I want you to go to the rear Sandy,' he went on, 'and keep a look out in case that fighter tries to have another pass at us. Open up the freight hatch and keep in contact over the refuelling intercom. It still seems to be working.'

'What about you Desmond? Are you O.K.?' Laura leant over and asked him as the Purser hurried away to do as he was told. Her face was scratched over the forehead, she had rolled up her sleeves and there was blood on her hands from where she had been helping the Professor. 'I'm fine.' He smiled briefly. 'How about you?'

'Nothing worse than a bump on the head,' she told him. 'Will that other aeroplane come after us do you think:'

'He's crazy if he does, but I'm afraid it's possible,' he answered grimly. 'One thing at least is that he will have found it pretty difficult to get into position for a take-off run for a while thanks to the swell we kicked up as we left. I reckon that will have given us several minutes start, which with luck will mean we will be too close to New York by the time he catches up.'

Conditions at the lake were in fact even worse than Desmond had guessed. The slipstream of the flying-boat had driven the Supermarine hard aground on the muddy shore below the house. Leaping out on to the bank, and for the moment ignoring the escaping airliner, Jarrett ran down the jetty till he came to the tangle of broken timbers at the end. Fully one third had been torn away by *Caterina*'s hull, only a few bits of shattered planking remained in the still swirling water to show where it had been.

Of Susie there was no sign. The girl had disappeared completely, her body evidently sucked under by the flying-boat's wake and like that of the crewman who had started the shooting, swept out into the middle of the lake. There was not a trace left of either of them. A deep, bitter anger welled up within Jarrett as he gazed at the desolate aftermath of the brief but violent battle. There had been no need for any of it. The man who had died had killed himself and Susie and probably many others as well and all to no purpose.

Rage and frustration at the collapse of his plans, combined with grief at the death of the girl and the destruction of the dreams he had had for them both, left him empty of all save a desire to be revenged on the flying-boat and its crew, who had been responsible. Running back up the jetty, he pushed the silver fighter off from the mud and clambered aboard again.

Two Marine Corps TBD-1 Devastator torpedo bombers had just taken off from the airbase at Floyd Bennet Field and were heading out towards the gunnery practice range off the coast of New Jersey at an altitude of ten thousand feet. The Devastators, the standard U.S. Naval and Marine bombers were all metal, low winged mono-planes, with an eight hundred horse power engine giving a top speed of two hundred and six miles per hour. Normally carrying a crew of three, pilot, bombardier and radio officer/rear gunner, seated one behind the other in tandem; they were on this occasion flying without their bombardier, who had no part to play in gunnery practice.

In the cockpit of the lead aircraft, Lieutenant Phil DeMartino heard the voice of his rear man, twenty-one year old Sergeant Al Murray crackle unexpectedly over the intercom. 'Skipper, the base has just been on the air,' he called excitedly. 'We're to break off and head over to Manhattan. It seems some looney in a home-made fighter is taking shots at an airliner and we've been ordered to see him off.'

'They want us to do what?' Phil replied in amazement. He had heard Al's words perfectly clearly but found them almost impossible to believe. 'Are you being serious?'

'Never more so,' the young sergeant's voice came back happily. 'They say we are the nearest planes in the sky carrying ammunition and we're to get on over.' He sounded cheerful at the prospect; Phil could picture him in his exposed, rearward facing open cockpit, grinning as he cocked his gun, the prospect of actually being able to shoot at a real target for once, was plainly one he was looking forward to.

The Devastator's armament consisted of one fixed, forward firing .30 calibre machine gun mounted on the right hand side of Phil's windscreen, and a similar weapon fixed on a scarf mount giving limited traverse in Al's position, firing rearwards. Hardly an excess of weaponry with which to tackle a fighter, Phil thought as he reached up to cock the gun beside him. Glancing out at the aircraft flying alongside his starboard wing he saw his fellow pilot Bob Wood had just done the same and was giving him a thumbs up sign. Evidently he was confident enough.

'O.K.' he called back to Al. 'Manhattan it is,' and banking hard round to port he set a course towards the north.

Jacquetta d'Este and Andy Draper had each been made comfortable on beds in the midship cabin. Their injuries had been expertly attended to by the Professor who had worked imperturbably away at his task, seemingly unworried by any thought of danger to himself. In this he had been aided by Laura and Charlotte who had acted as assistants and nurses.

With the arrival of the pair of Devastators to protect them, the passengers had been allowed back to their seats. The Professor and Laura had returned to the flight deck to take a second look at Ralph Kendricks' wound, which though not serious, was causing him pain. Draper had been given an injection of morphine and lay drugged and semi-comatose; Jacquetta's injury however had been less severe; the bullet had scored along the side of her left shoulder, stinging and breaking the skin, but fortunately inflicting no further damage. Sitting up in bed she was discussing with Rashid their position together now that her husband had learnt the truth about them both.

'What can we do?' she was saying despondently, 'there is so little time left. We are practically at New York now. What is going to happen when Luca tells the authorities about you?' Already the aircraft was wheeling over the Queen's district of Long Island and was losing height, slipping down through the air as it swung in along the line of the Hudson River towards the airport at La Guardia. Through the window on her left Jacquetta could see the magnificent panorama of lower Manhattan spread out beneath them, the gleaming towers of the immense sky scrapers stretching up through the haze in the midst of the busy harbour; a maze of interlocking waterways and islands held together by the slender spans of innumerable bridges in a complex and delicate tracery. Ordinarily she would have been fascinated by this view of the richest and most powerful city on earth, but as it was, however, she could think only of the imminent arrest and deportation it signalled for her lover.

As if on cue Luca appeared in the doorway; now that the emergency was over he had recovered his customary suavity of manner and with a smugly complacent smile, he answered his wife's question for her. 'I can tell you exactly what will happen, my dear,' he said. 'The Americans will have no choice but to deport a man who has not only entered the country on a false passport but has, in addition, threatened the life of an accredited diplomat. In which case I shall at once, acting on behalf of our government, request that he be returned to Italy to stand trial for his crimes. The verdict will not, I think,' he concluded, 'be hard to predict.'

'You may not find me so easy to dispose of Baron,' Rashid retorted, proudly rising to his feet and stepping threateningly towards the Italian. 'And come what may I shall somehow have my revenge on you. Of that you may be sure.'

Luca continued to smile. 'I anticipated your attitude,' he remarked coldly. Bringing his hand out from behind his back he levelled the pistol he had been concealing at the young Sheikh. 'So I intend taking no chances. You will now please hand me over your gun. If you refuse,' he added as Rashid glared at him defiantly, 'I can assure you I shall have not the slightest compunction in shooting you where you stand.'

As he spoke Pat Jarrett opened fire on the flying-boat again.

Despite the superior speed of the Supermarine Jarrett had underestimated the lead which the flying-boat had acquired and by the time he was in a position to make his second attack, *Caterina* was already passing over Queensboro Bridge and Welfare Island at a little over a thousand feet and Desmond O'Neill was preparing for the final approach to La Guardia six miles ahead round the bend of the East River.

Jarrett saw the two Devastators flying in close formation to either side but by now he had worked himself into such a state of pathological hatred and bitterness that he no longer cared who his opponents were or how great their numbers. The sight of the enormous city spread out beneath them in an endless sprawl served in a curious way to heighten his desperate need for revenge. It was as though the whole of New York had been selected as a gigantic backcloth against which the final act in the drama was to be played out.

Coming in from the west at eight thousand feet he was perfectly placed to swoop down out of the sun at the three unsuspecting aircraft. This time there was no reason to hold his fire or stick to pre-arranged plans; putting the sea-plane into a steep power dive he screamed down on the slow moving airliner as it came towards him.

All thoughts of his own survival or safety vanished as the Supermarine hurtled through the air, swallowed up in a red mist of battle frenzy. His brain singing with the force of the acceleration, he held the dive till the flying-boat's hull swam up to fill his sights, the black bead in the centre of the ring set squarely in the middle of her back between the wing roots. At a range of four hundred yards he pressed the firing button on his joystick and walked a stream of tracer into the helpless plane.

He felt the heavy vibration running through the fighter as the four Colts pumped their shells across the intervening space.

Travelling at three thousand feet a second the huge slugs tore into the white fuselage in a pulverizing blast which ripped through the mail room and into the passenger deck. Lifting the Supermarine's nose Jarrett watched the line of holes punched by the seven hundred grain bullets march across the hull and on to the innermost of the two starboard engines. Instantly a thick, oily trail of black smoke began to pour from the nacelle.

The crews of the Devastators had failed to spot the deadly silver racer streaking down on them from out of the sun. Not until they heard the rattle of Jarrett's guns and saw the airliner shudder beneath the terrible impact of his fire did they realize what was happening. As *Caterina* fell away towards the river, trailing smoke they saw the fighter flash by close overhead and the two pilots slammed their throttles open, flinging the Devastators into an urgent climb in pursuit.

Wrenching the stick hard back Jarrett pulled the Supermarine up sharply, and, as his speed began to fall away, flicked over to starboard and rolled out above them. Both rear gunners had swung their weapons up and were engaging him, but the pitiful fire from the single barrelled light calibre guns went easily wide. Pushing the fighter into another dive he cut down through the sky on top of them. Then even before the marines realized the danger they were in he had opened fire on Bob Wood's aircraft.

Holding his thumb on the button he raked the bomber with a full, five second burst. During that fraction of time the Colts, firing at a rate of eight hundred and fifty rounds a minute each, poured over one hundred and seventy bullets into the plane, with a total striking impact of over one ton. Against such appalling firepower the Devastator stood not a chance. With a bright orange flare from the exploding petrol tanks it blew up, disintegrating instantaneously into a cloud of fragments, which showered down on to the river.

Stricken with horror at the sight, Phil DeMartino hurled his machine into a tight turn, frantic to get clear before the fighter could lock on to his tail, but the Devastator was no match for the speed and manoeuvreability of the Supermarine. There was a series of stunning concussions at the rear of the fuselage and over his earphones he heard a scream of agony from Al in the rear cockpit. The elevator controls went heavy and the plane began to spin earthwards.

Caterina was still airborne. The inherent ruggedness and strength of the flying-boat had enabled her to withstand Jarrett's initial and shorter burst, and by a fortunate chance the stacked gold and mail sacks had absorbed a considerable proportion of the fire. Even so she had suffered grievous harm. One engine was already burning and the outer one on the port wing had taken a scatter of hits and was running raggedly. The hail of bullets had also sliced through the cables linking the wing flaps rendering the aircraft's rate of descent almost impossibly hard to control.

On the lower deck Andy Draper and Luca d'Este had died in the same instant, their bodies riddled bloodily by the Colt's fire. Only the shielding of the gold crates above them had saved Jaquetta and Rashid from a similar fate.

In the cockpit Desmond was struggling desperately to control the airliner. His one thought was to get down on to the water of the river before the fighter came back for a second pass at them or the remaining engines failed. The Triborough Bridge complex on Ward's Island loomed ahead of him, beyond that was Hell Gate Bridge. He was feathering the outer port engine to try and keep it going but the flames were spreading down the wing along the fuel lines. They must last out for another two or three minutes until they reached clear water to land on.

Behind him Laura screamed suddenly from the radio desk where she had been helping the Professor to bind up the wound in Ralph's chest. 'He's coming at us again!' Through the window of the navigation hatch she had caught sight of Jarrett plunging down on them again. At the same time Ralph shouted, 'Break to port, Skipper! Break to port!'

With no time to think any more of what the airliner could stand, Desmond drove the rudder into the floor and forced the stick hard over, peeling *Caterina* away low across northern Manhattan, praying that the sudden manoeuvre would throw the sea-plane off. Before they could claw away out of range however they felt the violent jarring shock of the machine-gun bullets impacting on the starboard wing and the tail, as the fighter swept past.

Above the noise of smashing metal which filled the cockpit, Desmond heard both the starboard engines break into a shuddering rattle of coughing and felt the immediate loss of power. Simultaneously the rudder assembly went slack beneath his feet as the concentrated fire ripped apart the flying-boat's tail.

Now with almost total engine failure, badly on fire and losing height rapidly, *Caterina* was limping out of control across Manhattan over the roofs of Spanish Harlem. Above them Desmond knew instinctively the Supermarine was looping round again to administer the coup de grace. Within seconds the airliner would be a blazing wreck plummeting down to crash on one of the most densely populated pieces of land in the world.

Miraculously no further passenger had been injured during the last attack, for the stream of bullets had missed the main fuselage, spending their force on the control surfaces and power plants. In the bloody shambles of the midship cabin, Jacquetta clung screaming to Rashid, as the sea of brown roofs below rose to meet them.

Yet as Jarrett powered his machine round over the Bronx to make his final pass, to his amazement he saw the shape of the remaining Devastator coming straight towards him, fire spitting from its single machine gun. Badly damaged as his aircraft was and with his rear gunner dead in his seat, Phil DeMartino knew that he had at all costs to stop the fighter from shooting the airliner down over central Manhattan. Pointing the Devastator at the attacker's nose, he kept his finger on the firing button.

Flames flicked along the gun ports of the sea-plane and he felt the bullets striking home around him but he held his course without flinching. Too late he saw the pilot of the other plane try to pull up in a last effort to scrape above him. At a closing speed of four hundred and fifty miles an hour the two aircraft smashed into one another and exploded in a terrific ball of flame which seemed to hang suspended in the air for a moment before toppling into the docks of the Harlem Riverside.

Caterina was now skimming the rooftops of Harlem's tenement blocks. There was no hope Desmond knew of their making the far side of Manhattan. Only the fact that the buildings in this part of the city were significantly lower than those to the south had delayed a crash this long. One last faint chance remained to them as they dropped through the few remaining feet of air.

Seeing the green expanse of Central Park opening in their path he yelled at the others behind him to brace themselves. With feet to spare *Caterina* flew over the buildings on Cathedral Parkway, and the ancient blockhouses round Harlem Meer. The green of the meadow beyond flashed by barely missing their keel, and there ahead of them lay the clear, hundred acre expanse of the Receiving Reservoir.

Caterina was at her last gasp. With three propellors twirling uselessly, and flames streaming back to envelope the whole of the port wing, she plunged bodily down into the water with a terrific violence which bounced her twice shatteringly clear of the surface, throwing up bursts of spray two hundred feet into the air. Surging through the waves created by her landing she sped helplessly towards the southern bank, to fetch up with another crunching impact which carried her halfway up the grass. There, battered, bullet riddled, but miraculously intact, she rested.

Dazed and stunned by the successive impacts of the crash, and their minds numbed, the passengers' instinct for survival drove them to their feet and sent them reeling through the smoke filled cabins towards the hatches.

The shock of the landing had flung all on board about like toys, and the floors were slippery with blood from the dead and injured. As well as killing Andy and Luca d'Este, the Supermarine's final pass had seriously wounded Stewart Curtis. Mrs. King had received a broken shoulder in her fall, but with characteristic determination had refused offers of assistance and, together with her husband had taken charge of the badly-shocked Siegret Wienzman. All three succeeded in making

478

their way forward to the Promenade Cabin hatchway which Sandy Everett had just managed to force open.

The drenching spray thrown up by the plane's crash-landing on the surface of the Reservoir had doused the flames pouring from the wings and it was this fact more than any other which saved the lives of *Caterina*'s travellers. Rashid seized Jacquetta in his arms and hastened out with her after the Kings. Closely followed by Arlette Ducroix, they stumbled thankfully out on to the grass of the Park before a swiftly gathering crowd of amazed spectators who hurried forward to help them.

In the after cabin Charlotte Curtis had escaped the burst of fire which had struck down her husband, but the shattering concussion of the crash flung her against the rear bulkhead knocking her unconscious for several seconds. Coming to in the smoke-choked cabin, she saw Stewart lying on his side near the door and a single glance at the ominously spreading, dark stains across his suit was enough to tell her of the seriousness of his injuries.

Terror gripped her at the thought of being trapped in the blazing aircraft, and she attempted to drag him through towards the hatch. The wounded man groaned, and a froth of red bubbles appeared at his mouth. His weight was too much for her, but her frantic cries for help brought Sandy to her aid.

Some little while later Desmond watched as the last of the ambulances moved slowly off through the crowd. The entire northern end of the park seemed to be filled with hordes of onlookers who had come to gaze at the huge, smoke-streaked hull of the flying-boat, lying half out of the water. Near at hand were parked four fire tenders summoned to the crash, their crews waiting idly by as *Caterina*'s remaining fuel was drained from her tanks. About them were grouped an ever-increasing swarm of police cars, and vehicles belonging to City and Airline Authorities and the cars of the scores of journalists and newsmen who had flocked to the scene.

It seemed likely that Stewart Curtis would succumb to his wounds. Should he survive it would only be to face a series of charges of fraud. Looking up at his former command Desmond shook his head in wonder, it was almost impossible to believe that anyone at all could have come out of her alive or that any aircraft could withstand so much punishment. All at once he gave a chuckle.

'What on earth are you laughing at?' Laura was standing beside him; Desmond slipped his arm through hers as he answered, 'I was just wondering,' he said smiling, 'how we're ever going to get her out of here again?'

And together they walked across the grass, their hands almost touching.

THE END